TRISTAN SLOWLY LOWERED HIS LIPS TO HERS

knowing even as he did so that he should be checking her pulse ... helping her to her feet ... calling a doc ...

His mouth brushed hers in a sweet, dry caress. An electricity more primitive than lightning arced between them, melting the neurons of Tristan's methodical left brain to mush. Her lips parted without hesitation beneath his gentle probing, dragging a hoarse groan out of him.

He surrendered those lips to nuzzle the satiny column of her throat, breathing deep of her fragrance. She smelled nearly as delicious as she tasted, more intoxicating than well-aged cognac or Chanel No. 5. She smelled like kittens napping in a rocking chair. Towering cedars strung with bows and lights. Chocolate-chip cookies fresh from the oven on a snowy winter night.

It was those dreams of a home he'd never had that finally allowed Tristan to identify her quaint perfume.

Cloves. Arian Whitewood smelled of cloves.

Arian welcomed Tristan's kiss with artless innocence. She moaned with disappointment that soon melted to delight when his lips abandoned hers to feather soft, provocative kisses along her jaw and throat.

He wanted more. She could deny him nothing ...

Also by Teresa Medeiros

Breath of Magic

Teresa Medeiros

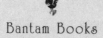

Bantam Books

2009 Bantam Books Mass Market Edition

Copyright © 1996 by Teresa Medeiros

All rights reserved.

Published in the United States by Bantam Books, an imprint of The Random House Publishing Group, a division of Random House, Inc., New York.

BANTAM BOOKS and the rooster colophon are registered trademarks of Random House, Inc.

Originally published in paperback in the United States by Bantam Books in 1996.

ISBN 978-0-553-59279-5

Cover art: copyright © 1996 by Alan Ayers

Printed in the United States of America

www.bantamdell.com

2 4 6 8 9 7 5 3 1

To Nita Taublib
for giving me the wings to soar

To Tommy and Jacque Pigage and
Brian and Vonda Gates.
God knew I was going to have
a tough year, so he gave me you for friends,
proving his infinite wisdom once again

And for Michael,
who makes me believe in magic every day we're together

ACKNOWLEDGMENTS

To the memory of

ELIZABETH MONTGOMERY,

whose wit, beauty, grace, and intelligence made every little girl of my generation long to be a witch.

Prologue

The media hadn't dubbed the four-thousand-square-foot penthouse perched at the apex of Lennox Tower the Fortress for nothing, Michael Copperfield thought, as he changed elevators for the third time, keyed his security code into the lighted pad, and jabbed the button for the ninety-fifth floor.

The elevator doors slid open with a sibilant hiss. Resisting the temptation to gawk at the dazzling night view of the Manhattan skyline, Copperfield strode across a meadow of neutral beige carpet and shoved open the door at the far end of the suite.

"Do come in," said a dry voice. "Don't bother to knock."

Copperfield slapped that morning's edition of the *Times* on the chrome desk and stabbed a finger at the headline. "I just got back from Chicago. What in the hell is the meaning of this?"

A pair of frosty gray eyes flicked from the blinking cursor on the computer screen to the crumpled newspaper. "I should think it requires no explanation. You can't have been my PR advisor for all these years without learning how to read."

Copperfield glared at the man he had called friend for twenty-five years and employer for seven. "Oh, I can read quite well. Even between the lines." To prove his point, he snatched up the paper and read, " 'Tristan Lennox—founder, CEO, and primary stockholder of Lennox Enterprises—offers one million dollars to anyone who can prove that magic exists outside the boundaries of science. Public competition to be held tomorrow morning in the courtyard of Lennox Tower. Eccentric boy billionaire seeks only serious applicants.' " Copperfield twisted the paper as if to throttle his employer in effigy. "*Serious* applicants? Why, you'll have every psychic hotline operator, swindler, and *Geraldo*-reject on your doorstep by dawn!"

"Geraldo already called. I gave him your home number."

"How can you be so glib when I've faxed my fingers to the bone trying to establish a respectable reputation for you?"

Droll amusement glittered in Tristan's hooded eyes. "I'll give you a ten-thousand-dollar bonus if you can get them to stop calling me the 'Boy Billionaire.' It makes me feel like Bruce Wayne without the Batmobile. And I did just turn thirty-two. I hardly qualify as a 'Boy' anything."

His fickle attention shifted to his fax machine. The display's artificial light carved hollows beneath his cheekbones and cast an eerie glow over his implacable features. As his deft finger tapped a button that would send a fax authorizing a corporate takeover of a multi-million-dollar software conglomerate, Copperfield wanted to tug his own sleek ponytail in frustration.

"How long are you going to keep indulging these ridiculous whims of yours? Until you've completely destroyed your credibility? Until everyone in New York is laughing behind your back?"

"Until I find what I'm looking for."

"What? Or who?"

Ignoring Copperfield's pointed question as he had for the past ten years, Tristan flipped off fax and computer with a single switch and rose from the swivel chair.

As he approached the north wall, an invisible seam widened to reveal a walk-in closet twice the size of Copperfield's loft apartment. Recessed track lighting illuminated each of his steps into the cavernous vault. Fearing that shouting across such a distance might actually produce an echo, Copperfield had no choice but to tag after him.

As Tristan activated an automated tie rack, Copperfield said, "Sometimes I think you flaunt convention deliberately. To keep everyone at arm's length where they can't hurt you." He drew in a steadying breath. "To keep the old scandal alive."

For a tense moment, the only sound was the mechanical swish of the ties circling their narrow track.

Tristan's shoulders lifted in a dispassionate shrug as he chose a burgundy striped silk to match his Armani suit. "Discrediting charlatans is a hobby. No different from playing the stock market or collecting Picassos." He knotted the tie with expert efficiency, shooting Copperfield a mocking glance. "Or romancing bulimic supermodels with Godiva chocolates."

Copperfield folded his arms over his chest. "Have you had my apartment under surveillance again or did you conjure up that sordid image in your crystal ball? At least I give chocolates. As I recall, the last model I introduced you to didn't get so much as a 'thank you, ma'am'! after her 'wham-bam.' "

Tristan's expression flickered with something that might have been shame in a less guarded man. "I meant to have my assistant send some flowers." He chose a pair of platinum cuff links from a mahogany tray. "If it's the million dollars you're worried about, Cop, don't waste your energy. I'm the last man who expects to forfeit that prize."

"Well, you know what they say. Within the chest of every cynic beats the heart of a disillusioned optimist."

Tristan brushed past him, fixing both his cuff links and his mask of aloof indifference firmly in place. "You should know better than anyone that I stopped believing in magic a long time ago."

"So you say, my friend," Copperfield murmured to himself. "So you say."

He studied the tie rack with a practiced squint before choosing a modest Brooks Brothers that would complement his eyes. He shoved it into his suit pocket, then pivoted only to discover that Tristan's exit had prompted the closet doors to glide soundlessly shut.

Copperfield rushed forward and began to bang on the seamless expanse with both fists. "Hey! Somebody let me out of here! Damn you, Tristan! You arrogant son of a—" A disbelieving bark of laughter escaped him as he braced his shoulder against the door. "Well, I'll be damned. What else can go wrong today?"

He found out an instant later when the mellow lighting programmed to respond solely to his employer's entrances and exits flickered, then went out.

The girl plopped down on the broomstick. Her skirts bunched up around her knees, baring a pair of slender calves shrouded in black stockings. A stray gust of wind rattled the dying leaves and ruffled her hair, forcing her to swipe a dark curl from her eyes. Gooseflesh prickled along her arms.

Shaking off the foreboding pall of the sky, she gripped the broomstick with both hands and screwed her eyes shut. As she attempted the freshly memorized words, a cramp shot down her thigh, shattering her concentration. She tried shouting the spell, but the broomstick did not deign to grant even a bored shudder in response.

Her voice faded to a defeated whisper. Disappointment swelled in her throat, constricting the tender membranes until tears stung her eyes. Perhaps she'd been deluding herself. Perhaps she was just as wretched a witch as she'd always feared.

She loosened the taut laces of her homespun bodice to toy with the emerald amulet suspended from a delicate filigree chain. Although she kept it well hidden from prying eyes and ignored its presence except in moments of dire vexation, she still felt compelled to wear it over her heart like a badge of shame.

"*Sacre bleu*, I only wanted to fly," she muttered.

The broomstick lurched forward, then jerked to a halt. The amulet lay cool and indifferent over her galloping heart.

Afraid to heed her own fickle senses, she slowly drew the gold chain over her head and squeezed the amulet. Leaning over the weatherbeaten stick, she whispered, "I only wanted to fly."

Nothing.

She straightened, shaking her head at her own folly.

The willow broom sailed into the air and stopped, leaving her dangling by one leg. The stick quivered beneath her, the intensity of its power making the tiny hairs at her nape bristle with excitement.

"Fly!" she commanded with feeling.

The broom hung poised in midair for a shuddering eternity, then aimed itself toward the crowns of the towering oaks. It darted to a dizzying height, then swooped down, dragging her backside along the ground for several feet before shooting into another wild ascent.

She whooped in delight, refusing to consider the perils of soaring around a small clearing on a splintery hearth broom. The harder she laughed, the faster the broom traveled until she feared it would surely bolt the clearing and shoot for the distant moon hanging in the afternoon sky.

With a tremendous effort, she heaved herself astride the broom. She perched in relative comfort for a full heartbeat before the curious conveyance rocketed upward on a path parallel with the tallest oak, then dove downward with equal haste. The ground reached up to slam into her startled face.

She wheezed like a beached cod, praying the air would show mercy and fill her straining lungs. When she could finally breathe again, she lifted her throbbing head to find the broom lying a few feet away.

She spat out a mouthful of crumbled leaves and glared at the lifeless stick.

But her disgust was forgotten as she became aware of the gentle warmth suffusing her palm. She unfolded her trembling fingers to find the amulet bathed in a lambent glow. Her mouth fell open in wonder as the emerald winked twice as if to confirm their secret, then faded to darkness.

She was too captivated by her discovery to see the gaunt figure who unfolded himself from the shadows of the forest. A grim smile of triumph twisted his lips as he turned toward the village, the half-light of the rising moon caressing the elegant threads of silver at his temples.

PART I

Thy sweet magic brings together
What stern Custom spreads afar;
All men become brothers
Where thy happy wing-beats are.

—Johann Christoph Friedrich von Schiller

Enter these enchanted woods,
You who dare.

—George Meredith

1

If anyone had dared to inform Miss Arian Whitewood that it might prove hazardous to practice witchcraft in the colony of Massachusetts in 1689, she would have scoffed in their face with all the saucy immortality of any twenty-year-old. Anyone, however, did not include her stepfather, for whom she harbored a great deal of respect and a somewhat stilted affection. So she sat in the ladder-backed chair facing the stone hearth, her hands folded demurely in her lap, and listened wide-eyed to his diatribe against Satan's servants and black magic.

His rehearsed speech seemed to embarrass him more than it did her. He clutched a slim prayerbook in one hand and fidgeted with his iron-gray hair with the other. His gaze persisted in straying to a spot just over her head.

Arian's buckled shoes tapped out a merry rhythm on the freshly sanded floor as her stepfather raved on about some irksome cow that refused to give anything but curdled milk for Goody Hubbins. As she glanced at the willow broom leaning innocently against the hearth, her lips twitched with remembered amusement.

"Arian!" Marcus Whitewood bellowed, his faded blue eyes capturing her gaze. "Have you not heard a word I have said? Do you not realize your soul is in grave danger, child?"

She swallowed a sigh. "Forgive me, Father Marcus. My thoughts wandered. Pray do continue."

Her bored resignation sent Marcus's hand shooting through his hair again. "Only yesterday Goodwife Burke claimed her Charity was reading her catechisms when you did pass by the window and the girl went into fits."

"Fits of boredom most likely," Arian muttered beneath her breath. She didn't dare tell Marcus that the horse-faced Charity had come pounding at their door only two nights ago, begging Arian to cast her future in a cup of moldy tea leaves.

"I accuse you of nothing, daughter. But I thought you safer warned of the talk in the village. 'Tis not only your soul I am troubled for."

Arian groaned. "I shall never be a Puritan and they know it. I only attend their interminable meeting to make life easier for you. They've hated me from the moment I set foot in Gloucester."

Marcus's frown softened. He remembered that moment vividly although it had occurred over ten years ago. He had stood on the dock, wringing his hat in his hands until it was past all repair. A silent prayer had risen unbidden to his lips when a tiny vision in a scarlet cape had come sauntering down the ship's ramp, clutching a valise with the bored assurance of a practiced traveler.

His rehearsed words of welcome had died in his throat as the jaded pygmy surveyed him from heels to head and demanded in a voice two octaves too deep for its owner's petite stature, "Where is my mama? Has she run off again?"

His stepdaughter had grown a few scant inches

since then, but her husky voice and snapping dark eyes could still make a man swallow his words.

She folded her arms over her chest in a gesture of rebellion Marcus had come to know only too well. " 'Twas my fluency in French and my ruffled petticoats they did not care for. My grandmama believed a traveling child should be well dressed."

"Your grandmama also believed in witchcraft, young lady." He shook a forefinger at her. "She was a fanciful old Frenchwoman who poisoned your innocent mind with her black arts."

"White arts," Arian bit off. "Grandmama was a Christian. It broke her heart to send me away. She lived less than a year after my departure."

Arian blinked back a hot rush of tears. Her dear, pudgy grandmama had not known she was sending Arian to a stern stepfather she had never met and a mother who would be dead before she arrived.

Marcus tilted her chin up with one finger, forcing her to meet his gaze. "I promised your mother I would offer you both a home and a name. Even when Lillian was too weak to speak without coughing up blood, her thoughts were of you. She had great hopes of building a life here for the three of us."

His wistful smile gave Arian a glimpse of the adoration that had drawn her frivolous mama to this plain, stoic man. She looked away, knowing herself an intruder on his lost passion for a woman Arian had hardly known and never liked.

Marcus gruffly cleared his throat. "You are an innocent, Arian. An easy mark for the devil. He could prey upon your childish potions and playacting. I know you intend no harm, but the villagers do not. They see a willful girl who is different from them and it makes them afraid."

"But I haven't concocted a single potion since you burned my powdered mice feet and poured out my bat's blood," she assured him earnestly.

He shuddered and placed a firm hand on her shoulder. "Allow me to pray for your soul, daughter. Let us kneel and ask the Almighty Lord to purge you of the seeds of black magic your grandmother planted in your heart."

Even as she slipped obediently to her knees, Arian's heart cried, *White magic!*

Knowing protest was futile, she arranged her skirts to cushion her knees for an ordeal that could last for hours. Marcus eased into a steady drone, repeating prayer after prayer from the slender book. A trickle of sweat crawled down Arian's side beneath the scratchy linsey-woolsey of her dress.

She opened one eye to find Marcus's head bowed and his eyes closed. Eager to test her newfound talents, she narrowed her eyes, focusing all of her attention on a pewter candlestick that rested on the mantel. The candlestick just sat there—a mocking blob of inanimate metal. Desperate to prove her powers were her own, but loath to admit defeat, Arian drew her folded hands inward to grasp the emerald amulet. Her fingers began to tingle.

A gap slowly widened between the gleaming base of the candlestick and the wooden shelf. A mischievous smile curved Arian's lips. She swung her head from side to side, sending the candlestick into a sprightly jig.

"Arian!"

Marcus's roar splintered her concentration. The massive candlestick crashed to the hearth only inches from his kneeling form.

Arian gasped. "Forgive me, Father Marcus . . . I never meant to . . ."

Her protest faded as he scrambled to his feet, his face ashen. "You seek to do me harm, daughter?" Throwing a hand over his eyes, he cried, "I cannot bear it!"

He stumbled out the door into the windy night, leaving Arian to wonder if she had just alienated her only ally in this heartless land.

*   *   *

The moon had drifted high in the sky before Arian heard Marcus's disheartened tread on the stairs. She sat before a cheval glass in the shadowy loft, working a hairbrush through her mass of frizzled curls. The brush caught in a painful tangle as Marcus's bedroom door creaked open, then shut with a mournful thud.

Taking up her candle, Arian paced to the shuddering windowpane, her eyes searching the night for an unknown comfort. Resting the candlestick beside her, she curled up on the narrow sill and dragged a threadbare quilt around her shoulders. Clouds sped across the moon, making her wish she could fly away with them.

She had thirsted for magic most of her life, believing its power might quench the yearning in her soul. A yearning honed by years of being shuffled from household to household at the whim of her mother's wealthy lovers. Her only stability had been a battered book of fairy tales sent to her on her third birthday by a grandmama she had yet to meet.

She had immersed herself in exotic kingdoms ruled by wizards, witches, and raven-haired princes, far preferring them to the whirl of frenzied gaiety punctuated by her mama's brittle laughter, the clink of wineglasses, and unfamiliar masculine murmurs.

The rabid snarl of quarreling voices had shattered her sleep more often than not, leaving her trembling in the darkness and trying to remember where she was. It was only after she had fumbled to light a candle and begun to leaf through the gilt-edged pages of her beloved book that she would begin to remember not only where she was, but *who* she was as well. Or at least who she longed to be.

Often after such a night, her mother would emerge, her ethereal beauty enhanced by tragic pallor, and inform Arian that it was time to pack. Before the day was over, Arian would be settled in another house and her mother in another man's bed.

Arian rested her forehead against the cool glass. Her precious book of fairy tales had been lost during the grueling voyage to the Colonies and her mother now slept for all eternity beneath the stony Massachusetts sod. All that remained of her past was an emerald amulet—a trinket she had always regarded with a curious mixture of pride and contempt.

Arian drew the amulet from her nightgown, viewing it with newfound respect. Until that afternoon in the clearing, her clumsy attempts at spell-casting had always failed her. She shivered with mingled fear and delight at the memory. The raw power strumming across her nerves had been like being kissed by a bolt of lightning. Perhaps her natural talent for witchery had just needed a fresh focus. She'd read many tales of such charms and talismans, necessary only until the novice witch developed faith in her gift.

Arian longed to discover what other wonders she might be capable of, but after her disastrous encounter with Marcus, she feared invoking her powers without a compelling reason.

She closed her fist around the amulet, wishing it could be a source of comfort as well as contention.

Her eyes fluttered shut as she snuggled deeper into the quilt. But instead of dreaming of a raven-haired prince who possessed the power to break Gloucester's dark enchantment with a single chaste kiss, she dreamed of a man with hair the color of sunlight and eyes of glittering frost.

She moaned softly in her sleep as the wick of the tallow candle sputtered in its drippings and drowned itself into darkness.

The meeting house was cool, the oppressive heat of summer vanquished by the autumn winds. Arian smoothed her skirts and stole a glance at the man beside her.

Her stepfather's profile was as impenetrable as it had been at breakfast when all of her cheery attempts at conversation had been rebuffed by the stony set of his jaw. He had left the hot corn mush, smothered in the sugary molasses he loved untouched on his wooden trencher. Draining the well water from his mug, he had risen and started for the meeting house without a word, giving Arian no choice but to slap a white bonnet askew on her head and trot after him.

The Reverend Linnet's voice swelled, its arresting timbre undiminished as he plunged into the third hour of his sermon. As he accented his threats of fiery retribution by slamming a fist on the pulpit, his words penetrated Arian's fretful musings for the first time.

"Aye, my brethren, the Almighty Lord led us to Gloucester. He rescued us from evil and delivered us from the temptation of lives of ease bought with the lifeblood of our faith. He carried us over the sea to this new land. He protected us from tempests and disease."

Arian thought grimly of her mother, who had died choking on her own blood.

"But wherever there are godly men on this earth, there are devils to tempt them." He lowered his voice to a hollow whisper that could still be heard throughout the hall. "Never forget the words of the Lord written in Job: 'When the sons of God came to present themselves before the Lord, Satan came also among them.' "

Arian glanced at the rapt faces around her, both disgusted and slightly envious that they could find a worthy message in the man's theatrics.

"It is because we are good that Satan sends his servants among us. Satan is clever. He knows what tempts us. I hasten to remind you that Lucifer was the most beautiful angel in the heavens. No star shone brighter than Lucifer's glorious face. Never forget lest you be drawn into beauty's snare. Would Satan send ugliness among us to lead us astray? Would he send a heinous monster to plague our cattle and cast our innocent children into fits?"

A blanket of ominous silence drifted over the hall. People turned to one another, their eyes questioning.

"No!" The Reverend's voice rang out in a shout. "There is beauty among us. And there is evil among us, too. There is evil in this very room."

A collective gasp rose from the pews. Arian drew in a ragged breath, but found herself unable to release it as the Reverend Linnet looked straight over the heads of those seated in front of her, paralyzing her with his gaze.

"Satan's angels stalk us. Wild and wanton creatures fly in the night, howling at the moon. Simple tools dance with a life of their own. We can deny it no more. Satan and his servants are abroad in Gloucester." Then more gently, "Now bow with me and repeat the Lord's Prayer."

Arian sat frozen, the breath oozing from her body as Marcus's head bowed with a terrible finality. Only one head remained upright. Only one pair of eyes remained open. The Reverend Linnet stood tall and straight at the pulpit, his eyes devouring her with an unholy hunger. The Lord's Prayer flowed smoothly from his lips in blatant mockery of his searing gaze.

Arian choked back a cry, terror rising in her throat. She rose and fled down the long aisle between the pews, mercifully unaware of the hollow silence that descended over the congregation and the single tear that splashed on Marcus Whitewood's folded hands.

Arian ran toward the only home she had known in this foreign land. Marcus's clapboard house sat placidly in the middle of the clearing, the sparkling indifference of its windowpanes mocking her agitation.

She clutched her aching side as she flew up the stairs to the loft, half expecting to hear the angry roar of a mob behind her.

Golden sunshine beamed through the window, thawing the numbness from Arian's mind. She paced the narrow attic, reviewing every scrap of thought she had ever had concerning the handsome minister who had come to their village the previous spring.

He had spoken to her often as she left the meeting house, clasping her hand in his warm, dry palm. Charity Burke had simpered each time he smiled at her, while Goodwife Burke had whispered to Arian that he had received several invitations to marry since arriving in Gloucester. Now Charity was having fits and naming Arian as her tormentor.

Arian's hands shook with impotent rage. She had to admire Linnet's craftiness in making his accusation prior to the Lord's Prayer. Everyone in Gloucester knew that a witch could not recite the Lord's Prayer aloud. The hundreds of times she had repeated the prayer in the past would be forgotten as word of her flight from the church spread on the wings of malice.

But why in God's name did Linnet seek to destroy her? Did he truly believe her a servant of Satan?

Dropping to her knees beside the bed, Arian scrabbled in her stationery box for a sheet of foolscap and a feathered quill. Time was all she had and it was running out like the sands of an hourglass. Seized by inspiration, she began to scribble madly, pausing to chew on the quill's feather while she searched her brain for a word that rhymed with "newt."

Arian was standing at the window when Marcus rounded the bend, his shoulders set in sharp angles of defeat. After several moments, his leaden footsteps sounded on the stairs. As the door creaked open, Arian turned to face him.

He gazed at the floor, his hands hanging limp at his sides. "I sought the good Reverend's help last night. I did not know he would make my confession public."

"It seems the *good* Reverend surprised us all."

Marcus lifted his head. His pale blue eyes were darkened by torment. "He convinced Constable Ingersoll not to come for you. He agreed I should be the one to fetch you for questioning. The villagers trust me." The burden of their trust lowered his shoulders another inch.

Arian dreaded his answer, but was still compelled to ask. "Do you think me wicked?"

He could not meet her steady gaze. "Your mother was wayward before she discovered the grace of God."

Arian snorted. "God's grace must be bountiful indeed if He forgave her sins."

"Don't succumb to blasphemy, child. Remember the commandments. You must honor your father and mother."

"I'd have been more than happy to honor my father if my mother had only bothered to get his name." She could not resist giving the amulet a brief caress as an old and familiar bitterness welled in her throat. "So you find me not wicked, but wayward. As my mother was."

"I think you are playing a child's game your grandmother taught you. But I know you have powers. And such powers cannot come from God." His voice cracked beneath the strain. "The Good Book speaks plainly on the subject of witchcraft."

"I am familiar with the scripture. 'Thou shalt not suffer a witch to live.'" Arian rested a hand on his forearm, thinking it odd that she should be the one to comfort him. "Shall we go?"

He pressed his lips briefly to her hair. "Do not cry, child. I could not bear it."

"Don't be absurd, Father Marcus. Witches don't weep."

Arian's trembling lips belied her words.

2

Arian's steps did not falter until they came in sight of the muddy road thronged with villagers. Marcus gently propelled her past Charity Burke, who stood with her mother's hands on her shoulders, her eyes averted. To hide a glimmer of shame? Arian wondered.

"Bow your head, witch! You are exposed! Repent of your wickedness!"

Arian halted at Goody Hubbins's rasping cry, meeting the accusing gaze of the shriveled spinster with head held high.

Goody Hubbins shrank away from her. "The witch is cursing me! I cannot breathe! Help me! Lock her away!" Clutching the loose folds of skin at her throat, she swooned into the arms of the widow behind her.

Before Arian could defend herself, Constable Ingersoll snatched her from Marcus's arms. A lone man stood before the shed that served as a jail for the settlement, his tall hat blocking the sunlight. Arian fought the urge to spit in his face as she recognized the *honorable*

Reverend Linnet. He swept open the door of the shed so Ingersoll could herd her inside.

Arian was the only one to hear the Reverend's hissed whisper. "Sell me your soul, witch, and I shall save you."

The door slammed, shutting her away in the dark.

Arian shivered, battling hysteria. The dank straw littering the narrow cell reeked of musty things that skittered and rustled along the walls. A shy cough sounded behind her. Arian whirled around, squinting into the gloom to find a tiny gnome of a woman with long, matted hair squatting in the corner.

"Dinna fear, lass. I'm a thief, not a murderer. Ye must be the young witch. I heard 'em speak o' ye." Arian realized that she too could hear the rising voices of the villagers in the square. The crone's lilting burr disintegrated into a girlish giggle. "They're no more fond o' me than ye. They clap ol' Becca in the stocks on the morrow . . . or hang me."

It wasn't difficult for Arian to imagine how the shriveled Scotswoman had ended up in the jail. Despite having fled the persecution of bigotry themselves, the Puritans had little tolerance for anyone who did not share their narrow view of the world. Before Arian could contemplate sharing the woman's grim fate, the door swung open to admit Marcus and Linnet. Becca shrank into the hay.

Marcus twisted his hat in his hands. "The good Reverend has been gracious enough to offer us his help."

"How noble of him." Arian glared at Linnet, feeling as if she had little left to lose.

Marcus missed the man's baneful smile. "Aye, daughter. He has been kind enough to offer you a home in your time of need." A sickening suspicion took root in Arian's mind. "He has offered to take you in and drive out the demons that possess you."

Linnet smiled with gentle benevolence. "I seek

only to follow an example of a colleague of mine in Boston—a Reverend Mr. Cotton Mather. He recently opened his own home to a young girl possessed with strange fits." Arian squelched a shiver as his hungry eyes raked her. "In all modesty, I must say it takes a devout man to undertake such a challenge."

Marcus beamed. "If you will agree, daughter, we will present our case to the villagers. The good Reverend will use his influence to persuade them to our side. What think you of his generosity?"

Arian closed her eyes to blot out Marcus's hopeful face. "I think," she said softly, "that the good Reverend can go straight to hell."

Marcus's mouth fell open. Linnet's jaw clenched, a rhythmic tic pulling the skin tight. Arian heard a faint rustle in the hay behind her.

Linnet grabbed Marcus by the collar and shoved him toward the door. "Flee, Goodman! 'Tis Satan who speaks through this willful child. You must not be privy to such perversity."

Marcus stumbled out. Linnet slammed the door and whirled on Arian, his eyes narrowed. She locked her knees, refusing to let them crumble. In all of her admiration for his fine looks, why had Charity Burke never noticed the lines of cruelty etched around his sensual mouth?

That mouth curved in a tight-lipped smile at her defiance. "You dare mock me. Do you know what will happen to you without my intervention? You'll be tried before the magistrates and a jury. If you're found guilty of witchcraft, you'll be hanged." The back of his hand crept up to stroke her cheek. "It would be a shame for such lovely flesh to melt in the fires of hell."

She recoiled from his touch. "You'll taste the fires of hell long before I will, sir. You have no evidence to convict me."

His throaty chuckle unnerved her. "Oh, no? The villagers are examining my evidence as we speak. They have in their hands a book of childishly scrawled rhymes they believe to be spells, several mysterious vials, and a certain willow broom." He advanced on her, backing her against the wall, his voice deceptively soft. "Of course, they all know the French are more vulnerable to the attentions of Satan because of their dark and sinful natures . . . their insatiable hungers . . ."

As he reached for her, Arian turned her face away, her skin crawling at the prospect of his touch.

"I need you, Arian," he whispered hoarsely. "I've searched the world over for you."

She gasped with shock as he plunged his hand into her bodice. It reappeared clutching the emerald amulet. He snapped the chain with a single vicious twist, then cradled the emerald in his palm, his eyes inscrutable.

Arian snatched for it. "Give that back, you wretch! You've no right!"

He dangled it just out of her reach, his eyes sparkling with dark mischief. "You shan't fly away from me, little witch." Dropping the amulet into his pocket, he pulled open the door. "Don't fret, Miss Whitewood. You'll only hang if the mob doesn't take you first."

The door slammed in her face. Arian gazed at it, despair dampening her fury. By stealing the amulet, she feared he had robbed her of any hope of escape.

"What be yer turrible crime, lassie?" came a voice from the corner.

Arian started, having forgotten she was not alone. She slid down the wall, propped her elbows on her knees, and buried her chin in her trembling hands. "I went flying during a full moon."

Arian stood on the parapets of a majestic tower, wearing shimmering white robes and waving to her adoring minions. They lifted their voices in praise to her beauty and prowess as an enchantress. As she tossed them a gracious kiss, their chorus of adulation swelled to a mighty roar.

"Kill the witch!"

Arian's eyes snapped open as the dream vanished. The thunder of approaching footsteps shook the tiny shed. She sprang to her feet, ignoring the protests of muscles cramped from being curled into a protective ball since Linnet had slammed the door on her hopes several hours before.

The door flew open. Two men appeared, their burly shoulders silhouetted against the moonlight. Arian choked back a scream of pure terror. As they grabbed her arms and shoved her through the door, she caught a glimpse of a tiny figure slipping away into the night.

The men dragged her through the narrow streets to the roared encouragement of the mob. A spiteful jerk of her hair brought tears stinging to her eyes. She blinked them away only to catch a glimpse of Goody Hubbins's twisted face. Her feet skidded in futile rebellion as they abandoned the village for the countryside, exchanging the briny scent of the sea for the oppressive threat of an approaching storm. Without warning, Arian was flung to her stomach in the dew-soaked grass.

"Fly away now, stubborn witch!" hissed a voice above her.

Arian slowly lifted her throbbing head. A pair of buckled shoes sprawled arrogantly in the grass, only inches from her nose. Shaking off the arms that bound her, she scrambled to her feet to face Linnet. The sleeves of his shirt were rolled up as if he were prepared to do nothing less than the work of God. Dread crept through Arian as she recognized the black chasm slicing through the night behind him.

"Bring a torch," he commanded. "Let us put this witch to the test."

Arian's fury infused her with daring. She grasped Linnet's starched collar and jerked him down to her eye level. "What have you done with my stepfather? He would never have allowed this."

Linnet caught her wrists, squeezing them until

pain forced her to loosen her grip. "He's on his way to Boston to fetch a magistrate for your trial."

"Why, you treacherous bas—"

"Bind her," he instructed.

A boy twisted a length of rope around her hands while another man knelt to tie her feet.

Linnet leapt to a rock, torch in hand. An uneasy hush fell over the mob. "You are all familiar with the validity of the water ordeal. We throw the girl into the pond. If she floats, Satan has saved her. If she sinks, she is innocent."

"And drowned before you imbeciles are quick enough to pronounce it," Arian cried, struggling against her bonds.

"Silence her. She will have her say," Linnet commanded. The boy clamped a sweaty palm over her mouth. Arian tried not to gag. "The girl's own stepfather came to me with tears in his eyes and confessed she had tried to murder him by dropping a candlestick on his head while he prayed for her immortal soul."

The crowd gasped with horror.

Linnet's voice rose. "But the candlestick that almost deprived the devout Goodman of his life was not wielded by human hands. Indeed, it danced in the air of its own volition while this harlot of Satan laughed with pleasure."

Goodwife Burke shrieked and fainted into her husband's arms. Arian rolled her eyes in disgust and sank her teeth deep into the boy's hand. He yelped and pushed her away, but before she could flee, Linnet sprang off the rock and wrapped an arm around her waist.

His breath scorched her ear as he cried, "Speak, witch! Say what you may in your defense! Deny that these devil's toys belong to you."

Arian watched helplessly as several women paraded past, displaying her vials, her moth-eaten ledger, the precious herbs she'd spent years foraging for in the forest. Last of all came Goody Hubbins, triumphantly waving the willow broom.

"I witnessed the woman riding astride this devil's device with my own eyes," Linnet shouted. "Sailing across the moon to rendezvous with her master."

A man shouted something about copulating with the devil that set Arian's cheeks aflame. Jeers and laughter greeted his words. The torches cast menacing shadows over the familiar faces, distorting them into nightmarish fiends. Buffeted by terror, Arian swayed in Linnet's arms, her consciousness hanging by a slender thread.

He dug his fingers into her shoulders. "Speak, witch! Proclaim your innocence if you dare."

Arian's eyes flew open as righteous fury buoyed her sinking courage. Her throaty voice cast a pall of silence over the clearing. "I am no servant of Satan! I am innocent!"

"What of these devil's tools?" came a cry. "Do you deny they were found in your lair?"

"And what harm are they? A bit of badly written poetry? A hearth broom? An herb I use to season stew?"

A woman waved a cloudy vial in the air. "I know of few enough stews that call for 'crumbled adder's tongue,' nor do I care to."

Arian waited for the laughter to die, her chin held high. "I practice *white* magic. I am a good witch, not a servant of Satan."

Several of the villagers exchanged uncertain glances.

Linnet bestowed an indulgent smile upon them. "The church does not recognize white magic. All magic comes from Satan and proclaims the evil of its doer." Arian smashed his toes with her heel in impotent rage; Linnet pinched her sharply.

If she ever intended to put her faith in her own talents, now was the time, Arian thought grimly, relaxing against Linnet's chest in apparent surrender.

"This is your last chance, *ma chérie*," he whispered. She stiffened with surprise as he slipped into her native French without so much as a stammer. "If you'll commit yourself into my hands, the two of us can rule this pathetic little world together." Returning his attention to the crowd and his language to clipped English, he asked, "Have you anything more compelling to say in your defense, Miss Whitewood?"

Arian knew Linnet was giving her one last chance. One last chance to denounce her magic and surrender herself into his hands. One last chance to sell her soul to a devil more cunning than any cloven-hooved monster feared by these villagers.

"Aye, I have something more compelling to say," she cried boldly. "Time halts but keeps on flowing. The winds cease but keep on blowing."

A blast of hot wind whipped through the clearing.

"Love hates but keeps on growing," Arian screamed, fighting the crippling fear that without the amulet, she had no chance of success. Even her fanciful grandmama had never done more than dabble with herbs and indulge in wishful thinking.

Linnet tossed his torch to a nearby man and dragged her through the high grass toward the murky pond. Arian's voice rose to a shriek.

> *A door opens, slamming shut.*
> *A knife seals, then makes the cut.*
> *The witch says absolutely . . . but . . .*

The wind gathered force, whipping her hair across her face. A clap of thunder sounded. Lightning sizzled across the sky. Goody Hubbins hurled the broom into the pond, then fell to her knees, covering her ears with her hands.

Arian drew in a last frantic breath as Linnet lifted her up the steep embankment and shoved her into the chill water. She sank like a rock. Her hands twitched against her bonds. She kicked off her heavy shoes, her legs tangling around the broomstick in a desperate search for stability. She fought to remember the rest of the spell before her lungs exploded.

Oh, yes. The ingredients. *With hellebore and eye of newt, belladonna and ginger root, griffin's claw and ash and soot.* But there were no griffins in Gloucester, Arian thought dolefully. As far as she knew, there were no griffins anywhere except in that ridiculous fairy book. And "soot" didn't really rhyme with "newt" or "root," did it?

She was sinking, fighting against the primal urge to open her mouth and seize a breath.

If only . . . she thought.

If only Linnet had never witnessed her inauspicious flight . . .

If only Marcus had loved her enough to trust her . . .

As if in a distant dream, she heard Linnet's enraged bellow and old Becca's lilting words, "Ye be a bonny witch and I be a bonny thief. Ye take yer charm, lass. It rightly belongs to ye."

A splash echoed in her roaring ears with hollow finality. The emerald amulet floated past her eyes and drifted behind her. She caught the chain, clutching at it with rapidly numbing fingers.

If only . . .

Her mouth opened of its own volition, gasping for air, but finding only water.

3

Arian prayed every prayer she could remember, both Catholic and Puritan, but unconsciousness eluded her. The pressure swelled. Water strangled the air from her lungs, the blood from her veins, the marrow from her bones. Her knees rammed into her chest with a heart-stopping jolt. She hurtled forward, the dizzying motion spinning her end over end until she feared her neck would surely snap.

The pressure worsened for one endless moment. Then the earsplitting roar of shattering glass surrounded her. The impact severed her bonds, setting her free. Free to breathe. Free to wrap her fingers around the dear, familiar shaft of the broomstick. Free to soar.

Arian opened her eyes to find herself astride the broom, sailing high above a patchy skein of clouds. The amulet's chain was still wrapped around her tingling fingers. The skirts of her dress flapped behind her, drying rapidly in the brisk wind. The inky blackness of night had faded to the mellow glow of morning. Her relief at discovering she was still alive was so keen that for a moment she forgot to be afraid. She whooped with triumph, relishing the music of her voice before it could be snatched away by the gusty breeze.

The broom angled downward, parting the clouds to reveal a looming expanse of land and water. Had Arian's knees not been clamped around the broomstick, they would have knocked together in terror.

The stony Massachusetts countryside had vanished. In its place was a vast bulwark of towers stretching to the water's edge.

"Oh, dear Lord, I am dead," Arian muttered, frowning in disappointment.

The monstrous glass-and-steel structures did not at all resemble the pearly gates of heaven she had so optimistically envisioned. Far, far below, a multitude of little yellow wagons went creeping along a web of tangled byways.

Arian slammed her eyes shut and tightened her death grip on the broomstick, rendered both giddy and dizzy by the inconceivable height. If, perchance, she was wrong about her mortal status and took a dive similar to the one she'd taken in the clearing, the broom would be of little use except to sweep up her pulverized bones.

The broom listed hard to the right. Arian's eyes flew open and she found herself heading straight for the mouth of a fat chimney. Squealing with alarm, she jerked up on the stick only to be enveloped by a cloud of smoke.

She emerged from the sallow fog coughing violently and batting at the air with her free hand. It seemed there was little she could do to correct the broom's course. It persisted in heading straight for one of the tallest towers, a shimmering structure that insinuated itself like a sleek needle into the fabric of the sky.

Mustering her courage, Arian jerked a crude knot in the chain and slipped the amulet over her head before tossing back her damp hair in a manner she deemed suitable for a flying enchantress. Whether she was to be

greeted at her final destination by Saint Peter or Beelzebub, she refused to arrive a quivering mass of terror.

But that was five seconds before she realized the
bristles of her broom were on fire and ten seconds before the dragon swooped out of the clouds and descended upon her with a mighty roar.

Copperfield was forced to shout over the deafening thunder of the helicopters buzzing the walled acre of grass
Lennox Tower modestly called a courtyard. "Are you
happy now, Tristan? You've got yourself a bona fide media circus and you're the only ringmaster in town."

From his leather chair behind the conference table
on the stage, Tristan drew a dark slash through another
name and called out, "Next."

A poodle-permed contestant wearing a flowered
house dress trotted forward, waving a tiny pink sweater.
"If you'll give me twelve hours, Mr. Lennox, I swear I'll
find the missing Pekingese this sweater belongs to."

The woman grunted as a reporter elbowed her out
of the way to thrust a microphone in Tristan's face. "Is
it true, Mr. Lennox, that a computer simulation has confirmed that Richard Rastasi of Iraq has bent the handle
of a spoon a trillionth of a centimeter using only the
power of his mind?"

Tristan calmly pushed the microphone aside.
"Next."

"But I found my husband's car keys under the
couch cushions and they'd been missing for over a year!"
The contestant cursed in fluent Yiddish as one of Tristan's assistants gently led her away.

Copperfield rubbed his throbbing temples. "I knew
I should have taken five extra-strength aspirin this morning instead of only three." A turbaned swami carrying
basket, cobra, and flute glided forward from the milling
crowd. Copperfield groaned. "Or maybe a bottle of Pro-
zac."

He shot the sky a nasty look. The sporadic roar of

the helicopters certainly wasn't helping his head. Both the *Global Inquirer* and the *Prattler* had been circling like vultures since dawn, their parasitic photographers hanging out open doors, telephoto lenses in hand. He wondered who at the *Prattler* fancied himself such a wit as to have had their helicopter painted to resemble a rather myopic shark.

"Next," came Tristan's cool command. His pen descended with a methodical slash as the swami slunk away. A flashbulb popped, invoking a sullen hiss from the cobra.

"How can you be so calm?" Copperfield asked. "Your credibility is in tatters. The front office has already fielded calls from Ricki Lake's booking agent, *America's Oddest People*, and four major stockholders offering referrals to their therapists."

Tristan doodled a Pekingese that looked more like a cloud with legs on the steno pad before shooting Copperfield an arch glance. "Maybe you should review the numbers of those therapists. You look as if you could use some analysis."

Copperfield threw up his hands in frustration. "Oh, do forgive me if spending the night on the floor of your closet aggravates my neuroses."

Tristan shrugged, looking anything but repentant. "I thought you knew where the emergency release was."

"It was a little hard to find in the dark. If you hadn't sent Sven to let me out this morning, I'd still be fumbling through your silk pajamas. And does any human male really need fifty pairs of silk pajamas?"

Tristan's gaze flicked to Copperfield's chest. A knowing smile quirked his lips. "Nice tie. It matches your eyes."

Their exchange was interrupted by a flurry of discord near the bank of glass elevators. "Unhand me, you Visigoth!" shouted a cultured voice. "You're wrinkling my cape."

As the top-hatted figure broke from his captors and

sped toward the stage, Tristan settled back in his chair, his legendary composure growing even more dangerous. An unnatural hush fell over the crowd. The reporters edged nearer, nostrils twitching like predators scenting the coppery tang of fresh blood.

Never one to squander a potential audience, the newcomer swept off his glossy top hat to reveal a leonine mane of snowy white hair. "Wite Lize, illusionist extraordinaire, at your most humble service." He flicked the lid of his cane; a bouquet of carnations popped into existence.

The antiquated trick was greeted by a smattering of cautious applause.

The helicopters had withdrawn for the moment and Tristan's words shredded the tense silence like slivers of glass. "Get him out of here."

Captained by Sven, a burly Norwegian whose budding acting career had been tragically cut short when he was fired from *Baywatch* because of his irresistible compulsion to gaze lovingly into the camera, Tristan's legion of omnipresent bodyguards moved in. They were distinguishable from the crowd by the suspicious bulges beneath their gray jackets and the regulation Ray•Bans they wore despite the overcast sky.

The intruder wagged a chiding finger at them. "I wouldn't do that if I were you, gentlemen. According to the newspaper, this contest is open to all. I have just as much right to that million dollars as anyone. If you cause me so much as a twinge of mental anguish, I shall have to call my attorney." He fished around in his top hat, drawing out first a squirming rabbit, then a cellular phone from its interior. A little girl clinging to her mother's hand squealed with delight.

Tristan's fingers twitched, snapping the pen in two.

Copperfield smiled, rather enjoying his employer's discomfiture. "He has a point. Another lawsuit would only generate more negative publicity."

"He may have a point, but we have a restraining

order. Would you rather I ordered Sven to shoot him on sight?"

"Sven," Copperfield called out, already envisioning the grisly headlines. "Would you please escort Mr. Lize to the nearest exit?"

The little girl started to cry as the bodyguards seized the magician by the arms.

"You'll have to forgive Mr. Lennox, child," Lize crooned. "He doesn't like it when you make things appear." His veneer of civility crumbled as they dragged him toward the exit. "You only know about making things disappear, don't you, Lennox?" Shoving his face into a reporter's TV camera, he snarled, "Ask him about my son. Ask him how he made my son disappear all those years ago!"

The familiar accusations continued to ring in the air long after Wite Lize was gone, but Tristan simply flipped to a fresh page on the steno pad, chose a solid-gold Cross pen from the breast pocket of his suit, and murmured, "Next."

It was almost a relief when the hollow *thud-thud* of a returning helicopter broke the awkward silence. The mother knelt to dab at her daughter's cheeks, shooting Tristan a reproachful glance. "Now, honey, I told you before we left home that there was no such thing as magic. Poor Mr. Lennox simply has more money than he has common—"

The rest of her words were drowned out by a scream of pure terror, so shrill it pierced even the rhythmic clamor of the helicopter's blades.

The little girl pointed heavenward, a snaggle-toothed grin transforming her tearstained face. "Look, Mommy—the Wicked Witch of the West!"

Tristan came to his feet. "What the hell . . . ?"

Copperfield was so busy gaping at his employer's astounded expression that he failed to look up until the crowd let out a collective gasp.

"That's odd," Tristan murmured, following the er-

ratic path of the smoke trail across the sky. "I don't remember authorizing a skywriter."

Copperfield's own jaw dropped as he realized the
trail of smoke and cinders was being shed by a flying
broom. A flying broom piloted by a petite brunette
whose terrified shrieks verged on deafening.

Copperfield winced as the contraption did several
clumsy loopedy-loops around the helicopter, narrowly
missing its twirling blades. Never one to disdain a photo
opportunity, the *Prattler* photographer leaned out for a
clearer shot only to drop his camera and grab for his
safety strap when the helicopter swerved, avoiding a col-
lision with the soaring spire of the Chrysler Building by
a hairsbreadth.

Choosing discretion over valor, the helicopter
wisely retreated. A curious downdraft seized the broom,
slowing it to a near float. It came tumbling end over end
toward the courtyard, the squeals of its rider growing in
volume with each dizzying flip-flop. The squeals ended
with an ominous thud.

Tristan was the first to reach her. Before Copperfield could even recover from his shock and leap down
from the stage, Tristan was kneeling in the grass, the
stranger's head cradled in his lap.

From the haste with which Sven dropped to one
knee, tossed back his sun-streaked mane, and drew his
sleek 9-millimeter, Copperfield suspected the bodyguard had been waiting for just such an opportunity his
entire film career. "Step away from her, sir," he commanded, doing his best Schwarzenegger. "She could be
an assassin."

His employer gave no sign that he'd heard the
warning, much less had any intention of heeding it. With
a tenderness Copperfield had forgotten he was capable
of, Tristan brushed a curl from the woman's pallid brow.

Her lashes fluttered open to reveal dark luminous
eyes. She blinked up at Tristan, her expression quizzical,
then lifted a trembling hand to touch his cheek. A lop-

sided smile curved her lips. "Good heavens. You must be Lucifer."

As her fingers curled into her palm and her eyes drifted shut, Tristan lifted his helpless gaze, giving Copperfield a jarring glimpse of an emotion he hadn't seen in his friend's eyes for over a decade.

Wonder.

4

Arian's fingers glided over the sheets, puzzled to encounter the sinful sleekness of satin instead of the scratchy weave of faded homespun. One of her mama's lovers had insisted on satin sheets. Had it been the petulant Pierre or the mustachioed Jacques? A duke or a musketeer?

Snuggling deeper into the firm tick, she murmured something half English and half French, all vowels and slurred consonants. She could sleep away the entire morning if she liked. Her mama's temper was capricious at best and if Arian dared trouble her before noon, she was likely to get a hairbrush hurled at her head. Arian winced at the thought. Her head already ached as if she'd forgotten to duck.

She rolled to her back and knuckled open her eyes, expecting to see a carved cherub leering down at her from a gilded tester.

The heavenly creature glowering down at her possessed neither dimpled cheeks or a simpering pout. His honey-hued hair had been cropped above the ears, accentuating the chiseled strength of a brow creased with determination. A tantalizing hint of a cleft marred a chin that would have been too pretty without it. His slightly off-center nose was complemented by the jaded quirk of his lips.

Arian's eyes lingered there, captivated by the insouciant grace of that mouth. He was less cherub than rebellious angel—divine, seductive, and dangerous enough to imperil her vulnerable soul.

As if he also possessed the power to read her thoughts, he said, "I suppose you were expecting Lucifer? My competitors have called me much worse on occasion, but even they've never accused me of impersonating the Prince of Darkness."

She jerked her gaze from his lips to his eyes, the sharp motion making her head throb. She touched her fingertips to her temples, remembering through a muddled haze her dizzying flight, her desperate attempt to elude the dragon's steely claws, her reckless plummet from the sky.

She would have sworn this man had been waiting to catch her. That his strong, warm hands had soothed her brow. That his pewter-gray eyes had misted with tender concern.

Those eyes were narrowed now, the mist in them chilled to frost. Arian had awakened once as a child to find one of her mother's paramours sitting on the edge of her bed, gazing down at her in just such a predatory manner. Her shrill scream had jarred her mama from a champagne-induced stupor and Arian had been shipped off to live with her grandmama three days later.

She snatched the sheet up to her chin, knowing Marcus would have been gratified by the unexpected surge of Puritan modesty. "You should be ashamed of yourself, sir. Leering at a defenseless maiden while she sleeps. Have you no scruples?"

"None to speak of." He stroked his immaculately shaved chin. "The face of an angel. The voice of a siren.

Charming." The flinty gleam in his eyes warned her he was in little danger of being enchanted.

Arian dared a peep under the sheet and was mollified to find her drab Puritan garments intact. She was even more relieved to discover the amulet still draped around her neck. A single lamp burned high on the wall, its flame as disarmingly steady as the stranger's gaze.

"Where am I?" she whispered, peering around in a vain attempt to escape his scrutiny. "What is this place?"

"Lennox Tower."

Unable to resist the magnetism of those eyes, she stole a sidelong glance at him. "And you, sir, would be . . . ?"

"Tristan Lennox. You disappoint me. Didn't you bother to do your homework before staging that idiotic stunt?"

"Home work?" Arian parroted, wondering if his French would be as incomprehensible as his English.

"I find it difficult to believe your employers didn't provide you with a detailed dossier on Lennox Enterprises. Shareholder profiles? Stock portfolios? A current photo of the CEO?"

She shook her head, but he mistook her confusion for denial.

He arched one tawny eyebrow. "The rules and restrictions of the magic competition?"

Arian seized eagerly upon the only phrase she understood. "Magic?"

He tossed a folded sheaf of paper in her lap. She recognized it as a newspaper, similar to the pamphlets she'd seen distributed on the street corners of Paris as a child. Pamphlets denouncing the extravagant pensions Louis bestowed on his nobles or deriding the excesses of his most recent mistress. Still eyeing Lennox warily, she wiggled to a sitting position and tilted his offering so she could read it. The bold script seemed to leap out at her—*One Million Dollar Prize Offered for Proof of Magic.*

Arian jerked the paper up to her nose, fearful her eyes would reveal a glint of avarice. "One million dollars? 'Tis an uncommon amount of wealth, is it not? Just how many francs would that be?"

"Sorry. I don't do foreign exchange rates in my head."

Lowering the paper, she wrinkled her nose hopefully at him. "Did I win?"

His sharp bark of laughter erased her timid smile. The wintry spice of his cologne made her nose tingle as he leaned forward. She shrank back into the pillows.

"That remains to be seen." His tone swerved from menacing to conversational with dizzying swiftness. "But if I'm not able to discredit you for the clever little fraud you obviously are, what name would you like on your check—Glenda, the Gold-digging Witch of the North?"

Arian felt the blood drain from her cheeks. She'd barely just arrived in this curious place and this arrogant stranger was already accusing her of witchcraft. He had judged and convicted her without a trial. The hint of mischief playing around his mouth warned her he was capable of far more deliciously diabolical punishments than the Reverend Linnet had ever plotted.

But Linnet had been a thorough tutor. She would never again be bullied into confessing anything. Not without first considering the possibility that this man's magic competition might have been nothing more than bait to lure some unsuspecting witch into his trap.

Folding her arms over her chest, she said coolly, "My name is not Glenda. 'Tis Arian. Miss Arian Whitewood." She sniffed disdainfully, wishing her nose was less pert and more aristocratic, then uttered the four words Marcus had so frequently used to explain her many eccentricities. "I am from France."

"And how many frequent flyer miles did you earn crossing the Atlantic on your broom, *Miss* Whitewood?"

When she only blinked at him to hide her bafflement, he swore beneath his breath and rose from the bed. Arian's relief was spoiled by a shiver. An unnatural chill seemed to permeate the air in his absence. As he crossed the enormous salon, her gaze drifted back to the newspaper, only to be riveted by the innocuous line of print at the top of the page.

October 25, 1996.

5

The newspaper tumbled from Arian's numb fingers just
as the floor-to-ceiling curtains parted to reveal a radiant
galaxy of stars through a wall of sheer glass.

Her host was no less enigmatic by starlight than in
shadows. He swept out an arm toward the dazzling vista.
"Well, Miss Arian Whitewood from France, welcome to
New York City."

If he had said, "Welcome to paradise," Arian would
have been no less astounded. She could not choke so
much as a gasp past her constricted throat. She had lived
the past ten years in a world bereft of beauty. Drawn by
its irresistible temptation, she slipped from the bed, tugging her skirts down to shield her ankles from Lennox's
probing gaze. She sidestepped him, gliding forward until
she could press her thirsty fingertips to the cool glass.

It was only then that she realized the lights were
not stars at all, but thousands upon thousands of lamps
glowing from the windows of soaring towers. " 'Tis a
wonder they haven't burned the city to the ground," she

murmured, awestruck by the discovery. "Not even Paris has so many candles."

They gazed upon the marvel from an unthinkable height. Arian made the mistake of glancing down only to discover a multitude of similarly lit processionals creeping along the broad avenues far below. Dizziness washed over her in waves as she comprehended for the first time just how far she'd strayed from home. Her ears began to roar. Her vision blurred. Terrified of humiliating herself by swooning in front of this indifferent stranger, she fumbled at the window for a latch, frantically seeking a breath of fresh air.

She swayed, but before her knees could buckle, his hands were there to cup her shoulders, their warmth palpable even through the hardy weave of her sleeves.

"The windows are hermetically sealed," he said softly. "They don't open."

Even as Arian accepted his unspoken invitation to lean against him, she could not help but wonder what manner of man would be so extravagant as to fashion his walls of windows, yet so foolish as to shut out all the lovely things that could drift through them—crisp autumn breezes, the cheery song of a thrush, the aroma of honeysuckle on a sultry summer day. An unwelcome trace of pity softened her wariness.

Her curious intimacy with a stranger only intensified the alien nature of the landscape. A keen sense of isolation swept through her as she realized that everyone she'd ever known had been dead for centuries— Marcus, Charity Burke, even the Reverend Linnet. She would have thought it impossible to yearn for Gloucester, but even the village's uncompromising harshness seemed preferable to starting over one more time.

She had little choice, she reminded herself sternly. Until she could figure out which miscalculation in her spell had brought her to this place, she would simply have to shrug off her fears and do what she'd done her entire life—pretend to belong somewhere she never would.

She lifted her head to discover her host wasn't admiring the magnificent view, but her pensive reflection. Their gazes merged in the glass, and for a fleeting moment, the loneliness echoed in his cool gray eyes created the disconcerting illusion that he was more lost than she was. Before she could deem it anything more than a trick of the light, his gaze lowered to the amulet.

"What's that you have there?" he asked, guiding her around to face him. "A crucifix to ward off vampires and marauding chief executives?"

" 'Tis nothing," she mumbled, tucking it into her bodice. "Just a worthless trinket."

Too late, it occurred to her that dropping the amulet down her dress only presented the avaricious Mr. Lennox with an irresistible challenge. She stiffened, expecting him to plunge his greedy hand between her breasts as Linnet had done. But his warm knuckles barely grazed her collarbone as he snagged the amulet's chain with a deft grace infinitely more dangerous than Linnet's pawing. 'Twas as if he sought to pilfer not only the amulet, but the heart that lay beneath it as well.

He held the emerald up to examine it. "A striking piece. Is it antique?"

"You might say that."

"The setting is rather unusual. Where did you get it?"

The casual question did not fool Arian. "I did not steal it, sir, if that's what you're asking." She lowered her eyes, fearful his crystalline gaze might unearth long-buried seeds of deceit. " 'Twas a gift from my mother."

The emerald cast a sparkling prism of light across Lennox's implacable features. "Ah, a woman of impeccable taste."

"Except when it came to men." As Arian's nervous gaze licked up and down Lennox's lean length, taking in his flawlessly tailored breeches, crisp waistcoat, and tan shirt unbuttoned at the throat to release a sprinkling of golden hair, she breathed a silent prayer of thanksgiving that she hadn't been similarly cursed.

The amulet twirled before his hypnotic eyes as if it belonged there, giving Arian a brief moment of horror. What if he innocently gave voice to his unspoken wish that he'd never laid eyes on her? Would she pop back into the bottom of that murky pond in Gloucester or simply cease to exist altogether?

She snatched the amulet from his hand, knowing even as she did so that she was being ridiculous. Lennox was but a mere mortal. She was the witch. The amulet was simply a channel for her powers, not the source of them.

Lennox obviously wasn't a man accustomed to having anything snatched from his grasp. His face hardened into a dispassionate mask. "So tell me, Miss Whitewood, how did you accomplish your cheap little trick? Was the broom radio-controlled? Digitalized? Motorized? Was that how the fire started? A gasoline leak? A flaw in the motor? You do realize that they're disassembling what was left of the device in my laboratory even as we speak."

Arian was too dazed by his barrage of questions to fashion a coherent denial. "I don't know . . . I don't remember . . ."

As he backed her against the window, danger roiling off him like woodsmoke, she became thankful that it didn't open. "Just who the hell are you? A con artist? A corporate spy? One of those leeches from the tabloids? Or did Wite Lize send you?" She wouldn't have thought it possible, but his expression darkened further. Her knees began to tremble again, but this time he made no gallant move to steady her. "Such a ridiculous stunt would certainly have appealed to his flair for the dramatic."

Arian didn't know whether to be grateful or unnerved when a polite cough sounded behind Lennox. "If this is a formal interrogation, Tristan, shouldn't the lady have an attorney present?"

Lennox swung around. "Dammit, Cop! Don't you ever knock?"

Arian's relief at having his wrath shifted to a new target was eclipsed by horror as she saw the man standing behind him. She clapped a hand over her mouth too late to muffle a shriek.

They both stared at her as if she'd lost her wits.

She lowered her hand and pointed a quivering finger at the intruder. His black, unpowdered hair had been sleeked back in a leather thong. "H-h-he's an Indian!"

The two men exchanged a bemused glance.

"Don't be alarmed," Lennox said, arching a wry brow. "He's entirely domesticated. He hasn't scalped anyone since the *Wall Street Journal* accused me of insider trading in eighty-nine."

The savage gently extended his sun-bronzed hand, as if fearful any sudden moves might cause her to bolt. "How do you do, ma'am. I'm Michael Copperfield—Tristan's legal counsel, PR advisor, and token Native American."

Arian still hesitated, remembering how the Reverend Linnet had preached that all Indians worshiped the devil as their master. But the good reverend had also accused her of fornicating with Satan and tried to drown her.

She spread her skirts and bobbed a timid curtsy before placing her hand into Copperfield's. Instead of bringing it to his lips as she expected him to do, he pumped it up and down in a most curious manner. Compared to the wintry gaze Lennox swept between the two of them, the savage's twinkling brown eyes radiated warmth.

"Cop majored in law and minored in public relations," Lennox offered. "He's a living oxymoron."

Arian gasped at his blatant rudeness. "The poor

fellow can't help it if his wits are not as keen as yours.
There's no need to insult him."

Lennox stared at her for a long moment. Then his
lips curled in a tender smile that conveyed his sarcasm
more effectively than a sneer. "We seem to be experi-
encing a slight language barrier. Miss Whitewood claims
she's from France."

The Indian snorted. "So did the Coneheads."

"Are you implying she's an alien?"

"No, but the *Prattler* is. The *Global Inquirer* insists
she's Elvis's illegitimate daughter. They're both begging
for exclusive interviews."

The men towered over Arian, making her feel like
one of the squat dwarves in her grandmama's fairy book.
As they continued to discuss her as if she weren't even
in the room, she glanced down at her feet to make sure
she hadn't accidentally rendered herself invisible.

Her ears pricked up when Copperfield said, "She
did bang her head a pretty good one. Maybe she honestly doesn't remember crash-landing in the courtyard.
She might have a temporary case of amnesia."

"Temporary and selective. You watch too many
soap operas, Cop. She might have an evil twin, too."

"Yeah, and you might have a nice one somewhere," the Indian shot back, his mutinous tone making
Arian want to applaud.

Lennox pivoted on his heel.

"Where are you going?" Copperfield demanded.

"To find some answers," Lennox snapped, shooting Arian a glance rife with menace. "I'm sure as hell not
going to find any here."

Copperfield stared after him, a bemused smile
playing around his mouth. "Congratulations, Miss
Whitewood. I do believe you've cracked the ice
prince's façade. I haven't seen him in such a temper in
years."

"I was under the impression that was his usual temper," she replied glumly, wondering why she cared.

He shrugged. "Tristan's not such a bad sort. He never forgets a friend." The Indian's smile lost a fraction of its warmth as he turned his piercing gaze on her. "Or an enemy."

When Tristan strode into the dimly lit Security Command Center of Lennox Tower, the guard on night duty almost choked on his doughnut.

The former marine jerked his booted feet off the semicircular control panel, leaped out of his chair, and sucked in his paunch with an audible hiss. "Sir!"

In his present mood, it was no great challenge for Tristan to suppress his smile. At least the man hadn't saluted him. "At ease, Deluth. You've got powdered sugar on your upper lip."

Deluth swiped at his mouth, his paunch reinflating. "Sorry, sir. I wasn't expecting you."

Tristan didn't waste time pointing out that if the man had been doing his job, he would have seen his boss approaching the Command Center on security camera number 638, which would have given him ample time to hide both the box of doughnuts and the crumpled issue of *Playboy* sticking out from beneath his chair. He could hardly blame the guard for being surprised by his sudden appearance. Although Tristan had designed every fiber-optic circuit in the room, he had never deigned to make personal use of them.

Due to the late hour, glowing banks of monitors revealed screen after screen of empty offices, shadowy elevator shafts, deserted stairwells, and numerous entranceways guarded by uniformed security personnel. Tristan had long ago learned to shrug off accusations of paranoia. He lived with the knowledge that all the security guards and sophisticated surveillance equipment in the world wouldn't stop his enemy from destroying him.

"Activate the cameras in the penthouse," he commanded, sinking into the swivel chair the guard had abandoned.

"But, sir, I have strict orders never to activate those units unless you're out of the building."

Tristan cast him a look of deadly patience. "And who do you think gave those orders?"

Deluth scratched his head, his florid brow beginning to sweat. "Y-y-ou, sir," he ventured.

"That's right. And who signs your paychecks?"

"You do, sir."

Tristan continued to stare at him.

Deluth hunched over the panel, swapping two panoramic views of the courtyard for opposing views of the penthouse interior. Tristan leaned forward to adjust the toggle switch until the suite's single bedroom sharpened into crisp focus.

His mysterious guest was wandering the spacious room, her hands linked at the small of her back as if she were an inquisitive child fearful of touching something that might give her a nasty shock. As Tristan zoomed in on her, he was the one to receive the nasty shock. Arian Whitewood was no child. She might be dressed like some poor relation of the Addams family, but not even the hideous cut of her dress could disguise the fact that her petite body was ripe with womanly curves.

Tristan grimaced as he felt something panting down the back of his neck. He swiveled around to discover Deluth hanging over his shoulder, his beady eyes bright with interest.

Refusing to examine his sudden urge to shove the doughnuts, box and all, down the burly ex-marine's throat, Tristan bit off a single word. "Out."

This time, he didn't have to repeat himself. Tucking the box of doughnuts under his arm, the guard retreated, clearly more relieved than offended by his dismissal.

Tristan turned back to the monitor, coolly observing his quarry and wondering what mad impulse had prompted him to have her installed in his suite. In his bed. When she'd collapsed in the courtyard, Sven had rushed forward to take her from his arms, but Tristan's first instinct had been to shield her from the flashing cameras and shouting reporters. Cradling her slight form against his chest, he'd made a beeline for the express elevator and stabbed the button for the ninety-fifth floor. Habit, he supposed. The penthouse had always been his only refuge from the dogged persistence of the press.

But his careless act may have worked to his advantage. As long as she resided in the Tower, he would be able to monitor her every move until he could formulate a plan to discredit her.

The curious creature was all hair and eyes. A mass of corkscrew curls tumbled to her waist in a natural tangle no expensive perm could duplicate. The elfin delicacy of her features only magnified her dark eyes. He scowled at her image. She reminded him of those pathetic prints of sad-eyed waifs that had adorned the walls of the orphanage where he'd grown up. Her eyebrows were striking slashes against skin so pale as to be nearly translucent.

"Don't they have tanning booths in France?" he muttered.

Despite his conviction that she was the worst sort of fraud, he could not help being intrigued by the Gallic lilt of her husky voice and her quaint mannerisms. The girl had curtsied to Copperfield. Copperfield, for God's sake!

When she had awakened to find him looming over her, she had snatched the blankets up to her chin as if she were the vicar's daughter and he was some mustache-twirling villain from some Off-Broadway Gilbert and Sullivan revival bent on ravishing her. Remembering how she had looked with her rosy lips parted in sleep, her dark hair spread across his pillow as if it belonged there, Tristan shifted irritably.

Even more perplexing than her manners had been the hint of fragrance that clung to her skin. His mental scan of potential perfumes had yielded nothing. It wasn't Beautiful or Obsession or even some Chanel of obscure numerical origin. Tristan despised any puzzle he could not solve. Her elusive scent had made him inexplicably hungry, tempting him to brush aside that beguiling cloud of hair and nuzzle the skin of her throat until he identified it.

He watched through narrowed eyes as she picked up the remote control and idly trailed her fingers over it. Her mouth formed a startled O as a panel in the far wall hissed open to reveal a thirty-five-inch screen with the *Nick at Nite* logo emblazoned in the corner and the manic figures of Samantha Stevens and her very first Darrin cavorting across it. The girl drifted toward the television, her eyes widening to enormous proportions as a young Elizabeth Montgomery twitched her nose, sending Dick York into an eye-rolling, foot-stomping tantrum. Maybe he should have Cop check to see if there had been any recent escapes from Bellevue.

He became even more puzzled when she pressed her nose to the screen, then turned her head to peer both ways. He had once seen a cat do the same thing before circling the television to make sure the tasty little people trapped inside hadn't escaped out the back. When the girl straightened, her pert nose was smudged with dust. Tristan made a mental note to fire his cleaning service.

Still casting the television furtive glances over her shoulder, she crept toward the bedside table where the sleek Swedish telephone sat.

His ugliest suspicions confirmed, Tristan flicked the switches that would allow him to monitor her conversation and trace the call. He had hosted the magic competition with the slender hope of capturing a deadly shark only to end up netting a harmless guppy. Even as he settled back in the chair to nurse a twinge of gloating satisfaction, his methodical mind sorted through her possible contacts.

Would she call her editor at the *Prattler*? The CEO of one of his major business rivals? Wite Lize? Or perhaps another partner in her cunning scheme to swindle him out of a million dollars—some faceless lover who would mock Tristan's gullibility before whispering all the tender, wicked things he would do to her when they were reunited?

Tristan stiffened, wondering where that last wayward thought had come from. He'd never been a man given to flights of fantasy, especially when it came to women.

The girl held the phone in her hand for several minutes, her expression intent, before pushing the first button. The shrill beep jangled Tristan's nerves. Like a panther poised to pounce, he waited for her to complete the connection.

The notes meandered on, one after the other. Tristan leaned forward, frowning. No exchange took that long to dial—not even an international one.

His disgust shifted to bewilderment as the jumbled notes merged into a winsome melody. He sank back in the chair, stunned to realize she was punching out a halting rendition of "Frère Jacques" on the numbered buttons, much as a toddler might pick out the notes of "Mary Had a Little Lamb" on a toy phone. An unprecedented tightness seized his chest, so intense he briefly entertained the notion that he might be having a heart attack.

"If you'd like to make a call, please hang up . . ."

The mechanical voice startled him almost as badly as it did the girl. She dropped the phone as if it had bitten her, severing the connection, and collapsed into a sitting position on the bed.

As she gazed around the enormous suite, Tristan could not help but wonder if she found it as sterile as he had deliberately designed it to be. To his chagrin, the room's icy elegance only emphasized her disheveled charm. Her shoulders rose and slumped in a soundless sigh. Tristan had never seen anyone look quite so forlorn. He fought a brief surge of horror at the prospect of being a helpless witness to her tears.

But instead of crying, she simply curled up in the middle of the bed without bothering to draw the covers over her. The television bathed her in its impersonal light.

His eyes were drawn against their will to the slender legs tucked into the protective half-moon of her body. Her heavy black stockings were ripped just below the knee, revealing a pale strip of calf. A raw pulse of desire in his groin startled him.

If he was so inclined, he knew he could thumb through Deluth's well-worn copy of *Playboy* and find gorgeous women in varying states of dress and undress, their lush, silicone-enhanced bodies contorted in every provocative pose he'd once dreamed of as a lonely adolescent. There was no reason that innocent glimpse of flesh should quicken his breath or make his mouth go dry with want.

Tristan sank back in the chair, running a damp hand across his mouth. It was probably just the novelty of seeing so little flesh when he was accustomed to seeing so much. Or perhaps he'd been working too hard after all. He was going to have to take Copperfield up on his offer to fix him up with another one of those gaunt, hollow-cheeked model friends of his.

Almost as if his unnatural twinge of hunger had disturbed her, the girl reached to tug the homely skirt down over her legs. With one abrupt motion, Tristan switched off the camera, feeling like the very worst sort of voyeur.

Arian awoke the next morning with a feline stretch and a sated yawn. She burrowed into the fleecy pillow, thinking to steal another hour's sleep, then sat bolt upright as she remembered where she was.

New York City. Nineteen ninety-six. In Tristan Lennox's bed.

A brisk hint of his cologne still clung to the satin sheets.

Arian sprang to her feet in one lithe motion, beset by a ridiculous pang of guilt. 'Twas hardly her fault she found the decadent fragrance intoxicating. The most exotic aroma she'd smelled on any man in the past ten years had been the sweat of hard work mingled with the stench of cod and the earthy musk of cows and pigs.

The sunshine streaming through the wall of glass did much to dispel the desolation she'd experienced the night before. 'Twas impossible to gaze down upon the bustling avenues and not feel a surge of exhilaration. She'd never seen so many people in one place, all rushing like industrious ants to somewhere even more compelling. She pressed her nose to the window, wishing she could throw it open and absorb the sounds and smells of this thrilling century.

Her expectant smile faded as if a cloud had passed over the sun as she recalled the disconcerting sensation of pewter-gray eyes studying her reflection in the glass. From the tips of his shiny leather shoes to the tawny sheen of his hair, her host had exuded a masculine confidence so powerful it bordered on arrogance. Shuddering, Arian remembered another arrogant man, a man willing to debase and even drown her if she refused to bow to his will.

Tristan never forgets a friend. Or an enemy.

Copperfield's gentle warning drifted back to haunt her. Arian had no intention of being either friend or enemy to Tristan Lennox. She simply wanted to discover what manner of colossal blunder had sent her crashing into his life.

She'd found it impossible to think last night with her body battered by exhaustion and her mind muddled with shock, but today her musings felt as crisp as the sunlight.

" 'Time,' " she muttered, pacing the thick carpet while she struggled to recall the hastily scrawled words of her spell. " 'Time halts, but keeps on flowing . . . ' "

It had been her rather ambitious intention to freeze Linnet and his bloodthirsty minions in time while she made her escape. She had never dreamed her clumsy spell-casting would send her hurtling over three centuries into the future. She nearly stumbled, her chagrin tempered by belated awe and burgeoning excitement. Why, her powers must be far greater than she'd ever dared to hope! But were they great enough to return her to 1689 where she belonged?

Her spirits plummeted as she recalled the grim fate that awaited her there. If her current luck prevailed, she'd arrive just in time to hear Linnet mouthing some sanctimonious words over her freshly dug grave.

Time, Arian thought, jerking up her head. She had manipulated time once. What was to stop her from doing it again? What if she returned herself to Gloucester the day before Linnet witnessed her disastrous broom flight? She might have to experiment with several different spells, but if she were successful, the dastardly minister would have no motive for persecuting her and no evidence to convict her. Instead of dying a premature and tragic death, she could resume her barren existence as Gloucester's social pariah.

She groaned, rubbing her temples as her dragon-induced headache threatened to return. 'Twas too easy to envision her hair dulled with dust, her hands callused and raw from milking cows and scaling codfish, her spirit broken from battling petty Puritan intolerance. How long would it be before she withered into a dry and bitter old crone like Goody Hubbins?

She surveyed the alien landscape outside the window with a fresh eye. Perhaps there was a different future for her than the one she'd just imagined—a future within the future. There was certainly little enough to bind her to the past. Her grandmama was dead, and while she was undeniably fond of Marcus, her very presence in his household threatened his good standing within the Puritan community. Gloucester was already beginning to seem like nothing more than a dim memory of a vaguely disturbing dream.

She would have to rely on her wits to convince the skeptical Mr. Lennox that she belonged in his century. A bitter smile curved her lips. Her father was no more to her than some nameless actor, but at least she'd inherited an innate talent for mimicry. It had served her well when she was being jerked from household to household, from France to the Colonies, and from the decadent splendor of King Louis's court to a desolate Puritan village. She had adapted her speech patterns, mannerisms, and behavior to fit other people's expectations of her with such consummate skill that sometimes even she forgot who she was.

As she sank down on the edge of the bed to ponder her plan, something rustled beneath her feet. She glanced down to discover the newspaper Lennox had waved beneath her nose the previous night.

One Million Dollar Prize Offered for Proof of Magic.

She snatched up the paper, her eyes narrowing with a cunning that would have had Marcus dropping to his knees to pray for her eternal soul. If she was going to survive in this foreign time without depending on anyone but herself, she would need more than just her wits and her erratic witchcraft. She would need resources.

She pored over the article, muttering beneath her breath the phrases she did not comprehend. Her resolve grew stronger with each word she read. She had met the conditions of Lennox's competition. She had proved to him that magic existed. She deserved the prize.

She hugged the paper to her breast, her heart skipping with excitement. One million dollars would be more than enough to allow her to bid the haughty Mr. Lennox a hasty farewell and book passage to France. She could purchase a cottage like her grandmama's in the middle of some secluded forest. She sighed with yearning, already picturing the ivy creeping up its weathered stone walls.

There she would be free to grow her own herbs, compose spells, and test the limits of her God-given gifts without the constant fear of discovery. After a decade of practicing her magic in Marcus's grimy cellar with only indifferent spiders for company, the cozy vision made her throat tighten with longing.

Her wistful smile faded as she drew the amulet from her bodice. With wealth of her own, she would never have to rely on the capricious affections of men for food, lodging, or happiness. She would never be coerced into becoming the mistress of some wealthy nobleman, then have to endure being passed to another man and another bed when he tired of her. She would never become what her mother had been.

The emerald sparkled in the sunlight with a clarity uncommon to stones of its ilk. What would happen if she simply wished for wealth? she wondered idly. Given the amulet's perverse inclination to woo disaster, she feared she would find herself buried beneath a spill of gold doubloons or spitting out francs. When it came to something as mundane as currency, she'd rather take her chances with Lennox than trust her unpredictable talents.

But how to convince him she was no fraud and coax him into surrendering his prize? Tossing aside the paper, she rose to pace the salon with fresh urgency. The solution to her dilemma was simple enough—perform magic for him. But after her encounter with the Reverend Linnet, she feared putting her faith in any man. Especially a man as dangerous as Tristan Lennox. He claimed to seek magic, yet spoke of witches with icy derision. For all she knew, he might be just another ambitious witch hunter seeking to slip a noose around her slender neck.

She touched her throat, suppressing an involuntary shudder. There must be some way to learn if witches were still being persecuted in this age. If she could prove Mr. Lennox more enlightened than his ancestors, she would be free to demonstrate her powers, collect her reward, and begin a new life for what she prayed would be the last time. As soon as she could do so without arousing suspicion, she would seek out the library. Her gaze drifted to the soaring ceiling. Surely a mansion this grand had a library.

As Arian secured the amulet in her bodice, a twinge of discomfort reminded her that she had more pressing needs at the moment than knowledge or money.

Twenty minutes later, when Sven Nordgard's shy knock received no reply, he nudged open the bedroom door of the suite to find his employer's guest on hands and knees peering beneath the bed.

"Got to keep the cursed thing somewhere, doesn't he?" came her distinctly annoyed mutter. "Or perhaps His Lordship is too superior to need one."

Sven flipped up the lenses of his sunglasses to study the intriguing angle of her pert rump, unsure whether he should back out or proceed. He'd always been more comfortable dealing with terrorists than women.

"Miss?" he said timidly.

She jerked, striking her head on the enameled footboard with enough force to make him wince.

"Please, may I be of some assistance, miss?"

She climbed to her feet, glaring at him and rubbing her head. Even with his limited deductive skills, Sven could not help but notice that she kept shifting restlessly from foot to foot. "You may stop sneaking up on me, sir."

He lowered the lenses of his sunglasses and ducked his head. "Mr. Lennox sent me to see what you would like for breakfast. There is yogurt and fresh bagels with fat-free cream cheese, wheat-germ waffles, bran muffins, and always I can squeeze the fresh juice for you. Orange. Grape. Tomato. Pineapple. Peach nectar. Apple. Pear . . ."

As he recited the vast array of beverages favored by his employer, the woman's fragile complexion grew even pastier. When he reached "mango," she began to sway. Alarmed, he rushed forward to steady her.

She clutched his massive arm, her face crumpled in abject misery.

"What is it, miss? Are you sick?"

She studied his face, as if weighing whether or not she dared confide in him. Her pallor was replaced by a furious blush as she stood on tiptoe and whispered something in the general direction of his ear.

He frowned down at her. "I am sorry, miss. My English is not so good. I know not of this pot."

Heaving an exasperated sigh, she dragged his ear down to her mouth to hiss something even more explicit.

"Ah!" He felt a broad smile crack his stoic face. "I understand."

Thankful to have found a task he felt competent to execute, he tucked her small hand in the crook of his arm and led her to an expanse of wall textured with flocked paper. He punched a shiny black button, unable to resist a tiny flourish as he did so.

The wall slid open, eliciting a gasp of pure astonishment from his companion. She drifted ahead of him into the spacious room.

She glided past the Italian marble of the sunken whirlpool tub and matching pedestal sinks without a second glance. She paid little heed to the plush mauve carpet crushed beneath her feet or the twin brass shower heads wrapped in a frosted glass enclosure. Not even the thick burgundy towels draped over the electronic towel warmer were enticing enough to lure her rapt attention from the gleaming object perched beneath a tasteful Andrew Wyeth print.

She drew her gaze away from it only long enough to flash Sven a grin of utter delight. "Why, 'tis the grandest chamber pot I've ever seen!"

Tristan's Gucci loafers didn't make even a whisper of sound as they traversed the wide corridor to the boardroom of Lennox Enterprises. Since it was Sunday morning, the maze of offices flanking the hall had been deserted by all but his most conscientious employees. In defiance of superstition, Tristan had located his corporate headquarters on the thirteenth floor of the Tower.

Copperfield marched at Tristan's side, frantically shuffling a stack of manila files. "The press are clamoring for some answers about the girl. I've fielded interview requests from the *Times*, the *Post*, *People* magazine, and Jay Leno. What should I tell them?"

"Tell them I have no comment at this time."

The rhythm of Copperfield's steps faltered. "Let me clarify this. First you offer a million dollars to the first scam artist clever enough to con you. Then some woman dressed like the corpse from an Amish funeral flies in on a burning broom and crash-lands in your arms in front of a thousand witnesses and you have no comment?"

"That's correct. Until I have some concrete answers, I see no point in whetting their appetites. You know as well as I do that the scent of blood will only send them into a feeding frenzy."

Copperfield jotted a notation in a margin before slapping one of the files shut. "So what are you planning to do with her? Keep her prisoner in your penthouse tower like some princess in a medieval romance?"

"She's no prisoner," Tristan replied, his bland expression costing him more effort than usual to maintain. "She can leave anytime she likes."

"Then I suppose it's pure coincidence that her baby-sitter just happens to be a six-feet-four Norwegian armed with a Glock nine-mil and a Walther PPK he's convinced once belonged to James Bond."

The perpetual sarcasm in Tristan's voice ripened. "I confess. You've found me out. I gave Sven strict orders to shoot her in the back if she tries to leave, then heave her body down the nearest elevator shaft."

Although Tristan would never have admitted it, he wasn't sure if Sven's presence was supposed to deter Arian from leaving or deter him from spending any more time than necessary in her presence. After his brief flirtation with espionage, he had spent a restless night on the sofa in his corporate office.

He had removed the temptation of further nocturnal spying by disabling the penthouse security cameras before leaving the Command Center. He could care less if Deluth or any other of his security guards spent their on-duty hours ogling Miss Whitewood's nubile legs, but he despised the thought of them trespassing on her solitude—intruding upon her private melancholy as he himself had been guilty of doing. He'd rather let Sven do his dirty work for him.

Dousing a flicker of shame with a shot of cynicism, he said, "Miss Whitewood didn't seem to have any engagements more pressing than collecting her million dollars." He threw open the boardroom door. "If this meeting proceeds as planned, I'll allow you the pleasure of personally evicting her from my suite."

As soon as they entered the boardroom, it became evident that nothing was going to go as planned. Instead of the beaming faces Tristan had expected, they were greeted by a variety of expressions ranging from glum defeat to utter despondency. The heavy drapes had been drawn to ward off the morning sunlight, only adding to the aura of gloom.

"Good morning, ladies and gentlemen," Tristan said briskly, settling into the sleek leather chair at the head of the oak conference table.

As Copperfield slumped into the chair at his right, an assistant melted out of the dark paneling to place a cup of steaming black coffee at Tristan's elbow.

Tristan eyed the five men and three women seated around the long table, knowing they were the most gifted panel of computer programmers, physicists, chemists, and engineers ever assembled in the United States under one corporate banner. Yet at the moment they were all avoiding his eyes as if they heartily wished they possessed one-way plane tickets back to their countries of origin.

"I trust you have the results we discussed," he said, his smile deceptively gentle.

Several members of the panel made a great production of rifling through the mountains of computer printouts that littered the table, but it was Gordon Montgomery who lunged to his feet.

Tristan had always admired the Scotsman's frankness. Montgomery was also the only man in the room with an IQ higher than his. The convex lenses of his glasses magnified his red-rimmed eyes. "I'm turribly sorry, sir. We've worked the whole night through, but have nothin' of any significance to report."

"Nothing at all? Not even the chemical composition of the device? Theories on its potential methods of aviation?"

Montgomery shook his head, his uncombed nest of ginger hair making him look more like a scientist of the mad variety. "We've dissected the thing into microscopic cross sections and done magnetic resonance imaging until we're bug-eyed, but I'm tellin' you, sir, it's nothin' but a pile of splinters and a heap of scorched straw—a bloody broom!"

Tristan took a sip of the coffee. Its bitterness wasn't nearly as keen as his disappointment. After his lapse of judgment in the Command Center last night, it somehow seemed even more imperative that he prove Arian Whitewood nothing more than a conniving little fraud. "Then we simply have to assume the motor fell off in flight, causing the crash."

Copperfield's smile was a fraction too smug for Tristan's comfort. "It's a pity most standard kitchen brooms don't come equipped with flight recorders and little black boxes."

Tristan spared him a brief, but icy glare. "All right then, Montgomery. Have your technicians map the surrounding city blocks into quadrants and begin combing the area for debris. Tomorrow morning, we'll—"

"Uh-um, excuse me, Mr. Lennox." Sven's shaggy blond head appeared in the crack between door and frame.

"What is it, Sven?" Tristan demanded, unable to suppress a tiny thrill of alarm. He knew it would take nothing less than a bomb threat or a call-back audition for *Baywatch* to make his bashful bodyguard brave the corporate offices without his permission.

Despite his agitated state, Sven could not help giving the security camera mounted in the corner a come-hither look as he rounded the table. He cupped his massive hand around Tristan's ear and whispered something.

Tristan frowned, thinking he couldn't possibly have heard him correctly. Sven straightened and beckoned him toward the window. Nearly quivering with curiosity, Copperfield beat them both around the table to tug open the drapes, flooding the paneled gloom with sunlight.

Exchanging baffled glances, the scientists lined up on either side of Tristan as he peered down into the courtyard thirteen stories below. At first glance, everything appeared to be as orderly as it should have been on a peaceful Sunday morning.

"There, sir." Sven pointed one of his beefy fingers. "The fountain."

Tristan narrowed his eyes, realizing that the majestic geyser designed to be the focal point of the courtyard had fizzled to a lethargic sputter. Even as he watched, it diminished to a trickle, then to a pathetic little dribble.

Ever the pragmatic engineer, Gordon Montgomery clapped him on the shoulder. "Somethin' seems to be bottomin' out the water pressure, sir."

"Something," Tristan concurred, knowing no amount of restraint in the world could hide his darkening expression. "Or someone."

As he turned on his heel and strode from the boardroom, Sven and Copperfield exchanged an apprehensive glance, forging an unspoken agreement that it would be wiser not to follow.

7

When Tristan stepped off the penthouse elevator, he was bombarded by billowing clouds of steam. His irritation mounted as he felt his raw silk suit wilt against his frame like an overwatered daisy.

After slamming the door of his private office to protect his computers from the humid assault, he headed for the bedroom, muttering dire imprecations beneath his breath. A thunder resembling that of Niagara Falls was rumbling from the open door of the bathroom.

He plunged through the veil of mist, too angry to care if the idiotic Miss Whitewood was fully clothed or dressed in nothing but bubbles and a smile. Which didn't explain his stab of disappointment at finding her still wearing her shabby shroud.

Water poured from the brass faucets of the tub in steaming gouts. Both sinks were running full tilt as were the twin shower heads. Their roar muffled his arrival, leaving him free to observe his guest gleefully flipping the handle of the commode, then bouncing backward to admire the result. As soon as the tank stopped running, she would repeat the ritual—flushing, chortling with delight, then watching intently as the water drained from the sparkling basin.

Tristan wrenched off the bathtub, then waited for a lull in the water pressure to lean into the shower. Just as he was giving its crystal knob a vicious twist, another shift in pressure sent a gush of warm water cascading over his head. The commode's roar subsided to a trickle, leaving no sound in the room except the steady *plop, plop* of water dripping off the cuffs of his trousers to soak his newly installed Berber carpet.

Arian slowly turned around. She eyed him from head to toe before bobbing a wary curtsy. "Good day, Mr. Lennox. Is it raining outside?"

Her baffled blink left no doubt as to how ridiculous he must look with his painstakingly applied mousse dripping into his collar and his two-thousand-dollar Valentino suit plastered to his body. In contrast, the steam had coiled her hair into an enchanting halo of ringlets and made her skin look as dewy as the petals of a lily. The injustice of it infuriated him.

"Of course it's not raining! Are you out of your mind?" His bellow echoed off the tile walls, making her flinch.

Clearly assuming his question was a rhetorical one, she cast the toilet a last wistful glance before sidling past him. "Remarkable plumbing. I had heard of such marvels being installed in the new palace at Versailles, of course, so you mustn't think me an utter bumpkin."

A bumpkin was by far the most flattering description Tristan was entertaining at the moment. "They don't have tanning booths *or* indoor plumbing in France?" he growled, snatching a towel from the warmer and stalking after her.

She evaded his question by nearly colliding with a wide-eyed maid carrying a breakfast tray and several newspapers. It didn't improve Tristan's temper to realize the woman had overheard his uncharacteristic outburst.

As Arian intercepted the tray with a husky moan of anticipation, the succulent aroma of bacon wafted to his nose. Sven must have ordered from the deli downstairs, Tristan thought, unconsciously licking his lips as he eyed the thick slabs of pork. He would never allow such artery-hardening slop in his private kitchens.

"Thank you ever so much," Arian said, tucking the newspapers beneath her arm as Tristan's scowl sent the maid scurrying from the suite.

Still glowering, he toweled the moisture from his hair while Arian settled herself cross-legged on the bed and began to shovel in forkfuls of fried egg as if she'd never heard of a fat gram. He couldn't remember the last time he'd seen a woman eat without berating herself for enjoying it.

"Oh, Lord, I was ravenous," she mumbled, tearing off a generous bite of the bacon. "I feel like I haven't eaten in over three hundred"—she glanced up to meet his frosty gaze before swallowing with an audible gulp—"hours."

She drained a mug of hot chocolate, leaving Tristan to covet the enticing mustache of marshmallow foam adorning her upper lip.

"Would you care for some?" she asked, proffering a plump cinnamon roll studded with raisins.

"No, thank you," he said stiffly, the wheat-germ waffle he'd choked down at five that morning lying like a brick in his stomach. "I've eaten."

He regretted his haste the moment Arian's dainty coral tongue caressed a dab of icing from the pastry. Her moan of delight made his gut contract with longing. He wanted to snatch the roll from her and wolf it down in one gulp. Shocked by the outlandish impulse, he wadded the towel into a ball and hurled it into the corner.

"I didn't come here for breakfast, Miss Whitewood. I came to ask you a few pertinent questions."

"Then I hope you'll be satisfied with my answers. I've always been told I'm frightfully impertinent."

He tore his gaze away from her winsome grin. "My technicians are presently combing the streets surrounding the Tower for debris from your crash. I was hoping you might save them some of their valuable time by explaining to me just how you came to be *soaring* past at the precise moment of the magic competition."

"I don't remember." She polished off the cinnamon roll and began licking each finger in turn like a fastidious little cat.

Riveted by the innocent display of eroticism, Tristan suddenly had trouble remembering his original question. "You don't remember what?" he repeated faintly.

"I don't remember how I came to be flying past. I'm afraid I hit my head when I crashed and have been afflicted with an unfortunate case of . . . manesia." She set the tray aside, looking immensely pleased with herself.

Tristan didn't know whether to laugh or back away and call the Centers for Disease Control in Atlanta. "You wouldn't, by any chance, mean 'amnesia'?"

He had to give her credit. She recovered with nothing more than a thoughtful blink. "That's right. Amnesia. Sometimes when you have it, you can't remember what it's called."

Her guileless expression only intensified his desire to strangle her. He locked his hands behind his back to stifle the urge and began to pace at the foot of the bed. "Allow me to clarify your assertions. You hit your head. You have amnesia. But you do remember that your name is Arian Whitewood, you come from France, and you'd like very much for me to reward you a million dollars."

He pivoted on his heel to discover that instead of hanging on his every word as any one of his underlings would have done, her attention had strayed to the scattered newspapers. He wondered if it had been Copperfield's idea of a joke to send up not only the Sunday-morning editions of the *Times* and the *Post*, but special rush editions of the tabloids as well. Arian didn't seem the least bit distressed by the *Prattler*'s depiction of her as a bug-eyed first cousin of E.T., but she was gazing intently at the cover of the *Global Inquirer*.

"They're saying I might be this man's daughter," she said, her expression oddly earnest. "He looks like a pleasant enough fellow. Do you see a resemblance?" She held the cover next to her face to reveal a sulky young Elvis in the prime of his prepolyester career.

Tristan's cynical laugh was curbed by the wistful note in her voice. He curled his upper lip in a sneer that rivaled Elvis's to hide its jarring effect on him. "Let me guess. You've forgotten your father's name as well."

She lowered the paper, meeting his gaze evenly. "I don't believe I ever knew it."

Tristan would have found her confession less disturbing if it had been tainted by even a hint of his own bitterness. Eager to escape her large, liquid eyes, he strode over to the wall, his temper so feverish the automatic sensors sent the closet doors shooting open with a *whoosh* instead of a hiss.

He snatched down the handsome Panama he'd bought to wear on the beach at Martinique during a vacation he'd never found the time to take, marched back across the room, and tossed it into Arian's lap. "Pull a rabbit out of my hat."

Cradling the hat between her palms, she peeped over the brim, then indulged him with the sort of cautious smile one might reserve for an escaped lunatic. "Well, now, I can't very well pull one out if you haven't put one in."

He blinked at her, alarmed that her logic was starting to make sense to him. "I don't want you to pull out a rabbit that's already there. I want you to conjure one up out of thin air like bad magicians have been doing for centuries." He nodded toward the hat. "Go on. Snap your fingers. Twitch your nose. Cross your arms and blink. I don't give a damn how you do it, but if you can pull a bunny out of that hat in the next five minutes, I'll call and have Copperfield cut you a check for one million dollars."

Tristan was startled to realize he meant it. His carefully preserved peace of mind was worth more to him than a paltry million. He would forgo the satisfaction of proving this woman a fraud if he could just get her out of his life. And his bed.

She glanced at him, then back at the hat as if she were warring with some powerful temptation. One of her hands fluttered toward her chest and that unusual necklace of hers before curling into a fist and falling back to her lap.

"I won't," she whispered, bowing her head so that a curtain of hair fell around her features.

She wasn't getting off that easy. Tristan reached down and flipped back the dark veil, regretting the casual motion the instant he felt the silky stuff cling to his fingertips. An elusive ribbon of scent drifted to his nostrils, making them flare with primitive hunger. "Won't or can't?"

"I don't . . ." She faltered when her eyes met his.

He leaned down until his lips were only a whisper away from hers and gently offered, "Remember?"

She recoiled, her dark eyes snapping. " 'Tis the truth, sir. Whether you choose to believe it or not. And if you refuse to recognize flying as magic, then I can't see how dragging a hedgehog out of a chapeau is going to sway you."

Tristan allowed the skein of hair to escape his fingers, unable to remember the last time anyone had dared to defy him. Even Copperfield's thinly veiled insults were little more than petulant digs to his vanity. What surprised him most was that Arian's petty rebellion provoked grudging respect instead of frustration.

He straightened, forcing his shoulders into a parody of his effortless shrug. "Very well, Miss Whitewood. I'll continue to investigate your claim. But if you have a sudden uncontrollable urge to bend your jelly spoon with your mind, levitate a bagel, or even perform a card trick or two, do have Sven send for me."

Her outraged gasp warned him he'd finally managed to offend her. She pursed her generous lips in prim displeasure. "Playing cards, Mr. Lennox, are naught but tools of the devil."

Tristan had no answer for that but to turn on his heel and flee to the nearest sanctuary. Snatching up the phone, he barked, "I'll be working in my private office for the rest of the day. I'm not to be disturbed."

But even as he slammed down the receiver on the befuddled operator, he knew his command had come a day too late. Arian Whitewood had already disturbed the rigid calm he'd perfected over the past ten years. Cracked the veneer of reserve that kept him sane when fury and regret threatened to overwhelm him. She'd even had him challenging her to do magic, for God's sake! As if a belief in such nonsense was anything more than sheer lunacy. What idiotic thing would he do next? Beg her to put a hex on his business rivals before his next conference call? Hell, maybe she could even kiss his nose and turn him into a prince. The image didn't make him smile as it should have.

He swiveled his chair around and propped his feet on the windowsill, shivering as the icy air blasting from a floor vent struck his soggy suit. The autumn sun bathed the tinted windows in a golden haze, but its warmth failed to penetrate the climate-controlled environment.

He hadn't always been such a skeptic. He had once believed in magic of another kind. A wizardry woven of microprocessors and binary codes with incantations measured in megahertz and gigabytes. But that was before reality had robbed him of his childlike faith in the wonders of technology and the workings of his own fertile imagination.

Years of being on guard made the nearly imperceptible sigh of the door opening behind him echo like a shout. Tristan swung around in the chair, prepared to blast Arian with a thunderbolt of his own if she'd dared to intrude upon his private domain.

Cop stood in the doorway, a sheepish grin on his face. "I thought you'd want to know I dismissed the meeting."

"Did Montgomery have any more brainstorms?"

"Sorry. He just kept shaking his head and mumbling, 'Puir lassie. Took a frightful tumble, she did.' "

Tristan bit off a succinct oath. "So just how in the hell am I supposed to get rid of the 'puir lassie'?"

"You could throw a bucket of water on her and see if she melts?" At Tristan's glare, Cop hastily added, "Or you could pay her off. Offer her a few thousand dollars to perform a vanishing act. It worked on the woman who filed that paternity suit last fall."

"That's because I never touched her and she knew it. Shaking hands at an AIDS fund-raiser doesn't qualify as intercourse, not even in New York City." Tristan rose to stare blindly down at the distant streets below, jamming his hands in his pockets.

"Sven was able to get a valid set of fingerprints from the toothbrush you loaned her. We've already got the NYPD, Interpol, and our own private detectives running background checks of every criminal, con artist, and missing person matching her description. We should know something definitive by the end of the week."

"And if I don't want to wait that long to sleep in my own bed?"

Cop spread a magnanimous palm on his breast. "Why, I'd be delighted to book the beguiling Miss Whitewood a room at the Plaza or even put her up at my own loft. Located off Fifth Avenue with a breathtaking view of Central Park—" Tristan wheeled on him with such savagery that Copperfield took two hasty steps backward, despite the fact that the desk was between them. "Never mind."

The tension fled Tristan's body as quickly as it had come, leaving him weary to the bone. Unable to stomach Copperfield's speculative gaze, he turned back to the window, running a hand through his damp hair. "You're absolutely right. I'll talk to her first thing in the morning about moving somewhere else until we get her claim settled."

Even as Tristan acknowledged the rightness of his decision, he wondered why it left him with such a hollow feeling in the pit of his stomach.

8

Monday dawned with a crisp blue October sky and a media blitz more frantic than anything Copperfield had anticipated. The influx of press forced Tristan to close the fern-draped atrium of Lennox Enterprises to the public, but not before several resourceful reporters had wormed their way into his corporate lair. Sven was forced to run interference for him when he emerged from his office. Tristan knew if he gave the command, Sven would drop his shoulder and plow through the shouting mob like Emmitt Smith demolishing the Giants' defense on a lazy Sunday afternoon.

"Mr. Lennox, can you confirm that Miss Whitewood appeared to be riding a common kitchen broom?"

"No comment," he replied.

"Have you released the name brand of the broom? Was it a Tuff-Bristle or a Perfect Sweeper?"

"No comment."

"Sir, would you classify Miss Whitewood as a good witch or a bad witch?"

He refused to dignify that with any answer at all.

He had almost reached the elevators when a hacking cigarette cough brought him up short. He knew without looking what question would follow and exactly who would ask it. The *Prattler*'s Eddie Hobbes had spent the last ten years becoming the bane of Tristan's existence. Tristan even recognized the rustle of Hobbes's notepad as the man made a great show of pretending to consult it.

"Mr. Lennox, is it true that a Mr. Wite Lize, aka Mr. Leopold Finch, is still calling for local authorities to reopen the murder investigation of his son?"

Tristan turned, his eerie composure silencing the mob in mid-murmur. Hobbes wore a rumpled sports coat and was puffing on a fat cigar in flagrant defiance of the No Smoking sign posted directly over his balding head.

"As you well know, Hobbes," Tristan said, "there was no murder investigation. Arthur Finch disappeared nearly a decade ago and is officially listed as a missing person."

As Tristan coolly dismissed him by turning back to the elevator, the reporter snickered and elbowed the photographer next to him. "That's one picture you'll never see on any milk carton."

The shouting resumed with renewed vigor. "Mr. Lennox! Mr. Lennox!"

Tristan stepped into the sanctuary of the arriving elevator, leaving Sven to block the press's pursuit. As soon as the doors slid shut, he relaxed his rigid posture and sagged against the elevator wall, rubbing the back of his neck in a futile attempt to massage the stiffness from it. The leather couch in his office looked a hell of a lot more comfortable than it was. He bitterly hoped Miss Whitewood had spent a cozy night nestled between the satin sheets of his king-sized bed. He was on his way to ensure that it had been her last.

Who would have thought one small woman could throw his empire into such chaos? The Tower's phone lines had been jammed since dawn, leaving most of his fifteen thousand employees helpless to resume their duties. The wasted manpower galled him almost as much as the media's brutal siege.

Three altercations had already broken out between Tower security and the invading press, leaving behind a trail of smashed cameras and tape recorders that had Copperfield downing half a bottle of extra-strength aspirin in anticipation of a flurry of assault charges and civil lawsuits.

Copperfield might blame him for thrusting himself back into the limelight he hated, but Tristan was fully prepared to lay the blame where it belonged—at Arian Whitewood's dainty feet. Had she not staged such a flamboyant stunt, the press's attention would have waned by now or been distracted by some breaking scandal or juicy morsel of gossip. He was tempted to drag her downstairs and abandon her to their mercy.

Arriving at the penthouse, he strode off the elevator, prepared to do just that. The living room was deserted, the door to his private office still locked as he had left it.

A rhythmic roar drew him toward the bedroom. He hastened his steps, wondering what new calamity Miss Whitewood had devised to inflict on him. His unwanted houseguest was nowhere in sight. The roar intensified and he whirled around to find himself almost nose to nose with the helicopter hovering directly outside the window.

Even if the *Prattler*'s logo of carnivorous teeth and flapping tongue hadn't been stenciled on the craft's nose, Tristan would have recognized it by the predatory smirk of the photographer leaning out the door to get a clear shot of him.

Repressing the adolescent urge to flip the man off, Tristan satisfied himself with snatching the drapes shut. The thunder of the helicopter's rotors soon faded.

Tristan peered through the pearly gloom. "Miss Whitewood?"

Nothing. He checked the bathroom, but failed to find anything more incriminating than a dripping faucet and damp toothbrush. Apparently, the woman had decided her hoax wouldn't survive the scrutiny of his scientists and had chosen to spare him the unpleasantness of evicting her. He sank down on the foot of the bed and ran a hand through his hair, suddenly more weary than he had realized.

It took him a hazy minute to realize the bed was vibrating as if he'd just dropped a quarter into it. Utterly baffled, he flattened his palms against the mattress, but the strange quivering continued. He leaned over, gingerly lifted the bedskirt, and peered beneath the bed.

His eyes slowly adjusted to the murky light, but all he could see were a pair of black stockinged feet. "Miss Whitewood?"

The bed trembled with renewed violence. Dropping to his knees on the carpet, Tristan wrapped his fingers around the slender ankles attached to the feet and tugged. Arian slid out from beneath the bed, stiffer than an ironing board, her eyes clenched shut.

"Miss Whitewood?" he said, more gently this time.

Her eyes popped open, huge in her ashen face. Her dress was even more miserably rumpled than before and a litter of baby dust bunnies nested in her hair, validating Tristan's decision to hire a new cleaning service.

"Is it gone?" she whispered through her chattering teeth.

"The helicopter?"

"No, the dragon!"

Tristan mentally kicked himself for not having Cop follow up on that Bellevue connection. "You saw a dragon?"

"I did, sir. Right outside the window. He came swooping out of the sky at me with his teeth bared and his tongue flapping in the wind. I thought he was going to crash right through the window and—" She hugged herself as a fresh shudder raked her.

Wrapping an arm around her shoulders, Tristan eased her to a sitting position, caught off guard by his own primal impulse to slay her dragons, real or imaginary. Her pliant body trembled violently against his chest. She seemed so genuinely terrified that it was difficult to remember she was probably nothing more than a cunning actress.

Awkwardly supporting her weight, he plucked a dust bunny from her hair. "There's no need for you to be afraid, Miss Whitewood. What you saw wasn't a dragon. It was only a helicopter."

"A hell-copter?" she echoed, looking less than comforted.

" 'Helicopter,' " he repeated, wondering just how provincial France had become since his last business trip to Paris. "An aircraft designed to fly people from one place to another."

Arian was silent for a long moment as she pondered his explanation. "Then those men weren't inside its stomach?"

Tristan suppressed a smile. Being eaten by a dragon would have been a more than fitting fate for the *Prattler* photographer and his pilot. "No, they were simply riding *inside* the helicopter to reach their destination."

"Which was?"

Her innocent question reminded him that the men had been predators of a different sort. "Unfortunately, my window. They were trying to snap a photograph of you."

She blinked up at him. "A photo-graph?"

Tristan sighed and pinched the bridge of his nose. This was turning out to be a very long day. And it wasn't even noon yet. Too weary to attempt another explanation, he dumped her out of his lap and went to the dresser.

He chose a gold frame from its polished surface,

held it in front of Arian's nose, and tapped the glass with his forefinger. "A photograph."

Arian studied the smiling blonde, her expression almost wistful. "She's very lovely. Is she your wife?"

Tristan turned the picture around and frowned down at it. "I don't know who the hell she is. The interior decorator left her here." Shrugging, he replaced the frame on the dresser. "Anyway, the photographer might be an unscrupulous monster, but the helicopter itself is harmless. I have one just like it sitting on my helicopter pad on the roof. Would you like to go for a ride?"

Arian sprang to her feet, backing away from him as if he'd just offered her candy to get in the back of his limousine. "Oh, no, really I'm quite fine where I am. I'll just stay here, thank you."

Grateful to be reminded of his original mission, Tristan leaned against the dresser. "Actually, that's what I came to talk to you about."

Arian took the chair farthest from the window, as if she didn't quite trust his assurance that the dragon/hell-copter wouldn't return to rip her succulent throat out. She tried to smooth her wrinkled white cuffs, but whatever starch they'd once absorbed was long gone. Unnerved by the pathetic display, Tristan scowled down at her. He'd be glad when both she and her pitiful dress were gone. He couldn't bear watching her mope around his suite like some forlorn waif from the cast of *Les Miserables.*

His voice came out more brusque than he intended. "You and I need to discuss the future."

Her eyes widened and the skin around her mouth went pinched and pale. "The future?"

"Specifically, your future. Your near future. And exactly where you'll be spending it."

She smiled, looking oddly relieved. "Oh, *that* future."

"I'm afraid your presence here is making the day-to-day operations of Lennox Enterprises nearly impossible to execute. My scientists are currently making every effort to investigate your claim to the prize money, but until they reach a conclusion"—Tristan made a deliberate effort to gentle his voice—"I think it would be best if you sought accommodations elsewhere."

Arian's smile faded, then reappeared with suspicious brilliance. She rose from the chair and extended her hand. "Your hospitality has been more than generous, Mr. Lennox, but I would never presume to overstay my welcome."

Her rapid assimilation dizzied him. He had expected to find himself battling arguments, tears, and a demand for an extravagant housing allowance, but it was almost as if she were accustomed to being kicked out of places with little or no notice. Her graceful capitulation pricked a conscience he hadn't realized he still possessed.

She was already turning to go when he blurted out, "I'd be more than happy to book you a room at a nearby hotel."

"Oh, that won't be necessary." She waved a hand at him, her tone almost breezy. "I simply can't bring myself to accept another moment of your charity. But you needn't fret about me. I'm perfectly capable of looking after myself."

Then she was gone, sailing through the gaping doors and leaving him standing alone with his mouth hanging open.

The doors slid closed. Arian's disappearance was followed by muffled thumping and a mumbled French curse.

"Miss Whitewood?" Tristan ventured.

Puzzled silence.

"That's the closet."

An invisible sigh was followed by a small, defeated, "Oh."

Tristan squeezed his eyes shut and counted to ten before tripping the switch that would free her. She emerged from the darkness, blinking up at him like a rumpled baby owl.

He pointed toward the living room. "That's the way out."

Her smile betrayed only a faint decrease in wattage. "Of course. I knew that."

He leaned one shoulder against the doorjamb and watched with morbid fascination as Arian marched toward the elevator, her confidence undaunted. He winced in anticipation of her slamming into the sealed doors, but she skidded to a halt a mere inch from breaking her pert nose.

She studied the doors, her brow puckered in a frown, then tried backing up and approaching them from a new angle. Tristan felt his lips twitch with a reluctant smile. Shooting him a distracted glance, Arian braced her narrow shoulder against the doors and shoved. When that failed to budge them, she began to claw at the seam between the doors, her frustration starting to show.

Tristan rolled his eyes heavenward. His business rivals might think he was a sadistic son of a bitch, but he couldn't quite bring himself to cast this particular lamb to the wolves. Whether she was a conniving fraud or simply deluded, the snarling pack of reporters would tear her from limb to limb before she ever set foot outside the building. He had his own scars from their teeth to prove it.

As if to affirm his decision, the helicopter swooped into view of the living room windows, its mighty roar shuddering the triple-glazed glass. Arian ceased her assault on the elevator and spun around to plaster herself against the wall.

It wasn't the visible effort with which she swallowed her terror, but the tremulous smile she summoned for his benefit that made Tristan take a step toward offering her shelter in his arms.

There be dragons.

The ancient warning popped into his head without preamble. He hesitated, the throb of the helicopter's rotors drowned out by the thudding of his heart in his ears.

He knew he should march over and snatch the living room drapes closed, but the prospect of once again being entombed in his own penthouse made his gut clench with primitive claustrophobia.

For ten long years, he'd been a prisoner of his wealth. A prisoner of his regrets. A prisoner of the past. He'd erected an impregnable fortress in the very heart of New York City only to find himself trapped inside a cage of glass walls and steel beams.

But Arian's courageous smile made him believe escape was possible. Escape to a haven of blue skies, autumn breezes unpoisoned by smog, a far horizon unspoiled by the jut of skyscrapers. Her smile also reminded him that if his enemy had breached his defenses as easily as she had, he'd be dead right now.

The helicopter edged nearer. The photographer leaned out, positioning his telephoto lens for a close-up. Tristan crossed the room in three angry strides, grabbed Arian by the hand, and stabbed the elevator call button. The doors slid open without protest, earning a disgruntled look from his companion.

"Where are you taking me, Mr. Lennox?" she asked as he dragged her into the elevator.

He shot her dress a disparaging look. "Bloomingdale's."

9

As the service elevator lumbered its way toward the
ground floor of Lennox Tower, Tristan studied Arian
from the corner of his eye. He had to bite the inside of
his cheek to keep from making the obvious crack about
a French maid. The dowdy black dress he'd pilfered
from Housekeeping wasn't much improvement over her
original costume, but at least he'd been able to coax her
into leaving off the white apron.

Their departure had been delayed for over an hour
while he combed Lennox Enterprises for a suitable pair
of stockings. An ambitious young executive had finally
rushed up, waving the spare package of panty hose she
carried in her briefcase for just such emergencies. While
visibly appalled by their sheerness, Miss Whitewood's
misgivings had been mollified by their modest hue.

Black.

Tristan fought the urge to chuckle. Arian's eyes
might be hidden behind the oversized pair of Ray•Bans
he'd confiscated from Sven's extensive collection, but
her head was tilted at the perfect angle to study the rap-

idly descending numbers above the door. At first Tristan thought she was counting floors, but then he realized she was muttering a fervent stream of Hail Marys. If she got any paler, she'd be transparent, he thought, his amusement spoiled by an annoying twinge of pity.

"Try to relax, Miss Whitewood. It's an elevator, not a death trap."

She offered him a wan smile. " 'Tis a bit like traveling in an oversized coffin, is it not?"

"After my security teams clear the Tower of all press, I'll take you for a spin in the express elevator. It's designed to travel from the penthouse to the ground floor in under fifty seconds."

Arian clutched her stomach. "Forgive me, Mr. Lennox, but I was under the impression this was going to be my last ride. Aren't you escorting me to my new lodgings?"

Tristan could feel her unflinching scrutiny, even through the tinted lenses of her glasses. "I've reconsidered my decision. It shouldn't take my staff more than a few days to verify your claim." *Or more likely, to prove you're nothing more than a conniving charlatan.* "There's no reason you can't remain my guest until then. And since you may be forced to address the press yourself before this is all over, I'm taking you to Bloomingdale's to choose some more suitable clothing."

He drew his own pair of Oakleys from the pocket of his Burberry coat and slipped them on to let her know the matter had been settled and no arguments to the contrary would be tolerated. But Arian didn't look surprised, merely thoughtful.

When the elevator doors groaned open, she bounded through them as if fearful the steely jaws would snap shut and crush her. Tristan could still hear the hungry buzz of the reporters swarming the main entrance to the Tower, but the alley outside the service entrance was deserted, just as he had hoped. The press would never expect him to make such an obvious escape. He was a little disconcerted himself to realize he hadn't left the Tower on foot since its construction had been completed over seven years ago.

He caught Arian's elbow and guided her toward the street, frowning as he felt her stumble. He'd deliberately borrowed a pair of low-heeled pumps, yet she was teetering along as if they were spike heels from a Frederick's of Hollywood catalogue.

He shot her feet a puzzled glance, noting the problem immediately. "Your shoes are on the wrong feet."

Although the dress only fell to mid-calf, she still lifted its hem to examine them. "No they're not. They're my feet," she assured him.

Blowing out a breath of exasperation, he knelt before her and lifted each foot in turn to remove the pumps, giving her no choice but to clasp his shoulder for balance. As he cupped her right foot in his palm to slip on the appropriate shoe, his thumb lingered against its delicate arch, beguiled by the warmth of her skin through the sheer nylon. Her fingers tensed on his shoulder. He glanced up to meet her wary gaze, feeling unaccountably guilty.

Realizing how ludicrous he must look playing Prince Charming to her Cinderella in the middle of a graffiti-spattered alley, he crammed her foot into the other shoe, ignoring her wince.

She continued to stumble along, this time because she was staring so intently at her feet. "Imagine that. A different shoe for the right and left. Who would have thought of anything so clever?"

Their sudden emergence onto Fifth Avenue spared Tristan from coming up with an answer to that ridiculous question. As he paused to turn up the collar of his coat, the bustling crowd threatened to swallow Arian's slight form. She craned her neck to gape up at the surrounding skyscrapers, outwardly oblivious to the dirty looks of the pedestrians forced to bump and jostle their way around her. As she reached the curb, a horn blared, forcing Tristan to lunge forward and jerk her out of the path of a speeding taxi.

"If you don't watch where you're going, you'll be spending the next few nights at the hospital. Or the morgue," he snapped as he herded her into the flow of pedestrian traffic. His heart was galloping along at twice its normal rate, reminding him that he was long overdue for a checkup.

Unfazed by his rebuke or her narrow escape, Arian threw back her shoulders and took a deep breath, drawing the cheap rayon of the uniform taut across her breasts. "I adore October! The air is so sweet and crisp. Isn't it glorious?"

Tristan averted his gaze from her chest and sniffed cautiously. "All I can smell are exhaust fumes."

"Why, would you look at that charming lamp!" She snatched his hand right out of his pocket and dragged him over to examine a perfectly ordinary crosswalk signal.

Arian seemed to have found her balance while Tristan was the one left stumbling to keep up as she tugged him this way and that, pointing and chattering at sights he had passed a thousand times, but never noticed through the smoked glass windows of his stretch limousine.

He was almost enjoying the rare anonymity of being part of a crowd. He was accustomed to heads snapping around and a path magically opening wherever he went, but if anyone glanced at him today, they would simply see a well-dressed man with a petite, dark-haired young woman clinging to his hand.

Encouraged by Arian's rapt attention, he sought to explain the formula he'd developed to help pinpoint any avenue address. "If you'll drop the last digit of the address, divide the remainder by two, then add or subtract the key number offered in several prominent travel guides, you'll be able to discover the nearest cross street." When she failed to compliment his genius, he spun around, realizing too late that his hand was empty and Arian was nowhere in sight.

His surge of panic receded when he saw a flash of black going round and round in one of the revolving doors of Trump Tower, much to the annoyance of the scarlet-coated doorman and the amusement of the gathering crowd. It took Tristan three circuits to rescue Arian, and by the time he succeeded, she was so dizzy and breathless with laughter she had to lean on his arm for support.

Her delight lingered until they passed a corner cart where the aroma of roasting wieners threatened to send her into a frenzy of near-religious ecstasy.

"Would you care for a hot dog?" he asked stiffly, wondering if the vendor had change for a hundred or took American Express.

"A hot dog? No, thank you," she said weakly, backing away from the cart. At first Tristan feared it was his own sneer of distaste that had spoiled her eagerness, but she was gazing at the skewered sausages with something more akin to horror. "Some of the poor in Paris considered cat a great delicacy, but I never could bring myself to try it."

She withdrew with a forlorn little sigh, leaving Tristan to choke back his laughter as he realized just how badly she had misconstrued his offer. He was about to explain when she seized his arm and tugged him into the doorway of Tiffany's.

Peeping around his shoulder, she said, "Don't look now, but those men are following us."

Ignoring her hissed dictate, Tristan threw a casual glance over his shoulder. Five burly, gray-suited men were huddled in front of a toy store, their efforts to look inconspicuous failing miserably. One of the men seemed to be admiring his reflection more than the charming window displays.

"Those men are paid to follow us," he whispered back. "They're my bodyguards. I arranged for them to delay their departure until Cop could divert the press's attention, but I would never leave the Tower without them."

Arian stole another look. "Why, you're right! There's that kind Mr. Nordgard. Sven!" she trilled, waving wildly. "Oh, Sven!"

Tristan pulled her hand down. "For God's sake, don't wave! You'll blow his cover and then he'll sulk for the rest of the day because you recognized him in his Ray•Bans."

Arian drew off her own sunglasses to reveal a pensive frown. "Why do you require guards, Mr. Lennox? I can't imagine a man like you being afraid of anything."

"The streets of New York can be a very dangerous place." Her luminous brown eyes reminded him that there were more subtle dangers than gang members or kidnappers. "Only a fool wouldn't be afraid," he added lightly, tucking a wayward strand of hair behind her ear.

If he expected her to linger at Tiffany's to admire the costly trinkets she planned to buy with his million dollars, he was sorely disappointed. She forsook the glittering window display without so much as a longing glance when a policeman mounted on a handsome sorrel came trotting past.

"Oh, sir! Please, sir, might I have a moment of your time?" Arian cried, bounding after the horse before Tristan could restrain her.

The officer slowed, guiding his mount in a prancing circle. The mouth above his helmet strap looked as if it hadn't cracked a smile since the early eighties. He shot Tristan and his trench coat a suspicious glance. "Is that fellow bothering you, ma'am? Are you in need of assistance?"

By the time Tristan reached the duo, Arian was already explaining. ". . . it's just that she's the first horse I've seen in New York. I was beginning to fear there weren't any left."

"Bathsheba's been with the force for five years

now, ma'am. I'm the one who named her," the officer confided, his stern mouth softening in a bashful grin. But his suspicious glower returned when he shifted his gaze to Tristan. "A little warm for that coat, isn't it, sir?"

Tristan summoned a genial smile instead of tearing open the front of his coat and flashing his Armani suit at the man. "I'm just recovering from a nasty head cold."

Arian stroked the horse's velvety muzzle, her other hand absently toying with her necklace. "You're quite the beauty, aren't you?" she crooned. "I wish I had an apple to—"

The horse tossed its mane with a raucous whinny before lowering its head to nuzzle Arian's skirt pocket. Its teeth emerged with a fat red apple clenched between them.

The cop chortled with delight, but Arian looked nearly as stunned as Tristan suspected he did.

"Thank the pretty lady, Bathsheba," the policeman commanded, but Bathsheba was too busy gulping down the apple core to comply. "Good afternoon, ma'am. I get the feeling you're not from around here, but I hope you enjoy your stay in the Big Apple." The cop nudged his horse into a saucy trot, his expression so smitten Tristan half expected him to tip his helmet to Arian like some noble gentleman of yore.

He, however, was more chilled than charmed by her resourceful trick. He stood directly behind her, near enough to warn, but not to threaten. Near enough for the distracting perfume of her hair to sweeten the exhaust fumes.

"I thought witches only offered apples of the poisonous variety," he murmured.

Arian's tension was palpable, even in her off-key laughter. "'Tis fortunate the mare didn't pull a rabbit out of my pocket. At least I can claim the apple came from my breakfast tray."

"Oh, you can claim whatever you like, Miss Whitewood." The bustling crowd seemed to perform its own vanishing act as Tristan whispered into her ear, "But I'm not required to believe you."

"Excuse me, honey, but our children's department is on the eighth . . ."

The clerk's nasal whine trailed off as Arian freed the velvet skirt she'd been fondling and turned away from the rack.

"Oh," the woman said. "You ain't a little girl." She worked her jaw in tireless rhythm, like a cow chewing its cud, as she eyed Arian up and down, taking in her severe dress, her scuffed pumps, her unbound mass of curls. "Our cosmetics department is on the ground floor if you're interested in some ashes to go with that sack-cloth."

Arian fingered the amulet, thinking she just might turn the condescending creature into a dormouse, but Tristan rescued her from the temptation by emerging from the other side of the rack and drawing off his sun-glasses.

The clerk swallowed whatever she'd been chewing with a gratifying gulp. "Why, Mr. Lennox! I didn't recognize you!"

He offered her a smile that was scathing in its tenderness. "Obviously." Arian fought the urge to squirm as he slipped a possessive arm around her waist. "But if you're too busy to assist me in selecting an extensive new wardrobe for my guest, we'll just be on our way to Bergdorf Goodman's."

The woman almost fell off her pointy heels in her rush to block his path. "Oh, no, Mr. Lennox. We always have time for you at Bloomingdale's. If you and the lovely young lady will follow me . . . ?" Patting her shel-lacked helmet of hair with a trembling hand, she ush-ered them into a private salon.

"What country is she from?" Arian whispered. "I don't recognize her accent."

A shadow of a smile touched Tristan's mouth. "A sprawling kingdom called Queens."

Arian found the salon's rose-colored carpet, walls, and settee soothing to her nerves. She still hadn't recovered from her recent brush with disaster. Given the capricious nature of her magic, she was fortunate she hadn't turned herself into an apple and been gobbled up by the horse. More than ever before, she must remember to heed Marcus's sage advice to "be careful what she wished for." Especially when Tristan Lennox was around.

She stole a glance at his implacable profile. More disturbing than the literal fruits of her error had been the figurative ones. Wariness and suspicion had cast a shadow over the convivial mood they had so briefly shared. 'Twas probably just as well. There had been a fleeting moment, when he had gazed into her eyes and touched her hair, that she had been tempted to confide in him. To spill the entire sordid story of her flight from Gloucester and Linnet's clutches.

He was presently explaining to the fawning clerk how her entire wardrobe had met with an unfortunate accident. Arian glared at his broad back, having been present when he'd ordered that her one and only dress be tossed into something called an incinerator. It was only after she'd protested that he'd agreed to have it laundered, then removed to the darkest, most inaccessible recesses of his closet.

The clerk soon disappeared through a narrow door, but instead of bringing fabric samples for Arian to peruse, she returned with a single glass of champagne balanced on a silver tray. A fat strawberry floated in its effervescent depths.

"Why, thank you, Louisa. You always remember my strawberry." Tristan removed his coat and lounged back on the settee, favoring the woman with a genuine smile.

Arian's stomach did a strange little flip. Even she

could not deny the devastating charm of the man's smile. It crinkled his eyes and erased the stern furrow from his brow. His long fingers cupped the bowl of the champagne glass with maddening grace as he plucked out the strawberry and brought it to his lips.

"Anything to please, Mr. Lennox. That's our policy at Bloomingdale's. Especially for you." The clerk's coy nudge indicated she was willing to go beyond the call of duty to ensure his satisfaction.

Repulsed by the woman's obsequious manner, Arian assumed the haughty demeanor her mama had always affected when rebuking her paramour's servants. "Pardon me, madam, but weren't you about to measure me for a gown?"

The woman started as if just remembering Arian's presence. "Measure you? Don't you know your size?"

Reluctant to display her ignorance, Arian glanced down at herself, then ventured, "Little?"

The clerk exchanged a bemused glance with Tristan. "Maybe I'd betta measure her."

Drawing a writing pad and a yellow tape from her dress pocket, she circled Arian like a starched buzzard, clucking ominously beneath her breath. As the woman knelt to measure her inseam, Arian began to regret drawing attention to herself, especially when she noted the amused twinkle in Tristan's eyes. He lifted the champagne glass to his lips, but it failed to hide his smirk.

Louisa slid the tape beneath Arian's upraised arms, then gave an admiring whistle. "You got some hefty boobs for such a tiny frame."

Tristan choked on his champagne. Arian didn't know whether to sink through the floor in mortification or laugh at his discomfiture.

"Why, thank you," she replied instead, drawing in a breath that showed her assets off to their best advantage. Her generous figure had been an ongoing source of consternation for Marcus as well. There were some

God-given charms even a homespun bib could not disguise.

Louisa poked her in the breastbone, deflating her sinful pride. "You ever think about having those things reduced? My uncle Maury in Queens is one of the best plastic surgeons in New York. I could give you his number."

Arian hesitated, unsure what a "numba" was or if it was appropriate to accept one if offered.

"That won't be necessary, Louisa," Tristan recovered himself enough to say. "Just bring us a sampling of your petite fall collections, then leave us in private."

Arian managed to avoid his eyes until Louisa returned to thrust a bewildering array of garments into her arms. She had assumed the woman would bring patterns or fashion dolls, not tailored gowns. As the woman shooed her into a curtained antechamber, Arian threw a panicked glance over her shoulder at Tristan only to have him heft his champagne glass in mocking salute.

Tristan sipped the champagne as he waited for Arian to emerge, idly wondering if a rich red or a cool turquoise would best offset the midnight hue of her curls. He glanced at his Rolex, noting that fifteen minutes had already passed. He waited fifteen more before scowling at the curtain. It hung limp, not even stirring in the draft from the air-conditioning.

"Miss Whitewood?" he called out, struggling to soften the edge of impatience in his tone. "Would you like to come out and show me what you've tried on?"

Silence.

Setting the champagne glass aside, Tristan rose and went to the curtain, battling a strange premonition that he would pull it back to find the alcove empty. That Arian might have vanished as abruptly as she'd appeared in his life. He reached for the curtain.

A faint scuffling noise accompanied by muttered French curses made him jerk back his hand. He took several hasty steps backward as Arian emerged, noting with wry humor the color of the dress she had chosen. Black.

The slim Chanel sheath was far more flattering than the borrowed uniform, but its sleek lines were spoiled by the wad of fabric she'd clenched at the small of her back.

Her face was red and unshed tears of frustration glistened in her eyes. "Silly frock has no buttons or frogs. How on earth am I supposed to fasten it?"

"Have you tried the zipper?" he suggested gently.

When she only blinked up at him, he turned her around and pried her fingers from the rayon. He caught the tongue of the zipper between his fingertips and eased it upward, noting with idle appreciation the tiny dimple at the base of her spine. The skin of her back was as soft and pale as if it had never known the kiss of the sun.

He was forced to lift her hair to complete the task, the casual motion releasing a cloud of fragrance. He secured the zipper and backed away from her, in danger of becoming intoxicated from more than just the champagne.

She gave her hips an intriguing little wiggle. " 'Tis far too small. I can barely breathe."

"Try one of the others, then," Tristan snapped, growing rather short of oxygen himself. He gave her a none-too-gentle push toward the dressing room and returned to the settee to drain his champagne.

Both bemused and irritated by her modest tastes, Tristan watched as she modeled one selection after another: a black Missoni turtleneck; a demure gray Donna Karan suit with Peter Pan collar; a long-sleeved Versace dress trimmed with virginal cuffs identical to the ones on the dress he'd wanted to burn. When she ducked into the alcove to change for the final time, Tristan rubbed his clean-shaven chin in exasperation.

Arian had displayed her humble choices with such

pride that he hadn't the heart to tell her she could have found any one of the outfits a few hundred dollars cheaper at a convent's garage sale.

Her innocent enjoyment was alarmingly contagious. He'd bought clothes for women before, but most of them had been content to be handed his Gold Card and curtly dismissed. None of them had sought his opinion on hem length or twirled around as if a homely black pair of leggings was a Dior original.

Arian emerged from the dressing room just as Louisa trotted back into the salon, nearly buried beneath a mound of iridescent taffeta. "Thought you might want to take a look at this. It's so rare to find a Givenchy in the little lady's size."

"Oh, how lovely!" The wistful cry spilled from Arian's throat before she could stop it.

Thrusting her own pile of garments into Tristan's arms, she rescued the emerald-hued gown from the woman's clumsy hands, unable to resist the temptation to hold it against her and test its length. Instead of dragging the floor, the pleated skirt swirled around her ankles in a perfect bell. Her mother had often worn fabrics so fine and rare when Arian was a little girl.

She remembered sneaking downstairs once during a ball, peeping through the gilded banisters to watch her mother glide through the intricate steps of a court dance with the grace of a young queen. To Arian's adoring eyes, her mama had seemed the most beautiful woman in all the world. Arian stroked the lustrous fabric, allowing herself a stab of grief for the first time since her mother's death.

The gown elicited a pang of primal yearning, not just for its elegance, but for all it represented. Beauty. Grace. A world where every pleasure was not condemned as sin.

Her face must have betrayed her longing, for Tristan softly said, "Why don't you try it on? It suits you."

"C'mon, honey," the clerk urged, throwing him a

knowing wink. "It might set Mr. Lennox back six months of Lamborghini payments, but he obviously thinks you're worth it."

Arian felt herself go hot, then cold, as she realized what the woman believed of her. She shouldn't have allowed it to catch her by surprise. After all, how many times had she seen her mother barter both body and soul for a scrap of silk or some shiny bauble?

She lifted her head, expecting the woman's crude assumption to have restored the mocking sparkle to Tristan's eyes. But they were as gray and inscrutable as a December sky.

Even with his arms full of women's garments and a disheveled lock of hair falling over his brow, Tristan managed to appear a portrait of casual elegance. She remembered the damning familiarity with which the clerk had greeted him, the fresh strawberry in his champagne. He probably brought all of his mistresses to this place.

"I don't want it," Arian declared, thrusting the billowing temptation back into the clerk's arms. " 'Tis a sickly hue that would make me look bilious in the moonlight."

She moved to stand stiffly by the door, deliberately ignoring Tristan's gaze and the clerk's crestfallen pout. Let the woman think they were having a lover's spat if it so pleased her.

"Have these wrapped and delivered along with an assortment of the appropriate foundation garments," Tristan commanded, handing over Arian's choices and peeling a tip from a fat wad of bills.

"Yes, sir!" Louisa replied, tucking the hundred dollar bill in her bra.

Arian's pride would not let her steal even a last wistful glance at the crumpled gown. So she missed the cryptic signal Tristan gave the simpering clerk behind her back.

* * *

As they strolled toward the Tower, Tristan stole a puzzled glance at Arian's stormy profile. She hadn't laughed or spoken once since they'd left Bloomingdale's private salon, not even when he'd coaxed her into trotting down the up escalator, offered to give her a spin in a revolving door, and pointed out Sven crashing into a girdle display because he insisted on wearing his sunglasses indoors.

He should be the one brooding, he thought grimly. He'd wasted an afternoon of invaluable time playing personal shopper, leaving his corporation to defend itself against the press's ruthless assault.

He clenched his teeth against a sigh, wishing he could forget the naked longing he'd glimpsed on Arian's face before she'd thrust the Givenchy gown back at the harried clerk. He'd been a fool to let it affect him. Women had been using that look for centuries to beguile men into begging, borrowing, or stealing whatever their calculating little hearts desired.

He'd traveled several long, angry strides before he realized that Arian was no longer at his elbow. He whirled around to discover she'd pressed her palms and nose to a store window like a child at a bakery counter. She was studying a display of orange and yellow boxes. Halloween films, he noted indifferently, no doubt teeming with ax-wielding maniacs and decapitated babysitters.

"Is this place a library?" Arian asked, her face showing its first trace of animation in over an hour. "Might I go in and examine the books?"

Tristan glanced up at the yellow block letters of the towering sign. "It's not a library. It's a video store."

"Vi-de-o?" She sounded out the word as if it were utterly foreign to her.

"You know—a place to buy and rent movies." She continued to look blank. "I know the French have movies because I've been forced to sit through several of them. Subtitles? Sad clowns? Brigitte Bardot?"

Nothing.

Tristan sighed and reached for the door handle. She hung back, shooting him a furtive glance from beneath her lashes. "You've already been far too generous, sir, and I don't wish to keep you from your work. Perhaps Mr. Nordgard could escort me back to the Tower?"

Tristan recognized a dismissal when he heard one. He gave her a cold smile. "You're absolutely right, Miss Whitewood. I've neglected my duties long enough."

He crooked a finger at Sven, who was lurking behind a nearby Italian ice stand. Sven came trotting over, visibly pouting to be summoned in so ignominious a manner in front of his colleagues.

Tristan handed him a credit card. "The lady has carte blanche. See that she gets whatever she wants."

As Tristan watched Arian vanish into the store's interior, he was almost grateful to her for rekindling his suspicions so effectively.

10

The Manhattan skyline glittered like a freshly cut diamond, radiating beauty, but no warmth. Tristan gazed at it through jaded eyes as he brought the tumbler of Scotch to his lips. The digital clock on his desk silently heralded the arrival of midnight.

"The witching hour," he murmured, lifting his glass in a bittersweet toast.

Another man might have identified the emptiness inside of him as loneliness, but Tristan had long ago learned to endure his own company as penance for his mistakes.

Exhausted from dodging press and having photographers masquerading as window washers popping up outside his corporate suite, he had cocooned himself in his private office shortly after leaving Arian to Sven's care. It dismayed him to discover the infusion of fresh air had blunted his brain's efficiency instead of sharpening it. He'd caught himself snapping at his personal assistant, yawning over the quarterly reports, and shivering at the stifling chill of the air-conditioning, which he always insisted be set to a comfortable and ecologically sound seventy-two degrees.

When Sven had returned with his written report detailing Miss Whitewood's every gesture and blink, Tristan had snatched it out of his hands, eager to search for evidence of her duplicity. The single sheet of paper now lay crumpled on the floor beside his overflowing trash can.

Contrary to Tristan's hopes, Arian hadn't attempted a rendezvous with a potential accomplice or even eluded Sven's surveillance long enough to use a public phone or restroom. The only anomaly Sven had noted in her behavior was her panicked dive into an open manhole when a helicopter had passed overhead.

Shaking his head, Tristan drained the Scotch and rose from his desk, forced to accede the day an abject failure. He could only hope tomorrow would be more productive. If his team of scientists couldn't give him the ammunition he needed to discredit Arian, perhaps his army of private detectives could.

He emerged from his office into the darkened living room, nearly tripping over a brightly colored gameboard that attested to Sven and Arian's evening activities.

"Candy Land?" he muttered.

Monopoly he could understand, but what was the point of playing any game where you couldn't charge exorbitant rent for hotels or bankrupt your opponents?

His bedroom door was cracked ajar, allowing a strip of flickering light to escape. He shot the room a hostile look, resenting its occupant anew for making him feel as if he should tiptoe across his own suite.

He was reaching to summon the elevator when the muffled sound of weeping drifted to his ears.

Tristan froze, his finger poised above the glowing call button. He wanted nothing more than to retreat to the plush sofa in his corporate office and seek the oblivion of sleep.

Torn between an infuriating sense of helplessness

and his desire for escape, he slowly lowered his hand. Surely any man who could compute the independent variables of logarithmic functions in his head could comfort a crying woman. After all, it was only a logical process of isolating the problem, formulating an acceptable hypothesis, and providing feasible alternatives. She'd probably lost a round of Candy Land or was sulking because she thought he hadn't overridden her feeble objections and bought her the Givenchy dress.

Tristan's purposeful stride did not falter until he eased open the bedroom door.

Arian was perched in the center of his bed, her attention riveted on the unearthly blue glow of the television. Relief surged through Tristan. She was undoubtedly engrossed in one of those sentimental "chick flicks" Copperfield adored—*Love Story* or perhaps *An Affair to Remember.* After the older boys at the orphanage had teased him mercilessly for crying when Bambi's mother died, Tristan had vowed to never again let his own emotions be so manipulated.

He started to withdraw, but a pathetic hiccup enticed him into the room. Arian was oblivious to his presence, offering him an irresistible opportunity to study her.

She sat with her legs tucked beneath her, a soggy bowl of popcorn cradled in her lap. She'd pinned her clean, damp hair in a careless knot at her nape using a duo of mismatched tie clips. The shirt from one of his own pairs of silk pajamas draped her slender form. Black, of course, he noted dryly.

Several empty video cases were scattered across the bed. He tilted his head to read their titles: *Bell, Book, and Candle, I Married a Witch, Escape to Witch Mountain, The Witches of Eastwick.* He shook his head in wry disbelief. Even the thick-headed Sven should have been able to detect a discernible pattern and included it in his report. She was probably researching the proper deportment for a con artist masquerading as a witch.

A reluctant smile touched his lips as he watched her dab at her nose with a drooping sleeve. Unlike most women of his acquaintance, she didn't cry as if she lived in mortal terror of smudging her mascara. If he lingered long enough, he suspected he'd catch her blowing her nose on the sheets.

A fat tear rolled down her cheek. Her breath caught in a piteous sigh.

"Arian?" he said softly, the casual intimacy of the rumpled bed and moody lighting making "Miss White-wood" seem too formal.

She cast him a beseeching look. Tears spiked her lashes, making her eyes look even larger. He realized she'd been aware of his presence the entire time, but too engrossed in the film to care. "Did you see it? That nasty Dorothy dropped a house on the poor witch. The inno-cent creature was just minding her own business, then *splat!*"

Tristan slowly turned his head to gaze at the tele-vision. He had expected to find Deborah Kerr in a wheel-chair or Ali McGraw gasping her last, not a chorus line of munchkins gleefully chirping, "Ding-dong, the witch is dead!"

"Horrid dwarves," Arian muttered, staunching a fresh spill of tears with the hem of the satin sheet. "Should have known they'd take that bratty Dorothy's side."

Reeling as if he, and not the unfortunate witch, had just had a house dropped on his head, Tristan stared at Arian as if seeing her for the first time. Copperfield might have shed a sheepish tear when Old Yeller died, but Tristan had never encountered anyone so tender-hearted as to weep for one of the vanquished witches in *The Wizard of Oz.*

His natural inclination to laugh was overwhelmed by a far more unnatural inclination to gather Arian into his arms. To lower his lips to her face and kiss away each salty tear in turn. To part her trembling lips with his tongue and . . .

Shaken, he picked up the remote and thumbed off the TV. "The witch was wicked," he said flatly. "She deserved to die."

He tossed the remote on the bed and walked away, convincing himself that he had only imagined the flicker of fear in Arian's eyes.

The hillside blazed with the light of a hundred torches. Arian backed toward the yawning chasm, preferring its certain doom to facing the creatures that came shambling out of the darkness.

The beasts stalked her, their soulless eyes glowing yellow out of empty sockets. An icy claw brushed her throat. As she recoiled from the skeletal face of Goody Hubbins, a scream caught in her throat, choking her with blind terror.

"Halt!" came a cry from the top of the hill.

The Reverend Linnet stood silhouetted against the moon, a black cape swirling around his ankles. The brim of his tall hat shadowed his features. Her accusers shuffled backward until she stood alone at the edge of the pond.

Linnet pointed a finger at her trembling form and uttered a single damning word. "Witch!"

She went tumbling into the water, but before its murky blackness could enfold her, the man on the bluff drew off his hat. The moon spun his hair into purest gold and frosted his gray eyes with moonbeams. The last sound she heard before the icy water closed over her head was the mocking music of Tristan Lennox's laughter.

"Holy Mother of God," Arian gasped, sitting straight up in the bed.

Desperate to escape the lingering miasma of the nightmare, she threw back the satin coverlet and bounded out of the bed, sending a stack of video cases cascading to the floor.

She had hoped to learn about this society's attitude toward witches from their amazing miniature plays, but the videos had only left her more confused than before. In *I Married a Witch,* the groom viewed his bride's magical talents with amused tolerance while in *Bell, Book, and Candle,* the hero lived in mortal terror of falling beneath an enchantress's spell. In *Escape to Witch Mountain,* two children were persecuted and terrorized because of their supernatural powers. Most disturbing of all, *The Witches of Eastwick* actually *were* in league with the devil! Arian blushed anew to remember the lewd acts they'd offered to perform on a smirking Satan.

Huddled beside the bed, she rubbed her arms through the thin silk of her borrowed nightshirt. Beads of rain had begun to pelt the windows and there seemed to be no escaping the artificial draft that cooled the air. 'Twas almost as if the chill of that watery grave still clung to her.

Remembering that there was a fireplace in the spacious salon off the bedchamber, Arian padded in that direction. The drapes had been drawn and a single lamp left burning, enclosing her in a cocoon of understated luxury.

A dejected pair of potted ferns flanked the fireplace. The sunken marble hearth felt like a chunk of ice to Arian's bare feet. She peered into the polished brass grate, but found its interior as pristine as its exterior, with no sign of ash or ember. She reached up the chimney, thinking to dislodge the flue and start a blaze of her own, only to discover its narrow opening had been bricked shut.

Shivering, she straightened, both puzzled and exasperated. Winter was drawing nigh and a crackling fire on a damp fall day was a pleasure no man should deny himself.

The sight of a sleek ebony urn sprouting a profusion of blossoms cheered her. She drew the vase off the mantel and buried her face in its blooms only to recoil as she encountered the scratchiness of silk instead of the velvety softness of fragrant petals.

Her pensive frown deepened as she returned the vase to the mantel. Flowers woven of silk? A bricked-up hearth? Windows that did not open? Portraits of women he'd never met? Was there nothing in Tristan Lennox's life that wasn't an elaborate illusion? Or were his hollow surroundings only a reflection of the man himself?

The witch was wicked. She deserved to die.

His callous words haunted her. How was she ever to determine if his exquisitely polished exterior hid a man's vulnerable heart or simply a shriveled kernel, as dry and bitter as wormwood?

She ambled around the elegant suite, hoping to find some clue to his character, some evidence to prove her nightmare had been only an echo of her fears instead of a dire warning.

It was almost as if the salon had been deliberately cultivated to protect its occupant's secrets. The rich cream of its walls, carpet, and settee was unbroken by a single splash of color. There were no cozy quilts to snuggle beneath on a snowy winter night, no leather-bound books scattered across the lacquered tables to expose his favorite authors or private passions. Perhaps he had none, Arian thought, running her finger along a sterile expanse of wall. The notion made her feel strangely melancholy.

She wandered over to an Oriental secretary and tugged open a drawer, ignoring a twinge of guilt.

Her search yielded only a stack of cream-colored stationery engraved with Lennox's name, its edges precisely aligned to match the rim of the drawer. An exploration of the drawer beneath revealed a row of pens, neatly grouped by color and type. Arian sighed. Perhaps she'd been ignoring the obvious all along. Perhaps the salon's very barrenness revealed Lennox's nature more clearly than any discarded volume of poetry or threadbare pillow.

Perhaps he was nothing more than a methodically tidy man. A man who loathed any disruption of his orderly routine. Her lips curved in a rueful smile. If that were so, he must truly despise her and the chaos her unconventional arrival had created.

She was sliding the bottom drawer into place when it hung on something she could not see. She reached into its recesses, drawing out a crumpled pamphlet printed on glossy paper. Her breath came a little faster. It wasn't the pamphlet itself that excited her, but the very disregard with which it had been shoved to the back of the drawer.

"Forbes?" she whispered, smoothing the wrinkles from the slick cover. "November nineteen ninety-five?"

It wasn't the bold script of the unfamiliar title that made her heart leap, but the portrait beneath it. Not a portrait sketched by an artist, she quickly realized, but a photo-graph, an eerie likeness similar to the one of the woman on the bedroom dresser. But this was no stranger.

This was Tristan Lennox, captured for a moment in time in a thousand subtle shades of gray. Tristan as she had first seen him—waistcoat unbuttoned, shirt open at the throat, one arm draped casually over bended knee, sandy lashes unable to completely veil the steely glint in his eyes.

Tristan Lennox—Boy Billionaire or Financial Wizard?

The snide caption beneath the photograph jarred her from her reverie. She flipped impatiently through the pages until she found another photograph of Tristan, this one captured while he sat at the far end of a long, polished table. The artist's choice of angles made him look undiminished, yet very alone.

Eager to scan the article, Arian groped blindly for the settee behind her. Perhaps now she would learn something of her enigmatic host more beneficial than his weakness for wheat-germ waffles or his distaste for disorder. Many of the modern terms eluded her, but she struggled to piece together the fragments of Tristan's life into some recognizable pattern.

The article made scant mention of his early life except to report that he'd been raised in a Boston orphanage. Arian felt a twinge of pity, although she knew instinctively that Lennox would despise her for it.

In 1986, at the age of twenty-two, he'd sought a patent on a computer microprocessor so fast it had made the 386 then in use look as if it were standing still. Within three years he had parlayed his discovery into a Fortune 500 company and added the feather of corporate raider to his cap. Arian studied a rare smiling image of Tristan. 'Twas only too easy to envision a dagger clamped between his gleaming teeth. What could a "corporate raider" be if not a polite euphemism for "pirate"? She wrinkled her nose in exasperation. 'Twas like trying to make sense of a foreign language.

Turning the page, she read aloud, " 'While many express grudging admiration for his meteoric rise in the competitive world of high finance, Lennox's legendary ruthlessness has earned him more than a few enemies.' " The paragraph concluded with a quote from one of his many detractors (who had allegedly begged *Forbes* to let him remain anonymous for fear of retaliation): "Everything the son of a **** touches turns to gold. It's almost like he has some sort of supernatural power. Like he sold his ****ing soul to the devil or something."

Arian slowly lowered the magazine. Having been the victim of just such gossip herself, she knew how insidious its poison could be, yet she could not quite suppress a shudder of foreboding.

She muddled along through another page, then, frustrated by the obtuse blathering about "CPU's" and "motherboards," began to study the accompanying photographs instead: Tristan stepping into a long, black wagon that resembled a horse-drawn hearse without a horse; Tristan touring something called a stock exchange. Arian was baffled by the absence of cows or pigs in the background. Tristan resplendent in black breeches and tailed coat, smirking down at the hollow-cheeked brunette on his arm; Tristan exchanging the brunette for an equally emaciated blonde. Beset by an unfamiliar pang, Arian touched her slightly rounded belly through the silk nightshirt, feeling plump for the first time in her life.

She sought the next page only to discover it was missing—not neatly excised as she would have expected, but ripped out by the seams, leaving only a jagged edge where it should have been. A curious chill crept over her, but it was banished by a treacherous swell of warmth when her gaze lit on the final photograph of the piece.

Tristan standing in a lumpy shirt etched with the letters MIT, his striking eyes almost hidden by a pair of thick, wire-rimmed spectacles. A lock of uncombed hair fell over his brow, and Arian absently touched the page, thinking to brush it back. He looked so young, so painfully awkward—his smile shy and uncertain, yet full of hope for the future. She searched, but could not find even a shadow of the cynical, dangerous man he would become.

She read the caption beneath, groaning at being presented with yet another challenge to her limited vocabulary. Hugging the pamphlet to her chest, she promised herself she would corner Sven first thing in the morning and force him to explain exactly what a "geek" was.

11

The laboratory staff of Lennox Enterprises stood at rigid attention, looking less like a delegation of the most brilliant scientists and technicians in the world than a defeated army facing a firing squad. A firing squad consisting of only one man, a man whose caustic tongue contained all the firepower necessary to annihilate them.

Tristan knew his pleasant smile had developed a distinctly unpleasant edge over the past three days. "So, Montgomery," he said, pacing the immaculate white tile as a possible prelude to offering the engineer a last cigarette. "After seventy-two hours of gathering data, plotting flight trajectories, and analyzing theories, you have only one conclusion to offer me."

The imposing Scotsman was all but squirming in his brogans. "Aye, sir. The wee lass was ridin' a broom."

Tristan paused, keeping his eyes downcast. His staff drew in a collective breath, waiting for his temper to ignite like carbolic acid pitched on a Bunsen burner.

But when Tristan finally lifted his gaze to their anxious faces, his countenance was that of a condemned man. "Very well. Resume your duties."

Starched lab coats rustling, they fled to their work stations, leaving Copperfield to unfold himself from his post by the door and follow Tristan into the corridor.

"Any word from Interpol or the local police?" Tristan asked.

Copperfield shook his head, falling into step beside him. "Lieutenant Derschiwitz promised us some answers no later than Friday afternoon. So how is our wee enchantress doing?" he added, valiantly trying to inject a note of levity into a situation growing grimmer with each passing day.

"I wouldn't know. I haven't seen her since late last night. Sven says she's spent the morning wolfing down tubs of Häagen-Dazs and watching Jerry Lewis movies."

"Good God," Cop muttered. "She is French." He eyed the smudges of exhaustion beneath his friend's eyes with concern. "It's ridiculous for you to go on sleeping in your office, you know."

"The problem isn't where I'm sleeping, because I'm not."

"At least you're *not* sleeping with her," Copperfield said darkly. "Another paternity suit could cost you a hell of a lot more than a million."

Tristan knew the casual warning was meant to remind him that Arian was nothing but a ruthless scam artist, not inflict him with a stabbing pain in his chest. He slowed his pace, scowling. He'd already suffered a peculiar tightness in the region of his heart, then shortness of breath in Bloomingdale's private salon. As soon as he was rid of the troublesome Miss Whitewood, he promised himself, he would have his assistant schedule him an appointment with a reputable cardiologist.

He wasn't aware he was massaging the offending area until he caught Copperfield's uneasy glance. "Is something wrong?" Cop asked.

"Nothing a productive day at the office won't cure," Tristan replied, seeking solace in the only place he'd ever found it. "Did Miss Alonzo fax you those figures I requested?"

Copperfield winced. "I was waiting for just the right moment to tell you this, but I'm afraid the only thing Miss Alonzo faxed me was her resignation. She's lucky the tearstains didn't short out her fax machine."

"I was a little hard on her yesterday. Call her at home and tell her I'll double her salary if she can be here by one o'clock."

"Too late. Rumor has it that the *Global Inquirer* already tripled it in exchange for an exclusive."

The soft-spoken, efficient Miss Alonzo had been Tristan's personal assistant for over five years. Even as his lips tightened in a bitter smile, he wished he hadn't lost the ability to be surprised by her desertion. "I suppose every woman has her price, even one as devoted as Miss Alonzo. She also has an ailing mother to support. Send her a generous severance check and have the agency rush over a temp."

Arian had no inkling of Tristan's personnel problems when she tiptoed into the penthouse elevator late that afternoon. She suppressed a groan when she saw the abundance of numbered buttons on the panel. 'Twould take hours, perhaps even days, to search every floor of this monstrous mansion for a library. But she had little choice. Despite her prodding, Sven had been unable to provide her with any fresh insights into his employer's character. When she'd asked him what a "geek" was, the bespectacled behemoth had simply shaken his head and said, "My English is not so good. I think maybe is some kind of duck."

Arian timidly tapped a random button, then clutched her stomach as the conveyance took a dive. She was thankful it wasn't an express elevator. Despite Tristan's assurances to the contrary, she still wasn't convinced the narrow glass tube wouldn't send her hurtling toward a gruesome and inescapable death.

After Arian had wandered aimlessly through ten floors of nondescript corridors, earning nothing but indifferent shrugs and scathing glances directed at her bare feet in reply to her queries, a gruesome and inescapable death began to gain appeal. She almost wished she was back in her penthouse refuge watching *Bewitched* or playing Chutes and Ladders with Sven. A cry of relief escaped her when she spotted an elderly black man wielding a mop at the end of a lonely corridor.

He flashed her a grin that was more gum than teeth. "Hello, sweetheart. You lost?"

"More than you know," she confessed. "I'm trying to find the library. Doesn't anyone in the twentieth century read?"

He shook his head, clucking sadly beneath his breath. "Not as many as used to. Too many can't and them that can are too busy watching TV."

Arian sighed, beginning to fear her search for that other Tristan—the boy with the wire-rimmed spectacles and shy smile—was all in vain. "So there's no library." Her mind raced, seeking alternatives that might be more suited to this curious century. "Where would historical records be kept? Ledgers? Photo-graphs?"

The old man scratched his graying head. "Probably in Archives on the thirteenth floor."

"Oh, thank you, sir! You don't know how much you've helped me." Arian stood on tiptoe to kiss his grizzled cheek before racing for the elevator. She could only pray that thirteen would prove to be her lucky number.

Arian pushed open the first pair of frosted glass doors she came to on the thirteenth floor, sniffing hopefully for leather and mildew. She almost got her nose knocked off when a red-faced young man came charging through the doors in the opposite direction without even bothering to beg her pardon.

She hopped out of harm's way only to find herself plunged into a scene of utter chaos. Men and women rushed this way and that, darting in and out of tiny glass cubicles, waving fanfolded sheets of paper and bellowing orders. The deafening cacophony was underscored by inhuman beeps, shrill rings, and an incessant humming that jangled Arian's nerves even more than the discordant shouts. What a noisy century this was! Her overloaded ears could catch only snatches of conversation.

"Hobbes from the *Prattler* is on line three, but for God's sake, don't put him through."

"The minimicroprocesser diode stock just plunged over fifteen points. I'm not going to be the one to tell him. It's your turn."

"Like hell. I told him yesterday."

"Has anyone seen the messenger who's supposed to pick up the Delaney files? He wanted them sent over an hour ago. Oh, God, I'm dead. Why doesn't somebody just shoot me now and put me out of my misery?"

The last was uttered by a disheveled young woman who punctuated her plea by banging her forehead on her desk.

"Excuse me," Arian whispered.

The woman's head flew up. She peered suspiciously at Arian through the strings of hair that had escaped her once tidy bun. "What the hell do you want?"

Although shocked by the casual profanity, Arian managed a polite smile. "I was wondering if you could direct me to—"

"Praise the Lord, I'm delivered! And so are the Delaney files!" The woman bounded up and snatched Arian's hand, dragging her through the fray toward a closed door. "What took you so long? That wretched temp is having hysterics and Mr. Lennox is threatening to throw her out the window."

Before Arian could even form a protest, the woman had thrown open the door and shoved her inside. "Here's the messenger you've been waiting for, honey," she called out in a singsong voice that held more than a trace of feline malice. "And you really should invest in a good waterproof mascara."

The woman slammed the door behind Arian, leaving her alone with a sniveling creature whose red-rimmed eyes were ringed with black smudges. She looked rather like a forlorn raccoon. Some sort of blinking, humming contraption was spitting out pages faster than her trembling hands could catch them.

This room was much more plush than the previous one, with thick mist-colored carpet and a wall of sparkling windows, yet Arian sensed it was only an antechamber for the haven guarded by a pair of ornate mahogany doors on the far wall. The sight gave her an odd shiver. She could not have said if it was anticipation or fear.

"I was looking for Archives," she blurted out. "Could you help—"

Leaving the curious machine to cough papers into the air, the woman rushed around the desk to clutch Arian's arm with such pathetic gratitude that Arian hadn't the heart to finish. "Oh, Gawd, I thought you were neva coming." She shot the mahogany doors a petrified look before hissing, "He accused me of calling a messenga service in Siberia."

Arian might have found the woman's overwrought terror amusing had she not known immediately who "he" was. Before she could explain her own predicament, stacks of cream-colored files were being thrust into her arms. She accepted them with a sigh of surrender. What harm would it do to simply relieve the poor woman of her burden and wait outside until the real messenger arrived? The files kept coming, the stack growing higher and higher until Arian was nearly buried behind them.

She would have never known one of the mahogany doors had swung open if the woman hadn't spun around with a horrified shriek, spilling the remainder of the files to the floor.

Arian would have recognized the acerbic purr anywhere. Its silky menace sent a jolt of warning coursing down her own spine. "My dear Miss Cotton, are you aware that you've cut off telephone conversations with two of my major stockholders, faxed my accountant's suggestions for creating tax loopholes to the IRS, and crashed the hard drives of not one, but two state-of-the-art computers?" His voice softened, growing lethal with tenderness. "Tell me, is it a policy of your agency to hire the competence-impaired?"

"He's a monsta!" the woman wailed. "I quit!" Bursting into tears, she fled the room, slamming the door behind her.

Although the stack of files shielded Arian until there was little visible of her but her sloppy chignon, a pair of legs encased in slim black leggings, and ten bare toes twitching with trepidation, she could still feel Tristan's scrutiny like a palpable thing. She slowly lowered the files to offer him a tentative grin.

"You!" His eyes narrowed as he peered over her shoulder as if expecting to find Sven lurking behind a potted fern. "Where the hell is Nordgard? If he's abandoned his post to sneak off to the gym and pump up those damnable pecs of his . . ."

Tristan left the ominous threat unfinished, but Arian still felt compelled to jump to Sven's defense. "He's still in the penthouse. He fell asleep watching an opera."

Tristan cocked a disbelieving eyebrow. "An opera? I didn't know Sven's tastes ran to the sublime. I thought he preferred *American Gladiators*."

" 'Twas a piece called *Guiding Light*. The music lacked substance, but the drama moved him to tears."

"Oh, *that* sort of opera."

Tristan advanced on her, but Arian stood her ground, determined to let him know she could not be bullied or intimidated. She drew in a breath for courage only to feel her will melting beneath the wintry spice of his cologne.

He leaned down until his nose was less than an inch from hers. Since his sandy lashes tended to fade against his golden skin, Arian had never before noticed just how sinfully long they were. "Can you type?"

"No, but I can milk a cow, clean a cod, churn a wicked tub of butter, and handstitch the entire alphabet on a sampler."

He blinked at her precisely three times before wheeling away to pace the length of the room. "This is all your fault, you know. If you hadn't staged that silly broom crash, the press wouldn't be camped on our doorstep, Lennox Enterprises stock wouldn't be plunging, and Miss Alonzo would be sitting behind that desk instead of spilling my most intimate secrets to the tabloids." He threw his watch a helpless glance, then ran a hand through his immaculate hair, rumpling it until he looked nearly as irresistible as the boy he had been. "It's already four-thirty," he muttered more to himself than to her. "We can stop answering the phones in half an hour."

He shot her a speculative glance before removing the files from her arms. His warm, competent hands closed over her shoulders, guiding her to the chair abandoned by the beleaguered Miss Cotton.

"Sit here," he instructed, his breath teasing the sensitive hairs at her nape. "And don't move. This is the telephone. If it makes a ringing noise, pick it up, hold it to your ear and say 'Hello.'" He demonstrated. "Tell whoever is on the other end of the line that Mr. Lennox is in a meeting and not taking any calls until tomorrow morning. If they insist on speaking to me, tell them I'm not here. Tell them I went home sick. Do you understand?"

"Yes, sir."

"And if you simply can't refrain from disturbing me

in the next thirty minutes, tap this button. I'll be able to hear everything you say."

"Yes, sir."

"And stop calling me sir!"

"If you wish, sir."

Growling beneath his breath, Tristan retreated to his office, slamming the door so hard it rattled the tasteful prints on the wall. Arian grinned as she leaned back in the chair and propped her bare feet on the desk, thinking she just might have stumbled onto the perfect opportunity to observe Tristan Lennox in his natural environment.

Although she still jumped every time the telephone jangled, Arian did not find her job overly demanding. She told three callers Mr. Lennox was in a meeting, two that he'd left for the afternoon, and one unpleasantly persistent fellow named Hobbes that Mr. Lennox had a mild case of the plague, but would be happy to speak with him on the morrow.

Sooner than she believed possible, the brass clock on the wall read five o'clock. She waited several minutes, but didn't hear so much as a murmur from the chamber's inner sanctum. She wandered to the window to discover the sun had dipped below the peaks of the tallest buildings, sending a premature twilight creeping over the city in muted shades of lavender and gray.

"Excuse me?"

Arian turned to discover a woman huddled in the outer doorway. The chaos in the offices beyond had subsided.

The woman was nervously twisting the gold band on the fourth finger of her left hand. "I was wondering if I could speak with Mr. Lennox?"

Arian opened her mouth, then closed it again. Tristan had given her no instructions regarding visitors. "I'm sorry," she finally said with genuine regret, "but Mr. Lennox is in a meeting."

The woman sighed, her plump face revealing a trace of weary bitterness. "That's what he told you to tell me, isn't it? I guess I can't blame him. I never had time for him so why should he clear his busy schedule for me?" She squared her shoulders as she turned to go, visibly torn between pride and defeat. "Just tell him to call his mother when he can spare a moment."

12

"Wait! Oh, please wait! Don't go!" Arian cried, rushing around from behind the desk to seize the stranger's hands. "I had no idea you were Tristan's mother."

The woman's hands were like ice, but she clung to Arian as if she'd been tossed a lifeline on a stormy sea. Knowing that Tristan had grown up in an orphanage, Arian was confused by his mother's existence. But there was no denying the resemblance. The years might have faded the gold in her teased hair to pale silver, but her eyes still glistened like pools of molten pewter. She was young, Arian realized with a faint shock, not much older than Arian's own mother would have been had she lived.

The woman's skirt and blouse looked slightly shabby, but freshly starched. A defiant hint of red tinged her lips. The obvious care she'd taken with her appearance touched Arian in a way she could not explain.

She squeezed the woman's hands, hoping to put her at ease. "Do come in and wait while I let Tristan know you're here. I'm certain he'll be delighted to see you."

The woman laughed shakily. "I wish I could be so sure." She cast Arian's naked feet a glance that was puzzled, but not unkind. "I don't believe we've met, although I must say you're much nicer than the lady who usually works in this office."

"I'm new around here," Arian offered, moving around the desk to tap the button Tristan had shown her. Clearing her throat, she announced with what she hoped was suitable pomp, "Mr. Lennox. Your mother is here to see you."

Several seconds of ominous silence followed. Arian was beginning to wonder if he'd heard her when a terse "Just a minute" emerged.

They waited in awkward silence, Arian struggling to keep her confident smile intact and Tristan's mother chewing her lower lip. When the door finally swung open, the first thing Arian noticed was that Tristan had donned his coat and smoothed back his hair. Not a strand was out of place.

"Hello, Brenda," he said coolly.

Arian recoiled. Had she dared to address her own mama by her Christian name, she would have gotten her mouth smacked for her impertinence.

"Hello, Tristan." The woman's stilted reply baffled Arian further.

Tristan consulted the calendar on his watch. "You're a little early this month, aren't you? It's only the twenty-ninth."

"Please," the woman whispered, giving her ring a violent wrench. "Could we talk inside?"

Arian held her breath, fearing that Tristan was going to be heartless enough to deny his mother's request. But he proffered her the door with a mocking flourish. Before he drew it shut behind them, he shot Arian a look of such icy displeasure she was surprised her hair didn't sprout icicles.

She sank back into the chair, oddly unnerved, then

shot straight up as Tristan's voice emerged from the box on the desk. "Would you care for a Scotch?"

His mother's answering murmur was nearly obscured by the clink of ice cubes tumbling into a glass.

Nagged by a twinge of conscience, Arian reached for the button, determined to silence the private exchange before it could progress. She might stoop to snooping through a man's personal belongings, but eavesdropping on his most intimate conversations was another . . .

"What is it this time, Brenda?" Arian withdrew her hand, riveted by the note of world-weariness in Tristan's voice. "An overdue insurance payment? Too many trips to the track? Or did Danny flunk another sobriety test?" Leather creaked and Arian could visualize him settling back in his chair, a tumbler of Scotch dangling from his elegant fingers.

Brenda's voice sounded suspiciously thick. "You don't have to be so cold. You might ask me how I've been."

"Why bother when we both know the question isn't 'How are you?' but 'How much?' "

His mother sniffed. "You could try to be a little more civil about it."

"Sorry." Tristan's voice could have cut a diamond. "My mother didn't teach me any manners."

Brenda's sniffling degenerated into heartrending sobs, muffled as if by her bare hand. Arian blinked back tears of her own and waited for Tristan to comfort his mother, as he had so tenderly comforted her when the hell-copter had frightened her.

But when his voice came, it wasn't gentled by compassion, but edged with desperation. "Christ, Brenda, take my handkerchief. You'd think your allowance would at least be enough to keep you in Kleenex."

Arian heard a scraping noise, as if a chair had abruptly been pushed back, then Tristan, his voice even bleaker at a distance. "Stop bawling and tell me what's wrong."

Arian swiveled around in her own chair, imagining him staring out over that same lonely vista of passing strangers and city streets.

"It's Ellen. She's pregnant." His mother's announcement was greeted by a silence so profound that Arian would have thought the box had malfunctioned if Brenda hadn't eventually scrambled to fill it. "She's my baby, you know—only seventeen. She won't even graduate until spring. And the boy . . . well, you know how boys that age are."

Tristan's harsh laugh made Arian hug a shiver away. "Does she plan to simply drop it off on somebody's doorstep like you did or get rid of it by more permanent means?"

"She wants to keep it. You don't know my Ellen, but she's a good girl, Tristan. She just made a little mistake."

Arian was crying openly now, the tears trickling down her cheeks before she could swipe them away.

"She'll be a good little mom, son, I know she will. If she just had some cash to make things easier . . . please . . . don't make me beg . . ."

Tristan's only reply was the rustle of paper being pulled from a drawer and slapped on a desk, then the scratch of a pen across it. "Here. Tell her there's more where this came from. Tell her I'm proud of her for accepting responsibility for her . . . little mistake."

Brenda's startled gasp revealed far more about Tristan's generosity than his terse instructions. "Oh, son, you're too good to us. Why, if you'd just let me bring my Ellen here to meet you, she'd throw her arms around you and give you the biggest—"

Tristan cut off the passionate declaration without a hint of remorse. "Don't come back on the thirty-first. I'll have my assistant mail your check."

Arian was still gazing out the window when Brenda

emerged from the office clutching a narrow rectangle of paper. From her reflection in the darkening glass, Arian could see that the woman had gnawed the rouge from her lips, leaving them pale and trembling. The sight failed to evoke even a ghost of Arian's sympathy.

"Good night, miss," Brenda shyly offered. "Thank you for your kindness."

A stilted "Good night" was all Arian could manage.

She remained curled up in the chair as true dusk fell, knowing she should retreat to the penthouse before Tristan emerged. She could only imagine how much he would loathe her if he knew she'd intruded on his private anguish.

But when she rose, a force more powerful than fear for herself drew her toward those mahogany doors.

Tristan hadn't lit a single lamp to shield him from the gathering darkness. He stood at the window, a lone shadow silhouetted by the city lights, a half-empty Scotch glass dangling from one hand, the other jammed into the pocket of his trousers. He'd shed his jacket and loosened his tie. His gaze narrowed on her reflection, forcing her to see herself as he must see her—as an insensitive stranger intruding on his solitude.

"It blinks, you know."

"What?" Arian had no idea what he was talking about.

He pointed to the reflection of the little black box perched on his desk—a box identical to the one in the antechamber. A tiny green light on its top was flashing. "The intercom. It blinks when it's activated."

A wave of shame passed over Arian, but there was no denying her guilt. She would simply have to brazen it out. "If you knew I was listening, why didn't you stop me?"

He shrugged. "Why bother? You'd have to stand in line to sell my pathetic secrets to the press. I can see the headline now—BOY BILLIONAIRE BILKED BY OWN MOTHER."

Arian perched on the edge of his desk, more disturbed by his sarcasm than she cared to admit. "I read somewhere that you grew up in an orphanage."

"So you assumed I was an orphan? Oliver Twist and all that romantic rot? Sorry to disillusion you, but orphanages take bastards, too."

Arian winced, but Tristan's expression never changed. Perhaps the label didn't bear the same stigma as it did in her own time. She could still remember the unkind remarks, the cutting slights, the pitying glances when the other children at Louis's court had learned she had a mama, but no papa.

"Your mother must have been very young," she said gently, wanting to pity the woman, but finding it nearly impossible in the face of his unflinching candor.

"Seventeen. Just like her precious Ellen." He took a sip of the Scotch. "I'm sure she convinced herself she was doing the best thing by giving me up. She couldn't have known there wouldn't be much demand for shy, brainy kids with stringy hair and Coke-bottle glasses. Most of my potential parents never got past the photo."

Arian wanted him to stop. He might be able to relate such a tale without betraying even a trace of emotion, but his passionless confession was flaying her tender heart to ribbons.

"I hated the ones who made it as far as the interview the most. They were all polite, of course. Painfully polite. But somehow that only made it worse."

She inched closer to him without realizing it. "What happened to your moth—to Brenda after?"

"Shortly after she left me on the orphanage steps with my name pinned to my shirt, she dropped out of high school to marry a construction worker, moved to a three-bedroom tract house in Newark, and raised three kids with good solid blue-collar names like Bill and Danny . . . and Ellen."

Arian had always longed for a sibling to ease her loneliness. "So you have brothers and a sister?"

Tristan swung around. She recoiled from the virulence of his expression. "No. My mother has other children."

Arian's fingers trembled with the urge to touch him, to comfort him. But before she could, his mask of icy indifference slipped back into place, warning her she would earn nothing for her foolishness but frostbitten fingers.

She clasped her hands in her lap to keep them from betraying her. "How did you and your mother come to be reunited?"

He propped his hip on the corner of the desk opposite her. " 'Reunited.' Such a touching word." His scathing smile implied the opposite. "Since I was never adopted, my name never changed and it wasn't that difficult for Brenda to trace me. She called three years ago to request a meeting. I canceled all of my appointments for the afternoon, put on my most expensive suit, my finest cologne, and waited for her to arrive."

"She didn't come?" Arian breathed, fearing the worst.

He lifted the glass to his lips for a long draw before answering. "Oh, she came. At two o'clock on the dot. Things were a little awkward at first, as you can imagine, but we managed to carry on a civil conversation. You see, I'd already decided to forgive her. Convinced myself that she didn't deserve to suffer any more than she already had. After all, she was just a girl when she gave me up. A 'good girl' who'd made a 'little mistake.' "

Arian's hands curled into fists as anger surged through her, anger toward the woman who'd dared to make this man feel as if he were nothing more than a careless blunder to be regretted for the rest of her life.

"Brenda chattered on and on about her second family. About her husband Earl, who'd been forced to go on disability after he suffered a back injury at work. About her oldest son Bill, who desperately wanted to attend an Ivy League school, but lacked the grades to snag a scholarship. About sixteen-year-old Danny, whose multiple DUI's had earned him a court-ordered stay at an expensive rehab center."

Arian could too easily imagine Tristan sitting behind this very desk, growing colder and colder as each of his mother's words drove an icy wedge of betrayal deeper into his heart.

"By the time she'd confided her own particular weakness—afternoon trips to the horse track to bet on the daily doubles, I knew she didn't want me any more than she ever had. She only wanted my money."

It was Arian's turn to rise and seek the window. Her turn to stare out over the lights of the city so Tristan wouldn't see the tears glistening in her eyes. She knew instinctively that he would scorn her pity. All she had to offer him was her rage.

"I wouldn't have given her an allowance," she said bitterly.

Tristan rose from his own corner of the desk, stunned by the ferocity of Arian's passion. He'd never had anyone to defend him before. Never even expected it. He'd always been content to stand on his own, as he had since the day he was born.

Yet there Arian stood, little more than a wraith in black leggings, black turtleneck, and bare feet, ready to do battle with any dragon who dared to cross his path, even his weak and calculating mother. Something irresistible and dangerous coiled through his belly.

"What would you have done? Put a curse on her?" Tristan spoke the words lightly to douse the tension smoldering between them, but when Arian spun around to face him, her wrath was still hot enough to strike sparks.

"I'd have thrown her out on the street. I'd have told her never to darken my doorstep again. Her or any other member of her rotten brood."

"Witch," he murmured.

Arian's eyes darkened with such wounded alarm

that he softened his accusation with a lazy smile before cupping her delicate jaw in his hand. "You beautiful, vindictive little witch."

Suddenly, Tristan wanted to taste her on his lips more desperately than he'd ever wanted to taste the Scotch. His groin stiffened with unbearable longing, fading his smile.

"Stop looking at me like that," he ordered.

"Like what?" she whispered, blinking up at him.

"As if I were a pint of Häagen-Dazs and you've been deprived of sweets for a lifetime." Tristan's fingers tightened on her jaw. He would have felt guilty for trying to frighten her away if she hadn't already scared the bloody hell out of him. Against his better judgment, his thumb strayed out to stroke her trembling lower lip. "Maybe I should just indulge your little sweet tooth. You know all my secrets, so maybe I can coax you into confessing a few of your own. I've always found pleasure to be a most persuasive incentive."

As Tristan drew her into his arms, Arian thought of a hundred secrets to tell him, a thousand things to confess. But her words melted into a broken sigh as he lowered his head to plant a kiss against the throbbing pulse in her throat. His tapered fingers caressed her nape with ruthless tenderness, sending languorous waves of delight tingling through her body. A sweet tongue of fire flickered to life low in her belly, threatening to become a roaring blaze with each sensual stroke of his fingertips. Not even the lecherous Reverend Linnet had dared to touch her with such shocking and exquisite familiarity.

Linnet's threats and bullying had failed to defeat her, yet Tristan mastered her with nothing more than a nibble of her willful flesh and a few practiced caresses.

"No!" Arian wrenched herself from his arms, stumbling backward into the desk.

He reached to steady her, whispering, "Arian, don't . . ."

She was deaf to his hoarse plea. Terrified she would find only a mocking reflection of her own carnal weakness in his eyes, she fled, realizing even as she did so that there was nowhere left to hide from her own folly. She'd already betrayed her most dangerous secret, the one she'd struggled to keep from herself since the first moment she'd laid eyes on Tristan Lennox.

His mother might not want him, but she, Arian Whitewood, most definitely did.

13

Wearing one of Tristan's nightshirts, Arian sat cross-legged on the carpet in front of the penthouse's living room window and watched the lights of the city wink to life through the falling curtain of darkness. She dug her tablespoon into the open pint of Häagen-Dazs and brought another mouthful to her lips. Never in her most decadent dreams had she imagined such a sinful delicacy. The sweet cream melted in her mouth, but the dark, rich aftertaste of the chocolate lingered. 'Twas like her encounter with Tristan the previous night. Bitter, yet sweet. Pleasure mingled with the threat of pain.

Not the sort of pain she had anticipated, either. Not a noose around her neck, but a man's fist closed snugly about her heart. She had misjudged him sorely it seemed, only to discover he was even more dangerous than she had feared. He might accuse her of being a witch, but he was the one guilty of weaving an enchantment more powerful than any spell her feeble magic could cast.

She set the frozen cream aside, her appetite deserting her. Tristan Lennox was nothing like the raven-haired prince she had always dreamed of. He was terse and mocking rather than patient and kind, wicked instead of noble, and possessed of a dark sensuality that precluded the spiritual. If she were wise, she would forget the million dollars and use the amulet to flee to some place or time where he could never find her.

Hugging her knees to ward off a chill, Arian wondered if Tristan was staring out another window at that very moment. The foreign city viewed through her pensive reflection had never seemed so vast or so lonely. Who did Tristan see staring back at him? she wondered. The accomplished, devastatingly handsome man he had become or the shy, homely boy he had believed himself to be?

She rested her cheek on her knee. Her heart ached for that boy. She wanted to draw him into her arms and promise him he would never be unwanted again. But Tristan had not been seeking solace when he'd drawn her into his arms. He'd wanted something more tangible than her pity or her comfort.

The harsh reminder sent her scrambling to her feet to pace the elegant salon. She would do well to remember that Tristan was no longer that boy. He'd molded himself into a ruthless man who took what he wanted without apology or regret. He was no different from any of the wealthy, powerful men who had offered her mama their protection. A "protection" that had lasted only until a younger, more lovely face had come along.

Yet Arian could still feel the tenderness of Tristan's long, elegant fingers cupping her nape, the scorching heat of his breath against her throat. Her mouth went dry with a primitive thirst. 'Twas as if he embodied every sin Marcus had ever warned her about. Every delicious temptation that had enticed her mama to give herself over to wickedness and self-indulgence. Such pleasures were as foreign to Arian as the sinuous whisper of silk against her skin.

Stifling a moan, she paused to cool her burning brow against the window. As it did every evening at this time, the encroaching darkness activated the lamp behind her, spoiling both her brooding and the melancholy beauty of the view.

She scowled at the lamp's reflection. She was growing increasingly weary of Tristan's uncanny magic. Having lamps flare to life and doors spring open without her assistance only seemed to emphasize her powerlessness at his hands.

Seized by inspiration, she snatched the spoon from the melting tub of cream, determined to wrest back some tiny measure of control over her destiny before it slipped out of her reach altogether.

"I need to borrow one of my ties," Tristan said, breezing into Copperfield's office that evening with an Ungaro suit coat draped carelessly over one arm.

Copperfield's fingers ceased their methodical tapping on the keyboard of his computer as he studied his boss over the rim of his reading glasses. "My, my, aren't we chipper tonight. What's the occasion? Foreclosing on an old folk's home?"

"Dinner date," Tristan replied, adjusting the cuffs of his shirt with a series of expert flicks.

Copperfield rolled his desk chair over to a steel file cabinet and yanked open the bottom drawer to reveal a colorful nest of ties.

When Tristan cocked a disbelieving brow, he shrugged without a hint of shame. "Sorry. It's a sickness." He watched as Tristan untangled a narrow black Ralph Lauren. "So why have you been reduced to borrowing from my pathetic stash? Did your little Rapunzel flush all your others or is she weaving a rope of ties so she can bust out a window and climb down the side of the building like King Kong?"

Tristan smirked at him. "Why climb when you can fly?"

"Ah, but you don't believe she can, do you?"

"That remains to be seen. Perhaps I can charm her into a little demonstration this evening over peach sorbet and a bottle of Dom Pérignon."

Copperfield snapped forward like a sleek spaniel going on point. "So the enchanting Miss Whitewood's agreed to be your dinner companion, eh? You're taking her somewhere French, I presume? Lutèce? La Caravelle?"

Tristan suffered a distinct twinge of conscience, leaving him no choice but to squelch Copperfield's eager grin before it could damage his resolve. "We'll be dining in. I'm taking her to bed."

Copperfield leaned back in the chair, steepling his fingers beneath his chin. As he'd expected, Tristan found the disillusionment darkening his friend's eyes much easier to withstand than his hope. He'd had ten long years to grow accustomed to it.

"So are you seducing her for information," Cop asked, "or just for the sheer greedy pleasure of it?"

Tristan steeled his expression to shield the treacherous direction of his thoughts. "Information, of course." He shrugged. "The pleasure will simply be a fringe benefit."

"Like dental insurance?" Cop's smile had a nasty edge. "And what makes you think she'll succumb to your charms? Do you find yourself that irresistible?"

Tristan blew on a cuff link and polished it on the opposite sleeve while considering his answer. The casual gesture did not betray the quickening of his pulse or the slow, hot throb of desire in his groin as he remembered the exquisite feel of Arian melting into his arms, heard her sweet sigh of surrender, and smelled that quaint perfume that clung to her hair and evoked such wistful yearning in him. But he was strangely reluctant to expose her vulnerability to anyone, even Copperfield.

"I can assure you that Miss Whitewood will have

every opportunity to resist me," he said. "I plan to seduce her, not molest her."

Copperfield surveyed him through narrowed eyes. "Brenda was here yesterday, wasn't she? Isn't that how it works? She screws you and you turn around and screw somebody else? Usually somebody who may want it, but doesn't deserve it."

Tristan jerked his head up. Only Copperfield would have dared such insubordination without fearing for his next paycheck. Copperfield, who had grown up in the orphanage alongside him. Copperfield, who had sworn pricking their fingers to become blood brothers forged a stronger bond than any mere accident of birth. Copperfield, who at ten years old had been adopted by a wealthy Cherokee attorney and his wife, leaving Tristan standing alone on the playground, feeling left out, left behind, and just plain left. Again.

"I find it a little ironic that you're defending Miss Whitewood's honor," Tristan said. "She's hardly some innocent victim. She only came here to fleece me out of a million dollars. And if my bumbling laboratory staff or my incompetent detectives don't provide us with some ammunition by the end of the week, she just may succeed."

"Well, then, I can hardly blame you for trying to get your money's worth, can I?"

Tristan slammed both hands on the desk. "Are you quite through with your interrogation, counselor?"

Cop lifted his palms in a gesture of surrender. "The prosecution rests." Thrusting the tie in his pocket, Tristan turned to go, but Copperfield's tone—musing, almost pleasant—made him hesitate. "Tell me, Tristan, when you look in the mirror, whose reflection do you see staring back at you? Yours? Or Arthur's?"

Tristan whirled around. For a furious moment, he mistook the ominous buzz in the air for the tension crackling between them. Then the fluorescent ceiling panel flickered, drawing both of their gazes upward. The suit coat slid from Tristan's arm, puddling on the floor.

The panel dimmed, leaving them in near-darkness, then blazed on again, twice as bright as before.

Their alarmed eyes met as they blurted out one word in the same breath.

"Arian."

The express elevator shot toward the roof of the Tower, its sole occupant pacing its narrow confines like a caged panther.

Tristan had deliberately chosen the glass-and-steel tube, knowing it was one of only three elevators in the Tower powered by the emergency generators. He paused to glare at the rapidly escalating numbers, mentally willing the red caution lights to stop flashing.

Resuming his pacing, he ran his fingers through his hair, tormented by images of Arian flushing his fax machine or deciding the whirlpool tub might be a handy place to rewire the stereo. If she had injured herself or destroyed the entire top floor of the Tower, he had only himself to blame. If he hadn't been ruthlessly plotting her seduction, he would never have given Sven the night off to audition for the Off-Broadway revival of *La Cage aux Folles*.

The elevator snapped to a halt. Tristan squeezed through the doors before they were half open. The night wind roared like thunder in his ears as he raced across the roof toward the red door marked Fire Stairs.

Battling the ruthless gusts, he tugged open the door, then plunged down the shadowy steps, praying the hidden passageway he'd deliberately designed in case a hasty escape became necessary wouldn't be blocked by a piece of furniture or fallen body.

Relief surged through him as the false panel of drywall gave easily beneath his hands.

He burst into the suite's living room only to be frozen into place by the sight of Arian perched on a chair, holding a metal spoon poised above the empty socket of a brass floor lamp. Fear washed over him in an icy cascade he'd known only once before.

"Arian! No!" he shouted, lunging toward her in what felt like slow motion.

She swung around, her pale face framed by a dark cloud of hair. He caught only a glimpse of her wide, startled eyes before the bowl of the spoon touched the naked connection and she went flying across the suite in a sizzling arc of white-hot light.

14

She was dead.

It was the only thought to penetrate the staggering numbness of Tristan's mind.

Arian was dead.

At first he believed the darkness and hush were inside of him, simply tendrils of the cold, black fog swirling through his brain. Then he realized the city itself had gone dark and mute, leaving a pale spill of moonlight as Arian's only shroud.

He drifted toward her small, still form, knowing in his more rational mind that there was something he ought to be doing. Shouting for help. Dialing 911. Administering CPR. But his habit of taking command of every situation had abandoned him.

Arian's ebony hair was spread in a shimmering fan around her shoulders, reminding him absurdly of Snow White in her glass coffin. Even in death, hadn't the deceptive blush of life stained Snow White's pallid cheeks? Hadn't her rosebud lips parted as if to welcome a kiss from a prince who might never come? Hadn't the creamy swell of her breasts tantalized every hopelessly naïve kid in the theater into daring to believe her chest would rise just one more time?

A wistful sigh feathered the air. It took Tristan a few moments to realize it was not his own.

Then without knowing how he got there, he was on his knees, cradling Arian's throat in a desperate search for life. He found it in the contagious warmth of her skin, the miraculous throb of her pulse beneath his fingertips.

Her eyes shot open, luminous even in shock. She blinked up at the ceiling several times, then quietly said, "I always thought getting struck by lightning might straighten my hair."

A breathless laugh escaped Tristan. He could not resist capturing one of the sable tendrils and tickling her nose with the tip of it. "I hate to disappoint you, but I think it's more curly than before."

She swore softly in French. Her gaze shifted to his face. She was looking at him as she had that day in the courtyard, her eyes misty with tenderness and invitation. That curious mixture of innocence and lust cast an irresistible spell over him.

Tristan slowly lowered his lips to hers, knowing even as he did so that he should be checking her pulse . . . helping her to her feet . . . calling a doc . . .

His mouth brushed hers in a sweet, dry caress. An electricity more primitive than lightning arced between them, melting the neurons of Tristan's methodical left brain to mush. Her lips parted without hesitation beneath his gentle probing, dragging a hoarse groan out of him.

He pressed his advantage, giving her his tongue and stealing hers away as he'd secretly yearned to do from the first time he'd held her in his arms. Then there had been a thousand witnesses. Now there was only the two of them, wrapped in a velvety fog of darkness that was no longer a threat, but a blessing.

Savoring the lush sweetness of her mouth, Tristan melted against her as if mere physical proximity could make them one. During his years in New York, he'd grown accustomed to women hewn only of planes and angles, with elbows sharp enough to puncture lungs and poke out eyes. But Arian hadn't had all the softness sucked out of her by a surgeon's wand. Everything about her was soft. Her hair, her breasts, her delectable lips.

He surrendered those lips to nuzzle the satiny column of her throat, breathing deep of her fragrance. She smelled nearly as delicious as she tasted, more intoxicating than well-aged cognac or Chanel No. 5. She smelled like kittens napping in a rocking chair. Towering cedars strung with bows and lights. Chocolate-chip cookies fresh from the oven on a snowy winter night.

It was those dreams of a home he'd never had that finally allowed Tristan to identify her quaint perfume.

Cloves. Arian Whitewood smelled of cloves.

With a growl of mingled hunger and repletion, Tristan sank his tongue deep into her mouth, knowing he was teetering on the dangerous precipice between frustration and ecstasy. He hadn't been this close to release without consummation since his clumsy fumblings in the back seat of a Toyota hatchback his sophomore year in high school.

Arian welcomed Tristan's kiss with artless innocence, blissfully unaware that it was only a shadow of his darker urges. Until she'd opened her eyes to find his wintry gaze melting with concern, she hadn't realized how badly she'd wanted him to look at her like that again. As if she were the only woman in the world who could soothe the stern furrow between his brows.

He cupped her face in his palms, holding her mouth captive for his tender possession. Deprived of sight by both darkness and desire, Arian teased up his shirtsleeves and blindly caressed his forearms. Their crisp dusting of hair thrilled her seeking fingertips.

She moaned with a disappointment that soon

melted to delight when his lips abandoned hers to feather soft, provocative kisses along her jaw and throat. He wanted more. She could deny him nothing. Even as she welcomed the delicious press of his weight against the cradle of her hips, some small, plaintive voice within her wondered if this was how her mother had felt when she'd given herself to Arian's father. And to all the men who had come before and after him.

As if in defiance of her doubts, Arian's hands grew bolder. She dared to caress the prickly softness of Tristan's nape, to rake her fingers through his short-cropped hair, enticing him to return his mouth to hers and deepen the demanding thrust of his tongue. Wicked tendrils of pleasure licked through her belly, incinerating her inhibitions.

At first Arian believed it was only her heart pulsing wildly between them, but then she realized it was the amulet. 'Twas as if the gem had absorbed the strange lightning and was throbbing in time to the thick, hot blood surging to all the forbidden reaches of her body. The rushing in her ears drowned out the whine of a distant siren, the renewed hum of the air conditioner, the muffled *ping* of the arriving elevator.

Copperfield's matter-of-fact voice washed over them like a bucket of ice water. "Sorry, Tristan, but you can't blame your precocious little witch for this one. It was some sort of citywide blackout. I called Con Ed and they said some idiot probably dropped his electric shaver in the bath—" He lurched to a halt on the verge of stumbling over their entwined bodies, then emitted a low whistle. "Well, I'll be damned . . ."

Arian squinted against the flood of light, fearing it was not Copperfield, but she who would be damned for her wanton behavior. After being cocooned in such seductive darkness, even the recessed track lighting Copperfield had switched on seemed unbearably harsh.

The light threw Tristan's broad shoulders into silhouette and cast an ugly shadow over what had been lovely in the darkness: the puffy tenderness of her well-kissed lips, the provocative juxtaposition of their bodies, the glint of raw hunger in Tristan's eyes.

Eyes that were glazing over with an impenetrable shield of frost even as Arian watched, leaving her with nothing but a scalding blush and a wretched sense of loss.

His lazy grace untarnished, Tristan rose to face his friend, dismissing her as easily as he flicked a speck of carpet fuzz from the sleeve of his shirt. Feeling nude instead of just mildly rumpled, Arian sat up and jerked the nightshirt closed at the throat.

Copperfield rocked back on his heels. "Well, well ... no wonder there are so many babies born nine months after a blackout."

Arian sensed the condemnation in Copperfield's eyes wasn't intended for her, but she still lunged to her feet, dragging the back of her hand across her tingling lips. "You might have warned me," she cried.

Tristan turned on her as if relieved to find an outlet for his own frustration. "I didn't think I had to warn you. Any three-year-old knows not to stick a spoon into an electric socket."

"I was trying to smother the flame at its source," Arian shot back at him. "I kept unscrewing the globe, but every time I screwed it back in, the lamp would come on again. But I wasn't talking about the lamp. I was talking about the baby. What if your impertinent kisses have gotten me with child?"

The anger fled Tristan's face, leaving him looking mildly dazed. "With child?" he echoed, as if she had spoken in a foreign tongue.

Copperfield frowned at his friend in blatant disgust. "Very intelligent, Lennox. This is New York City in the nineties, the woman is a total stranger, and you didn't even bother to use protection?"

"I didn't need any protection," Tristan said softly, the speculative gleam in his eyes deepening. "Except maybe from her." His deft fingers captured Arian's jaw in a mocking travesty of his earlier caress. "Would you care to repeat what you just said?"

Already sensing that she'd erred in some irredeemable manner, Arian pressed her lips together and shook her head.

Tristan's tender smile did nothing to relieve her fears. "Your selective amnesia must be flaring up again, darling. Allow me to refresh your memory. You said, 'What if your impertinent kisses have gotten me with child?' And to think, Cop," he tossed over his shoulder, "all these years I thought it was letting a woman drink after me that posed the danger." His narrowed eyes searched her face, their scrutiny so intense it made her want to squirm. "Who the hell are you, Arian Whitewood?"

Arian bit her lip to keep from spilling out the truth, knowing silence was her only defense. But Tristan wasn't offering pardon, only condemnation.

His expression resolute, he grabbed her hand and dragged her past a gaping Copperfield to the elevator.

Arian feared he was taking her somewhere to explain exactly how babies were conceived or perhaps even to show her. "Where are we going?"

His terse reply sent a shiver of foreboding down her spine. "On a witch hunt."

Arian trotted along behind Tristan in her bare feet, forced to take three steps to each of his determined strides. His possessive grip on her hand never slackened, not even when their trek through the endless corridors of Lennox Enterprises brought them face-to-face with several of his employees whose departures had been delayed by the chaos created by the brief blackout.

"E-e-excuse me, sir," yelped a shiny-faced young man, plastering himself against the wall as they passed. "Mr. Lennox! I thought you'd left for the day." A gawking woman vaulted out of their path, hugging her briefcase like a shield.

Although Tristan seemed oblivious, the astounded stares and shocked whispers made Arian want to cringe. She feared the immaculately groomed men and women all knew she'd been tussling on the penthouse floor with their employer. She might not have a scarlet letter emblazoned on her chest, but her lips were still moist and swollen from Tristan's kisses, her hair tumbled from his caresses. She slowed to tug the nightshirt down with her free hand, breathing a prayer of thanksgiving that it at least covered her naked legs to the knees.

Tristan's pace quickened. Stumbling after him, Arian glared at his back with mounting resentment. Did he seek to punish her for her carnal weakness or his own?

A shiny plaque engraved with tasteful script identified their ultimate destination as Lennox Labs.

Tristan shoved open the swinging door with the heel of his hand, revealing a group of workers hovering over glowing screens and glass tubes. Their expressions were no less startled than those they'd confronted in the corridor.

"Out," he commanded. "You have three minutes to clear the lab."

"Yes, sir!"

"Aye, Mr. Lennox!"

The white-coated figures scurried to obey, leaving Arian at Tristan's mercy. He dragged her over to a keypad on the far wall and began to tap out a complex string of numbers. As his fingers flew over the keys, Arian reluctantly marveled at their tapered grace. It already seemed a lifetime ago that they'd caressed her with such wrenching tenderness.

A hidden panel swished open.

As Tristan drew her into the room beyond, Arian knew instinctively that she was being granted entry to the inner sanctum of Tristan's domain. Merciless white light flooded the sterile chamber. There were no shadows here. Nowhere to hide.

Relinquishing her hand, he left her standing in the center of the room, a dark blot upon its dazzling purity. He stepped up on a shallow platform, bent over a panel, and began to flip switches and twist knobs. An ominous humming filled the air. The light flickered from white to pale green, casting a sinister mask over Tristan's handsome features. He shoved up his shirtsleeves, sending his cuff links bouncing across the room and revealing a tanned expanse of forearm. This was the real Tristan Lennox, Arian realized. With his polished veneer stripped away, he was as comfortable in these laboratory surroundings as any sorcerer of old.

"I designed this software to measure metaphysical telekinetic energy," he said, swiping a stray lock of hair from his eyes with a disregard Arian found dangerously endearing. He swiveled a glowing monitor around to face her. "This graph will fluctuate in the presence of any extrasensory manifestation stemming from aberrant brain wave activity."

Arian sniffed. "Aberrant? Are you suggesting I am a freak, sir?"

He straightened. "I'm suggesting you're a flagrant phony. But I thought it only fair to give you one last chance to prove me wrong before I call you a cab for the airport." He smiled sweetly and folded his arms over his chest in mocking challenge. "Or would you prefer a broom?"

Arian would have preferred to hurl a fireball hot enough to singe his smug eyebrows off. Instead, she crossed her own arms and glared at him, her muteness now more rebellion than defense. She refused to allow him to provoke or bully her into a confession. If he was seeking a witch, then he would hunt in vain.

He stepped down from the platform to circle her like the predator he had become. "What's wrong, Miss Whitewood? Cat got your tongue? I suppose you do have a cat somewhere, don't you? A big, black one that shape-shifts into a raven when the moon is full? Every good witch has a familiar, you know." He paused to chuck her under the chin. "And you are a very good little witch, aren't you?"

Arian clenched her teeth to keep from biting his finger. *You must learn to guard that temper of yours, daughter. 'Tis the meek who shall inherit the earth.* Chastened by the memory of Marcus's words, she fought to keep her anger at a low simmer.

"After all, you were clever enough to infiltrate my competition, my life . . ."—moving behind her, Tristan pushed aside the heavy fall of her curls, his heated whisper tickling the baby-fine hairs at her nape— "my bed."

Arian was shocked to realize his indrawn breath was no more steady than her own. Dropping her hair as if it were a nest of baby cobras, he strode back to the platform, putting as much distance between them as the lab would allow.

"I'm no fool, Arian Whitewood," he snapped, spinning around to face her. His normally imperturbable expression was so savage with desperation that she wondered if he was trying to convince her or himself. "And you're no witch. You're a fraud. A shameless cheat whose sole purpose in coming here was to swindle me out of a million dollars."

Nearly choking on a cry of denial, Arian drew herself up to her full five feet half an inch.

Tristan's voice softened with lethal scorn. "What really gets me is that I was actually on the verge of believing you . . . of believing in you. But you blew it with that pathetic performance upstairs. Too bad Sven wasn't there to witness your acting debut." His insulting gaze swept her rumpled form from head to toe, striking invisible tongues of flame wherever it lingered. "This is nineteen ninety-six, sweetheart. I'd be a hell of a lot more likely to believe you're a witch than a virgin."

Arian's hand closed around the amulet. The emerald pulsed against her palm like a sullen throb of thunder warning of a coming storm.

"Why, you couldn't pull a rabbit out of a rabbit hutch!" Tristan's contempt spilled like acid over the shame of her many failures. "You couldn't bend a spoon with both hands. You couldn't charm your way out of a paper—"

"Enough!" The cry of pure fury burst from Arian's throat at the precise instant the ball of lightning leapt from her outstretched fingertips, shooting straight for Tristan's head.

PART II

There be none of Beauty's daughters
With a magic like thee;
And like music on the waters
Is thy sweet voice to me.

—George Noel Gordon,
Lord Byron

Everything that deceives
may be said to enchant.

—Plato

15

"Sweet Jesu, I've killed him!" Arian clapped a hand to her mouth, gazing with utter horror upon the blackened, smoking crater where Tristan had stood. A sob escaped her parted fingers. "Grandmama always tried to warn me my tantrums were most unbecoming."

"I hope you'll forgive me if I agree with her." The wry, shaken voice came from behind the panel.

Arian's breath caught in her throat as a tousled golden head emerged, followed by a pair of broad shoulders. She was too giddy with relief to be gratified by Tristan's dazed expression, the rumpled condition of his shirt, or the smudge of soot marring his patrician nose.

Gripping what remained of the panel for support, he climbed to his feet, eyeing her with a curious mixture of awe and wariness. "You don't, by any chance, suffer from PMS, do you?"

Arian's first ridiculous urge to rush into his arms, smother his face with kisses, and beg his forgiveness was tempered by caution as she realized just what her ugly little fit had revealed. She no longer believed she could bear it if Tristan turned out to be cut from the same starched broadcloth as Linnet.

She lowered her eyes to hide her vulnerability. "The only thing I was suffering from, sir, was your heartless taunts."

Dragging his gaze away from Arian's averted face, Tristan glanced back at the computer monitor to confirm his suspicions. The wildly zigzagging line of the graph was off the scale. He reached over to gently flick off the machine before the influx of impossible data could crash its hard drive. His own senses threatened a similar overload. His ears still crackled and the stench of burning ozone flooded his nostrils. He stepped off the platform, his heart pounding wildly in his ears.

He suspected he would recover from his reckless dive behind the panel long before he'd recover from the shock of discovering that Arian's magic was no cheap parlor trick. In the instant before she'd blasted him, he'd seen no sign of a radio transmitter, no microprocessor, not even a puff of smoke or the betraying flash of a mirror.

There had been only Arian in his silk pajama shirt and bare feet, her dark eyes flashing with anger, her soft lips quivering because his cruelty had almost driven her to tears.

His unsteady legs betrayed him. He sat down abruptly on the edge of the platform, resting his hands on his knees to control their violent trembling. "Who the hell are you?" he whispered, searching her face.

Gazing into the molten pewter of Tristan's eyes, Arian realized he was no longer demanding, but pleading. A plea she found it nearly impossible to resist.

"I'm Arian Whitewood," she whispered back, spreading the oversized nightshirt to bob a shy curtsy.

"From France?" he added hoarsely.

She nearly blurted out the truth, but some small, superstitious part of her was hesitant to invoke the Reverend Linnet's name. The sin had been solely his, but the shame of that dark episode seemed to taint even this shadowless haven. She longed to leave Linnet and Gloucester in the past where they belonged.

Tristan watched Arian hesitate, saw the shadow pass over her face. How many times had he felt the presence of a private specter only to have Eddie Hobbes or some other reporter drag it into the sunlight for strangers to poke and prod? He certainly didn't want Arian or anyone else delving into his past or nudging his ghosts into wakefulness.

"Don't," he said, lifting his hand to stay her words. "All I asked for was proof of magic. You don't owe me anything beyond that." A choked laugh escaped him. "Unless, of course, the *Prattler*'s right and you really are a lascivious alien with insatiable appetites who's going to whisk me off to Venus and keep me in sexual bondage until I father a new race of superbeings." Tristan had frequently entertained such fantasies as a sex-starved, *Star Trek*–obsessed teenager, and to his keen chagrin, he discovered it wasn't such a stretch of his imagination to picture Arian in a silver foil bikini leveling a laser gun at his heart. Hell, she might not even need the gun.

Her cheeks had darkened in an endearing blush. "Don't be ridiculous. I'm only a witch."

"Only a witch," Tristan echoed, clambering to his feet. Wonder crept over him, as gently and irrevocably as a mist of green stealing over a slumbering garden. "Just a cauldron-stirring, lightning-hurling, broom-riding princess of darkness."

Arian sniffled. "I do believe that's the nicest thing anyone has ever said to me."

Tristan approached her with the respect he would have accorded her from the beginning had he not been so desperate to elude her enchantment. "I haven't been very nice to you, have I? I was a dreadful bully."

"An absolute wretch." Her voice subsided to a defensive mumble. "I could so pull a rabbit out of a rabbit hutch."

Tristan winced. "Lightning was too good for me. You should have turned me into a frog."

"A tadpole," she concurred with a sullen nod. " 'Twould have been no more than you deserved for—" She glanced up at him, her eyes brightening with poorly disguised hope. "Do you honestly believe I could? Turn you into a frog?"

As Tristan cupped her chin in his palm, his thumb strayed out to caress her parted lips. He had thought to wring a confession from them, but it seemed he would be the one compelled to confess tonight.

"Yes, Arian," he said softly. "I believe."

Beguiled by the reverent glow in his eyes, Arian wondered how she could feel so blissfully elated and so miserably uncertain at the same time. Beneath the guise of smoothing a wrinkle, she tucked the amulet into her nightshirt, praying Tristan's newfound faith was not misplaced.

When Tristan marched into Copperfield's office the next morning, clutching a paper sack from a nearby hardware store instead of a stack of files, Cop's scowl warned him that his allegiance had shifted. He might as well have had "Michael Copperfield, Defender of Chaste Witches" lettered in gold on his door. Tristan could have told his friend that his vigilance was unnecessary. He had every intention of protecting Arian from himself.

Copperfield snapped open a folder and used it to shield his mutinous expression. "Don't nag. I've been working on the Monkman account since dawn. I'll have a copy of my report on your desk by noon or you can dock my—"

"There's no rush. You've been working far too hard lately. Maybe you need a vacation." Gratified by the drop of Cop's jaw, Tristan added, "As a matter of fact, I've decided to take the day off myself."

His attorney couldn't have looked any more flabbergasted had Tristan announced he was donating all of his assets to charity and joining a Sicilian monastery. "But you haven't had a day off since nineteen eighty-nine!"

"Precisely my point." He planted his palms on Cop's desk, too wired with anticipation to care if his eyes betrayed his delight. "I want you to come with me. I have an extraordinary surprise for you."

"The ninety-six profit projections?" Cop ventured.

"Something a hell of a lot more interesting." He grabbed Copperfield's arm and dragged him toward the door.

Cop sniffed at his breath. "I haven't seen you this giddy since the Republicans reclaimed Congress. Have you been drinking?"

Although the Tower was still ringed with news vans and reporters waving microphones, the atrium of Lennox Enterprises was mercifully devoid of their shouting and jostling. Tristan had ordered extra security posted at each entrance with express orders to deny access to anyone who was not an employee or resident of the building. His refusal to comment on Arian's status had only whetted the press's insatiable curiosity. His lips twitched as he suppressed a calculating smile. The press conference he'd scheduled for noon should send them all scurrying back to their holes to sharpen their teeth and claws in anticipation of a fresh kill.

As they crossed the atrium, Sven ducked beneath a fern and fell into step beside them.

"Good morning, Nordgard," Tristan said.

"Morning, sir." The bodyguard's doleful expression implied it was not a good morning at all.

"So how did the audition go?" Tristan asked, ignoring Copperfield's startled glance. He wasn't exactly known for taking an interest in his employees' personal lives or even allowing them to have one.

"I didn't get the part," Sven confessed in his grave baritone. "They said I was too masculine." Tristan eyed the Norwegian's bulging neck muscles, wondering which role he could possibly have coveted in a play about two aging homosexuals. As they approached the elevators, Sven drew a flip phone from his jacket. "Shall I alert security team three, sir? Will you and Mr. Copperfield be leaving the building?"

"That won't be necessary," Tristan replied.

"Mr. Lennox has a surprise for me," Cop inserted coyly, earning himself an elbow to the ribs.

"Oh, goodie. I love surprises!" Sven exclaimed, visibly brightening.

Tristan paused. "I'm terribly sorry, Sven, but *you're* not invited." He thrust the paper sack he was carrying into the crestfallen giant's hands. "I have more vital security matters for you to attend to. I want these installed throughout the Tower before noon today."

Sven drew a piece of plastic from the mouth of the bag, looking more befuddled than usual. "What are they, sir? Bomb detectors? Some sort of newfangled wiretap?"

Tristan plucked the two-pronged device from Sven's hand and popped it into the nearest electric outlet. "I might be mistaken, but I believe they're called child protector caps."

* * *

Ash of brimstone and winter's thunder,
Tear the veil of heav'n asunder.
Leper's nose and lizard lips,
Make fire fly from my fingertips!

Arian's voice rose to a majestic crescendo on the last note of the spell. Her outstretched arm quivered with anticipation.

Nothing. Her fingers did not emit so much as a feeble spark.

Her shoulders slumped with disappointment as she examined the fresh tub of Häagen-Dazs she'd placed on the marble hearth. She poked at its ribboned surface to find it nearly as solid as when she'd removed it from the miniature freezer over the bar.

"What pathetic sort of witch can't even melt frozen cream?" she muttered, sucking her finger clean. Even the rich taste of the chocolate melting on her tongue failed to console her.

What more could she do? she wondered despairingly. She'd been up since dawn crafting a plausible spell. She'd drawn the salon's drapes and dimmed the track lighting to create a suitably spectral ambience. She'd even donned a midnight blue robe she'd found in the closet and brushed her hair until it crackled like a cloud around her face. A brief glance into the mirror above the mantel assured her she was the very portrait of a respectable enchantress.

All she lacked was talent.

Her frustration escaped in a gusty sigh. The amulet lay where she had forced herself to abandon it, glinting against the watered silk of an overstuffed ottoman.

Gathering up the skirts of Tristan's bathrobe so they wouldn't trip her, she marched over and glared down at the amulet. She was beginning to feel as if it weren't a charm, but a curse. The hateful thing seemed to be winking at her, taunting her for her incompetence. She was torn between snatching it to her bosom and flushing it down the chamber pot. It might enable her to claim the million dollars, but it also prevented her from satisfying her desperate, inexplicable need to prove herself worthy of Tristan's faith.

She'd slept little after he'd escorted her back to the suite last night, although he'd left her at the elevator with nothing more than a chaste peck on the brow. 'Twas almost as if their tender tryst during the blackout had never occurred. Arian eyed the plush carpet beneath the window where they had lain, stabbed by a fresh pang of longing.

Almost.

Driven by a compulsion born of both curiosity and

dread, she reached for the amulet with trembling fingers. Closing her fist tight about it, she extended her other hand, squinted at the container of frozen cream and whispered, "Burn."

A jet of flame ten feet long shot from her fingertips with a deafening *whoosh*. The frozen cream began to melt, then to bubble, finally boiling over until there was nothing left of cream or container but a lump of steaming cardboard.

Arian popped her smoking fingers into her mouth, extinguishing them with a sizzle. *"Sacre bleu!"*

Her awe eclipsed by crushing defeat, she hurled the amulet at the far wall, savoring a petty thrill of satisfaction when it ricocheted off and vanished amongst the plump cushions of the settee.

"Temper, temper, my dear," chided a mocking male voice.

Arian whirled around to discover the elevator had arrived just in time for Tristan to witness her tantrum. The second in two days, she reminded herself with a cringe of embarrassment.

"I—um—I couldn't get the clasp fastened," she offered lamely as Copperfield followed Tristan off the elevator.

If Cop was surprised to find her still in residence after last night's debacle, he hid it behind a sympathetic smile as the elevator departed.

Tristan's excitement was palpable, giving his step a buoyancy she'd never seen before. It both pained and warmed her to think she might be responsible for his transformation.

He clasped both of her hands in his. "I brought Copperfield here so he could experience a taste of what I experienced last night."

Arian's befuddled brain dismissed their encounter in the lab, remembering instead the lazy flick of Tristan's tongue over her lips. "I c-can't possibly . . ."

"Now don't be modest," he admonished. "I simply want you to demonstrate your powers for Cop."

It was Copperfield's turn to arch a skeptical eyebrow. "C'mon, Tristan. She's a charming girl, but even I never believed she possessed any sort of supernatural power. I'm a lawyer, not an idiot."

Tristan's coaxing smile threatened to melt Arian's bones more effectively than any fireball. He gently caressed the fine bones of her hands with his thumbs. "Don't be shy, Arian. Something simple will be fine. Just make yourself invisible or levitate an ashtray."

Drawing her hands from his, Arian backed toward the settee, scrambling for the words of a spell, any spell. Her mama had resided briefly with an English marquess who had quoted frequently from his favorite bard. "Uh, double, double, toil and trouble," she blurted out, "fire burn and cauldron bubble . . ."

"Cute," Cop said dryly, "but not highly original."

Arian stumbled over the hem of Tristan's robe. The back of her knees crashed into the settee. She sat abruptly, using the opportunity to reach behind her and dig beneath the pillows for any trace of the amulet.

Tristan shot Copperfield a warning scowl. "She's just suffering from stage fright. Give her a moment to compose herself."

Cop's own composure was slipping. "Oh, why don't you stop taunting the poor girl? It's like kicking a helpless kitten. You should be ashamed of yourself!"

Fearful they might actually come to blows over her, Arian wailed, "Scale of dragon, tooth of wolf!"

Both men stopped glaring at each other to gape at her, transfixed by her performance. She rooted frantically between the cushions, wincing as one of her fingernails tore to the quick. If she could just keep them distracted until she could locate the amulet . . .

"Eye of newt and toe of frog." She deliberately lowered her voice, weaving a husky enchantment that had little to do with the gibberish she was muttering. "Wool of bat and tongue of dog!" Inspired by the sparkle of approval in Tristan's eyes, she tossed back her head, sending a cascade of curls tumbling down her back, and waved her free arm gracefully in the air. The arch of her spine enticed the expensive silk to cling to her generous curves.

"Bewitching," Tristan murmured.

Copperfield rolled his eyes.

Arian suppressed a grunt of mingled triumph and frustration as the amulet's chain rippled like quicksilver through her fingers. The bard's overwrought stanzas were beginning to elude her as well. "Lizard's leg and owlet's wing; baboon's blood and—and piglet's . . . thing."

She made one last lunge beneath the cushions, her voice rising along with her desperation. She couldn't bear to watch Tristan's expectant smile fade to the same cynical sneer he had given his mother. "Snout of shoat and gall of"—her fingers brushed the smooth surface of the emerald. She seized it with a gleeful shout—"goat!"

The elevator doors slid open. One moment Sven stood there, his expression pleasantly vacant. The next, a fluffy, blond goat stood there, chewing his own beard.

16

Arian's intake of breath froze in a feeble squeak. Cop's cry of astonishment was drowned out by Tristan's triumphant whoop.

Tristan clapped his friend on the shoulder, nearly knocking him off his feet. "What are you staring at? Haven't you ever seen a goat wearing sunglasses before?"

Cop sank down on the ottoman, his bronze skin paling to a rather noxious green. Arian flinched as Sven trotted over and began to nibble on one of the potted ferns flanking the hearth. Moaning in mortification, she buried her burning face in the settee pillows, wishing she could burrow beneath them and disappear. She hadn't felt like such a dismal failure since she'd accidentally poisoned one of her mother's paramours with a love potion concocted of rotted eggs and wolfsbane. The man had survived but her mama had delivered a blistering tirade that had left her ears ringing for days.

"Arian?"

She heard Tristan's gentle query through a fog of

misery. Perhaps if she didn't answer, he'd just go away
and leave her to loathe herself to death. Something cold
and clammy nudged her arm. She slowly lifted her head
to discover it was Sven's snout. A familiar pair of mirrored lenses reproached her.

"Oh, Sven! What have I done?" She wrapped her
arms around the goat and sniveled into his silky pelt.

"Quite an impressive demonstration. It'll probably
take Cop a hell of a lot longer to recover than Sven."
Tristan's matter-of-fact tone stifled Arian in mid-sob.

She dared a glance at his eyes. They were twinkling with wicked delight. "You're not angry with me for
turning your bodyguard into a goat?" she whispered.

"You can turn him back into a big, dumb aspiring
actor, can't you?"

Sven tossed his flowing blond mane with an offended snuffle. Tristan gave his rump a friendly swat and
he went trotting over to butt the bedroom door.

Arian squeezed the amulet until it cut into her
palm, unable to completely disguise her bitterness. "I
think I can."

Tristan shrugged, the casual motion emphasizing
the exquisite cut of both his jacket and his shoulders. "If
not, we can always chain him to a stake in the courtyard.
Just think of the money Lennox Enterprises will save on
lawn care."

"Sweet Jesu, I'm so sorry," Arian wailed, burying
her face in her hands.

Tristan had to nudge her chin up with his knuckle
before Arian realized he had only been teasing her. His
fingertips brushed the curve of her jaw with jarring tenderness. "I'm the one who should be apologizing. You're
not some cruise ship magician. I shouldn't have expected you to perform on demand. But since Copperfield
will be finalizing the press arrangements for tonight, I
felt it imperative that he understand the magnitude of
what we're dealing with."

"Tonight?" Arian echoed, her chagrin replaced by a thrill of foreboding.

"Tonight?" Cop mumbled, watching Sven ingest a corner of the drapes.

Tristan began to pace the carpet, easily resuming his role of self-appointed master of all their fates. "I've booked the ballroom at the Plaza for a modest reception to be given in Arian's honor. I considered hosting it here, but thought meeting our enemies on neutral territory would be safer. Do you agree, Cop?"

"Neutral territory," Cop murmured, his dazed nod confirming that he didn't have the faintest idea what he was agreeing with. Sven lost interest in the drapes and wandered over to nibble on the hem of Cop's chinos.

"Am I in danger?" Arian asked, her longing for acclaim balanced by a far more healthy fear of condemnation. Although she'd left them over three hundred years in the past, the ugly snarls and shouts of accusation still echoed through her memory.

"Only if the press leaks any inkling that your powers might be genuine." Tristan dropped to one knee and cupped her hands in his. "They might not burn you at the stake in Times Square, but people do have a rather narrow-minded tendency to condemn what they can't explain."

" 'Thou shalt not suffer a witch to live,' " Arian murmured.

He squeezed her hands. "You could spend the rest of your life hiding behind locked doors, afraid to answer the phone, looking over your shoulder every time you hear a footstep behind you." From the bleakness shadowing his eyes, Arian knew he spoke from bitter experience. "If they catch even a whiff of mystery or scandal, they will hound you to the very gates of hell."

"Then why?" Arian withdrew her hands from his, unable to bear another betrayal. "Why are you throwing me on their mercy?"

"I'm not. I'm only going to toss them a bone. I'm

announcing the reception this afternoon at a press conference. That should start them drooling in anticipation. Tonight I'll publicly declare you the victor in our contest of wits and grudgingly toast your good fortune. Then I'll trade a few sly winks to let them in on our private joke."

"Which is . . . ?" Arian asked, failing to see the humor in her situation.

Tristan rose to his full height, his face transformed by a snide sneer. "That you're nothing but a cunning little scam artist who's managed to con one of the wealthiest men in the world out of a million dollars."

Arian recoiled from his contempt as if it were a blast of brimstone, fearing she had stumbled into one of her own nightmares. But that was before his sneer melted into a slanted grin. "Don't you see, Arian? Instead of thinking you're a witch, they'll think I've simply been duped. That I lack the evidence to prove you're a fraud. I'd much rather let them think you made a fool of me than risk exposing your rather *unique* talents."

Arian knew how expensive Tristan's concession would be to a man of his pride. Yet he made it without asking anything in return—not even the truth about her past. The wistful ache in her heart multiplied. She twisted the amulet's chain into a knot, wishing she had more to offer him than half-truths and blatant falsehoods.

"Oh, they'll request a few interviews and snap some photographs," Tristan continued. "They may even hound you for a few days, but after that, some more alluring scandal will grab their attention and you'll be free." His eyes betrayed a hint of wistfulness. "Free to start a new life without any of the baggage from the old."

"I didn't bring any baggage," Arian murmured. "I didn't have time to pack."

"God, it's brilliant," Cop muttered, his eyes slowly sharpening into focus. "You're giving them everything they think they want, yet nothing at all."

"Precisely," Tristan replied.

Cop pried his pants leg out of Sven's mouth and sprang to his feet. "And you're giving it to them tonight!"

"I thought you'd appreciate the irony," Tristan said, looking almost irresistibly smug. "And to think, you once accused me of having no imagination."

"What's so special about tonight?"

Tristan's eyes glittered with wicked mischief. "Why, Arian, I'm disappointed in you! Don't you know that tonight is the night when werewolves howl at the moon and witches take to the windy skies on their brooms? It's October the thirty-first." Tristan's voice lowered to an ominous purr, sending a shiver of dark anticipation tingling down her spine. "Halloween."

Never had a witch suffered such a heinous fate on All Hallows' Eve.

The foppish Antonio minced around Arian's stool, surveying her from all angles before bending over to slap another dab of paint on her face. "Can't have you looking like Casper the Ghost at the reception, can we, dear? With that complexion, you'll positively disappear next to the other guests."

"I rather wish I would," Arian muttered, rubbing her stomach to try and soothe the flock of butterflies that had nested there.

He tweaked her nose, his thin chest heaving with a heartfelt sigh. "If only Mr. Lennox had given us more time. I've got a surgeon friend in Queens who could chisel that little snout of yours down to absolute perfection."

Arian cupped a protective hand over the offending feature. "No, thank you. I've never been particularly fond of it, but I'd rather not have it whittled upon."

Antonio had arrived promptly at noon with a retinue of pink-garbed assistants and a trunk full of modern torture devices. Within minutes, he'd transformed the penthouse bathroom into a private chamber of horrors. While the sloe-eyed beauty expert claimed to be from

Milan, Arian noticed that in moments of extreme travail, such as when she'd protested that only harlots removed the baby-fine down from their legs, his Continental accent dissolved into a distinct drawl.

In the past four hours, Arian had had her legs waxed, her teeth whitened, her eyelashes curled, and her toenails painted a dazzling coral. Even as Antonio applied the finishing touches to her face paint, two Asian women were slathering her thighs with a gel the consistency of marmalade and wrapping them in sheets of cellophane.

"To melt the unsightly cellulite," one of the women whispered with a knowing wink. Arian had no idea what cellulite was, but she tried to look suitably ashamed.

Antonio smoothed her eyebrows with his fingertip. "I'll pluck these after I've finished with your hair. We don't want anyone mistaking you for Brooke Shields or Sam Donaldson, do we? But first comes the real challenge." Fully aware that he had the attention of everyone in the bathroom, he whipped the towel from her damp hair with a flourish.

Arian's curls tumbled around her face with their natural exuberance. Antonio circled her like a vulture, clucking dolefully beneath his breath. "Impossible. Simply impossible. Only an artist would even try . . ." He drew himself up to his full height and straightened his narrow shoulders. "But I, Antonio Garabaldi, am such an artist, and you, my dear, shall become my new masterpiece!"

Arian could not quite suppress a small scream as he snatched up a pair of gleaming shears and came at her with blades flashing.

Tristan fervently hoped none of his employees had seen their uncompromising boss enter the atrium elevator carrying a cardboard tub adorned with pink ribbon instead of his habitual briefcase. Beside him, a silent Copperfield rocked back and forth on his heels as the elevator ascended to the penthouse. Although they were on their way to reassure Arian that the press conference had proceeded exactly as planned, Cop seemed to be suffering from a severe case of second thoughts. Tristan gazed up at the flashing numbers and tried to ignore his friend's dour expression.

But neither of them could ignore the steady *chomp-chomp* coming from behind them.

They turned as one to find Sven munching salad from an enormous Styrofoam tray. He waved a laden fork at them and flashed his gleaming teeth. "From the deli downstairs. Is delicious. You should try."

As Tristan resumed his position, he whispered to Copperfield, "He doesn't seem to be any the worse for wear."

"That's easy for *you* to say," Cop hissed back. "He didn't eat the Chia Pet off *your* desk."

Tristan shrugged. Since Sven seemed to have no memory of his brief transformation, his bodyguard's compulsive craving for leafy greens was the least of Tristan's worries. He was more concerned with the inherent dangers of introducing a witch into New York society. As long as Sven didn't start nibbling on the drapes at the reception tonight or butt Dan Rather in the . . .

"Lieutenant Derschiwitz called before I left my office." Copperfield interrupted Tristan's mental review of potential disasters. "According to NYPD, FBI, CIA, and Interpol files, Arian Whitewood simply doesn't exist."

Tristan remembered the plush feel of Arian in his arms, the intoxicating taste of her lips. Arian Whitewood might be a witch, but she was no phantom.

His enigmatic smile only aggravated Cop's frown. "Derschiwitz still urged the greatest caution. He said some con artists are so clever they've just never been caught. What do you really know about this woman, Tristan? Has she discussed her past with you?"

"No." He shot Cop a meaningful look. "Nor have I discussed mine with her. She's entitled to her privacy just as I am. If she should decide to confide in me, I'll be very flattered, but I'm not going to go digging into her past like some tabloid—" Tristan strolled off the elevator just in time to hear Arian's muffled scream.

He shot toward the penthouse bathroom, charging through the open door before Sven could even drop the salad and draw his Glock.

The sight that greeted him was worse than any he might have imagined. A cloud of dark curls littered the Berber carpet. Scissor blades flashed in the air, dancing and darting with lethal skill. As the maniac wielding them lifted another thick sheath of Arian's hair to inflict a fatal snip, Tristan seized him by the yoke of his silk shirt and slammed him into the nearest mirror.

"Holy shit," Antonio bawled, his sophisticated accent disintegrating into a full-blown Georgia drawl.

Tristan released the cowering hairdresser, realizing with a stifled flush of horror what an utter ass he'd just made of himself. An even more horrible suspicion took root in his mind as Antonio slid down the mirror, landing in a boneless heap at his feet. Tristan checked his reflection and smoothed back his moussed hair before turning to face the havoc he had wreaked.

Antonio's pink-coated assistants were plastered against the shower stall, hands raised in surrender as they nervously eyed the gun Sven had trained on them.

"At ease, Sven," Tristan commanded wearily.

Sven relaxed like a well-trained Doberman, tucking his gun back into its shoulder holster and offering the fallen hairdresser a hand. "Hello, Andy."

"Hello, Sven." Antonio's nostrils flared in a haughty sniff as Sven tugged him to his feet.

"You two know each other?" Copperfield shot Tristan a disbelieving glance.

Sven shrugged his massive shoulders. "An actor has to eat. I worked as a manicurist and hairdresser before I became demolitions expert."

"Your employer is going to be needing an attorney

more than a demolitions expert by the time I'm through with him," Antonio snapped, brushing wisps of Arian's mutilated hair from the front of his shirt. Snatching up his overflowing trunk, he huffed from the room, his lackeys yipping at his heels like a pack of pink poodles.

Tristan gave Cop a discreet signal to follow, knowing he was a master at calculating just how much cash was required to heal a bruised ego.

Tristan flinched anew when he saw the amputated curls scattered around Arian's feet. Ten coral-tipped toes peeped out at him from the silky mass. He slowly lifted his gaze, wincing with the premature fear that he would find her as bald as a newborn baby.

An ethereal cloud of hair drifted around her face, framing her wary smile. "The poor gentleman was trying to cut my hair, not my throat."

At her gentle rebuke, Tristan cleared his own throat, but his voice seemed to have deserted him. He tugged at his tie, wondering why no else seemed to have noticed how airless the room had become.

Heartlessly oblivious to his mounting distress, Arian pointed at the cardboard tub peeping out from under the towel rack. "For me?"

As Tristan rescued his humble offering, he felt more than a little ridiculous—like a smitten suitor with a bouquet of roses in one hand and his heart in the other. He forced himself to relax his grip, knowing he'd look even more foolish with melted ice cream dripping in his Bruno Magli shoes.

He handed the Häagen-Dazs to Arian with a noncommittal grunt.

As she smiled up at him, flashing a shallow dimple he'd never noticed before, a giant fist seemed to reach out and seize his heart. "How did you know chocolate was my favorite?"

Unwilling to humiliate himself further by confessing he'd had one of the janitors dig through the penthouse trash for empty containers, he shrugged. "Just a hunch."

Sven examined the lopsided layers of Arian's hair. "I can fix," he announced with a confidence he'd displayed previously only when confronted by an armed mugger or a mass of plastic explosives.

As Tristan watched Sven's beefy fingers sift through Arian's hair, the pressure in his chest intensified to crushing pain.

Catching a glimpse of his pasty complexion in the mirrored tile over the sink, he backed away from Arian's stool. "If you'll excuse me, there are some last-minute details I need to attend to."

Arian and Sven exchanged a glance, their concerned expressions informing him they were as mystified by his odd behavior as he was.

Clutching his chest, Tristan staggered across the living room and into his private office. He slammed the door, then collapsed against it, mopping his clammy brow with his immaculate sleeve.

He'd been a bloody fool to ignore the warning signs: shortness of breath, chest pain, insomnia, inability to concentrate, sniffing at Arian's hair when he thought she wasn't looking.

He groaned. Christ, it was worse than he thought. He wasn't dying of a heart attack. He was falling in love with a witch. He didn't need a cardiologist. He needed an exorcist.

He scrambled for the Rolodex on his desk, his unsteady hands soothed by its cold, familiar contours. Of course it wasn't love, he assured himself as he began to flip frantically through the cards. It was only a painful infatuation, no different from those Copperfield suffered with comedic regularity. Just a crush, like the crush he'd had on Sylvia Throckmorton, a doe-eyed nymph who'd had the shiniest braces and largest breasts in his entire seventh-grade class. Beautiful, heartless Sylvia Throckmorton, who had dotted her *i*'s with hearts and sent his handmade Valentine back with RETURN TO SENDER scribbled on it in baby-pink lipstick.

He drew a card from the Rolodex and settled back in his leather chair to study it. His lust for Arian was simply the consequence of prolonged abstinence. It was no different from being tempted to gorge oneself on an unhealthy meal after fasting for an unreasonable number of hours. To his empty stomach, Arian was a chocolate-drizzled Hungarian torte—delicious but dangerous.

Proximity to another woman—any woman—would engender the same reaction, a theory Tristan was determined to prove as he leaned forward and punched out seven numbers in quick succession.

He tapped a pencil on the desk, undaunted by the breathy reply of an answering machine. When he finally opened his mouth, he was relieved to hear the clipped, confident tones that emerged. "Hello, this is Tristan Lennox. I know it's been a while and this is short notice, but I was wondering if you had any plans for tonight?"

Arian gazed at her reflection in wonder. She might be a witch, but Sven had proved himself a sorcerer to be reckoned with. Wielding only shears, hairbrush, and a mascara wand, he had transformed her into a vision of shimmering sophistication. He had sealed his magic with a puff of glittering fairy dust he called eye shadow.

In appreciation, Arian had ordered him a fresh spinach salad from the deli downstairs and pretended not to notice when he finished the salad and began to nibble on the Styrofoam tray. He had departed shortly after that to wrap up the security arrangements for the reception, leaving Arian alone with the stranger in the bathroom mirror.

She slid off the stool, trying desperately to stop admiring herself. Puritans shunned vanity, yet Arian was unable to resist a giddy spin of delight as she spread the folds of . . .

. . . Tristan's bathrobe.

An icy flush of panic seized her as she gazed down at the rumpled garment. She and Sven had been so preoccupied with her hair that it had never occurred to them she would need something to wear with it. She charged toward Tristan's closet with such haste that the electronic sensors failed to trigger the doors to open.

Muttering a curse on modern technology, she backed up and forced herself to walk sedately toward the seamless expanse. As soon as the walls began to part, she dove between them.

She found the stack of Bloomingdale's boxes she hadn't yet opened in a forlorn pile behind a rack of leather shoes. Dropping to her knees, Arian tore open the one on top, grimacing as a dove-gray skirt emerged without a ripple of grace. She tossed it over her shoulder and tore into the next box, moaning with regret as a shapeless shift the color of mud puddled in her hands. She remembered choosing these garments for their austerity and their modesty, the precise reasons she was rejecting them now.

She discarded two more boxes, shuddering with distaste. Sinking back on her heels, she breathed in the intoxicating musk of expensive leather and wondered what strange spell Tristan Lennox had cast upon her. Her longing that he recognize her as a witch had been overshadowed by an intense desire to make him look upon her as a woman. Intense and dangerous.

Hadn't she vowed never to entrust her happiness into a man's fickle hands? Her mama had been fool enough to do so only once.

Arian's vision clouded as she remembered a burst of cruel masculine laughter. *Don't be ridiculous, Lily. You're not the sort of woman a man marries.* From her hiding place, Arian had heard a door slam, a vase shatter against it, then the muffled sounds of weeping. She had come creeping out from under the testered bed where her mama had flung herself. Clambering up on the feather tick, she had stroked her mama's soft hair with her chubby little hands and whispered, *Don't cry, Mama. Please don't cry.*

Arian brushed a stray tear from her cheek, prepared to admit defeat and choose between the drab garments when she noticed the final box, this one a little larger than the others and banded with a bright gold ribbon.

Her hands lost their confidence, trembling slightly as she reached for the elegant box. She drew it into her lap and gave the ribbon a tentative tug. The top sprang open, spilling a river of iridescent taffeta across her lap.

Her breath caught with wonder as she freed the gown from its stifling confines. The shimmering folds captured the light, tossing it back in a verdant shade identical to the emerald in her amulet. A Givenchy, the clerk had called it in a well-deserved tribute to its designer. Arian had found it a wistful reminder of the grace that had been missing from her life for far too long.

Why don't you try it on? It suits you.

Tristan's soft-spoken invitation echoed through Arian's memory.

She had rejected his offer, yet he'd ignored her childish protests and rewarded her rudeness with kindness. Arian hugged the gown to her chest, promising herself that tonight she wouldn't be so hasty to decline the pleasures Tristan offered.

When Arian floated down the stairs to the private ballroom of the Plaza, she felt more like a fairy princess than a witch. The skirt of the Givenchy gown belled around her ankles, sheathed for the first time in a pair of sheer stockings. Her dark cloud of hair barely brushed her shoulders. Being relieved of so much of its ponderous weight had left her feeling lighthearted as well as lightheaded.

But nothing made her feel as buoyant as the naughty scraps of silk she'd found buried in the bottom of one of the Bloomingdale's boxes. The clerk's taste in

foundation garments ran to the decadent and Arian felt
deliciously naked beneath the sleek taffeta.

Her fingertips grazed the banister as if to keep her
from taking flight. Heads turned and conversation
ceased as she descended, making her bite back a smile.
She should have known Tristan would leave nothing to
chance. Sven had instructed her to ride the elevator up
two extra floors just so she could make such a striking
entrance.

She would have preferred to face the crowd for the
first time on Tristan's arm, but she was assured he had
only her best interests at heart when she'd peeked into
the freezer of the plush carriage that had delivered her
to the Plaza to find it stocked with not one, but three
different varieties of Häagen-Dazs.

Tristan's *modest* reception included hundreds of
guests, a dozen chandeliers dripping with crystal prisms,
a full orchestra, a bubbling champagne fountain that shot
ten feet into the air, and an imposing ice sculpture of a
pointy-hatted witch in full flight perched upon a gleaming broom. Arian hadn't witnessed such splendor since
her childhood days at Louis XIV's court.

She had to struggle not to hasten her steps as she
saw the man awaiting her at the foot of the stairs. She
had seen men wear naught but black during her years
in Gloucester, but she'd never seen a man wear black
like Tristan Lennox—not as a somber denial of light, but
a sensual embrace of darkness. His tuxedo was the perfect foil for the crisp white of his shirtfront, the molten
sunshine of his hair. As their eyes met, his lips quirked
in that wry smile Arian was beginning to crave with such
alarming hunger. She wiped her damp palm on the banister, praying no one would notice.

Lifting his hands, Tristan applauded her arrival
with lazy grace.

Arian froze, paralyzed by the resulting thunder
of approval that swept through the ballroom. It seemed
she was finally to be praised instead of condemned, sim-

ply because this generous man had deemed her worthy of it.

She knew her heart was in the tremulous smile she gave him, but by the time she noticed the willowy beauty clinging to his elbow, it was too late to snatch it back.

17

A camera flashed, blinding Arian, then another. She dreaded the thought of having her humiliation frozen for all time, but welcomed the harsh sting of the lights. Perhaps she could blame them for the mist of tears in her eyes.

A microphone was thrust in her face. "Miss White-wood, is it true that Mr. Lennox has decided to reward you the million dollars?"

"Any chance of us printing a schematic of that broomstick, Miss Whitewood?"

"Are you a practicing member of Wicca, Arian, or do you profess to worship Satan?"

The voices around her rose to a shrill cacophony, vying with each other for the privilege of screeching her name. Arian's brittle smile never wavered. Her mama might have had many weaknesses, but Arian had never seen her crawl before any man.

As soon as she felt the warm hand cup her elbow, she knew who it belonged to. Although furious that he should be the one to come charging to her rescue, she

resisted her first impulse to jerk away from his possessive touch and allowed him to lead her through the
crowd to a stage adorned with a podium and a microphone of its own.

"Ladies and gentlemen." Tristan silenced the
crowd with little more than an artfully crooked eyebrow.
"Patience, please. I haven't forgotten that I promised you
an impromptu press conference before we get down to
the far more pleasurable business of celebrating Miss
Whitewood's good fortune."

The questioning murmurs escalated. Shading her
eyes against the lights, Arian spotted Copperfield directly in front of the podium, his usual sunny expression
replaced by a fretful scowl. Tristan's companion stood
beside him, her short-cropped auburn hair clinging to
her skull in a sleek cap. The rail-thin woman smiled
up at Tristan, the proprietary gleam in her eye unmistakable.

"When I sponsored the magic competition," Tristan was saying, "many of you thought I'd overloaded my
own circuits. But as you all know, exposing phonies who
prey on weak-minded individuals for profit has become
something of a personal crusade of mine. I don't have to
tell you how surprised I was when Miss Whitewood's
broom came sailing over the wall of Lennox Enterprises."

"Not half as surprised as I was," Arian muttered,
earning her a sidelong look that she ignored.

"Are you still implying she's a phony?" a woman
near the front called out.

Tristan managed a smile that was even more enigmatic than usual. "I'll let you draw your own conclu-
sions. But since the young lady was clever enough to
outwit me, I'd prefer to believe she possesses a rather
high degree of supernatural powers." The crowd exchanged chuckles and knowing smirks.

"Hey, how 'bout a demonstration?" shouted a balding reporter who had accessorized his tux with a T-shirt that had a bow tie stenciled on it.

Tristan slipped a protective arm around Arian's waist; she held her breath to avoid inhaling the wintry enchantment of his aftershave. "What did you have in mind, Hobbes? That she make a few of your ex-wives disappear?" That crack won Tristan a laugh from his enthralled audience.

"Just a few of their lawyers," the reporter shot back, blowing a flawless smoke ring toward the stage.

A woman crowned by a neat blond chignon appeared less than amused by the banter. She tapped her pen on her open pad. "What's the purpose of bringing us here tonight, Mr. Lennox? Do you feel you owe Miss Whitewood a public apology for insinuating she was a fraud?"

"Oh," Tristan said, drawing a folded piece of paper from the breast pocket of his tuxedo as if he'd just remembered it was there. "I owe Miss Whitewood far more than an apology. I owe her a million dollars."

The crowd gasped as Tristan unfolded the oversized bank draft and pressed it into Arian's limp hand.

She stared dumbly at his offering, knowing she should be delirious with joy. Everything she'd ever wanted was finally within her reach. Magic. Wealth. Freedom from the demands and manipulations of men like Tristan Lennox.

But as the cameras flashed and Tristan graciously stepped back to let her bask in the adulation of the crowd, Arian couldn't help but feel as if she'd lost far more than she'd gained.

Tristan lifted the beveled rim of his champagne glass to his lips, his gaze following Arian as she wended her way through the teeming mob of well-wishers. Copperfield hovered at her elbow, self-appointed to fend off the press's more probing questions and to make sure Arian didn't turn some avid reporter into a porcupine.

Where the hell was Sven? Tristan wondered, noting that his bodyguard's assigned post by the north doors was vacant. With Eddie Hobbes sniffing around, he could hardly afford any gate-crashers. Especially one as potentially disastrous as Wite Lize. He finally located the burly Norwegian grazing at the salad buffet. Tristan rolled his eyes heavenward, thankful that Sven was using a plate instead of diving headfirst into the endive.

If Arian's gracious smile was frayed around the edges, Tristan was the only one who seemed to notice. He had expected her to squeal with delight when he had awarded her the check, not murmur, "You're too generous, sir," in that husky contralto of hers that always sent dark shivers of desire down his—

"Tristan?" He became aware of graceful fingertips stroking his sleeve.

There was no need for Tristan to glance down at his date. Even in flats, she stood over six feet tall. "Hmm?"

Cherie Boldiszar sucked in her cheeks, emphasizing her Slavic cheekbones. "When you didn't call after our last date, I didn't expect to see you again."

Tristan didn't remember their last encounter as a date, but as a sweaty coupling between virtual strangers. "I'm terribly sorry. Business, you know," he muttered, his gaze drifting back to Arian.

The Hungarian supermodel might wear tinted contacts to correct her nearsightedness, but she wasn't blind. She nodded in Arian's direction. "Charming, isn't she? Like a young Audrey Hepburn."

"Enchanting," he murmured.

He had mourned the loss of Arian's frizzled curls as if he'd shorn off each one personally, but he had to admit her new cut flattered her. When she turned her head just so, her hair swung out to reveal the delicate curve of her jaw, the exotic tilt of her eyes—those sparkling, fathomless eyes.

Cherie sighed. "I wonder what her plans are. With

a million dollars in her purse, she can go anywhere. Do anything."

Cherie's dreamy words startled Tristan from his reverie. He was so used to planning everything down to the minutest detail that it had never occurred to him that Arian might possess plans of her own. Plans that did not include him. Contempt at his own shortsightedness made him drain his champagne in a single swallow. It lingered on his tongue, as corrosive as acid.

What had he expected? That Arian would continue to live in his penthouse, sleep in his bed, wear his pajamas? He had no claim on her. She wasn't a share of stock he could buy or some faltering company he could plot to take over, however dangerously appealing the idea.

Cherie's hot breath grazed his ear. Arian would have had to stand on a stool *and* her tiptoes to accomplish such a feat. "I was hoping that when you were done baby-sitting your little prodigy, we could go back to my place for a drink. I've got a bottle of Glenlivet I've been saving just for you."

Tristan turned to stare at her, belatedly remembering that his sole purpose in asking her out had been to forget Arian Whitewood for a few hours.

As Cherie ran her tongue over her collagen-enhanced lips in an invitation no man should be able to resist, he understood what she was offering. A casual coupling with no emotional obligations. Fleeting release from the exquisite tension in his trousers. Safe sex in a dangerous world. If he pressed, she would snap open her Chanel purse and pull out a clean bill of health from her gynecologist and a package of foil-wrapped party favors.

She was also offering him the perfect opportunity to break the spell Arian had cast over him before he was lost altogether.

"I am parched," he murmured, capturing Cherie's hand to draw her toward the moonlit balcony that overlooked Central Park. "Why don't we whet our thirst before we go?"

The witch was crying.

Fat tears trickled down her cheeks, cutting rivulets in her smooth flesh. Her nose dripped, growing more hooked with every moment spent beneath the glaring spotlights.

Arian gazed up at the melting ice sculpture, her own heart aching with empathy. She feared that if she started crying, she, too, would melt into a miserable puddle on the black satin tablecloth. Just as Tristan had predicted, the press's fickle attention had waned, leaving her to prop her chin on her hand and watch the merriment swirling around her with morose fascination.

Tristan might be a million dollars poorer, but he hadn't lost his wicked sense of humor. In deference to All Hallows' Eve, he had had the ballroom decorated with towering cornstalks, fat orange pumpkins, and crackling sheaths of red, gold, and yellow leaves. The waiters wore black masks and champagne flowed from the mouths of leering gargoyles into clinking glasses while the orchestra thumped out the chords of a rousing ditty called the "Monster Mash." The wanton gyrations of the dancers horrified Arian, but she could not stop her own willful feet from tapping to the song's provocative rhythm.

Her gaze met Sven's across the teeming ballroom and he wiggled his beefy fingers at her. He was wending his way among the tables, eating sprigs of parsley from abandoned plates. Copperfield had been ambushed by one of the *Prattler* reporters in the far corner and was gesticulating wildly in a futile bid for freedom. Tristan and his lovely companion had vanished.

"Just one more photo, Miss Whitewood? I'm working my way through college." The pleading voice and earnest face belonged to a freckled young man who dropped to one knee at her feet and pointed his camera at her like a musket.

Sighing, Arian drew the bank draft from her tiny gold purse and held it beneath her chin, forcing a wan smile. He snapped three photos in quick succession before melting into the crowd without so much as a "Thank you."

Arian was left holding the prize she'd fought so hard to win. The artistic flourish of Tristan's signature only reminded her that she had been nothing more than a brief diversion in his jaded life. A business transaction that had cost him more than he'd planned, but nothing so dear as his heart.

That revelation had been driven like a stake through her own heart when Tristan had led her from the dais after the presentation of the check and casually introduced her to his companion. When he'd given the gaunt beauty's name the French pronunciation, Arian had been forced to grit her teeth against a wave of spiteful jealousy. The spark of genuine friendliness in the woman's azure eyes had only made her feel worse. Especially when all Arian really wanted to do was turn her into a codfish and dump her in the champagne fountain.

The true torture had begun when they'd been compelled to pose for several publicity photos. Arian had stood stiffly in Tristan's pseudoembrace, despising the provocative heat of his hand against her naked back.

A tray appeared in her line of vision. "Champagne, miss?"

"No, thank you," she murmured, stuffing the check back into her purse. "I don't indulge in spirits."

The tray flipped over to reveal a porcelain cup, but the champagne glass still clung miraculously to its bottom, its liquid intact. "How about some nice hot tea, then?"

Arian laughed, charmed by the clever trick despite her melancholy. A scarlet-coated waiter was beaming down at her, his blue eyes twinkling merrily through the eye slits of his mask.

"How ever did you do that?" she exclaimed.

He wagged a white-gloved finger at her. "Shame on you, young lady. It's very poor etiquette to ask a magician to reveal his secrets."

Arian sat up straighter in her chair. It had never occurred to her that there might be others in New York who shared her talents. The possibility of meeting a kindred spirit relieved her loneliness the tiniest bit. "You're a sorcerer?"

"A master illusionist, my dear. Specializing in fabrications, deceptions, and prevarications."

Arian frowned. "Lies?"

"Mr. Lize to you, my dear. Mr. Wite Lize at your humble service." He executed a debonair bow and pressed a kiss to the back of her hand before handing her the cup of tea. "You looked as if you needed cheering."

Charmed by his gallantry, Arian took a sip of the steaming brew. It tasted just like her grandmama's always had—more sugar and cream than tea. The familiar warmth threatened to melt the lump of misery lodged in her throat.

"Exquisite," he murmured.

"Pardon me?" Arian replied, nearly choking as she lowered the cup to find the grandfatherly figure gazing hungrily at her bosom. She'd become even more sensitive about her generous figure after noticing the relative concavity of Cherie's chest.

The old man stroked the face of her amulet with one gnarled finger. "Such an exquisite gem."

Arian tried not to recoil from the fruity stench of his breath. " 'Tis a family heirloom," she said, indulging in a petty fib of her own.

"I thought it might be a gift from Mr. Lennox. They say he has impeccable taste in both jewelry and women."

The tea, despite its sweetness, had left a bitter taste in Arian's mouth. "So I've discovered."

Mr. Lize's probing gaze shifted to her face. "Oh, dear. I hope you haven't fallen prey to his seductive wiles."

Arian stiffened. "Of course not. We have a business arrangement, nothing more."

His voice lowered to an urgent whisper as he squatted in front of her. "Then you are wise as well as lovely and gifted. Lennox's magic is dark and tainted by his ambitions. Things, and people, who are no longer useful to him have an uncanny way of disappearing."

Arian leaned away from him, alarmed by his vehemence. "I don't know what you're talking about."

"You will."

The certainty in his tone chilled her. Over his shoulder, she saw Sven start toward them. Her eyes must have betrayed her relief, for the old man's glower was replaced by a benevolent smile. He snapped his fingers in her face, making her flinch, but her annoyance changed to delight when a small bouquet popped into existence.

Sven elbowed one of the dancers out of the way, reaching into his jacket. Wite Lize pressed his offering into Arian's hand and whispered, "Beware the warlock."

When Arian glanced up from the bouquet, he was gone, vanished as if into thin air. Sven's hand emerged from his jacket, clutching a fistful of carrot sticks. He began gnawing on one as he loomed over her. "Was that man disturbing you?"

"No," Arian murmured, knowing she was lying. The old man's enigmatic words had disturbed her deeply.

While Sven shambled off in search of some cucumber dip she studied the bouquet of paper flowers, bemused by its whimsy. Closer examination revealed that it was fashioned from a single sheet of paper clipped, then fanfolded into separate blooms. She smoothed it on the table, puzzled by the nagging familiarity of its ragged margin.

A tiny thrill of foreboding crawled up Arian's spine as she recognized it as the missing page ripped from the *Forbes* pamphlet she'd discovered in Tristan's penthouse. The text had been methodically inked out, leaving only a grainy black-and-white photograph.

Tristan in yet another incarnation, bearing far more resemblance to the boy he had been than the man he would become. Tristan being led away by two uniformed men, his shoulders slumped, his wrists bound by a pair of silver shackles. He had glanced back at the camera in an unguarded moment, his expression dazed as he peered through strands of hair badly in need of a trim. A surge of tenderness tore through Arian. She wanted to reach out to him, to stroke his cheek and smooth his hair and tell him that everything was going to be all right.

But the betrayal that haunted his eyes told her that nothing had ever been right again after that moment.

She reached to touch him anyway, but her hand froze an inch from the page as she recognized the spattered stains on his shirt and hands. Blood. Dark, profuse, and damning.

Her hand trembled as she withdrew it.

Beware the warlock.

As the stranger's cryptic warning echoed over the strident wail of the orchestra, Arian crumpled the page in her fist.

Hadn't she, too, been the victim of gossip and slander and false accusations? She would never convict Tristan without a trial. She would seek him out and ask him to explain what terrible crime that dazed, shackled boy could have committed.

She rose, stuffing the sheet of paper and all of its ugly insinuations into her purse.

* * *

Arian was forced to battle her way through the crowd. The steady flow of champagne had loosened both tongues and inhibitions. Someone had dimmed the chandeliers, enticing the dancers to bob and jerk to the throbbing beat of the orchestra. Shadows contorted their faces into writhing masks and a thin haze of cigarette smoke hung over the room, stinging Arian's eyes.

She bounced up and down on tiptoe, then clambered up on an abandoned chair, but still could not distinguish Tristan, Sven, or Copperfield from the seething mob.

Her foot smashed a miniature pumpkin as she jumped down and began to elbow her way through the crush, repeatedly asking, "Excuse me, but has anyone seen Mr. Lennox?"

Her plea earned her nothing but disinterested shrugs and pitying smiles. She'd barely traveled three feet before a trio of squat men blocked her path.

"Trick or treat, honey!" bellowed a balding, rotund reporter with an equally fat cigar dangling from between his lips.

Tristan had called the man by name, Arian remembered through a haze of desperation. They had even shared a joke. Perhaps the man was a friend of Tristan's.

She clutched the sleeve of his jacket. "I'm looking for Mr. Lennox. Have any of you gentlemen seen him?"

"What do you need a stiff like Lennox for when you've got me?" The man's fetid breath made her nose wrinkle. She was doubly horrified when he wrapped an arm around her waist and dragged her into a sweaty bear hug. "How 'bout we go back to my apartment for an interview? You could give me a little exclusive ... or something?"

If Arian could have reached her amulet at that moment, she would have given the wretch something he wouldn't have soon forgotten. As it was, she could only stomp his toes with the heel of her slipper in helpless outrage.

He released her with a startled yelp. His companions howled with laughter.

As Arian turned to flee, the man covered his embarrassment with an ugly snort. "I wonder how the little witch got her start—performing tricks or turning them? She must be damn good. Even for Lennox, a million dollars is a lot to pay for a whore."

Arian froze, her blood chilling to ice. The laughter and music faded to a dull roar in her ears.

Had Tristan's attempt to protect her misfired so miserably? Was that what they were all thinking? That she was nothing but a conniving harlot who had seduced him into surrendering the prize?

Suddenly she wanted Tristan with an intensity that shook her. Not to confront, but to touch. She wanted his arms to shield her from the darkness as they had the night of the blackout. She wanted his kiss to wash the bitter taste of the reporter's slurs from her mouth.

A crisp breeze cut through the haze of smoke, rattling the sheaths of leaves and cooling Arian's burning cheeks. Her gaze shifted to the open balcony doors and all they promised. Fresh air. Escape. Freedom.

Painfully aware of the leering eyes gnawing at her spine, she straightened her shoulders and marched through the doors, the skirt of the Givenchy gown billowing behind her like a sail.

Later she would have good reason to be thankful she wasn't touching the amulet, for at the precise moment she saw Tristan devouring the lips of the woman in his arms, she wished herself anywhere else in the world, even at the bottom of that murky pond in Gloucester.

18

Tristan Lennox was blushing. He might not have recognized the foreign sensation had it not crept over him with such excruciating slowness. As he met Arian's accusing gaze, the guilty flush crawled up his throat, over his jawline, and into his cheeks, kindling a fire that refused to be quenched. Arian had no claim on him, yet he felt like a straying husband caught with his pants around his ankles.

Even more damning was his body's perverse response to her unspoken condemnation. Cherie had been twined around him—soft, yielding, her open mouth requiring little persuasion—and his body had reacted with nothing more than mild interest. Yet there Arian stood, glaring daggers at him, her lips compressed to a line he doubted even his skilled tongue could penetrate, and he went as ramrod stiff as her spine. He thrust Cherie away from him, fearing the sudden violence of his erection would betray him.

The sparkle in Arian's eyes seemed to have intensified. "*Pardonnez-moi, monsieur.* I did not mean to intrude."

With a snap of her skirts, she stalked back into the ballroom, flinging a last reproachful glance over her shoulder.

Tristan had never found jealousy particularly arousing before. He had always made it his policy to discourage clinging women or avoid them completely. So why did the flash of temper in Arian's eyes, so at odds with her prim demeanor, make him long to crush her in his arms, to kiss her until her every breath resounded with his name? He took two steps toward the door, then one back toward his date.

"Go after her," Cherie said, making shooing motions with her elegant hands. He shot the model a rueful smile, keenly regretting that he hadn't sent flowers after their last encounter.

When Tristan was gone, Cherie plucked her champagne glass from the ledge and lifted it in a wistful toast. "Good luck, little witch. Maybe you can turn that gorgeous ogre into a prince after all."

Tristan darted after Arian only to find himself plunged into a nightmarish whirl of motion and noise, underscored by the bass throb of Michael Jackson's "Thriller." In his absence, the party had disintegrated into an orgy of revelry. The writhing shadows robbed him of the advantage of recognition, forcing him to shove and elbow his way through the mob, two steps behind Arian's determined strides.

They were still separated by a wall of seething flesh when Eddie Hobbes shifted his cigar to the corner of his mouth and called out, "Change your mind, honey? Come on over to my place. I'll show you a few tricks if you'll treat me real nice."

Tristan lunged forward, his hands curled into fists, just as Hobbes's cigar exploded in his face. Arian never broke her stride, never spared the man so much as a disdainful glance. The reporter blinked, his startled eyes pools of white in his round, blackened face. His companions thumped him on the back and howled with laughter. Tristan might have found the effect comical as well if icy beads of dread hadn't just broken out on his brow. For a dangerous moment, he had allowed himself to forget that Arian was perfectly capable of defending herself.

"Arian!"

He shouted her name, but his hesitation had cost him precious seconds. She was already several feet ahead of him. He prayed some irresponsible janitor hadn't left a mop out. He could only shudder to imagine her soaring between the chandeliers, cackling her wrath like the Wicked Witch of the West. He was less afraid of the havoc she was capable of wreaking than of exposing her extraordinary gift to the media.

"Hey, Miss Whitewood, how about one last head shot?" As if invoked by Tristan's fears, a freckled photographer thrust his camera into Arian's face.

Tristan winced as the camera sailed out of the young man's hands, then went darting back at him, its shutter clicking with wild abandon. The photographer recoiled, blinded by his own flash. Howling with alarm, he stumbled over his own feet and went crashing into a table full of astonished guests.

From the corner of his eye, Tristan saw Sven snap to attention, alerted by the commotion. He gave his bodyguard a terse signal, one also witnessed by Copperfield, who began to work his way toward Arian from the opposite corner of the ballroom.

As Arian sailed past the frozen witch, a network of cracks shot through the ice sculpture, widening until the thing cracked open like an egg, eliciting new trills of alarm from the crowd. The champagne fountain was similarly afflicted by her approach. A golden geyser shot straight toward the ceiling, drenching the shrieking guests. Ducking beneath the effervescent spray, Tristan made a mental note to rent the film version of Stephen King's *Carrie* for Arian to watch if he made it out alive.

As she stormed through the nearest exit, Sven closed in on her from the left, Copperfield from the right. But Tristan was the only one near enough to sprint through the double doors before they could slam shut in Sven's startled face.

Tristan skidded to a halt on the marble tiles, realizing that if he didn't act quickly, Arian might soar right out of his life without so much as a backward glance. "Has anyone ever told you you're cute when you're mad?"

Arian shuddered to a halt before swinging around to face him across the chasm of the deserted foyer. "No," she bit off.

He allowed a mocking smile to curve his lips. "Good, because they would have been lying through their teeth."

Actually, Tristan was the one not being completely honest. With her eyes darkened to volatile lakes of brimstone and her delicate chin squared in defiance, Arian was not cute. She was breathtaking. But if he had any hope of shaming her into compliance, he couldn't afford to let her know it.

He jerked a thumb toward the ballroom where the shrill screams and panicked cries were being underscored by the bass thump of fists hammering at the door. Sven's, he suspected. "That was quite an impressive performance back there."

Tristan noticed for the first time that Arian was methodically squeezing her necklace in her pale fist. "I'm delighted that you enjoyed it, sir, but it wasn't intended for your benefit."

He cocked an eyebrow. "Oh, wasn't it? I was most definitely under the impression it was *my* head you wanted to dunk in the champagne fountain." Tristan rested his hands on his hips. "Why don't you stop punishing those innocent people, Arian? Why don't you turn *me* into a warthog or fry *me* to a crisp with one of those lightning bolts of yours?"

As Tristan faced her, the taste of another woman still on his lips, Arian's eyes narrowed to glittering slits, making him believe she just might give him cause to regret his careless challenge.

He pressed his tenuous advantage, crossing to her, stopping near enough to watch the pulse flutter in her throat, to smell the tantalizing fragrance of her hair. "Go on, Arian. Do it. After all . . ." He gazed down into her eyes. "I'm the one you want."

Her hand slowly uncurled from the necklace. She lowered her lashes, but not before he caught a glimpse of raw longing followed by a flicker of despair that only succeeded in shaming him instead of her.

The ballroom door behind them shuddered beneath a massive blow. Sven would probably call for a battering ram if the door refused to give way beneath his shoulder.

His anger rekindled by the impossible situation, Tristan seized Arian's wrist and dragged her toward the fire exit. "They all think I'm a sadistic bastard anyway. Let's get the hell out of here before they decide this was anything more than just a nasty Halloween prank."

As Tristan shoved Arian into the waiting limo, the Plaza's lobby doors burst open, spilling out a torrent of dripping, irate partygoers. Arian caught a brief glimpse of Sven's frantic face before Tristan slid into the plush seat opposite her and slammed the door.

"Drive," he snapped.

"Where to, sir?" replied the startled driver, shoving a carton of Chinese take-out beneath the seat.

"Anywhere. Just drive until I tell you to stop." Tristan leaned over to jab a button, insinuating a wall of opaque glass between the front and back seats.

They rode in frigid silence, Tristan gazing out the tinted windows as if the murky streets beyond represented his only escape from her. Arian stole a glimpse at his averted profile, her misery increasing with each revolution of the limousine's sleek wheels. Her temper had bested her once again, making her behave more like a harpy than a witch. She clutched the tiny gold purse in her lap, but both the million-dollar bank draft and the *Forbes* clipping seemed to have faded to insignificance the moment she'd seen Tristan kissing another woman.

I'm the one you want.

Arian nibbled on her lower lip, haunted by the damning echo of truth in Tristan's smoky taunt. The vehicle sped up, crossing a bridge to leave behind cramped city streets for rolling countryside.

When Tristan opened the refrigerator to pour himself a generous Scotch, Arian reached past him into the freezer, her fingers closing instinctively around a frosty tub of Häagen-Dazs.

Cherie's svelte figure fresh in her memory, Arian rejected a teaspoon in favor of a tablespoon. She dug into the frozen treat, spitefully hoping the stuff would make her fat. So fat Tristan would have to pry her out of the limousine.

He loosened his tie and downed the Scotch in a single swallow before shifting his gaze to her face. His eyes glittered like diamonds of frost in the shadowy interior.

Unnerved by his predatory silence, Arian spooned a ribbon of chocolate courage into her mouth. "Why don't you just shout at me for ruining your clever plan?"

"And risk being turned into a weasel? I don't think so."

Arian's appetite vanished. She shoved the ice cream back into the freezer, hating him more for spoiling even that simple pleasure. "Don't be ridiculous. You're not afraid of me."

His eyes lost their mocking light, going as hard and flat as a winter sky. "Oh, but that's where you're wrong. You scare the bloody hell out of me, Arian Whitewood. You have from the first moment I laid eyes on you."

Arian's bravado faltered. "But I would never harm you . . ."

"You already have. You cut me to ribbons every time you look at me with those big, brown eyes of yours and tempt me to believe in magic, in innocence, when I know in my heart that they're nothing more than a cruel illusion. A petty trick. Just like love."

To her horror, Arian felt tears well in her eyes. "I never asked you to believe in love. I only wanted you to believe in me."

He closed the distance between the seats, capturing her shoulders and giving her a savage little shake that dislodged the tears from her lashes. "Well, I don't. You're nothing more than a beautiful figment of my imagination, no more real than the Loch Ness monster or the Holy Grail." His accusing gaze dropped to her parted lips. "If I were to kiss you right now, you'd probably go up in a puff of smoke."

Arian did not stop to ponder the consequences of winning this argument. She simply twined one arm around Tristan's neck and drew his lips down to hers. He accepted her invitation with a hoarse growl that was half plea, half warning, but the taste of her fallen tears soon gentled his kiss.

Arian's senses were consumed by the rough velvet of Tristan's tongue probing her mouth, the smoky, bittersweet blend of Scotch and chocolate, the powerful purr of the motor beneath them as the limousine shot through the night, hurtling them toward some dangerous precipice.

As Tristan coaxed her tongue into mating with his, it wasn't Arian who melted to vapor, but every other woman he'd ever kissed. Every woman he'd drawn into his embrace and beneath his body. Every woman who wasn't Arian.

He enfolded her in his arms, content for the moment just to breathe her sighs and try to translate the soft, broken words she murmured against his mouth. He longed to entice other French words from her lips. Tender words. Erotic words. Pleas, demands, and promises he would be helpless to resist.

"Do you still believe I'm only a figment of your imagination?" she whispered, her eyes luminous in the darkness.

"I don't give a damn if you are," he replied, realizing it was true.

He no longer cared where she came from or what unusual powers she possessed. He only wanted to hold her, to revel in her warmth and substance, to nuzzle her throat and inhale the bewitching scent of cloves from her hair. He stroked one finger down the creamy valley between her breasts before filling his hands with their plush warmth. Her nipples pebbled beneath the sleek taffeta, beguiling him anew with their responsiveness to his touch.

The shock of Tristan's hands claiming her breasts should have offended Arian, but she could only gasp with wonder at the unexpected rightness of it. His tapered fingers eased the gown from her shoulder, his seeking lips following their path. The chill of the air-conditioning puckered her breast an instant before the heat of Tristan's mouth closed over its turgid peak.

Arian's halfhearted protest melted to a moan of raw pleasure as he drew her nipple into his mouth, suckling fiercely, not as a child, but as a man—with a man's formidable hungers and undeniable needs. Nectar surged between her thighs in an invitation she had not planned to offer, but was helpless to rescind. Her hands caught at his hair, although whether to hinder or prolong that terrible delight, she could not have said.

"You're so sweet," he said thickly as he took her mouth again. "So damned sweet."

He continued to sample the honeyed softness of her lips while his hands wandered beneath her skirt to shackle her ankles with irresistible tenderness. His palms drifted over the gossamer silk of her stockings, caressing her calves, lingering to stroke the sensitive skin behind her knees. Arian felt them fall open, betraying her without so much as a twitch of moral outrage.

Perhaps if he would only stop kissing her with such tender ferocity, she could catch her breath, gather her wits long enough to . . .

But when he sought to draw his mouth from hers, she was the one who beckoned him back with a wanton flick of her tongue. Shuddering with reaction, he caught the backs of her thighs and drew her beneath him on the broad leather seat. A pang of mingled fear and longing tightened Arian's belly. She had succeeded in shattering Tristan's shield of frost only to risk being incinerated by his hard, hungry heat.

"Are you trying to bewitch me?" he whispered hoarsely, tracing her earlobe with feather-soft kisses before thrusting his tongue into the delicate shell of her ear.

Arian moaned. He was the one casting a spell of sensual languor over her. A spell woven tighter with each kiss, each caress. But as he eased his weight to the side, she realized it was not his own pleasure he sought, but hers. Even as he fondled her breasts with one hand, teasing each peak to an aching bud between thumb and forefinger, his other wandered farther up her skirt, sliding past the naughty lace of her garter to pet the tingling skin of her inner thigh. Each deft stroke brought his fingertips nearer to that part of her that was melting and throbbing in anticipation of his touch.

When his fingers finally brushed her through that illicit scrap of fabric, Arian arched off the leather seat with a sharp cry. The damp silk seemed to dissolve beneath his hand, making the shock more intimate than if he'd touched her naked flesh. Her knees drew inward in instinctive shyness.

"It's all right, angel," he murmured against her lips.

"Just close your eyes and open your legs. I swear I won't hurt you."

Arian buried her burning face in the crook of his throat, whimpering a denial, but her traitorous body refused to deny itself the indulgence he was so unselfishly offering. She stole a peek downward. Her skirt still clung to its pretense of modesty, only making what Tristan's hand was doing to her beneath it more irresistibly carnal.

Her head fell back and she gasped with delight as his thumb and forefinger slipped beneath the silken barrier to part her nether curls. Never in her wildest fantasies had she dared to contemplate a sin so dark, so sweet, so deliciously wicked as the play of Tristan's fingertips over her swollen flesh. A spool of raw need unwound from each skillful flick of his thumb as he teased and tormented the fragile bud he found there to throbbing delight.

His thumb continued to apply that exquisite friction, even as his long, slender fingers dipped lower, probing gently until Arian's moans melted to sobs and her body began to shudder with wave after wave of primal ecstasy.

Arian slowly became aware of Tristan kissing the tears from her cheeks. Still lost in a haze of pleasure, she pressed against him, sending her forgotten purse tumbling to the floor of the limousine with a jarring jingle.

Even for Lennox, a million dollars is a lot to pay for a whore.

Don't be ridiculous, Lily. You're not the sort of woman a man marries.

Arian stiffened as a murky current of shame began to seep through her delicious languor.

Everyone knows the French are more vulnerable to the attentions of Satan because of their dark and sinful natures . . . their insatiable hungers . . .

The Reverend Linnet's voice joined the damning

chorus, paralyzing her in her compromising position—
fingers tangled in the wheaten silk of Tristan's hair,
breasts bared and flushed with satisfaction, thighs
spread in wanton invitation, the hollow between them
aching to be filled. She could feel the fierce nudge of
Tristan's need through the fine linen of his trousers.
That uncompromising ridge of male flesh made her realize that Tristan would have to give her more than his
kisses to get her with child. Much more.

"Kiss me, Arian," he urged, smoothing her sweat-
dampened hair from her cheeks.

Arian closed her eyes and turned her face away
from him, wishing fiercely that she were still Catholic.
That her sins could be absolved with nothing more than
a mumbled Gloria Patri and a dozen mea culpas. How
many times had she seen her mother go to confession
the morning after she'd given herself to another lover
and beg forgiveness from some faceless priest?

If she gave herself to Tristan, she would be no better than what those men at the party had said she was,
no better than her poor misguided mama. She might
have no pride where Tristan Lennox was concerned, but
she still had her virtue—a tarnished treasure she was
beginning to despise.

"I can't . . ." she whispered, knowing he must think
her the worst sort of hypocrite to take her pleasure, yet
offer him nothing in return. A hot, bitter tear squeezed
past her tightly clenched lids.

Tristan was nearly wild with the urge to press Arian back against the butter-soft leather and finish what
they'd started, but instinct warned him that her mind
wasn't as deliciously prepared as her body.

"Don't cry, sweetheart," he murmured, brushing a
gentle kiss over the tip of her nose. "I know it can all be
a little overwhelming. Especially the first time. There's
no rush. We've got all night." He chuckled softly. "The
limo even has an extra gas tank."

"You don't understand," she said fiercely. "I *can't*."

"If it's getting pregnant you're worried about, you don't have to. I'll take care of that." He reached around to his back pocket for his wallet and the insurance he always carried there. Insurance against bringing any more "mistakes" like himself into the world. "I'll take care of *you*."

"Like you take care of Brenda? With a sneer of contempt and a monthly allowance?"

Tristan frowned, feeling suddenly chilled. Arian pushed at his chest, making him feel like some sort of sleazy date rapist, but he couldn't quite bring himself to let her up.

"Arian, please . . ." He realized with a shock that he would beg for this woman. Would go down on his knees for her even if his only reward was to taste the honey his touch had coaxed from her body, to make her cry out his name and weep with pleasure again. "Please, Arian. Let me love you."

"No," she whispered.

As his own plea echoed through Tristan's head, the chill spread. Why in God's name hadn't he said, "Let me make love to you"? Why had he trusted her with his most shameful secret, a secret he'd hoarded since childhood—that he needed someone to love more than he'd ever needed someone to love him?

He shoved himself away from her and settled in the opposite seat, watching her struggle to rearrange her clothing with dispassionate eyes.

He shouldn't have to ask why. Arian obviously didn't want him. Not like he wanted her. He closed his eyes against a wave of pain, surprised that another verse of that old familiar song could still cut so deeply.

"Why?" he asked anyway.

Arian's hands trembled as she smoothed her skirt. " 'Twould be a sin." She hung her head as if the confession itself were something to be ashamed of.

"What a quaint notion." Tristan's bruised pride compelled him to reduce their encounter to its lowest common denominator. "In this day and age, it's hardly considered a sin for two consenting adults to indulge in a little recreational sex."

"It's not?" For a moment, Arian looked almost hopeful. Then her face fell anew. "Sin is sin in the eyes of God in any age, I fear."

He would have liked to mock her. Would have liked to laugh out loud at the absurdity of her views. But the wistful regret in her smoky eyes stopped him.

"And just what terrible sin would we be committing to offend this God of yours?" he asked. "Not adultery I'm assuming, since to my knowledge neither one of us is married."

"Don't you see? That's precisely my point. We would be committing fornication."

Tristan had never found the archaic word with its biblical undertones particularly erotic, but the sight of Arian's lush lips wrapped around it did dangerous things to his resolve. "So if we were married, it would be perfectly moral—and legal—for us to"—he hesitated, tempted by spite to use an even cruder word—"fornicate?"

"Of course it would," Arian earnestly assured him. "It would even be expected." She sighed. "But I'm afraid I cannot in all good conscience give myself to a man I'm not wed to. 'Tis a gift I'm bound to bestow only upon my husband." She stole a hopeful glance at him. "Do you understand?"

"Oh, I understand perfectly."

Tristan had been forced to deal with his share of gold diggers since making his fortune, but never one as shamelessly manipulative as this woman. Never one brazen enough to huddle across from him like some rumpled angel, her skin still flushed from the pleasure he had given her, and boldly state her demands.

The ice floe reached his heart, blocking off that sweet, brief shaft of radiance that had been Arian in his arms. A radiance that had made him dream of a Connecticut farmhouse with hardwood floors and a kitchen that smelled of freshly baked bread and cloves. A place where every child was wanted and mistakes conceived out of love were celebrated instead of regretted.

As that happily-ever-after dream went up in a puff of smoke, his lips curved in a calculating smile. The irony amused him. After years of knowing he could have anything he desired and desiring nothing, the one thing he wanted had just been jerked out of his reach.

But if Brenda had taught him anything, it was that everything had a price—a winning streak at the tracks, a mother's love, even Arian Whitewood's precious virginity. Arian's price was just a little steeper than most. A million dollars wasn't quite enough. *He* wasn't enough. She would settle for nothing less than a joint checking account, a Gold Card with her name embossed on it, and a fat chunk of diamond for the third finger of her left hand.

And his name.

"I guess you're just an old-fashioned girl, aren't you?"

Her voice broke on a heartwrenching little hiccup. "You don't know the half of it."

Tristan tapped the button on the leather armrest, activating the intercom. "Take us back to the Tower, Barrett."

"Yes, sir," came the dutiful reply.

As the road unfurled beneath them like the twitching tail of a sleek black cat, Arian shrank into the corner of her own seat, shivering with misery. The drafts blowing from the silver vents felt like a spring breeze compared to the arctic blasts rolling off Tristan. He was staring out the window, his features carved in ice as he watched the countryside give way to city streets.

He was probably just rehearsing the most polite way to tell her farewell, Arian thought, as the driver guided the limousine into the Tower's private parking stable. Or perhaps he wouldn't even bother. Perhaps he would just order one of his many servants to fetch a broom from housekeeping and shove her off the roof.

The limo rolled to a halt in the cavernous stall. As Tristan's emotionless voice came floating out of the shadows, Arian cringed, already anticipating the worst.

"We'll be married the Saturday before Thanksgiving if you don't have any objections. That should give my consultants ample time to plan the wedding."

The driver whisked open the door in Arian's astonished face. Before she could coax her limp limbs or her stunned brain into action, Tristan had slipped past her, leaving behind nothing but an intoxicating whiff of his cologne. His clipped footsteps were already fading before Arian shook off enough of her bewilderment to realize he hadn't even given her a chance to accept or reject his unconventional proposal.

19

Something was banging on the bedroom door.

Arian stumbled out of Tristan's bed, rubbing her raw eyes and wondering if she was awake or if this was just another of the disturbingly vivid dreams that had plagued her throughout the night. As she bumped her shin on the footboard, pain jolted up her leg, assuring her this was no dream. The sun slanted through the drawn drapes, warning her it was nearly noon.

Biting back a curse, she limped toward the door, her bleary mind still haunted by echoes of her sleep-induced fantasies. She had been at a ball, she remembered through a drowsy fog, drifting down a marble staircase into the waiting arms of her black-garbed prince. She sighed with longing, but that innocent vision was consumed by one so sinfully and deliciously carnal it brought a flush of mingled lust and embarrassment stinging to her cheeks.

"Naughty girl," she mumbled to herself. "What would Goody Hubbins say?"

Her dreams had become even more preposterous

as the night wore on, culminating with Tristan asking her to be his bride. Arian stumbled to a halt, almost pitying herself for letting such a ridiculous fancy send a thrill of pure joy shooting through her heart.

"No more chocolate cream before bedtime," she muttered, shaking off the poignant daze.

The banging on the door had ceased, but Arian would have sworn she heard a faint roar, like that of the ocean at low tide or the murmur of many voices. She pressed her ear to the door, frowning. Perhaps it was just Sven watching cartoons again.

She dragged open the door and padded into the living room, indulging in an enormous yawn. "All right, Sven. None of your saucy Monsieur Roadrunner and his annoying 'beep-beep' before I get to watch *Dreaming of Mademoiselle Jeannie*."

At least twenty pairs of eyes swung around to blink at her. None of them were Sven's.

Arian put a hand to her tangled mop of hair, then lowered it as if it would be enough to shield a figure barely confined by the rumpled silk of Tristan's nightshirt. She stumbled backward toward the bedroom, but her escape route was cut off by a matronly woman bearing a thick stack of pamphlets.

"Good morning, Miss Whitewood. Mr. Lennox asked me to scour the newsstands for these. He said he hoped you would find them inspiring."

The woman dropped the pamphlets into Arian's arms and retreated with a motion that was only a bob short of being a curtsy. Arian caught a brief glimpse of a lady in white on one of the glossy covers. Nuns? she thought, her confusion growing. Why was Tristan sending her pamphlets about nuns?

She had little time to ponder for it was as if the woman's approach had released a floodgate of jabbering strangers.

"Miss Whitewood, if you would just sign this release form in triplicate, Mr. Copperfield can put the paperwork for the prenuptial agreement into motion."

She recoiled from the gold pen thrust in her face.

A gaunt woman darted at her, her lips pressed in a disapproving line. "As soon as you've chosen your gown pattern, I must insist you schedule an appointment for a fitting. Mr. Lennox has left us so little time." She rattled a yellow tape, glancing hopefully at Arian's breasts. "Perhaps I could even measure you now."

Arian tried to retreat, but they stalked her across the carpet, honking like a flock of geese.

"Would you prefer shrimp canapés or goose liver tartlets at the reception?" snapped a foppish fellow with a petulant smirk.

An elderly priest beamed down at her. "Mr. Lennox has declined premarital counseling, but I wanted you to know I was available if you wished to discuss issues of intimacy such as . . ."

". . . smoked caviar or baby ducklings? If you'd like, we can roll and butter . . ."

". . . the finest bakery in New York," exclaimed an enormous man wearing a white apron dusted with flour. "I did Trump's wedding cake, you know. Both of them."

"Bavarian meatballs or escargots? You are French, aren't you? I must wire Paris immediately. We simply can't do a Gallic theme at the reception without fresh snails."

Arian collapsed into a sitting position on the ottoman, the voices blurring into a meaningless cacophony. They seemed to be speaking neither English nor French, but some other language beyond her comprehension. If it hadn't been for the solid object poking her rump, she might have thought she'd drifted into another bizarre nightmare. She briefly considered touching the amulet and wishing them all away, but a twinge of conscience prevented her. She wasn't quite sure where they'd end up.

It wasn't until the panel on the opposite wall hissed

open that she realized she was sitting on the remote control. Her bewildered attentions were easily distracted by a thirty-five-inch color image of Tristan's face.

"Quiet!" she pleaded, rising to her feet.

Her pursuers fell into a reverent hush, automatically stepping back to clear a path between Arian and the television. Still clutching the stack of pamphlets, she drifted toward the screen, mesmerized by the unholy beauty of Tristan's features. She wanted to groan with disappointment when they were replaced by an image of a somber stranger wearing a tan coat and clutching a microphone. She realized with an uneasy start that he was standing in front of the Tower.

"So who is this resourceful sorceress who's cast her spell of matrimony over the billionaire once voted America's most eligible and unattainable bachelor?" he intoned. "No one seems to be sure, but early this morning in a press conference that stunned both the business and entertainment communities, Tristan Lennox announced he would wed Miss Arian Whitewood on November twenty-third in a lavish ceremony to be held at Saint Paul's Chapel on Broadway."

The last cobweb of slumber drifted from Arian's brain on a breath of shock.

The reporter continued. "The enigmatic computer magnate claims he and his bewitching fiancée intended to announce their engagement at a reception held last night at the Plaza, but a Halloween hoax got out of hand, resulting in a visit from the New York Fire Department and early cessation of the festivities."

Just like her peculiar dreams, Arian thought. Cameras flashing in her face; Tristan in the arms of another woman; a black limousine thundering through the night.

"Shall I have this cleaned for you, ma'am?" asked a maid, holding out the crumpled Givenchy gown.

Not dreams, Arian realized with a start, but memories. Every last one of them.

Tristan waiting for her at the foot of the stairs.

The exquisite gentleness of his hands on her. And in her.

His brusque declaration before he'd exited the limo.

Totally oblivious to the expectant silence of the maid, Arian glanced down at the pamphlet on top to discover a beaming young woman, radiant in white satin. Not a nun, but a bride. A *Modern Bride,* according to the elegant script etched above her billowing veil.

Arian slowly lifted her gaze to the screen to find herself staring into the mocking eyes of her future husband.

Copperfield stormed into Tristan's office without bothering to knock and slapped a legal-sized sheet of paper on the desk.

"The Monkman report?" Tristan queried, arching an eyebrow.

"My letter of resignation. I quit!"

Tristan plucked up the letter, drew open a filing-cabinet drawer, and dropped it inside. It drifted down to rest on top of a heap of identical letters. "That's only the third time this month. You're slipping."

Copperfield shook a finger at him. "I mean it this time. I've had enough of your sadistic little games."

Tristan settled back in his chair, propping his foot on the opposite knee. "It was the press conference, wasn't it? Did I make a grammatical error people are going to attribute to you? Did I accidentally call Arian my 'finance' instead of my 'fiancée'?"

"Precisely my point. You obviously don't need my help to manipulate the press. You had them slavering at your feet." Cop snorted. " 'Resourceful sorceress,' indeed!"

Tristan could not resist a feline smirk of satisfaction. "I was rather proud of that one."

"Well, I'm glad you're limber enough to kiss your

own ass because Michael Copperfield won't be around to do it any more."

Copperfield stalked toward the door, his pace slowing by imperceptible degrees with each step. Tristan watched the brass hand of the clock on his desk tick away the seconds, counting beneath his breath. It was a game they played, seeing how far Copperfield could actually get before Tristan called him back. He waited until the second hand reached the twelve, until Cop's hand curled around the doorknob in arrested slow motion.

"Don't go."

Copperfield pretended to waver until Tristan rolled his eyes and added a weary "Please."

The attorney returned to drop into the leather chair on the opposite side of the desk. It was the absence of Cop's usual sulk that made Tristan realize how deeply he had wounded his friend. If discovering the staggering extent of Arian's ambitions hadn't left Tristan so numb, he might have felt a stab of regret.

"I'm your best friend," Cop said. "Hell, I'm your only friend. If you can't confide in me when you fall in love, who can you confide in?"

Tristan shuffled a stack of papers from one corner of his desk to the other, avoiding Cop's eyes. "I never said I was in love."

"Don't be ridiculous. Of course you're in love. Up until Arian and her magical broom swept you off your feet, if anyone so much as hummed 'The Wedding March' in your presence, you'd run screaming from the room."

"Love isn't the only reason for getting married. There's always companionship."

"Get a cat."

Tristan leveled an acid glare at him. "And sex."

Cop leaned forward, dropping his voice to a mocking whisper. "This is the nineties. I hate to be the one to break it to you, but you don't have to be married to have sex."

"You do if you want to have it with Arian White-wood."

Cop sank back in the chair. "You've got to be kidding. Well, if you plan to marry every virgin witch you meet, I should warn you that bigamy is illegal in this state." When Tristan's face failed to betray even a flicker of amusement, Copperfield's smile faded. "Christ, this isn't just another Halloween prank, is it? You really intend to go through with it."

In reply, Tristan selected a folder and handed it across the desk. "I've already sent Dauber from Legal to get Arian's signature on the release forms. When he returns, you can start work on the prenuptial agreement."

Cop turned the file over in his hands, a troubled frown creasing his brow. "You're the very soul of romance, aren't you? How did you persuade Arian to marry you? Drop to one knee, clap a hand over your heart, and quote the latest divorce statistics?"

"I should think you'd be applauding my foresight. Aren't you the one who's always reminding me that nothing lasts forever?"

Copperfield's sigh was almost wistful. "I guess so. But maybe some things should." He fixed Tristan with a troubled stare. "Has it occurred to you that there may be inherent legal difficulties in marrying someone who doesn't seem to exist?"

Tristan nodded toward the file. "You'll find in there triplicate copies of Arian's birth certificate and proof of United States citizenship."

Cop sat up straighter. "How on earth did you get your hands on those?"

"I bought them."

Cop slumped. "Oh. I thought maybe she'd finally confided in you. You know, someday you're going to run into something or someone that you can't buy."

Tristan feared his wry smile reflected his bitterness. "I haven't yet."

Cop opened the file to examine the forged documents. "I know how you despise publicity. Why the press conference? The lavish wedding? Why not a quick trip to a justice of the peace?"

"Why, Cop, I'm disappointed in you! Aren't you supposed to be the guardian of my public image? It would hardly do for the CEO of Lennox Enterprises to go jaunting off to Vegas to be married by an Elvis impersonator." He tapped his gold pen on the desk, unable to keep the edge from his voice. "I want my bride to have only the best. I want to give her a wedding day she'll never forget."

"And a wedding night?" Cop tilted his head to the side, his eyes narrowing with unabashed suspicion. "Why are you *really* doing this?"

Tristan kept his voice brisk and businesslike. "Because we live in civilized times. It would be politically incorrect to throw Arian over my shoulder, carry her off to my cave, and ravish her until she can't walk."

"But you believe a marriage license will give you permission to do just that?"

Tristan shrugged. "According to her."

"So this is only a marriage of convenience, eh? You get laid and she gets . . ." Cop trailed off, scratching his head. "What does she get? A company car? A gold watch on your fiftieth anniversary?" His bright, dark eyes took on a shrewd gleam. "Or a quickie divorce in Reno a few weeks after the wedding?"

Tristan leaned back in his chair, the steely glint in his eyes warning Copperfield that further probing would be less than prudent. "Don't worry about my bride. I can promise you that I'll personally see to it that she gets everything she deserves."

Arian had never even allowed herself to dream that a man like Tristan Lennox might seek to make her his wife.

She had little time to ponder her amazing fortune for her every waking moment in the next week was consumed by an endless parade of dressmakers, bakers, caterers, lawyers, photographers, and travel agents who waved fabric swatches, recipes, shrimp canapés, incomprehensible contracts, and soothing photographs of sandy beaches and swaying palms beneath her nose until she wanted to scream.

She had never suspected how genuinely tiresome it would be to have her every wish catered to. If she even hinted she might prefer smoked salmon to goose liver pâté, it appeared like magic at her fingertips for her to sample.

She was thumbing through a bulging book of satin swatches one morning when she stumbled onto the one area where she would not be allowed to have her own way.

She inspected the pristine samples, unable to restrain a dubious sniff. "I really don't care for white. It dirties so easily. Don't you have anything in a nice sensible black?"

The impeccably coiffed woman who had introduced herself as a "professional bridal consultant" favored Arian with a patronizing smile. "We do have some lovely peaches-and-creams in our fall collection, but I'm afraid Mr. Lennox insisted on white. He said to remind you it was a symbol of *purity*." The woman punctuated the statement with a suggestive wink.

Arian blinked back at her, wondering if she was being mocked, but before she could press, the elevator spilled forth another torrent of fawning attendants.

Arian began to wonder if the genteel assault hadn't been deliberately choreographed to distract her from the fact that she hadn't caught so much as a glimpse of her fiancé since he'd announced to the entire world on national television that she was to be his bride.

Perhaps it was only a quaint custom of this century to separate bride and groom before the wedding. But that did not explain Copperfield's inexplicable absence from her life or Sven's pensive mood.

She even braved the telephone late one night only to have a disembodied voice inform her that Mr. Lennox was no longer in residence in the Tower, but had booked a suite of rooms at the Carlyle. She replaced the phone in its cradle, her unease growing as a vivid image of Tristan entangled in Cherie's arms shadowed her memory. She forced herself to shake off the ridiculous fancy. After all, he wasn't marrying Cherie. He was marrying her.

She'd managed to dismiss the more unpleasant aspects of that fateful night, shoving the tiny gold purse with its million-dollar bank draft and crumpled photograph of a shackled Tristan into the bottom of a drawer. The past was no longer of any import, she reminded herself sternly, only the future.

The gifts began to arrive the following week—shoes, scarves, earrings, bracelets, necklaces, and box after box of garments in every fabric and hue of the rainbow. Most of them were suited for the coming winter, cut from rich wool or heavy linen in vibrant shades of pumpkin and crimson. Each item Arian tried on was a flawless fit for her petite form. She spent hours surveying herself in the bathroom mirror, turning this way and that as she tried to imagine herself on Tristan's arm. But the image kept melting to mist before fully crystallized.

One morning Sven delivered a tasteful gold box labeled Victoria's Secret. Arian drew off the lid to find a diaphanous gown nestled in a bed of silver foil.

"How beautiful!" she cried, holding it to her chest an instant before realizing the garment was utterly sheer.

She lowered it, swallowing nervously, then bent to fish a provocative scrap of fabric from the bottom of the box. She poked her fingers through a slit in the silk and wiggled them at Sven. "What do you suppose this is? Some sort of veil?"

The stoic Norwegian blushed to the roots of his

tinted hair before padding over to whisper something in her ear.

Arian turned an even darker shade of pink. "Oh, my!" she breathed, eyeing the naughty undergarment with a mixture of apprehension and appreciation. "No wonder Victoria kept it a secret!"

Arian dutifully reminded herself this was the happiest time of her life and she ought to be savoring every second. Not only had she escaped the grim shadow of her past forever, but she was free to forge a bright future in the arms of the man she loved. Yet as each day passed without so much as a curt message from Tristan, her foreboding deepened until it lay like a dead weight in the pit of her stomach.

The flood of gifts climaxed on a rainy Monday with the arrival of her engagement ring. A pair of uniformed guards hung back at a respectful distance as the somber-faced Tiffany's executive snapped open his leather case to reveal a thick gold band crowned by a diamond the size of a small egg.

"It's . . . um . . ." Arian swallowed a grimace of distaste before choking out, "Lovely."

She had never seen anything so vulgar. She had to suppress a shudder when the gentleman pushed the glittering rock onto her finger. It seemed to weight her entire hand, shackling her to her flourishing sense of dread with an invisible chain.

That evening Arian stood at the living room window, relishing a moment of precious solitude as she gazed through the veil of rain that had fallen steadily throughout the long, gray day. With its multitude of lights blurred by mist and the rain-slicked streets below deserted by all but the most intrepid travelers, the city resembled a desolate kingdom abandoned by its king.

Rain coursed like teardrops down the cheeks of her pensive reflection. Where was Tristan now? she wondered wistfully. Was he thinking of her as she was thinking of him, dreaming of the day when he would become her husband?

"Husband," Arian whispered, the word more sweetly potent than any incantation.

But her engagement ring glittered like a chunk of ice on her finger, causing a cold splinter of doubt to pierce her heart.

Half-opened boxes littered the suite behind her, spilling their dazzling array of treasures across the settee and over the squat ottoman. As Arian turned to survey them, she realized precisely what was troubling her.

Tristan wasn't treating her like a cherished bride-to-be. He was treating her like a mistress.

Keeping her confined in this penthouse tower with servants to satisfy her every whim. Showering her with extravagant gifts. Ordering that her opinion be consulted on matters of little or no import. How many times had she seen her mother condescended to with just such a damning mixture of affection and contempt?

But when night fell and shadows crept across the rumpled sheets, her mother had been expected to provide something in return. Tristan had rewarded her with all the pleasures and privileges of being his courtesan, yet asked for nothing in exchange.

Yet.

Arian scooped the sheer negligee out of its box to finger the gauzy material. The delicate fabric snagged on her engagement ring. Were the sumptuous gown and garish diamond tokens of Tristan's devotion, she wondered, or simply payment in advance for services to be rendered on their wedding night?

In less than one week, Tristan was to become her husband. When the lavish wedding was over, the smoked caviar had all been eaten, and the guests had gone, would he come to her in love? Or would he seek her out to take his pleasure with icy hands and a stranger's eyes, making a mockery of their tender vows? Arian shivered, knowing she could not bear it if he did. A mistress might have the luxury of refusing her lover, but a wife renounced that right when she made her sacred oath before man and God.

Arian had hoped her love for her husband would be sufficient to make a marriage. Many women of her acquaintance, both in France and Gloucester, had settled for far less. But suddenly she realized that she could not take that oath without knowing if Tristan returned her love. Wadding the negligee into a careless ball, Arian tossed it at the hearth and strode for the elevator.

The corridors of Lennox Enterprises were deserted, the offices hushed and darkened. Arian padded through the gloom, encountering only a lone security guard who retreated with a deferent tip of his cap the moment he recognized her. At least Tristan hadn't ordered her shot on sight, she thought with a grim smile.

She pushed open the frosted-glass door leading to his inner offices, almost missing the cheerful chaos she had witnessed on her first visit. The phones hung mute in their cradles, their jangling voices silenced by the lateness of the hour. For all Arian knew, Tristan might have already retreated to his swank suite at the Carlyle.

But some tingling awareness tugged her onward, past the deserted desks and empty glass cubicles to his assistant's office. A thin sliver of light shone from beneath the mahogany doors guarding his office.

As Arian crept toward that lonely oasis of light, she wondered if this was how Tristan's mother felt when approaching her son's corporate throne each month— mouth dry and palms damp like some unworthy suppliant, fearful for her welcome. For the first time since their initial meeting, Arian felt a twinge of sympathy for the woman.

One of the doors was cracked ajar so it took only a gentle push to ease it open. Tristan sat behind his massive desk, studying a thick sheaf of papers. A brass desk lamp cast a golden glow over his inclined head. The pool of light only succeeded in deepening the hungry shadows that hovered around him.

Arian would have sworn she hadn't made a sound, but his head flew up as if she'd whispered his name. His hair was tousled from repeated finger-rakings and a pair of gold-rimmed spectacles perched low on his nose. In that unguarded moment, Arian knew that he could never be a stranger to her. She knew him as well as she knew the rhythmic cadence of her own heart.

But that illusion was shattered when he drew off the spectacles and smoothed back his hair before glancing over at the calendar perched on the edge of his desk. "Good evening, Miss Whitewood. My assistant didn't make me aware that you'd scheduled an appointment."

20

Arian forced herself to tread lightly, both toward Tristan's desk and around his invisible wall of wariness. "But we do have an appointment. A very significant one. This Saturday at two o'clock in the afternoon at Saint Paul's Chapel."

He leaned back in his chair, as if to put a few more valuable inches of space between them. "I'm well aware of that. I had to sacrifice one of the clerks from the mail room to address the invitations."

Arian could not resist widening her eyes in mocking disbelief. "I hope it wasn't too great an inconvenience."

"It was," he said shortly. "But I recovered. Now what can I do for you this evening? It's late and I've got some important reports to finish."

More important than you.

Arian heard the words as clearly as if he had spoken them aloud. She stiffened, realizing that she could no more ask this aloof stranger if he harbored some small morsel of affection for her than she could implore a wolf to lick her hand without biting it off. Was this what their marriage was to be? she wondered. Tristan shut up in his office until the wee hours of morning while she tossed and turned in their lonely bed?

She shifted her weight from foot to foot, wishing desperately that she had contrived some other excuse for her visit. Tristan had already inclined his head and begun to scratch notes in the margins of his precious report.

"I was wondering if you preferred rose petals or orange blossoms?" she finally blurted out.

"Rose petals," he said without looking up. "I'm allergic to orange blossoms. They make me sneeze."

Arian made a spiteful mental note to call the florist and order orange blossoms. She circled behind his chair, wishing for the courage to touch him. To seek out some hint of the man who had stroked her to shivering ecstasy, then dried her tears of release with his kisses. But Tristan's back was rigid, his long, graceful fingers wrapped so tightly around the monogrammed pen that his knuckles were blanched.

She leaned over his shoulder, so near that if he turned his face a quarter of an inch, their lips would graze. Her fingertips tingled with the urge to caress the golden hint of beard that shadowed his jaw. "And where would you prefer to honeymoon? Aruba or Aspen?"

"Aspen. I prefer the cold."

Arian should have anticipated his answer. Coaxing a response from him was like trying to strike a spark off a block of ice. She straightened, her defeated sigh ruffling his hair.

With lightning speed, he swiveled the chair around to face her. "What's really bothering you, Arian? Is the credit limit on your American Express card not generous enough? The diamond in your engagement ring a tad small for your tastes?"

Arian might have jerked off that ring and thrown it in his smug face had she not recognized the same note of thinly veiled contempt he had hurled like a weapon toward his mother. It was the voice of a wounded boy lashing out at those he believed had wronged him.

She backed away from him a step, allowing a hint of her own anger to show. "Forgive me for disturbing you, *Mr.* Lennox. I just thought you might want to help me plan the ceremony. It is *your* wedding, too, you know."

He tapped the pen on his knee and surveyed her through narrowed eyes, his expression so ruthlessly pleasant it almost made her wish he still wore his apathetic mask. "Try not to think of it as a wedding, but as an acquisition or a business merger. When the echo of the church bells has faded and the last grain of rice has fallen, you'll have what you wanted." His voice softened to a smoky murmur. "And I'll get what I want."

For a tantalizing instant, the veil of frost dropped, giving Arian a glimpse of the embers that smoldered behind it, embers glowing hot enough to leap into flame at the slightest provocation. An answering flicker of triumph sprang to life in her own heart.

Tristan might have thought his financial analogy would elude her, but she hadn't been reading the *Wall Street Journal* from front to back every night for the past two weeks for nothing. "I'm looking forward to it, sir. Some mergers turn out to be very profitable. For both parties involved."

With an enigmatic smile that was a mocking twin of his own, she turned on her heel and stalked out, barely resisting the petty urge to slam the door behind her.

She had learned both less and more than she had sought tonight. Tristan might not love her, but he still wanted her. Badly.

And for now, that would just have to be enough.

Arian stepped off the penthouse elevator to the strident jangling of the bedroom phone. She rushed across the suite to answer it, entertaining the absurd hope that Tristan might have repented of his boorish behavior and was calling to beg her forgiveness.

"Hello!" When there was no response, she realized she was bellowing into the earpiece.

She reversed the receiver and tried again.

A raspy voice floated out at her, sending a prickle of foreboding down her spine. "I can see you've failed to heed my warning, young lady. What a pity."

"Mr. Lize, is that you?" Arian felt compelled to whisper, although there was no one to overhear her.

A petulant sniff confirmed the caller's identity. "How did you know it was me? I am a master of disguise."

"Why, of course you are." Arian sought to soothe the old man's ruffled vanity. "But how could I fail to recognize you when your kindness made such an impression on me at the Halloween reception?"

"Apparently, I'm not the only one who made an impression on you that night. I hear you're to become Mrs. Tristan Lennox on Saturday."

"And you're calling to offer your congratulations?"

"No, my condolences."

Arian fumbled for the bed behind her, her knees growing weak with dread. "Mr. Lize, if you've called to speak ill of my betrothed—"

He interrupted her, his voice crackling with urgency. "I must meet with you. Friday afternoon at three o'clock at the cafe on the corner."

Arian wavered, thinking that she really ought to summon Sven and let him deal with the tenacious meddler.

Wite Lize took advantage of her hesitation. "Lennox is a very powerful man. Once he has you in his clutches, he'll never allow you to speak to me." A tense pause. "Please. Arian . . ."

Arian squeezed the phone, her knuckles going white. Oddly enough, it was not the plea, but the use of her Christian name in this century of so many strangers that swayed her. "I'll consider it, but only if you'll tell me why you bear such a grudge toward my future husband."

All traces of pomp and bluster vanished from the old man's voice, leaving it dry and paper thin. "He murdered my son."

Arian had already started to shake when the line went dead with a hollow click.

21

Arian melted into the crowd streaming past the Tower by drawing the floppy brim of her hat over her pilfered pair of sunglasses, thankful that Tristan's tastes ran to the stylish and Sven's to the functional. She had escaped the penthouse with surprising ease, shooing away the last of the fretful caterers and exhausted dressmakers and informing Sven that she planned to spend the afternoon soaking in a steaming bubble bath in preparation for tomorrow's wedding.

A wedding that would never take place if the persistent Mr. Lize had anything to say about it.

Garbed in one of the smart little crimson suits Tristan had bought for her and a pair of white gloves, Arian marched down the teeming sidewalk. Marcus would have scolded her for wearing the devil's color, but Arian didn't care. If Wite Lize didn't stop spreading his malicious accusations, she was fully prepared to give him an earful of unholy hell.

Her host was disguised as a strolling Gypsy, which only made it that much easier for Arian to recognize him.

He rushed forward to lead her to a corner table, the drooping ends of his fake mustache quivering with eagerness. "Miss Whitewood! How kind of you to come! I knew you wouldn't be so heartless as to leave an old man stewing in his regrets. I took the liberty of ordering you some herbal tea."

Arian started to remove the sunglasses, then thought better of it. If her eyes betrayed so much as a flicker of doubt in Tristan, she did not want Wite Lize to use it as a weapon against her. She drew off her gloves instead. "I didn't come here to sip tea with you, sir. I came to defend my fiancé's honor."

Wite Lize snorted. "Tristan Lennox doesn't know the meaning of the word."

Arian started to rise, but he seized her hand with such pathetic desperation that she hesitated. His rheumy blue eyes crinkled in plea. "Don't go. Please. Not until you've heard me out."

Arian sank back down in the chair and unfolded her napkin. "Have you always hated Tristan so bitterly?"

"Not always. Once I loved him like a son. Nearly as much as my own son."

"The son you claim Tristan murdered." Arian had thought saying the words aloud might rob them of their weight. She was wrong.

"Arthur," Wite Lize provided, smiling wistfully. "My sweet, brilliant boy."

Arian took a sip of the tea to hide a wince of empathy. She didn't want to picture this Arthur. Didn't want to evoke even a shadow of his memory.

"Arthur and Tristan roomed together their very first semester at MIT. A university in Boston," he added, noting her confusion. "Judging by outward appearances, they had much in common—brilliant minds, a love of computers, a shameless talent for hacking, and boundless imagination. One was dark, one light, yet they were enough alike beneath the skin to have been born brothers." Wite Lize took a sip of his own tea, his eyes focused on the past. "Tristan had no kin of his own so he would spend the holidays with Arthur and me in our tiny Greenwich Village apartment. We didn't have much money, couldn't even afford a Christmas tree some years, but he always seemed so pitifully eager to be part of our humble little family."

Arian shifted uncomfortably in her seat, more vulnerable to Tristan's phantom than she had been to Arthur's. Arthur was already lost. That bright-eyed boy Tristan had been might still be saved.

A ghost of a grin tugged at the old man's lips. "We used to laugh about how they would buy a Christmas tree bigger than the one in Rockefeller Center once they'd made their first million." The smile twisted into a sneer. "Lennox was true to his word. Every year, he puts up that very tree in the courtyard of his kingdom."

"Mr. Lize, please . . . I don't have much time."

"No, you don't." His pitying gaze unnerved her, especially when it drifted down to caress her amulet. "After Arthur and Tristan graduated, they bought several used computers, leased a cockroach-infested brownstone, and hung out a sign that read Warlock, Inc."

Beware the warlock.

Wite Lize's eyes were sharp enough to note her shiver. He did not seem displeased by it. "The name was meant to be an inside joke, but Arthur had a theory. He believed that the same laws that have ruled the universe since the beginning of time—the fundamental principles that govern mathematics, music, science, and magic—could be accessed through the central core of a computer."

Arian might know nothing about computers, but she knew too much about the capricious nature of magic to dismiss Arthur's theory as madness.

"He and Tristan slaved day and night, going without food, without sleep, driving themselves half insane trying to design a software program that would allow them to test Arthur's theory."

"And did they succeed?"

"I was performing at a seedy club in SoHo one night when Arthur called and left me a message." With the unsettling dexterity common to magicians, Wite Lize whipped a small silver box out from under the tablecloth and pushed a button.

"Dad? Are you there, Dad?" Arian started when a disembodied voice floated out of the device—a young male voice, wild and almost feverish with excitement, yet eerily familiar. Arian supposed she could hear an echo of the father in the son. *"If you're there, for God's sake, pick up! We're onto something big here. Something huge! Something that could bring us both riches and fame beyond our wildest imaginings."* The voice lowered to a croaked whisper. *"I've got one last virus to exterminate. I'll call you first thing in the morning."* A brief pause. *"And, Dad . . . I love you."*

Wite Lize's knobby finger shook as he punched off the device. A film of tears dimmed his eyes. "That was the last time I ever heard my son's voice."

Arian patted her trembling lips with her napkin and gathered her gloves, desiring nothing more than to cling to the bliss of ignorance. "I'm sorry, Mr. Lize, but if that's all the evidence you have, then I'll be on my—"

"Sit!" the old man barked.

Arian sat.

He drew a leather-bound book out from beneath the tablecloth, making Arian want to steal a peek just to see if he had any rabbits or bouquets of flowers stashed under there as well. As he flipped open the book and shoved it across the table at her, she prayed she wasn't to be subjected to snaggle-toothed baby portraits of the noble Arthur.

But the face beneath her fingers was as familiar to her as her own and twice as dear. She thumbed through the scrapbook, her fingers going numb as she discovered page after page of Tristan's golden image tarnished by ugly slurs and black innuendo.

MAGIC, MURDER, AND MAYHEM IN MIDTOWN MANHATTAN!

WARLOCK MAKES PARTNER DISAPPEAR!

TRISTAN LENNOX: BOY BILLIONAIRE OR BLOODTHIRSTY BUTCHER?

Credit for the more lurid headlines was invariably claimed by a Mr. Eddie Hobbes. For Arian, the very name was accompanied by a whiff of stale cigar smoke and a shudder of remembered humiliation.

She skimmed the articles, growing colder with each word she read despite the unseasonal heat of the November day.

Wite Lize leaned over and tapped a photograph of Tristan's image superimposed over a cage of bones. "He tore down the brownstone to build the Tower. There are some who whisper that he buried Arthur in the basement, then erected the Tower as a monument to his own greed and treachery."

Arian slammed the book shut, nearly catching the old man's finger. He shot her a wounded glare.

"How dare you!" she breathed. "You have no proof. You have nothing here but gossip and slander and vicious rumors."

"I have sworn affidavits from neighbors who heard angry shouts and the sound of a violent struggle near midnight that night. I have photos of Tristan Lennox being led away by the police with my son's blood smeared all over his clothes." Wite Lize's voice rose to an unholy thunder, evoking alarmed glances from diners at nearby tables. "And most damning of all, Miss Whitewood, *I have no son.*"

Arian flinched as if he'd struck her, but she refused to buckle. "If what you're saying is true, then why wasn't Tristan convicted of your son's murder? Why wasn't he sent to prison?"

"His attorney, the father of that renegade lawyer he has now, forced them to dismiss the charges during the preliminary hearing. His defense was simple—no body, no murder. To this day, my son is still listed as a missing person."

A waiter approached and Arian was forced to bite her tongue until he finished refilling their cups and drifted to the next table. "But why? Why would Tristan want to murder your son, Mr. Lize?"

"Greed. Ambition. An insatiable hunger for power." The magician lowered his voice to an urgent hiss. "Don't you see what he did? He wormed his way into our affections, knowing that it was Arthur's brilliance that held the key to everything he'd ever wanted. Arthur was always the leader, Tristan the follower. Ask anyone. Lennox hasn't invented so much as a mouse trap since Arthur died. The groundwork for the microprocessor that made him so filthy rich had been laid before my son disappeared. My only consolation has been knowing that Arthur must have taken the secret of that other breakthrough to the grave with him. That's why Lennox has spent all these years searching for it."

"The magic competition," Arian whispered, her misgivings chilling to dread.

"That's right. And all the bizarre conventions, symposia, and contests that came before it. He pretended to be a professional skeptic to infiltrate the ranks of the true believers. But I have every reason to believe he hunted for genuine magic in vain." Arian would have almost sworn his gaze flicked to her amulet again. "Until now."

"Until me?" she echoed, already knowing the answer he would give her.

"Precisely." The old man cocked his head like a bright-eyed bird, his expression winning, almost tender. "Oh, the press may brand you a fraud, but I know the truth. I saw the evidence with my own eyes. First at the magic competition when Lennox's goons were tossing me out of the building, then at the Halloween party. You have powers, Arian. Spectacular, miraculous powers, and Lennox can't wait to get his hands on them. And on you."

Arian shielded her face with her hat brim, not wanting the old man to guess Tristan had already had his hands on her. Even now, with doubts swirling through her head and her dreams crumbling to dust, the memory still had the power to evoke a shiver of raw desire. Could a murderer's hands be capable of such tenderness, such exquisite patience and skill?

Wite Lize passed her his napkin to use as a handkerchief, obviously believing his revelations had driven her to tears. His sympathy was even more grating than his bullying. "How did he manage to bewitch you, my poor dear? Did he whisper words of love in your ear? Pledge his eternal devotion?"

We'll be married the Saturday before Thanksgiving.

Arian stiffened, remembering words that were more dictate than proposal.

Try not to think of it as a wedding, but as an acquisition or a business merger . . . you'll have what you wanted. And I'll get what I want.

Tristan's own words damned him. She supposed she should be grateful that he hadn't insulted her with honeyed endearments or promises he never intended to keep. But she'd been so wrapped up in her girlish fantasies of wedding bells and everlasting love that she'd failed to heed his unspoken warning.

When Arian drew off her sunglasses and leveled an unflinching look at Wite Lize, her eyes were hot and dry. "You've made yourself quite clear about what Tristan wants from me. But what about you, Mr. Lize? What do you want?"

The old man reached across the table and cupped his gnarled hand over hers. "I need you, Arian."

I've searched the world over for you.

Linnet's hoarse whisper drifted across the centuries from another place, another lifetime, but it still made Arian's skin crawl. She jerked her hand out of Lize's reach, wishing she'd never taken off her gloves.

The old man failed to take offense. His words tumbled out, propelled by his eagerness to win her to his side. "Lennox is a very powerful man. He's spent the last ten years discrediting me, making everyone believe I'm nothing but a half-daft old geezer. That Hobbes fellow is the only ally I have left and even he's losing interest." His eyes took on a crafty slant. "But if Lennox's own fiancée turns against him, the police might listen. They might reopen the case and put him behind bars where he belongs."

Arian rose to her feet and drew on her gloves with a brisk snap. "I'm sorry I cannot help you, Mr. Lize, but my first allegiance is to my betrothed."

Lize's hopeful expression crumbled. He wrapped his hands around his cup as if to keep them from curling into fists and surveyed her from beneath his bushy eyebrows. "Loyalty is an admirable trait in a wife. I hope Lennox doesn't give you cause to regret it."

"So do I," she murmured, turning away from the table.

"Miss Whitewood?" Wite Lize didn't even bother to look up. He simply sat gazing into the bottom of his teacup, as if to divine both the past and the future in its dregs. "He never denied it, you know. Not even to his own attorney."

Arian stormed off the penthouse elevator, thankful for once for the unnatural chill of the air. She kicked off her heels and tore off her hat, sending it sailing in a futile attempt to cool her fevered brow. She wished she'd never left the climate-controlled environment. Never let Wite Lize pour his poison into her ears. Jerking off her gloves, she wadded them into an untidy ball.

It did not improve her bleak mood to discover her wedding gown had arrived from the bridal shop. The dazzling satin creation hung from a metal rack, its lace veil fluttering in the draft from the air-conditioning like a mocking ghost of all her dreams.

She wished she had chosen black, she thought bitterly. Black for treachery. Black for mourning. Black for—

"I think your bathwater's getting cold."

At the matter-of-fact male voice, Arian clapped a hand over her thundering heart and spun around. Copperfield was leaning against the bedroom doorjamb, his expression nearly as wary as her own.

"I went for a walk," she blurted out. "To get a breath of fresh air."

"You don't owe me an explanation. You're Tristan's fiancée, not his prisoner."

"Not yet anyway," she mumbled.

Copperfield padded into the living room with a graceful stealth that reminded Arian more of his ancestors than she cared to admit. But her expression betrayed her.

"You needn't look so nervous. I'm not going to scalp you." He held out a single manila file with a pen clipped to its edge. "I just need to get your signature on some legal documents."

"Very well." Arian took the file and sank down on the settee, eager to be rid of him so she could return to her tortured musings.

She automatically flipped to the last page, having grown accustomed to signing both releases and receipts in the past three weeks without having the faintest idea what they contained. But her eye was caught and held by the heading at the top of the page.

"Prenuptial agreement?" she ventured, rolling the foreign word off her tongue.

Copperfield shrugged, but seemed to be having difficulty meeting her eyes. "It's a standard prenup contract. Nothing out of the ordinary. I'm sure there's a French equivalent. I just don't know what it is. It simply means a binding agreement signed prior to the wedding to protect both parties."

"From what?"

Cop tugged at his ponytail, looking more uncomfortable by the minute. "From unforeseeable circumstances—marital discord, general incompatibility." He hesitated before gently adding, "Infidelity."

Dragging her bewildered gaze away from his, Arian flipped back to the first page and began to read. Cop draped one arm across the back of the settee, but his casual posture failed to mask his desire to be anywhere else in the world but where he was.

When Arian finally turned to the last page and lifted her head, she did not even try to hide the tears welling in her eyes or the defiant jut of her jaw.

Cop sighed. "He was more than generous, Arian. I even advised him against some of the more extravagant stipulations, but he insisted on them. In the event of a divorce, not only will he allow you to keep the million dollars you won from the competition, but you're also to receive a chateau in the south of France and alimony of three hundred thousand dollars a year for as long as you live, even if you should choose to remarry."

The tears trembled on Arian's lashes, but did not fall. "Are you familiar with the phrase 'till death do you part,' Mr. Copperfield?"

His wince was so subtle she might have imagined it. "I am."

"Where I come from, that vow is binding. It can't be dismissed by a man's whim or a signature on a scrap of paper."

Cop sprang to his feet, pacing in frustrated circles around the spartan coffee table. "Prenuptial agreements are merely a precaution, Arian. They don't make divorce inevitable."

Arian tapped the paper until it rattled. Cop stopped pacing as if riveted to the rug by her passion. "This paper gives Tristan Lennox the right to stand before God and man on the morrow and pledge his life to me. To come to our marriage bed and consummate that pledge, then to dismiss me as if I were no more than a common whore. Does it not?"

Cop stretched out his hands, pleading for her understanding. "It's only a formality. It would be unheard of for a man with Tristan's wealth to enter into a marriage without protecting his assets—"

"Does it not?"

"It does." Cop closed his eyes, sighing in defeat, but they flew open in shock at the furious scratch of pen against paper.

Arian signed her name through a blur of tears. Murder she might have forgiven Tristan, but this . . . ? This was a betrayal of everything she'd ever believed in. To make a woman your mistress might be a sin, but to make a mistress of your wife was an abomination. She would sign the hateful thing, then she would fling it back in Tristan's face along with his ring, his proposal, and the shattered fragments of her love.

As she crossed her t with an angry flourish, she noticed the line above Tristan's typed name was blank. A thoughtful frown quirked her lips.

When Arian rose from the settee, Copperfield was thrown off balance by the wicked glitter in her eyes and the dangerous brilliance of her smile. Remembering the destruction her temper had wreaked at the Halloween fete, he lurched forward to block her path.

"Now, Arian, it's not as if I've never been tempted to turn him into a pollywog myself."

"Don't be silly," she replied, sidestepping Cop with airy grace to summon the elevator. "I'm just going to get his signature on this document. You did say it was important, didn't you?"

Copperfield stopped just short of plastering his body across the elevator doors. "That would be a *very* bad idea. Tristan is in a meeting right now. He won't like being disturbed."

Arian's smile sharpened as she boarded the elevator. "Then I shall make every effort not to disturb him."

*   *   *

Intercoms beeped, telephones pealed, and heads popped out of doorways as Tristan Lennox's reclusive fiancée barreled through the corridors of Lennox Enterprises, ablaze with righteous wrath in her red Chanel suit and stocking feet. The office grapevine was ruthless in its efficiency, so ruthless that Tristan's freshly hired assistant was already rounding her desk to block Arian's path when she burst through the office door, still clutching the prenuptial contract in her white-knuckled hand.

The severe creature in the tweed suit and schoolmarm's bun towered over Arian. "I'm sorry, miss, but Mr. Lennox isn't in right now."

Arian had already suspected as much, but she dodged the woman and threw open the doors of Tristan's office anyway. She might have been at a loss had the assistant not betrayed herself with a furtive glance back at the outer offices. Elbowing her way past the woman, Arian marched back the way she had come, noticing for the first time another set of towering mahogany doors at the far end of a broad corridor.

The assistant trotted after her, her mouth pursed as if her high heels were pinching her lips as well as her toes. "Mr. Lennox is in the annual meeting of the executive board. He left express orders that he was not to be disturbed for any reason whatsoever." When Arian ignored her, the woman's tone chilled to ominous threat. "Please don't make me call Security."

Arian swept open the double doors to find herself the immediate focal point of over a dozen pairs of eyes. Some were young, most old, yet they all radiated a sort of shocked expectancy, a greedy anticipation of thrills to come. The board of Lennox Enterprises might reek of old money, but they were nothing but voyeurs of life. They would never be accused of witchcraft, nearly drowned, cast headlong into another century, discover the man they loved was possibly a murderer and most definitely a heartless knave, and have their own fragile hearts broken into smithereens. How Arian envied them their dull, complacent lives!

Tristan sat at the far end of the long table, his leather throne proclaiming him king of this lofty court. His expression was wary, revealing nothing.

The assistant elbowed Arian aside. "I'm terribly sorry, Mr. Lennox. I tried to stop her, but she wouldn't listen."

Tristan raised a hand. "That's all right, Mrs. Flanders. I'll take care of it."

The woman lingered, nearly licking her sparse lips in anticipation of Arian's comeuppance, but a pointed glance from her employer sent her scurrying for the door with an offended huff.

Tristan consulted his watch, his tone as mercilessly pleasant as Arian had known it would be. "Forgive me, darling. Did we have an appointment I forgot?"

Arian parried his bland smile with a tender one of her own. "No, precious. We didn't have an appointment. We *had* an engagement."

Alerted by her honeyed tone, Tristan cocked a warning eyebrow. "Is this something we could discuss later?" He indicated the eager faces that lined the table, the files and papers scattered across its gleaming surface. "As you can see, we're in the middle of something important."

Arian unfurled the prenuptial agreement. "What could be more important than protecting your ass—" She stumbled over the unfamiliar word, eliciting several poorly concealed smirks of amusement and one scandalized gasp from a blue-haired woman. "Your assets?"

Tristan's own lips twitched as if torn between a smile and a sneer. "This is neither the time nor the place, dear," he suggested gently, as if addressing a child. "I really think you should go."

Arian slammed both palms on the table in blatant challenge. "And if I don't, what are you going to do, sweetheart? Make me disappear?"

22

Arian's words lingered in the air like an echo of thunder. The board members slunk away one by one, leaving her to face Tristan down the long, empty length of the conference table.

Meeting his frosty gaze, Arian felt a flicker of genuine fear. She wouldn't have known her eyes had betrayed her had he not risen and gone to the window, as if he could no longer bear to look at her. She sank into one of the chairs a board member had vacated.

Tristan stared blindly down at the fountain in the courtyard below, his hands jammed deep in the pockets of his trousers. "I should have known it was only a matter of time. So who got to you first? Lize or Hobbes?"

"Lize," Arian said, crumpling the prenuptial agreement without realizing it. "He wanted me to go to the police with him. To convince them to reopen the case."

Tristan turned to face her, his expression weary. "Then why are you here instead of there?"

Arian swallowed a pretty lie. "I don't know. Lize was at the Halloween party. He showed me the photograph of you being taken away by the police. I saw the blood on your clothes . . . your hands . . ."

Tristan's eyes took on a predatory glint. He prowled around the table, each step measured by dangerous grace. He was stalking her, but Arian refused to cringe. Not even when he slipped his hands beneath her hair to cup her throat from behind, not even when his fingertips grazed the fragile pulse below her jaw that sought to throb a warning.

Her eyes fluttered shut as he leaned over and pressed his mouth to her ear, his voice a hoarse purr that sent a shiver of pure reaction down her spine. "You saw the blood, yet you let me touch you, let me put those same hands on you? A murderer's hands?"

He never denied it, you know. Not even to his own attorney. Oddly enough, it was Wite Lize's damning admission that gave Arian the weapon she needed.

"Where did you hide the body?" she whispered.

Tristan withdrew his hands as if her flesh had scorched him. She spun the chair around and faced him.

"Did you bury it in the basement of the old brownstone?" He backed away, but Arian bounced to her feet, stalking him as mercilessly as he had stalked her. "Or did you have his bones ground into mortar and poured into the foundation of the Tower?" She danced over to the wall and began to tap on it at irregular intervals. "Is his corpse rotting somewhere between these very walls? I've heard of murderers hiding the bodies of their victims within the hull of a ship, but legend has it that the ship will remain eternally cursed. Do you feel cursed?" she asked brightly. "Doomed? Damned perhaps?"

He was eyeing her as if she were his own personal Chanel-clad demon, sent from hell to prod his most painful scars with her pitchfork. "Damn you," he murmured. "How did you know?"

"That you were innocent?"

He nodded.

She favored him with her most winsome smile. "I didn't. Until just now."

Tristan took a step toward her as if he were seriously reconsidering the notion of strangling her.

Arian danced out of his reach, putting a chair between them. "Oh, I suspected all along that you couldn't have murdered Arthur. He was your friend. You loved him."

Tristan's bleak chuckle contained little humor. "That didn't stop him from trying to murder me."

Arian's smile faded. Sweeping a stack of papers out of the way, she propped her hip on the edge of the conference table. "Why?"

Tristan sank into a chair, shrugging carelessly. "I made a pizza." At Arian's baffled frown, he continued. "We'd been working day and night on my Warlock project, not eating, barely sleeping. Our nerves were frazzled, our tempers short, but we both felt we were too close to a breakthrough to quit."

"Your Warlock project? Wite Lize implied that Arthur devised the theory."

Tristan snorted. "He would. Arthur was nothing but a two-bit hacker. When I met him, he was earning beer money by breaking into the university's computer systems and changing grades. I was the one who convinced him he was wasting his talents."

"Go on," Arian urged.

"We were about to collapse from hunger so Arthur went out to get us a pizza. I stayed at the keyboard, inputting combinations of data strings. I was so damn tired." He rubbed his brow in remembered fatigue. "The numbers were all starting to blur together so I laid my head down next to the keyboard, thinking I would just steal a quick nap before Arthur got back. Right before I drifted off, I remember thinking how delicious the pizza would be, how steam would be rolling off the melted cheese, how the pepperoni would be just a little crisp around the edges. It was so real, I actually began to smell it. Then when I opened my eyes, the pizza was there, right beside my nose." Not even a decade of cynicism had completely erased the echo of delight from Tristan's eyes.

"At first I thought I'd slept longer than I meant to, but at that very moment Arthur came whistling through the door, pizza box in hand. He thought I was playing a joke on him. That I'd called and ordered a pizza while he was gone. It took me a long time to convince him that we'd finally done it—invented a computer program with the ability to convert thought energy into matter. A virtual tool for wish fulfillment."

"Magic," Arian whispered, her own eyes shining with the thrill of his discovery. It might be a different sort of magic than hers, but that didn't make it any less miraculous or worthy of wonder.

"Magic," he echoed, bitterness tinging his voice. "We toasted our success with enchanted pizza and a bottle of cheap Chianti, then dove right back into the work. I wanted to perform studies and trials, test the limits and quirks of the program, but Arthur insisted our first project should be installing Warlock into a microprocessor no bigger than the tip of my thumb. We were both giddy, nearly drunk with excitement, but by the second night, I was already beginning to have doubts."

"What sort of doubts?" Arian asked, leaning toward him.

Tristan's crystalline eyes clouded. "What if Warlock should fall into the wrong hands? What if it were to be used to fulfill the twisted wishes of a madman or a serial killer? How could such unlimited power not corrupt? I tried to discuss my fears with Arthur, but he just laughed and told me to stop being such a wuss. It was near midnight, but he encouraged me to go for a walk. He said some fresh air might clear my head."

"That was when he must have made the call to his father," Arian deduced. As she met Tristan's unflinching gaze, dawning horror tingled through her veins. "You!

You were the virus! The virus he planned to exterminate!"

Tristan nodded. "The police forced me to listen to that message over and over. I still hear his voice in my head sometimes, late at night when there's no one around." He rose and wandered back to the window. The shadows of impending twilight offered his profile sanctuary. "He was waiting for me when I walked in the door."

Arian wrapped her arms around herself to stifle a shiver, wishing they were Tristan's. She didn't have to ask what Finch's motivations had been. Greed. Ambition. An insatiable hunger for power. The very failings Wite Lize had attributed to Tristan. She wondered if the old man had suspected his son's treachery all along.

Tristan's mouth curved in a grim parody of mirth. "When I saw the knife in his hand, all I could think to say was, 'Shit, Arthur, why not a gun? You know how you hate to mop the kitchen.' He just lifted a finger to his lips, winked at me, and said, 'We wouldn't want to wake the neighbors, now would we?' "

But they had awakened the neighbors, Arian remembered. With angry shouts and the sounds of a brief and violent struggle. As Tristan gazed into the gathering darkness, Arian wondered if he saw Arthur's teasing smile or the mocking monster who had come at him from the shadows.

When Tristan finally spoke, his voice had been stripped of all passion. "We fought. He underestimated me. I hadn't watched Captain Kirk kick all those Klingon asses for nothing. The knife ended up embedded in his stomach. I tried to catch him as he fell and we both went down. There was blood . . . so much blood." Tristan drew his hands from his pockets, studying them as if he still expected to find a coppery stain beneath his manicured fingernails. "I tried to staunch the flow with my hands, but it just kept coming, welling out from beneath my palms, trickling between my fingers."

A tear slid down Arian's cheek and splashed on the prenuptial agreement. It chilled her to the marrow to realize Tristan might have been the one buried in the basement of the old brownstone. Arthur must have known that Tristan had no family and few friends other than Finch and his father. He must have believed that Tristan would never be missed. A fresh shudder rocked her to realize he had probably been right.

Tristan's hands curled into fists. "When his body started shaking, I thought he was coughing. Then I realized he was laughing. He flashed me his old cocky grin and said, 'Hell, Tristan, it was your turn to mop the kitchen anyway.' Then he opened his palm to show me the tiny microprocessor. I realized he had already programmed some sort of failsafe into Warlock—to help him escape in the event of a mortal injury. But before I could snatch the damn thing away, he disappeared. Right there in my arms."

"And you've been searching for him ever since, haven't you?" Arian asked softly, suddenly understanding his obsession with magic.

"How could I not?" Tristan spun around, his face ravaged by all the anguish and remorse he normally kept hidden behind his aloof exterior. "I'm the one who unleashed him! I'm the one who invented Warlock and placed such terrible power at his corrupt fingertips. I've had an army of detectives combing the world for nearly ten years, but it's as if he just vanished off the face of the earth."

"Does Copperfield know?"

Tristan shrugged. "I think he suspects that Arthur's alive. He never once asked me if I'd done it, not even when he convinced his father to take my case."

"You couldn't even defend yourself." Arian's heart ached anew as she realized how helpless and isolated he must have felt.

"No one would have believed me anyway, and I'd have spent the rest of my life in prison before I'd have told them about Warlock. I couldn't take the chance that some other madman might force me to re-create my work. I thought the magic competition might lure Arthur out. Not because he would need the money, but because he wouldn't be able to resist the urge to flaunt his survival in my face. Hell, if he hadn't been so damned arrogant, he'd have just stabbed me in the back while he had the chance and been done with it."

Tristan threw himself into a chair, running a hand through his hair. His expression reflected the same vulnerability that had shadowed the face of that bloodied boy in the *Forbes* photograph. Arthur hadn't stabbed him in the back; he had plunged that knife straight through Tristan's heart. A heart that had been seeping blood ever since.

Tenderness washed over Arian. For the first time, she understood what set her apart from her mother and what set Tristan apart from all the men her mother had bedded. Her mother had loved none of them, not even Arian's father, but Arian knew she would love this man until the day she died.

She circled the table, coming around to drop to her knees at his feet. She gazed up into his eyes, desiring nothing more than to banish the shadows from them forever. "Let him go. Arthur Finch is gone, maybe even dead. You can't spend the rest of your life atoning for his sins." She cupped his wary face in her hands before whispering fiercely, "Forget Arthur and love me, Tristan. Here. Now. Tonight." She pressed her lips to his, sealing her plea with a kiss. His lips parted in astonishment, allowing her tongue to slip between them and caress the delectable warmth of his mouth.

Tristan groaned his delight against Arian's lips. His first instinct was to seize what she was offering as ruthlessly as he'd seized everything else he'd wanted since Arthur's betrayal had drained the decency from his soul. He longed to lay her down on that triple-padded carpet and partake of her body's tender absolution.

She was yielding everything, yet asking nothing in return—no ring, no marriage license, no pious priest to pronounce them man and wife.

Arian's generosity proved just how wrong he'd been. She was no mercenary con artist peddling her body in exchange for his name. She hadn't rejected him out of malice or greed, but out of a genuine desire to save the gift of her innocence for her husband. It shamed him to remember how he had mocked her dearest principles. Principles she was now willing to compromise just to provide him with a few precious hours of solace and forgetfulness.

She relinquished his face to gather his hands in hers. Hands that had once been stained with a friend's blood. She pressed a fervent kiss to each of his palms, then kissed each finger in turn before resting her cheek against his knee. Tristan reached to stroke her bowed head, then hesitated, gazing at his trembling hand as if it belonged to someone else.

A lance of pain stabbed his chest, but this time he recognized the crushing ache for what it was. He was surprised Arian couldn't hear the crack of his heart breaking wide open to free all the love he'd been hoarding for a lifetime. A love that mocked his cynicism and dared him to believe in happily-ever-after and till-death-do-us-part.

She made a soft sound of protest when he gently disengaged himself from her embrace and moved to the table. He rescued the prenuptial agreement from the scattered papers and methodically ripped it into bits.

Arian nibbled on her lower lip as she watched him, her eyes dark and tremulous. She was petrified, Tristan realized, but no less willing to welcome him into her arms.

He thought his heart might stop altogether when she rose to her feet, drew the engagement ring from her slender finger and held it out to him. "Here. I won't be needing this."

He frowned down at it, having forgotten that he'd told his personal shopper to pick out the most expensive, most ostentatious ring in all of Tiffany's. It was even more hideous than he had anticipated—a garish mockery of the pledge it represented. But he supposed it would have to do.

He took the ring, closing his fist around it. "I wanted to believe you were nothing but a heartless gold digger, that you were only marrying me for my money. Well, I was wrong." Her expression brightened, then dimmed when he added, "My money's not enough for you."

Arian took a step away from him, as if to brace herself for a coming blow.

He ruthlessly closed the distance between them. "You're nothing but a greedy little witch who isn't going to be satisfied until you've stolen my heart, my soul . . . and my love. And now that you've succeeded, you have no choice but to marry me and make me miserable for the rest of my life."

Arian opened and closed her mouth with a reply that was half squeak, half squawk.

Tristan grinned and slipped the ring back on her finger. "I'll take that as a yes."

"But the p-p-prenuptial agreement," she sputtered. "You destroyed it."

"Damn right I did. And if you dare to divorce me, I'll take you for everything you're worth." He cupped her cheek, the breathtaking intensity of his gaze warning her he wasn't entirely joking. "If you break my heart, Arian Whitewood, you'll find yourself wandering the streets penniless, wondering where your next dish of caviar is going to come from."

"Bully," Arian whispered before flinging her arms around him with a cry of pure joy.

Clucking with mock dismay, Tristan threaded his fingers through her curls and gently tipped her head back. "You simply must make an effort to restrain your passions, Miss Whitewood. How else am I to cling to my virtue until you've made an honest man out of me?"

Her shining eyes blinked up at him. "But I thought you wanted—"

Backing her against the wall, he indulged her mouth with hot, wet, deep kisses until she thought the red Chanel suit just might burst into flames and sizzle right off her body.

"What I want," he finally muttered into her hair while she was struggling to catch her breath, "is for tomorrow night to hurry up and get here."

23

The exquisitely wrapped package arrived at the penthouse while Arian was still struggling into her wedding gown. Sven was already tipping and dismissing the messenger when she stumbled into the living room with the lacy waterfall of her train slung haphazardly over one arm.

"That lying wretch! He promised me he wouldn't buy me any more extravagant gifts." Arian heaved an exasperated sigh, but discovered it was impossible to even pretend to be angry at Tristan with the memory of his kisses still tingling on her lips.

She snatched the enticing box from Sven's hand. Perhaps Tristan had made good on his vow to replace her engagement ring with something half a dozen carats or so less obnoxious.

"That's odd," she said, examining the box from all sides. "It seems to have holes in it. Do you think the messenger dropped it?" She lifted it to her ear, giving it a tentative shake. Her eyes widened as she met

Sven's bewildered gaze. "That's even odder. It's rumbling at me."

"Drop it!" Sven's shout startled her into obeying. He caught the package before it could hit the rug and raced for the bathroom, holding the box at arm's length.

Arian crept after him, utterly baffled by his behavior. At the sound of running water, she peeped around the bathroom door to discover that Sven had thrust the package into one of the sinks and turned on the faucet full force.

The wrapping paper and fragile cardboard disintegrated beneath the gushing water, revealing a sopping wet occupant who was no longer rumbling its satisfaction, but yowling at the top of its tiny lungs.

"Sven!" Arian cried, rushing in to scoop the bedraggled ball of fur into her cupped palms. "You ought to be ashamed of yourself! Tormenting an innocent creature in that manner! There, there, nice kitty," she murmured, dabbing at its dripping whiskers with the tail of her train. The kitten sneezed and she shot Sven a reproachful look. "I won't let the bad man hurt you."

"I thought it was a bomb," Sven confessed sheepishly, still eyeing the tiny termagant as if it might explode.

The kitten's yowls had subsided to piteous mews. Arian bit back a wince of pain as it hooked its needle-sharp claws into the bodice of her dress and clambered toward her shoulder. A row of seed pearls popped off and bounced into the shower, but all was forgiven when the enchanting bit of ebony fluff began to nuzzle Arian's ear.

Deafened by the kitten's blissful purr, Arian reached past Sven and gingerly peeled the sodden gift card from the rim of the sink. The unmistakable scrawl was blurred, but still legible: *Every good witch should have a familiar. And you're the best damn witch I know.*

A warmth that had both nothing and everything to do with the darling creature cuddled beneath her chin spread through Arian's veins like chocolate syrup. Tristan couldn't have chosen a more appropriate wedding gift to celebrate their love. At first Arian thought the distant ringing was simply her heart caroling a joyous tune, but a shy cough from the direction of the living room warned her it had been the chime of the arriving elevator.

"Barrett here, ma'am. I've brought the limousine around to take you to the chapel."

Arian's head flew up. "Oh, my! The chapel! The wedding!" She thrust the kitten toward Sven. "Could you please find little Lucifer a basket? I want to take him with me."

Sven backed toward the sunken whirlpool tub, shaking his head with renewed violence.

Arian sighed. "Don't tell me a strapping fellow like you is afraid of a kitten."

The bodyguard signed a cross on his burly chest. "Black cats are bad luck."

"And Norwegians are overly superstitious and given to disagreeable bouts of gloom." Ignoring the sputtered protests of both man and cat, she deposited the kitten in Sven's mighty paw.

Tripping on her starched petticoat, Arian rushed from the bathroom, leaving Sven and Lucifer to eye each other with the wary suspicion of lifelong enemies.

Arian's wedding ring was everything her engagement ring was not—exquisite, delicate, tasteful. As Tristan slid the band of beaten gold on her trembling finger at the priest's command, he whispered that it was an antique, over seventy-five years old. Arian wondered what he would say if he knew his bride was even more of an antique, over three centuries old.

Someday she would tell him, she promised herself. Someday when they were lazing on the front porch of their Connecticut farmhouse, watching their grandchildren romp through the autumn leaves. But today was a day for both of them to leave the past behind.

Arian was thankful Tristan had insisted she wear white to symbolize their fresh beginning. The puffed sleeves of the princess-cut bodice bared her shoulders to the golden glow of the Waterford chandeliers. Sven had helped her pile her hair high on her head, then secured the rebellious curls with a tiara woven from silk blossoms and baby's breath. The emerald amulet provided a single teardrop of color against her snowy bosom.

Arian felt no need to invoke its magic. She could never have composed an incantation more enchanting than the priest's "I now pronounce you man and wife." As she turned up her face to seal their vows, Tristan's tender kiss cast a spell that would last a lifetime.

"Ladies and gentlemen," the beaming priest intoned, turning them to face the packed pews. "It is my privilege to introduce Mr. and Mrs. Tristan Lennox."

Thunderous applause rocked the elegant chapel. Arian gazed over the sea of smiling faces and squeezed Tristan's hand, marveling at how love had turned a city full of strangers into friends.

Before she even had time to catch her breath, they were swept down the aisle and out the towering doors of the chapel. A shower of orange blossoms tossed by cheering well-wishers enveloped them in a fragrant cloud, eliciting a flurry of sneezes and a reproachful glance from her new husband. As Tristan followed her into the waiting limo, Arian barely noticed the lowering clouds or the chill bite of a wind that whispered of early winter.

As the majestic limo rolled toward the Carlyle Hotel where the reception was to be held, Arian settled in the crook of her husband's arm, seized by an almost painful shyness. Tristan's long, tanned fingers stroked the ivory skin of her forearm, evoking provocative memories of their last encounter in a limousine. She stole a peek at his face. He was watching her with an irresistibly roguish smile that warned her he was thinking exactly the same thing.

If anyone awaiting their arrival at the Carlyle noticed that the limo circled the block six times or that the bride and groom emerged from the back seat rumpled and slightly dazed, they were too polite to do more than elbow one another knowingly and share an envious wink. Arian licked her puffy lips and managed a shaky smile for the flashing cameras, her cheeks aflame.

Even Sven and Lucifer seemed to have declared a truce in honor of their nuptials. When they reached the lavish banquet room where the reception was to be held, Arian discovered Sven ignoring the shocked stares of the society matrons to feed the kitten bits of smoked caviar from his plate. The women looked even more scandalized when Sven swiped a sprig of miniature roses from one of the centerpieces and began nibbling on it. Arian breathed a silent prayer of thanks that she hadn't turned him into a man-eating tiger instead of a goat.

When the leader of the string quartet prodded Arian and Tristan into claiming the floor for the first dance, Lucifer bounded down from the white satin tablecloth and frisked around their feet, shamelessly trying to catch a ride on Arian's train.

Drawing her as close as the orchestra's chaste rendering of Aerosmith's "Amazing" would allow, Tristan plucked a stray orange blossom from Arian's hair. "Happy, Mrs. Lennox?" he murmured.

"Delirious, Mr. Lennox," she replied, resting her cheek against his starched shirtfront and thinking how lovely it would be to wake up tomorrow morning with her cheek pressed to his bare chest.

As the second dance began, other couples swirled into motion around them, pointing and laughing at Lucifer's antics.

"That's strange," Tristan said, watching a pony-tailed Native American who looked suspiciously like his best man lead a statuesque auburn-haired beauty onto the dance floor. "I don't remember inviting *her* to the wedding."

Arian craned her neck to peer around his shoulder before smiling smugly. "You didn't. But don't they make a lovely couple?"

Copperfield spun Cherie into a dramatic dip, giving Arian a thumb's-up sign as he did so. "Someone seems to think so," Tristan replied, resting his chin on his wife's upswept curls. "Is that how you spent your morning? Brewing love potions for all my old girlfriends?"

As the music soared and the wine flowed, Arian grew more and more distracted. She kept glancing toward the doors, searching each new flurry of arriving guests for a familiar face.

Tristan gave his bride a possessive squeeze, bemused by her mounting nervousness. "If you've changed your mind, it's too late. I'll never let you go now. Especially not before I . . ." He inclined his head, muffling the delicious details of his sensual promise against her ear.

Arian blushed prettily, but as she searched his face, her sober expression lingered. "I just hope you'll like your wedding present as well as I like mine."

Her back was to the door a few minutes later when Tristan muttered, "What the hell . . . ?" Arian stiffened, but her guileless face betrayed nothing, not even when Tristan leveled a ferocious scowl at her. "Who the hell taught you to use the telephone?"

"You did," she reminded him, smiling sweetly. "Go on," she urged, giving him a slight shove toward the door. "Go play the gracious host. 'Tis your duty."

Tristan obeyed, but not before tugging the lapels of his gray morning coat straight and smoothing back his hair. Her heart stuck somewhere between her chest and her throat, Arian watched her gorgeous husband weave his way between the dancers to greet his mother.

Brenda hovered at the door, striking in a dark blue

dress adorned with a rhinestone stickpin. Arian didn't realize she was holding her breath until she saw Tristan bend stiffly to accept his mother's awkward hug, then flash a cautious smile at Brenda's reticent entourage.

Forcing Lucifer to find a new target for his pouncing attacks, Arian scooped up her train and wended her own way through the crowd to her husband's side, never more certain that she belonged there.

As she approached, Tristan drew her into their intimate circle. "I'd like all of you to meet Arian, my new wife. Arian, you've already met my mother." Two lanky young men flanked Brenda, as if to protect her from some unforeseen assault. "This is Bill. And Danny." The men, barely more than boys, greeted Arian with nods and bashful grins.

A plain girl clutching the arm of a boy even younger than Bill or Danny hung back behind them. Tristan drew her forward, handling her with a care that only made Arian adore him more. "Arian, this is Ellen." His brief pause spoke volumes. "My sister."

The girl's face broke into a shy smile and Arian realized she would not be plain for long. Arian had seen that smile before—on a bright, lonely boy who had grown up to rule an empire and steal her heart.

Arian beamed at the girl. "Why, Ellen, you're every bit as lovely as your mother! We're so glad you could come."

Arian's warm welcome seemed to melt the girl's shyness. "And I'm so glad Mr. Len—uh, Tristan—um, my brother"—this with a nervous glance at Tristan— "asked you to invite us. Mama nearly fainted after you called last night," she confided with a giggle. "We couldn't tell if she was laughing or crying. Then we realized she was laughing *and* crying. Oh," she exclaimed, drawing her reluctant companion forward. "And this is Phil. We're getting married in the spring, right after graduation." Phil looked a trifle pasty and inclined to bolt, but Ellen's possessive grip showed no sign of easing. "We're both starting at NYU next fall. I know it won't be easy, but love has a way of making things work out, doesn't it?"

"Yes, it does," Tristan murmured, wrapping his arms around Arian's waist. "But I'd still like to have a word with you, *son,* about your plans for my little sister."

"Why don't you dance with your mother first?" Arian suggested before her husband's glower could send poor Phil sprinting for the door.

Arian watched Tristan offer his mother an arm through a haze of happiness, praying Brenda would have the decency not to ask for an advance on her allowance during the dance. She sighed. She supposed she would have to stop meddling and let them work things out the same way mothers and sons had been doing for countless generations.

Arian barely had time to dance with Copperfield and rescue Lucifer from the irate caterer's clutches after he'd been caught licking the frosting from the wedding cake before she and Tristan were summoned to the front of the ballroom to share the toast that would signal dinner.

Tristan nuzzled her ear as if they'd been separated for hours instead of only minutes. "You're going to regret inviting your mother-in-law to the wedding when she starts giving you cooking tips and insisting we name our first baby after my uncle Felix."

"I didn't know you had an uncle Felix."

He gave his tie an irritable tug. "Neither did I."

An expectant spell fell over the crowd as one of the waiters handed Tristan a goblet of red wine. He gazed down into Arian's eyes with a sensual tenderness that stole her breath away.

His voice was smoky with the promise of pleasures to come as he lifted the goblet. "To my beautiful bride, who made me believe in the magic of true love."

The delighted applause was interrupted by droll

laughter. "Is it the magic of love you salute, Lennox? Or the love of magic?"

Dread rooted Arian to the floor as the crowd parted to reveal Wite Lize standing in the doorway, dapper in a black tuxedo, top hat, and flowing cape.

24

"Another of your mystery guests, my dear?" Tristan murmured through clenched teeth.

"I should say not," Arian replied, shooting him an offended glance.

As Wite Lize strode through the crowd, white cane in hand, Sven passed Lucifer off to Copperfield and bounded toward the front of the room, prepared to intercept the wedding crasher before he reached the bride and groom.

Arian placed a restraining hand on her husband's arm. "Please, Tristan," she whispered. "He can't hurt us anymore. Don't let him spoil our day by provoking you into tossing him out on his ear. He'd like nothing more than to make you appear the ogre in front of our guests."

She felt the ironbound muscles of Tristan's forearm slowly relax. He spared her a rueful glance, as if bemused by the ease with which she coaxed his surrender. "As you wish. Anything for my bride."

At Tristan's signal, Sven went to lean against the wall behind them, but kept his brawny arms folded over his chest in a threat that was impossible to misinterpret. Handing Lucifer off to Cherie, Copperfield rose to join him, adding his own warning to Sven's.

As Wite Lize approached, Tristan even managed a terse smile. "I had hoped the Carlyle might provide a higher quality of entertainment," he called out. "Yodeling, perhaps, or mimes trapped in invisible boxes."

Wite Lize sketched his host a mocking bow. "I believe your guests will find my feats of illusion as diverting as your own charade."

He swept off his top hat, sending a pair of snow-white doves fluttering toward the skylight to the appreciative "oohs" and "aahs" of the crowd. The guests broke into applause, obviously believing the caustic banter between Tristan and the magician was simply part of the show.

Arian clutched Tristan's arm, wondering what black mischief the incorrigible illusionist was up to now. He must be terribly bitter that his scheme to poison her against Tristan had failed. Now that she and Tristan stood together, united as man and wife, he was powerless to hurt them. Wasn't he?

Having won the delighted regard of the crowd by producing a bouquet of fresh lilacs from the top of his cane, Wite Lize pursed his lips thoughtfully. "For my next trick, I shall require a volunteer from the audience."

He paced back and forth, his cape rippling behind him as he pretended to assess the crowd for potential celebrities. Ignoring the frantically waving hand of a little girl, he spun around and pointed a finger at Arian. "What better helpmeet could I choose than the blushing bride herself?"

Arian recoiled from his outstretched hand.

"No, thank you," Tristan snapped, drawing her into the shelter of his side. "I'd rather not have my bride turned into a turtledove or sawn in half before the honeymoon."

The crowd booed and hooted their disappointment.

Lize cocked his head to the side, his expression insufferably coy. "What's wrong, Lennox? Afraid I'll make her vanish right before your eyes?"

Tristan tensed, and Arian knew he was only a taunt away from smashing his fist into the magician's smug face. She caressed the amulet, tempted to make the magician perform a disappearing act of his own.

"It's all right, Tristan," she said instead, her voice ringing high and clear in the taut silence. "I'll help him with his silly old trick."

"Arian, I really don't think—"

But she had already stepped out of the protective circle of her husband's embrace to face the magician.

"Ah!" Wite Lize exclaimed. "Brave as well as beautiful. Lennox is a lucky fellow, is he not?"

The guests dutifully applauded her boldness while Tristan gazed on in stormy disapproval, his knuckles blanched around the stem of the goblet.

"Follow the motions of my hands," Wite Lize instructed the rapt crowd, wiggling his fingers in front of Arian's face until her eyes crossed in annoyance, "and witness an amazing feat of prestidigitation. With my stunning sleight of hand, I shall create fire in the bosom of this lovely ice maiden."

Crowning his motions with a dramatic flourish, Wite Lize pointed at Arian's chest. A miniature lightning bolt crackled from his fingertip, provoking charmed applause and squeals of delight from the younger members of his audience.

Arian yawned. As lightning bolts went, it hadn't been particularly impressive. Her hair wasn't even standing on end.

Tristan looked more relieved than angry. "Your amateur pyrotechnics might be more impressive, old man, if you recharged that battery pack you've got stuck up your . . ."

His voice trailed off as the goblet slipped from his hand. Wine spattered like blood over the train of Arian's gown.

"Why, Tristan! What on earth—?" Arian glanced up from the mess to find Tristan staring at her chest, his face ashen.

"Where did that come from?" he asked hoarsely. Copperfield appeared behind him, as still and dark as his shadow.

Arian recoiled as Tristan took a step toward her. "What is it, Tristan? Don't stare at me so. You're frightening me."

Silence had fallen like a thunderclap over the banquet room and no one dared to stir. No one but Wite Lize, who was backing away from them with a look of grim triumph on his withered face.

"Where the hell did it come from?" Tristan repeated.

Arian shook her head mutely, afraid to even hazard a guess in answer to his cryptic demand.

He caught her by the shoulders, his hands as ruthless as they'd been gentle only minutes before. "The emerald! Where the hell did you get the emerald?"

Tears of wounded bewilderment flooded Arian's eyes. "I told you where I got it. My mother gave it to me!"

Her breath escaped in a shuddering sob as Tristan seized the delicate chain, just as Linnet had once done, and wrenched the amulet from her neck. He studied it for a moment, his face inscrutable, then held it up to the light, allowing the gem to dangle in a graceful arc directly in front of Arian's disbelieving eyes.

The emerald had cracked wide open beneath the shock of Lize's counterfeit lightning to reveal a tangled maze of wires. Hope died as understanding dawned. Not her magic. Never her magic. Always his.

Tristan's gaze traveled from the shattered gem to her face, his loving expression transformed by doubt.

Arian's shoulders slumped as everything she'd ever believed in—magic, faith, love everlasting—crumbled to ashes beneath the renewed suspicion in her husband's eyes.

Tristan dropped the amulet in his pocket, leaving her more utterly vulnerable to him than ever before. She was too numb with shock to even protest when he gave her a gentle push toward Sven and said, "I think you'd better get her out of here."

PART III

All the wild witches, those most noble ladies,
For all their broomsticks and their tears,
Their angry tears, are gone.

—William Butler Yeats

Make no little plans; they have no magic to
stir men's blood.

—Attributed to
Daniel Hudson Burnham

"Do you now or have you ever had any contact with a man by the name of Arthur Finch?"

"No," Arian croaked, hoarse from answering the same question for the thirtieth time in less than five hours.

"Was Finch the one who gave you the microprocessor and software program now being examined by my employer's team of scientists?"

"No."

"Then who gave it to you?"

"I told you a dozen times. I don't know what you're talking about. The necklace was a gift from my mother."

Her interrogator lit another cigarette and paced around the table, a sad sigh wafting from his nicotine-laden lungs. Levinson was the best to be had and his was a sigh that had broken the spirit of many an embezzler caught dipping their greedy hands in the company till. The private detective had learned his trade by grilling suspected shoplifters at Saks and was currently listed on the Lennox Enterprises payroll as a freelance interviewer. All tidy and perfectly legal.

"You are aware that fraud is a crime. It would be well within my employer's rights to call the police and have you arrested. If he should choose to press charges, Miss Whitewood, you could be facing not only extensive fines, but possible imprisonment of up to five to ten years." He fixed her with a basset hound's gloomy stare, looking as if his own heart were breaking beneath the burden of her noncompliance.

She didn't even blink. "My name is not Whitewood. It's Lennox. Mrs. Tristan Lennox."

He smoked in silence for several minutes before stubbing out the cigarette in the bottom of his Styrofoam cup. "Perhaps I'm not making myself clear. When was the last time you made contact with Arthur Finch?"

She simply glared at him. Mascara mingled with the smudges of exhaustion beneath her eyes. Her tiara of silk blooms had long ago listed to the left, freeing limp tendrils of hair to spill over her face. Her wedding gown was crumpled and stained, her shoulders slumped with fatigue. Watching from behind the two-way mirror in the Security Command Center control booth, Tristan was forced to flip off the hidden microphone and close his eyes, no longer able to bear her fierce and unyielding beauty.

As his strength ebbed, so did his resolve. Behind his aching eyelids, he saw Arian as she had looked the moment after she'd hurled the lightning bolt at his head. Her hair had tumbled around her shoulders like a little girl's and her crestfallen expression had captured his heart. He'd denied it to himself, but even then he'd known that the sweet, dark longing that quickened his pulse each time he looked into her trusting eyes could not be slaked with another woman. Sweet, tantalizing Arian, in his hands, but forever out of his reach. His dreams had been alight with her until the dawn.

But the dawn had brought with it an even more

bewildering set of doubts. He didn't want to believe the worst of Arian, but experience had taught him that cynicism might be his only defense against crushing disillusionment. It was all beginning to make a sort of horrible sense. By respecting Arian's privacy, he may very well have set himself up for the most vicious betrayal of all.

After all, she was a woman with no family, no past, and no legal identity. How difficult would it have been for Arthur to enlist her in his scheme? To outfit her with a disguised and enhanced version of Warlock and send her to infiltrate his camp? To arrange a clever little accident after which his grieving widow would inherit his entire fortune to be divided with her lover after a discreet period of mourning had passed?

His eyes flew open in an attempt to banish the taunting vision. Could he truly have been so blind? He had suspected Arian of conspiring with every lowlife in New York except the most obvious one. The one who knew he'd always been a sucker for a hard-luck story and a pair of big, brown eyes. Eyes that hadn't shed a single tear since her husband had had her escorted away from her own wedding reception before the shocked eyes of their guests.

Praying that Arian would say something, anything at all, to prove him wrong, he reached down and flipped the microphone back on. The private detective had shifted from accusing to tender, pressing a fresh cup of coffee into Arian's trembling hands before squatting down to peer into her chalky face. "Miss Whitewood, do you have any idea what would happen to a pretty little girl like you in a state correctional facility?"

"Shit! I don't know how much more of this I can take."

The vehement oath reminded Tristan that he wasn't alone in the narrow control booth. Copperfield, the author of said oath, sprawled on a stool at the end of the counter while Sven leaned against the back wall, as stalwart as a California redwood. Tristan tried not to look at the exhausted kitten sleeping in his brawny arms.

"Maybe you've got something you'd like to confess," Tristan suggested. "Have you been filching paper clips again? Forget to drop a quarter in the coffee-fund jar?"

Copperfield was no more amused than he was. "I'd confess to shooting Kennedy from the grassy knoll if it would shut Levinson up. How the hell can she stand it?"

"The door's not locked. She can leave anytime she likes." Tristan drained the cold coffee from the bottom of his own Styrofoam cup, savoring its bitterness.

"And did you bother to tell her that?" When Tristan averted his eyes, Cop said, "I didn't think so."

Tristan was thankful the booth was dimly lit. He'd allowed Cop to be the mirror to his soul for too damn long. He might be able to hide his own anguish behind an icy façade, but it would be reflected clearly in his friend's eloquent face.

Cop watched the tableau beyond the glass with the helpless fascination of a driver slowing down to gape at the bloody aftermath of an auto accident. Unable to look away despite his shame.

"Do you now or have you ever had any contact with a man by the name of Arthur Finch?"

Arian folded her arms on the table, then dropped her head onto them as if it had simply grown too heavy for her slender neck to support. Someone behind them made a dismayed noise. Tristan had no way of knowing if it was Sven or the cat.

He jabbed a silver button, activating the intercom between the chambers. "That will be quite enough, Mr. Levinson."

Arian didn't even stir when the detective and his hangdog expression vacated the room, leaving her huddled at the foot of the long table.

Cop dragged a hand over his mouth. "What now?

Thumbscrews? The rack? Some other hired thug to play good cop to Levinson's bad one?"

"Levinson *was* the good cop," Tristan replied, the grim twist of his lips making Copperfield look as if he wished he had a spare pair of thumbscrews in his pocket. Tristan rose from the stool, confirming his friend's worst suspicions. "Sven?"

"Yes, sir."

Tristan could not tell if the Norwegian's voice was laden with regret or reproach, nor could he afford to care. "Get that damn cat out of here."

Arian cradled her aching head on her arms, wishing desperately for a hot bath, a soft bed, and the tender solace of her husband's arms. A muffled groan escaped her as she reminded herself bitterly that wishing was as futile as longing for Tristan.

She possessed no supernatural powers. She was not, and had never been, a witch. Her magic had been nothing but a technological parlor trick, a cruel hoax that had preyed upon her childish dreams and deluded her into believing her own ridiculous fancies. A hoax that had stretched across three centuries to make fools of them all.

Beware the warlock.

She had refused to heed Wite Lize's warning until it was too late and now they were all paying the price. Her grief at losing her faith in magic paled next to the agony of knowing that Tristan believed she had deliberately betrayed him. Her breath caught in a strangled sob.

The door swung open with a muted click. She didn't have to lift her head to know who was standing there, but she did anyway.

Her husband had erased all traces of their union, changing into a pair of jeans and a gray cable-knit sweater. The faded denim molded itself to his hips and thighs and the inviting weave of the sweater made Arian want to bury her face against his chest and weep out her misery.

Copperfield slunk into the room behind him.

Tristan folded his arms over his chest, fixing her with a level stare. "Do you now or have you ever had any contact with a man named—"

"No!" Arian cried, coming to her feet. All the passion she'd kept suppressed during Levinson's endless interrogation boiled to the surface. "I never spoke with him. I never met him. I never even knew he existed until Wite Lize told me about him yesterday!" Yesterday already seemed an eternity away.

Tristan tossed a glance over his shoulder at Copperfield. "Methinks the witch doth protest too much."

"Don't call me that," Arian said fiercely, throwing herself back in the chair.

"What should I call you, then?" Tristan shot back, the rawness of his voice betraying both his desperate need to believe her and his fear of doing so. "Is Arian even your real name?"

Copperfield sank into a chair on the opposite side of the table in a futile attempt to stay out of the line of fire.

"Please, Arian," Tristan whispered. "Convince me that I'm wrong."

As Arian studied her husband's imploring features, she realized she might have only one chance to acquit herself. One chance to salvage her dreams and prove him worthy of the hope she still clung to.

"My name is Arian Whitewood," she said softly, adding "Lennox" just for the petty pleasure of watching Tristan flinch. "I was born in a small village in northern France in the year of our Lord sixteen sixty-nine."

It was Tristan's turn to sink into a chair. He chose the one farthest from her. "Go on."

Arian did. Keeping her voice painstakingly free of emotion, she told him about the years she'd spent with her grandmama in that sylvan forest, the grueling voyage across the seas to join her stepfather, those dark, lonely days in the Colonies. Her weary voice grew even more hoarse, but she pressed on, concluding with the persecution that had resulted in her exile from Gloucester and her haphazard flight across the centuries into his waiting arms.

When she'd croaked out the final word of her extraordinary tale, he sat in silence for several minutes, his face shielded by his hand. Arian sat up straighter, daring to dream, daring to hope. But the flicker of embarrassed pity in Copperfield's eyes crushed that hope an instant before Tristan's laughter came rolling out, black and mirthless in the sterile room. Arian realized too late that her improbable story had finally convinced him she was truly a fraud.

He rose to pace around the table, his scornful travesty of a smile wounding Arian more deeply than all the affronts that had come before it. "So now you've gone from bumbling witch to time-traveling Puritan. Was that the best alibi you could come up with? Your pathetic amnesia story was a hell of a lot more convincing and nobody believed it."

Arian glared at him. The "bumbling" stung. Even now. " 'Tis not an alibi. 'Tis the truth."

He paced behind her chair, torturing Arian with a whiff of his aftershave. Wistful tears welled in her eyes, but she struggled to blink them back before he reentered her line of vision.

"Your charming fiction failed to explain one thing. How did Warlock end up three hundred years in the past? Plainly enhanced and embedded in an emerald necklace draped around your lovely little neck."

"I don't know! I'm just as baffled as you are."

"Well, then, why don't we start with the necklace?" He planted both palms on the table and fixed her with the unblinking gaze notorious for sending his business rivals scurrying under conference tables. "Where did you get it?"

Arian averted her eyes, troubled by a flicker of shame. "My mother gave it to me."

Tristan straightened. "And who gave it to her?"

Arian twisted the crumpled folds of her train in her hands before mumbling, "An admirer."

Copperfield sank even lower into his chair, his face shadowed by misery.

Tristan's footfalls were utterly silent as he came around the table to stand behind Arian, near enough for her to feel the heat radiating from his body. She tried not to shudder when his powerful hands closed over her shoulders, bit her lip to keep from begging when his fingertips traced the delicate arch of her collarbone with unforgivable tenderness.

Copperfield stirred in his chair and Arian knew why he was there. Not to gloat, but to ensure that Tristan didn't do anything he might regret later. Like strangle his bride on their wedding night.

Her husband's voice did not so much threaten as beguile. "I know a little about these Puritans you claim as your contemporaries, my dear. I know that accused witches who chose to keep their silence were usually stripped and pressed to death with heavy stones."

Arian closed her eyes. Levinson's cruelty had been far easier to bear than Tristan's. At least it had been overt, not couched in malicious endearments and taunting caresses that only served to remind her of all she had lost.

When she opened her eyes, they were bleak with resignation. "She stole it. My mother stole the necklace."

Tristan paced to the other side of the table, looking grimly satisfied to have at least caught her in half a lie.

Arian forced herself to stop wringing her train. "My mother was a courtesan."

"A whore," Tristan amended dryly. "How fitting."

Arian flashed him a smoldering glance, but his sulky mouth did not betray even a twitch of contrition. "When I was a child, she was the pampered darling of many a nobleman at the king's court, but in her younger days, she wasn't quite as discriminating." Arian lowered her eyes, stumbling over a truth she'd never confessed to anyone. "She accepted an assignation with a handsome, charming young actor only to discover after their liaison that he was penniless. They quarreled bitterly, but before she stormed off, she managed to filch the necklace from his purse and drop it down her bodice." Since Copperfield's was the only remotely amiable face in the room, Arian directed her defense at him. "She didn't really consider it stealing. She truly believed he owed it to her."

"For services rendered," Tristan drawled. "A touching story, but that still doesn't explain how the necklace came to be in your possession."

"She caught me pawing through her jewel box one night when I was a little girl. By then she'd amassed quite a collection." The bitter note in Arian's voice left little doubt as to how Lily had earned her treasures. "Golden girdles, waterfalls of diamonds, ropes of pearls. When she came in and caught me fumbling through her things, I thought she was going to strike me. But she just laughed that tinkling laugh of hers, fished the necklace from the bottom of the chest, and tossed it to me." Arian's voice subsided to a whisper. "She said the worthless trinket was the only inheritance I'd ever receive from my father."

Arian lifted her eyes to find Tristan gazing at her with breathtaking intensity. For an imperceptible instant, his façade cracked, granting her a harrowing glimpse of his own anguish. An anguish that tempted him to believe her, yet refused to let him do so. An anguish that made her ache to reach out to him, even knowing that he would only push her away before she could do his wary heart any more harm.

She didn't have enough fight left in her to flinch when he leaned across the table to cup her cheek in his hand. "Every word that springs from that luscious little mouth of yours is a lie. Warlock has only been missing for ten years, yet you claim your mother stole it from one of her johns before you were even born. Now unless I'm guilty of corrupting the morals of a minor, that's a physical and chronological impossibility."

Arian longed to provide him with a clue to the puzzle, but she had none to give.

His hoarse whisper caressed her numb senses to agonizing life. "I'll give you twenty-four hours. If you haven't provided me with Arthur Finch's current location, I'll press charges for fraud and attempted extortion and have you prosecuted to the full extent of the law."

Arian sat as still as a marble statue, even when Tristan tore open the door to reveal Sven's hulking silhouette. "Take her to the penthouse. She might as well enjoy one last night of luxury at my expense." He spun on his heel, unable to resist a parting shot. "Sweet dreams, Miss Whitewood."

Sven was the only one left to hear her whisper, "Mrs. Lennox."

26

Sven stared straight ahead as the elevator ascended to the penthouse, no longer a bodyguard, but an armed sentinel who would no doubt be monitoring her every move, making sure she did not attempt an escape before the police came to take her away on the morrow.

Arian supposed he must hate her as well. Must believe her some heartless criminal involved in a nefarious plot to destroy his precious employer. Oddly enough, losing the Norwegian's uncomplicated regard struck a final blow to her composure. She was forced to turn her face away and dab at her nose with the train of her gown.

As they stepped off the elevator, Arian's foot snagged in the cumbersome skirt, ripping a delicate row of lace from the hem. She wanted to tear the hateful thing off her body with her bare hands and shred the rumpled satin to tatters. She would never wear white again, she vowed. White, with its deceptive promise of new beginnings and bright tomorrows.

Darkness had fallen and rain lashed at the win-

dows. Lucifer had curled up in the middle of the ottoman, soothed by the arrival of three cases of gourmet
kitten food and a shiny new litter box. As they entered,
he thumped down to the carpet, yawning a welcome,
then trundled over to greet them.

He butted his head against Arian's ankle in a
shameless bid for affection. She knelt to scoop him up,
rubbing his warm, furry body against her cheek.
"There's my sweet little devil," she crooned. "Have you
been lonesome without me? And to think, silly Sven said
black cats were b-b-bad luck." Her voice broke, her
shoulders convulsing with the wracking sobs she'd been
holding in ever since the moment Tristan's gaze had
shifted from suspicion to utter loathing.

She buried her face in the cat's silky fur, unable to
bear Sven's stoic indifference in the face of her grief.
Like Linnet, Tristan had condemned her without a trial.
And she would never be able to forgive him, not in this
lifetime or any other.

The very last thing Arian expected to feel was a big
hand awkwardly stroking her hair.

Copperfield was lying in wait for Tristan when he returned from the lab that night. He followed him through
his office door before Tristan could slam it in his face.
Ignoring his uninvited presence, Tristan went straight to
the bar, poured himself a neat Scotch, and downed it in
one gulp.

He poured himself another and went to the window, drawn by the kindred darkness of the rainy night.

Cop switched on the cozy glow of the desk lamp
and Tristan had to grit his teeth to keep from recoiling
from his reflection. He knew he felt like a savage, wild-
eyed beast. He just hadn't realized how much he resembled one. He abandoned the window, preferring
Copperfield's scrutiny to his own.

Cop eyed him up and down as if he didn't much

like what he saw. Tristan didn't think he could blame him.

His friend's disapproving gaze hovered at the glass gripped in his white-knuckled hand. "I would have thought you'd want a clear head to consider all of this."

Tristan took another generous swallow of the whisky. "The last thing I want is a clear head."

It should have been glaringly apparent that he wasn't fit company for other humans, but Cop propped his hip on the edge of the desk anyway. "Something keeps nagging at me," he confessed. "Why would Arian go to the trouble of contriving such an elaborate lie only to throw in the one element that made it impossible to believe?"

Tristan shrugged. "Maybe she believes it. Maybe Arthur has used Warlock to brainwash her and she's just another of his hapless victims. Maybe I should rush up to the penthouse, fall to bended knee, and beg her forgiveness for doubting her loyalty."

It took Cop a beat longer than usual to realize he was being mocked. He glowered at Tristan. "I'm no scientist, but you admitted yourself that the numbers don't quite add up. That the Warlock you designed would never have been capable of rearranging a human's molecules into a goat's. Or of making an inanimate broom fly."

"Finch has had ten years to bastardize my work," Tristan reminded him. "Ten years to toy with enhancements and modifications. For all we know, the damn thing could make a goat fly."

"What about time travel?"

Tristan shrugged. "We played around with the idea, but never managed to manipulate time by more than a few seconds. What are you suggesting? That Arthur bought himself a one-way ticket to the seventeenth century?"

Copperfield swore beneath his breath. "You won't

even let yourself consider the possibility that Arian might be telling the truth. You're too gutless to—"

Tristan slammed the glass down. Scotch splashed over the rim to drench the stack of unsigned contracts on his leather blotter. "They're carbon-dating the broom even as we speak! I've dispatched researchers to Boston and Gloucester to comb through any seventeenth-century records that might prove or disprove an Arian Whitewood's existence. But you know what? They won't find anything. And you know why? Because she's a heartless, lying witch. She lied about the necklace, she lied about Finch, and she lied when she said she loved me!"

Cop swallowed hard before blurting out, "I want to take Arian to a hotel."

"That's a bit unconventional, isn't it? It is *my* wedding night."

Cop refused to meet his eyes. "You can't just detain her against her will. That's kidnapping."

Tristan sank down in his chair, feeling an eerie composure creep over him, a composure more danger-ous than any of his ranting. He nodded at the phone. "If you think she'd be safer in police custody than with me, why don't you hand me the phone and I'll call them?"

Cop hesitated, then snatched up the receiver and held it out to him. "At least in jail, she'll have some legal rights."

Tristan ignored the offering, his smile ruthlessly pleasant. "Are you planning to defend her?"

Cop slammed the phone back in its cradle. "I'd rather defend her against you than defend you against rape charges."

Tristan's smile didn't flicker, although he stag-gered inwardly from the double blow. The blow of having his best friend think the worst of him and the blow of knowing he was dangerously near to the truth. He'd be a fool not to let Cop bundle Arian into the limo and get her the hell away from the Tower. Away from him.

He opened his mouth to say so. "No. I won't let you take her."

Cop stiffened. "Then my letter of resignation will be on your desk first thing in the morning."

Tristan didn't say anything flippant, didn't pull open the drawer to remind him of all the other times he'd threatened to quit, but hadn't. Throwing his boss one last pained glance, Cop started for the door.

Tristan watched him go, counting his faltering footsteps, watching the second hand on his desk clock sweep away twenty-five years of friendship. The brass hand crept toward the twelve; Copperfield's hand closed over the doorknob.

"Cop?"

Copperfield paused, too proud to beg.

"When Arthur disappeared and I was charged with his murder, you never once asked me if I was guilty. Why not?"

"You were my friend. I figured if you killed him, you had a damn good reason." Cop flashed him a tired ghost of his sunny grin. "I never liked the son of a bitch anyway."

He pulled the door shut behind him, leaving Tristan alone to watch the interminable minutes of his wedding night tick away.

The sky hurled inky gouts of rain against the windows. Thunder rumbled around the Tower like the low-pitched growl of some prowling beast seeking to claw its way into a man's soul. Tristan stood in his darkened office, worshiping the unholy chaos of the storm and sipping Scotch straight from the bottle.

He had thought the whisky might douse the flames raging through his brain. But it only seemed to feed them, sending them shooting higher and higher until the holocaust crackling in his ears threatened to engulf his will, his conscience, and his very sanity.

The clock on his desk read eleven forty-five. In fifteen more minutes, his wedding night would be over. Fifteen minutes with Satan nipping at his heels. Fifteen minutes of sucking smoke and brimstone into his tortured lungs. Fifteen minutes that would last the rest of his miserable, lonely life.

A flash of lightning blinded him, but did not erase the image imprinted on his memory. An image of a rumpled, battered Arian, her eyes darkened by despair, her shoulders slumped in defeat. He took a burning swallow of the liquor, despising himself for pitying her almost as much as he despised himself for still wanting her so badly.

She had dared to look at him as if he'd broken her heart. Dared to make him feel as if he were the one who had deceived and betrayed her.

Eleven-fifty.

Another flash of lightning, this one even more brutal than the last, showed Tristan what might have been instead of what was—he and his bride cuddled beneath the quilts of the king-sized brass bed in the honeymoon suite at the Carlyle; Arian's succulent lips parting to receive fresh strawberries dipped in champagne from his fingertips, her cheeks still flushed in the warm, sweet aftermath of their loving. Tristan swung away from the window to blot out the image, seared by a combustible mix of longing and lust.

Eleven fifty-five.

Arian had cost him everything. His humanity. His pride. His best friend. She'd left him nothing but the white-hot throb of his desire.

Eleven fifty-nine.

Tristan's fist swiped the clock from the desk before it could chime midnight, shattering time with a single swift blow.

*　　*　　*

Sven had locked out the penthouse elevator on the thirteenth floor just as his boss had commanded him to do, but all it took was a deft inputting of Tristan's executive code to send it soaring skyward.

Tristan was already envisioning his bride, her skin pale against the black satin sheets, her supple limbs sprawled in the innocent abandon of sleep. He would slip into the bedroom between flashes of lightning and gently cover her mouth with his own. He had no way of knowing if she would welcome or reject his embrace and no way of knowing if it still mattered to his jaded conscience.

The arriving chime of the elevator was drowned out by a sullen growl of thunder. Navigating the shadows, Tristan stepped over a limp puddle of satin before he realized what it was—Arian's wedding gown, peeled off and discarded like the hollow disguise it had been.

He paused to crush the costly fabric in his fist, his throat tightening at the lingering aroma of orange blossoms and cloves. He'd never wanted anything so badly as he wanted his wife at that moment. Not even revenge.

Letting the gown trickle from his fingers, he padded toward the bedroom and eased open the door. For an elusive instant as he stood there in the dark, he fancied he heard the mellow sound of her breathing, the echo of a wistful sigh.

Lightning flared, its eerie flicker illuminating the room.

The bed was empty. The sheets undisturbed.

Tristan tore through the penthouse in ten seconds flat, activating every door and switching on every lamp until the suite blazed with light. He looked under the bed, then charged for the closet, nearly battering the door down with his fists when it refused to open on the first try.

He kicked over racks of ridiculously expensive leather shoes and tore down entire rods of Armani suits, searching every corner, every shelf, and every crevice large enough to harbor a woman of Arian's size. When his search proved to be in vain, he spun around in the center of the enormous closet, his chest heaving with desperation.

A shelf perched high on the wall caught his eye. He stood on his tiptoes and felt along its length, some instinct already warning him what he would find.

Nothing.

No homely black dress with wilted collar and cuffs. No homely black dress that had made Arian look like an escapee from a witch-hunt reenactment at a quaint Salem inn. The sort of inn that attracted wealthy blue-haired widows and antique-seeking yuppies craving a supernatural thrill.

He staggered out of the closet, wondering if he could have been so terribly wrong. Wondering if Arian hadn't twitched her nose or crossed her arms and blinked herself right out of his wretched life.

As he wandered into the living room, his dazed perusal discovered what his frantic search had not—a panel of drywall propped against the wall like a piece of missing puzzle. It seemed Arian had exited his life by more conventional means than a broom—through his secret escape hatch, up to the roof, and down the express elevator to the street.

Sven, Tristan thought, shaking his head in disbelief. Who would have thought sweet, dumb Sven would have the guts to do what even Copperfield hadn't? Defy his boss's wishes and smuggle Arian to freedom.

A breeze that smelled of rain blew through the gaping hole, sending a scrap of paper fluttering off the coffee table. At first Tristan thought Arian had left him a note. *So long, sucker,* or some other such sentimental farewell scribbled on the back of one of their wedding napkins in her peach-flavored lipstick.

But closer examination revealed that she hadn't left him a note. She'd left him a message.

The million-dollar bank draft in Tristan's hand

bluntly informed him that wherever Arian had fled, she wasn't holed up in some luxury hotel in Arthur Finch's bed, giggling over her husband's gullibility. The check was no longer crisp and new, but worn and creased as if it had meant less than nothing to its temporary owner. A blotchy tearstain smeared the arrogant flourish of his signature.

Tristan sank to his knees on the floor, crumpling the check in his fist. He might have remained that way until his first anniversary if something hadn't butted up against his thigh.

He reached down blindly, encountering the beguiling softness of baby cat fur. The persistent creature began to worry his thumb.

Tristan detached its sharp little teeth before they could draw blood and cupped the tiny kitten in his palm, bringing it to eye level.

"You were her familiar," he said hoarsely. "You were supposed to take care of her."

The kitten retorted with a plaintive mew that sounded suspiciously similar to, *Like hell, bozo. That was your job.*

"Yeah, well, I blew it, too," he confessed.

Tristan rose, cradling the cat against his chest, and wandered to the window to gaze out over the vast and rain-drenched city. Arian was out there somewhere amid the shuffling homeless and street gangs and wailing sirens. Utterly defenseless. Without her magic. Without her cat. Without him.

And he would sell what was left of his worthless soul to find her.

27

"What do you mean you let her go alone? Are you out of your freaking mind?" Grabbing the gigantic Norwegian by the collar of his pajamas, Tristan hoisted him out of his bed and slammed him against the nearest wall.

It had taken Tristan over fifteen hours to trace Sven to this cozy TriBeCa walk-up. Fifteen hours of prowling the city streets in icy drizzle, shoving fliers printed with Arian's bridal portrait into every face he saw—drunk faces, white faces, black faces, sympathetic faces, suspicious faces, apathetic faces, frightened faces, hostile faces. He had attracted the usual share of predators throughout the day—baby-faced kids with fuchsia mohawks, pierced noses, and automatic weapons bulging beneath their leather vests, grizzled vets in camouflage pants with flat, lifeless eyes and needle-scarred arms. They would trail him for a few blocks, nudging each other or their invisible demons and hungrily eyeing his expensive coat, his leather shoes. But something in his unshaven face, something feral and slightly mad, would send them slinking away in search of easier prey.

Arian had been missing for almost twenty-four hours.

Tristan had spent the first three hours on the telephone, shaking down every police captain and precinct chief who'd ever entreated him to sponsor their annual charity ball. He didn't give a damn if he could hear their wives grumbling in the background or if their own muttered oaths changed to poorly suppressed mirth when they learned the billionaire hotshot from Fifth Avenue had *misplaced* his bride. All he gave a damn about was that they get on the phone and roust their grumbling men out of their warm, cozy beds to look for Arian.

Tristan spent three to five A.M. putting his considerable organizational skills to use. He called in most of his own staff, promising them triple overtime for working on Sunday, and helped them assemble and copy a hundred thousand fliers printed with Arian's likeness. He looked away each time a fresh stack emerged from the copy machine, each time he read the mocking words: *Reward for the Safe Return of Arian Lennox—One Million Dollars.*

But even when he'd been assured that half of his dedicated staff was saturating the city with fliers while the other half manned the Tower phones, even when he knew a veritable army of New York's finest was combing the city streets, even when he learned that no one of Arian's description had been admitted to any of the area's hospitals and the poor, strangled brunette lying on a cold slab down at the city morgue was some other man's wife or daughter, it still wasn't enough. So at dawn, when a bitter north wind was already threatening to turn the rain into snow, Tristan had turned up the collar of his coat and ducked out of the Tower on foot without his security detail for the first time in seven years.

Fifteen hours later, he was roughing up his own bodyguard in a bedroom draped in a dizzying array of paisley and chintz. "You just turned her loose? You didn't offer to go with her? To protect her? How could you do such a witless thing?"

Sven hung limp in his boss's grip, too stunned and remorseful to put up even a token protest. "She would not let me go. She said she'd already cost me my job and was afraid you'd send me to jail if you found us together." He hung his shaggy head in shame. "I did not want to lose my green card."

Tristan released him, biting off an oath. "If I hadn't been such a bastard, maybe none of this would have happened." He laughed bitterly. "But I'm damn good at it, you know. I've had a lifetime of practice."

He paced the small room, growing more claustrophobic with each pass. The proliferation of flowers and stripes was making his weary eyes cross. When he spotted the sleek Walther on the bureau, he knew exactly what he'd been looking for. As Tristan drew the gun from its leather holster, Sven threw his hands up, obviously thinking he was done for.

But Tristan simply checked to make sure the gun was loaded, then jammed it into the waistband of his jeans. "You head toward the Lower East Side. I'm going north. She might have sought shelter in the park."

"Sir?" Sven called out meekly as Tristan strode toward the door. "Am I fired?"

"Hell, yes, you're fired!" Tristan barked. "Now get to work!" Sven was still scratching his head, struggling to comprehend this bewildering turn of events when Tristan pivoted on his heel. "One more thing, Nordgard."

"Sir?"

Tristan's smile was almost conciliatory. "The next time you move, would you please take the time to upgrade the address on your personnel file?"

Tristan was already out the door before Sven's mumbled, "Yes, sir," could reach his ears.

* * *

Arian crept out from beneath the wilting hydrangea bush at nightfall to discover her hair had frozen and the icy drizzle had changed to snow. Although the swirling flakes were a vast improvement over the rain, the bitter wind cut through her dress like a blade. She rubbed her eyes, disoriented from sleeping the day through. She would have preferred to have stolen a few hours of sleep the night before, but every time she found a comfortable bench and dozed off, some uniformed man would poke her in the back with a stick and order her to move on.

After fleeing the Tower and wandering the city streets for what seemed like an eternity, Arian had discovered this pastoral haven. She had feared she might be terribly conspicuous in her tattered dress and tangled hair, but there were many others like her in this place. Lost souls wandering aimlessly down the darkened paths, some staggering and muttering to themselves, others pushing wheeled carts crammed with the meager extent of their worldly belongings. One old man huddled beneath a sodden blanket had fixed her with such a piteous look that she had knelt and pressed the wad of green bills Sven had given her into his palsied hand.

Some instinct told her there was nothing to fear from these kindred spirits. They, like herself, had been betrayed and abandoned by those they believed in the most.

The ones she feared were the ones who watched her from the darkness with sharp predator's eyes. The stealthy ones, who stalked her through the shadows, moving only when she did until the arrival of another surly officer would send them scurrying for cover, the predator becoming the prey. Those were the ones who had driven Arian under the hydrangea bush, forcing her to burrow beneath the fallen leaves like some small, frightened animal until sleep claimed her exhausted body.

She stretched as she emerged from her nest, but the motion failed to thaw her rusty joints. The sound of cantering hoofbeats, so woefully out of place in this harried century, made her heart beat a trifle bit faster. She barely had time to jump out of the way before a mounted patrolman went galloping past.

She stared after him, thinking he might be the same officer who had introduced her to his beloved Bathsheba.

He drew hard on his reins, wheeling his mount in a prancing circle. Pointing a black-gloved finger right at her, he shouted, "Hey, you there! Freeze!"

Beneath his helmet, he was just another stranger, no different from any of the others who had harassed her throughout the night. Since she was already freezing, Arian turned and fled, seeking the shelter of the towering trees. Hugging herself, she raced down the nearest path, weary of shadows and longing for the mundane comforts of lights and people.

It didn't take her long to emerge on another bustling city street. People rushed past, bumping and jostling her as if she were invisible, the collars of their heavy woolen coats turned up against the biting sting of the snow. They weren't like the people in the park. They obviously had somewhere warm and dry to go.

Their rudeness and apathy jarred Arian. When she had walked the streets on Tristan's arm, it was as if he had cast an invisible shield of protection around them both, forcing others to keep a polite distance or suffer the consequences.

But that magical shield had been withdrawn, she reminded herself bitterly, and the sooner she reconciled herself to its loss, the better off she would be.

The aroma of roasting meat drifted to Arian's nose, making her nostrils twitch and her mouth water with yearning. She hadn't realized how hungry she was until that very moment.

She followed the delectable smell to its source only to have her spirits plunge when a man poked his head out the window of a big silver wagon and bellowed, "Hot dogs! Git yer fresh dogs here!"

She watched steam waft off the fat sausages while her hollow stomach argued with her sensibilities, understanding for the first time why it was the poor who considered cat such a delicacy. Perhaps it was a good thing she had left Lucifer in the haven of the penthouse.

Arian had to stand on tiptoe to peer into the window of the wagon. "Excuse me, sir. Might I have a"—she could not quite suppress a tiny shudder—"sausage?"

Grease drizzled from the thing as he slapped it on a split roll. "That'll be three fifty."

Arian stared up at him blankly.

He leaned out the window, eyeing her ragged dress and the scuffed maid's shoes she had once worn to Bloomingdale's with a cynical eye. "Damn leeches," he muttered. "I'm sick of the whole lot of you. I'm already supporting your deadbeat generation with my hard-earned tax money and you still have the nerve to come begging for food. Hell, you probably make more bilking the government out of your welfare check than I do trying to make an honest living."

Arian began to back away from the wagon. She wasn't sure what she'd done to incense the man, but his already florid face was turning an alarming shade of scarlet.

"Go on!" he shouted. "Get the hell out of here! And while you're at it, get a job!" He punctuated his tirade by slamming down the wagon window, climbing into the front of the vehicle and racing off, gunning the motor so hard Arian was nearly smothered by billowing blue clouds of exhaust.

"Well!" she exclaimed, when she could strangle out a breath. "He shouldn't go around offering hot dogs to strangers if he's going to be so stingy about giving them away."

With a pathetic flounce of her wilted skirts, she

turned in the opposite direction and marched down the sidewalk, her ire increasing with each step. Her hunger only worsened her mood, and before she realized it, she had worked herself into quite a fine temper. And made an intriguing discovery.

Moping about feeling sorry for herself had only intensified her shivers, but being furious with the rest of the world invigorated her. Her face was aglow with heat, her fingers tingling with delicious warmth. She clomped along through the deepening snow, cursing hot dog vendors, the Reverend Linnet, Wite Lize, her anonymous papa, and every other faithless man born since the beginning of time. She hated them, she decided, but she hated her husband most of all. She hated him so much she nearly lost the rhythm of her stride and fell down.

She quickly discovered another benefit of her mounting wrath. As long as she was stomping and muttering beneath her breath, her face screwed into a fierce scowl, people tended to give her a wide berth. A few of them even went so far as to cross the street to avoid her. Their cowardice gave her a particularly savage satisfaction.

She traveled in that manner for several blocks, so lost in her vehement musings that she never noticed the decreasing crowds, the scattered gunfire, the perpetual wailing of the sirens, or the fact that most of the street lamps along the narrow avenue had been shot or broken out. But she could not ignore the bass throb of the music assaulting her ears. She paused, frowning. At least she thought it was music. There was no hint of melody, just an incessant beat, so deep and profound it shuddered the soles of her shoes.

The music seemed to be emanating from a dimly lit storefront with blacked-out windows and a lighted sign that read Woodrow's. At least Arian assumed it was supposed to read Woodrow's. Both *w*'s and an *r* had burned out, leaving a sputtering *oodo*'s in its place. It wasn't the exotic beat that lured her in, nor the enticing promise of shelter and warmth. It was the unmistakable aroma of roasting pork. Not dog, not cat, but pork. Already envisioning a steaming boar's head with a juicy red apple propped in its mouth, she pushed open the splintery door.

Arian could not have known what a sight she made. She stood framed by the swirling snow like an alabaster idol of a voodoo queen, her hair frozen into icy dreadlocks that would have been the envy of any Rastafarian.

A tense finger stabbed the button on a rectangular black box. The music stopped dead and everyone in the smoke-hazed room swiveled around to gape at her.

The lighting was so murky it took Arian nearly a minute of frenzied blinking to realize that every face regarding her with such an alarming mix of disbelief and hostility was a different shade of brown.

28

When Tristan burst through the ramshackle door of the Harlem club, gun in hand, the last thing he expected to find was his wife sitting next to a young black youth, picking out Motown tunes with one dainty finger on an old upright piano. Her other hand was occupied with what appeared to be the remnants of an entire rack of barbecued ribs.

Their eyes met, hotly, briefly, before she plunked out an off-key chord, dismissing him as if he weren't risking limb and life by charging into this Harlem dive to rescue her from God-only-knew what gruesome fate.

It was all Tristan could do to keep from groaning aloud when the lanky young man unfolded himself from the bench. His oversized khaki jacket sported the colors of one of New York's most dreaded street gangs. Two of his compatriots rose to flank him, folding their arms over their scrawny chests in deceptive repose while others watched from the smoky shadows, their eyes shining with wariness.

Their commander's intelligent gaze flicked to the

Walther, then back to Tristan's face. He sighed and
rolled his eyes, as if it were nothing out of the ordinary
for some wild-eyed, wealthy white man in Bruno Magli
shoes and a Burberry coat to bust into his establishment,
waving an antique automatic weapon. Expecting a bullet
to tear through his flesh at any minute, Tristan kept the
gun leveled at the kid's heart.

"Hey, man, chill out," the youth drawled in a soothing baritone. "We don't want no trouble here."

"I don't want any trouble, either. I just want my
wife."

The kid cast a puzzled glance over his shoulder.
"He your pimp?"

"No," Arian admitted sullenly, sucking one of the
ribs clean. "He's my husband."

Tristan's fierce relief at finding her was eclipsed by
a flare of irritation. Although damp and bedraggled, she
looked both well rested and well fed, two qualities that
had eluded him for more than thirty-six hours. As the
tantalizing aroma of barbecue wafted to his nose, his
stomach rumbled a protest at the injustice of it all. Fighting to hold the gun steady, he ran a hand over his haggard face, feeling hungry enough to eat an entire pig.
Raw.

"Arian," he croaked. "I'd like to take you home
now."

The budding Sir Galahad stepped between them.
"Don't hassle the lady, man. She don't have to go nowhere she don't want to." Another worried glance at his
lady fair. "He ain't a cop, is he, honey?"

Tristan held his breath, knowing that if Arian mis-
understood the question and said yes, she was about to
become a very wealthy widow. A lone cop in this particular section of Harlem was a dead cop.

She finished off the last rib and tossed it over her
shoulder. "No. He's a heartless wretch."

Tristan could not argue that point. As her cham-
pion drew an Uzi out from beneath his jacket and leveled

it at Tristan's head, he understood why the self-assured youth had looked less than intimidated by the Walther. "You want me to shoot him?"

Arian licked the dripping sauce from her fingers. She actually seemed to be considering the offer. Her brow finally puckered in a crestfallen scowl. "I suppose not."

Galahad shrugged and tucked the Uzi back into his jacket. Tristan took that as a cue to lower his own weapon. "Please, Arian. Come with me."

She rose from the bench, her dark eyes reflecting a bewildering array of emotions—longing, resentment, wariness. "Where are you taking me? Jail?"

This time the weapons emerged with a minimum of clatter, an Uzi or shiny Tec-9mm in the hand of every youth in the room.

Galahad looked distinctly sulky. "I thought you said he wasn't a cop."

Arian shoved the barrel of his Uzi aside with chilling disregard. "He's not. He doesn't want to take *you* to jail. Only me."

Ignoring the impressive arsenal, Tristan stretched out a hand toward his wife. "What I want is to take you home."

Arian took one reluctant step toward him, then another. Before she could change her mind, Tristan drew off his coat and swept it around her shoulders, realizing as he did so that her dress and hair weren't damp. They were soaked.

"You take care of her," young Galahad warned. "She's a little . . ." He tapped his temple in the universal symbol for "daft" before breaking into a broad grin that made him look even younger than the seventeen years old he probably was. "A few more piano lessons and I'd have had her doing a mean 'Tears of a Clown.' "

Grateful to the bighearted kid for far more than just not blowing his head off, Tristan reached for his back pocket only to realize he'd left his wallet back at the Tower. He eyed the youth's scuffed Army boots. "What size do you wear?"

Caught off guard by the question, he blurted out, "Ten."

Tristan reached down, tugged off his loafers and tossed them across the room. "They cost me five hundred dollars. If you can't wear them, you can always sell them. And if you ever need a job, come to Lennox Enterprises on Fifth Avenue and ask for Mr. Lennox. I could use someone like you in Security." He smiled wryly. "Or Legal."

Tucking Arian beneath his arm, Tristan guided her toward the door. She turned her earnest face up to him. "Did you know that all of these charming young Negro lads are freemen? Isn't that extraordinary?"

Tristan winced, hastening their steps, but the gang members only laughed, plainly more bemused than offended by her politically incorrect assessment.

As soon as they were out the door, Tristan grabbed her hand and began to run.

They had to run nearly a dozen blocks, the wet snow crunching beneath Tristan's socks, before they encountered a gypsy cabbie bold or stupid enough to cruise the fringes of Harlem after dark.

Tristan's possessive grip on Arian did not relent, not even when they were settled into a back seat that had spilled out more foam rubber than it had ever held. After peeling off his wet socks and stamping his frozen feet to restore feeling to them, he hauled her against his side, ignoring her wiggle of protest.

Arian hated to admit it, but she was actually grateful for the arm that bound her to Tristan's seductive warmth. Although the cab's ancient heater was roaring full blast, Arian could still see her breath. Her chill was returning with a vengeance to wrack her with helpless shivers. Tristan drew her even closer and she accepted his unspoken invitation to rest her cheek against his sweater-clad chest and warm her icy hands between his own.

"How did you f-f-find me?" she forced out between her chattering teeth.

"A cop in the park spotted you and said he thought you were heading north. It wasn't too terribly hard to track you," he added dryly. "There aren't that many Puritans in Harlem."

Arian cast his face a searching look, but his set features revealed less than nothing.

Traffic wasn't heavy on a Sunday night and they arrived at the front door of the Tower within minutes. The doorman rushed from his post to throw open the cab door, his face shielded from the cold by a heavy muffler.

"Pay the cabbie," Tristan ordered, whisking Arian past him and through the revolving doors to the lobby.

"Yes, sir! Whatever you wish!" the doorman called after them, tossing off a mocking salute. No one but the apathetic cabbie saw the malicious twinkle in his rheumy blue eyes.

By the time they reached the penthouse bedroom, Arian's shivers had deepened to shudders. She staggered beneath a flurry of sneezes. Fighting to maintain his usual brisk efficiency, Tristan whipped his coat from her shoulders only to discover her sodden dress was clinging to her skin like an icy shroud.

A pang of dismay seized him. Never had he so regretted not being able to offer her any of the trite, homey comforts he had so stubbornly denied himself. What good were the frivolous luxuries of silk pajamas and satin sheets to a body chilled to the bone? He wanted to button Arian into a long flannel nightgown, wrap her in a cozy quilt, and rock her to sleep on his lap in front of a roaring fire.

Brushing the snowflakes from his own damp hair,

he prowled the bedroom, seeking solutions and compromises.

Arian watched him, her apprehensive gaze reminding him that they had resolved nothing. A wall of mistrust still stood between them. But at that precise moment, Tristan didn't give a damn. He only wanted to make her stop shivering.

Suddenly inspired, he strode into the bathroom and wrenched on both faucets of the sunken whirlpool tub. Hot water poured out in steaming gouts. Fearing the harsh fluorescents might sting Arian's weary eyes, he dug several stubby candles out of the linen closet, lit them, and placed them around the tub's marble rim.

When he returned to the bedroom, Arian was fumbling with the buttons of her bodice, her fingers too stiff with cold to be very effective. Tristan eased them aside and took over the task, peeling the wet fabric from her shoulders. It wasn't until her small hand closed fiercely over his that he realized she wore no bra.

"It's all right," he said softly, gazing deep into her eyes. "I am your husband."

The argument didn't sound convincing, even to him, since he'd certainly done nothing to earn the privilege. But she relented anyway, allowing him to proceed. By the time he'd breached the last of the copious buttons and drawn the wet garment over her head, his own hands were shaking with want.

Gazing upon her unadorned flesh, it wasn't such a stretch of the imagination to believe she did not belong in his mundane realm of cellular phones and fax machines. With her damp curls tumbling about her face and her eyes burning with fierce pride, she possessed an ethereal, almost otherworldly beauty. She was part witch and part faerie, the sort of enchanted creature one expected to find perched on top of a mushroom or emerging from the heart of some exotic bloom, her milky skin glistening with nectar.

Tristan swallowed hard, his earlier hunger

eclipsed by a far more primal desire to make love to his bride.

But Arian was still trembling. More with shyness now than cold.

Tristan swept her up in his arms and carried her to the bathroom, allowing himself only the brief, guilty thrill of holding her naked body against his clothed one. He tested the temperature of the water before lowering her into the tub and turning off the faucets.

Arian sank into the steaming water and just kept going, her groan of innocent pleasure intensifying the pulsing warmth centered in Tristan's groin. She disappeared inch by voluptuous inch, submerging her slender waist, the generous swell of her breasts, her creamy shoulders, and finally her dark, tousled head.

Tristan was thinking he might have to dive in after her, and was rather relishing the prospect when she emerged, shaking water out of her eyes like an exuberant seal.

She flashed him a grateful smile that made his heart thunder in his ears like a kettledrum. "I didn't think I'd ever be warm again."

Tristan wasn't warm. He was hot.

Arian heaved a contented sigh as she leaned her head back against the rim of the tub and closed her eyes. The candles bathed her with flickering light and perfumed the air with the intoxicating scent of jasmine. The steam coaxed out pearls of sweat along the column of her throat and drew her hair into taut ringlets. The water lapped at the pale globes of her breasts just as Tristan longed to do.

When Arian opened her eyes, her husband was dragging his sweater over his head.

Arian had never before seen a man without his shirt. No matter how scorching the summer day, how grueling the task at hand, no Puritan male would ever consider removing his shirt in her presence. 'Twould have been judged as unseemly as stripping naked in the village square.

She could hardly squeal in maidenly indignation while frolicking about in his bath like a wanton mermaid, but she found it wildly unfair that Tristan's brazen display should leave her feeling even more exposed than her nudity. Surely he could hear each violent throb of her heart, each curious catch of her breath as her gaze was drawn as if magnetized to the crisp, golden whorls of hair adorning his chest.

"Sweet Jesu," she muttered, fearing steam was now roiling from her flaming cheeks.

Her blush deepened when Tristan's hand dropped to the button at the mouth of his jeans. Arian jerked her panicked gaze to his face. His eyes captured hers, their smoky depths glittering with an unspoken challenge she'd heard from a priest's lips only a day ago.

Speak now or forever hold your peace.

As he lowered the zipper and peeled the faded denim from his flesh, Arian could not have choked so much as a croak past her parched lips, much less a virginal protest. Her husband had been blessed with the face of a fallen angel and the body of a pagan satyr. Her exhaustion imparted a dreamlike quality to the entire scenario—one of those naughty dreams where she would wake up drenched with sweat and quivering with delicious anticipation.

As Tristan slipped into the water like a sleek merman, she clenched her eyes shut, a violent wave of shyness forcing her to pretend she was still alone.

But her fantasy did not withstand the moist, hot brush of her husband's lips against her own. When she opened her eyes, he was drawing her into the cradle of his legs, turning her so that her back rested against his chest. The lean, hard angles of his body were utterly foreign, yet fit her soft curves like fingers in a velvet glove. The water enveloped them in a warm cocoon as he reached for the sandalwood-scented soap.

Arian had expected to be punished for running away, not pampered, but Tristan bathed her like a cherished child, beguiling her with a tenderness that was almost chaste.

Almost.

He scooped handfuls of water over her breasts, then ran the hard, slick bar of soap over and between them with hypnotic grace until her rigid nipples glistened.

He poured shampoo into her hair, massaged her scalp until it tingled, then rinsed out the foamy lather by coaxing her to brace her weight against his own and float in the buoyant water. Arian could have drifted in that heavenly state for an eternity, especially with Tristan nibbling at the delicate skin of her throat.

Gently urging her to her knees, he washed her back, belly, and thighs, kneading her weary muscles until she felt the lingering tension drain from her body, leaving her blissfully relaxed—a limp, melting creature, utterly acquiescent to his touch.

Arian tossed back her hair in mingled shock and delight when he rubbed the softening cake of soap between her legs, lavishing the same tender attention on each hidden cleft and hollow. Lost in a haze of sensual pleasure, she barely noticed when the soap dwindled to nothing and Tristan's hands took up the erotic dance.

He glided them up her soap-slickened sides to cup her breasts from behind and below. Nipping the back of her neck in an age-old sign of mastery, he rolled her turgid nipples between thumb and forefinger, stroking gently and tugging hard until she felt every caress of his fingertips deep in her womb. Her broken gasps escalated into pants. Her back arched and her rump rose in primitive invitation, almost as if her body were begging for something only he could give.

But instead of taking advantage of her mounting need, he buried his face in her throat and whispered,

"It's all right, angel. This isn't a limo and we've got all night."

She turned her face toward his, blindly seeking, and he rewarded her with a hot, deep thrust of his tongue. "Does the tub have an extra gas tank?" she murmured.

She could feel his rakish smile against her cheek. "No. But I do."

He had somehow managed to work his muscular thighs between hers, so when he spread them, he spread her, too, exposing her throbbing core to every nuance of his touch. But he used only the middle finger of one hand to ignite that raw spark of pleasure sheltered by her nether curls, leaving the hollow below aching and unfulfilled.

As he intensified that exquisite friction, making her writhe with want, Arian struggled to remember that they were married. That all of this sensual decadence was perfectly legal and sanctioned by God. But it still seemed as if anything that felt this good must surely be a sin.

"Oh, please," she begged, teetering on the brink of ecstasy. She nearly sobbed aloud when her plea had the opposite effect. His finger slowed, stroking her with deliberate nonchalance.

"If I do, will you let me . . . ?" He pressed his mouth to her ear, whispering a suggestion so dark and evocative it brought a blush stinging to her cheeks.

Both shocked and aroused, she thrashed her head from side to side, then nodded helplessly. She would have promised him her heart, her soul, her first-born child, if he would just cease his diabolical torment.

He urged her back to that brink, then teased her to an abrupt halt again. "And then can I . . . ?"

Before he could even finish, she shouted, "Yes! Yes! But I don't think that's physically possible."

His chuckle was wickedness itself. "Oh, yeah? Just wait and see."

He leaned past her to flip on the whirlpool's jets. The warm water swirled and eddied around them as Tristan urged her nearer to one of the silver nozzles. Arian gasped as invisible tongues of water began to lick her throbbing flesh. When she might have recoiled, Tristan pressed himself against her from behind, the unyielding breadth of his big, warm body forcing her to sample every morsel of pleasure he would give her.

Arian could no longer tell where the water ended and Tristan's fingers began. They were both ravishing her with exquisite thoroughness, opening her like a flower to stroke forth the nectar within. She twitched with impending ecstasy, wondering if this was what it felt like to fornicate with a demon. To be enthralled by some powerful, invisible entity capable of stealing her mortal soul with his unholy kiss.

But Tristan was no demon. He was a warlock, weaving a spell of intolerable pleasure. When the first enchanting shudders wracked her body, he wrapped an arm around her waist and drove himself deep inside of her, filling a void she had never known was there.

Arian knew there was tightness and pain, but that pain was eclipsed by a pleasure so poignant, so intense, it seemed to sweep everything else out of its path. She moved against him in instinctive rhythm, her breath escaping in a strangled sob.

Tristan cradled Arian in his arms, binding her to his heart while he waited for her tender body to adjust to his crude invasion. He already knew he could be making a grave mistake. Arian wasn't the sort of woman to come equipped with a package of condoms and his wallet was in his office eighty-two floors below. But he'd never been skin-to-skin with any woman in his life and despised the thought of interrupting this indescribably sweet communion. And besides, Arian wasn't just any woman. She was his wife. Which he hoped excused, or at least explained, his dark and primal urge to spill his seed in her.

Both reason and conscience deserted him when she wiggled against him with a soft little grunt. An answering groan tore from his throat as he accepted her unspoken invitation to plunge himself deep into her tight, silky depths, then to withdraw and do it all over again. As that ancient rhythm seized them both in its irresistible grip, he braced his hands against the rim of the tub on each side of her, letting those pulsing jets of water work their own sorcery against their mated flesh. Arian's cry of surrender came a breath before his own as ecstasy thundered through them both, bewitching them with its raw and miraculous power.

He was doing it again. Taking care of her. Lifting her from the tub and depositing her on the plush rug. Choosing the thickest, fluffiest towel from the towel warmer and buffing her skin until it glowed. Arian sighed, drunk with languor. The water seemed to have soothed away any soreness she might have suffered, leaving an almost pleasurable tenderness in its place. She had even lost most of her shyness. Their nakedness, as husband and wife, somehow seemed both natural and right.

As Tristan dried her back, lingering at the rounded curves of her buttocks and the valley between them, she giggled. "We were in the bath so long, you'd think we'd be all withered up like prunes."

But when she turned around, her husband's wicked smile informed her plainly that that was not the case. She lowered her gaze, then desperately wished that she hadn't as her shyness returned with an almost audible thud.

"Oh, my!" she exclaimed. "You're not withered up at all!"

When he chose a fresh towel from the warmer, Arian thought he was going to cover himself. But instead he spread it on the carpet like a blanket of rose petals.

"Lie down," he commanded, a laughing glint in his eye.

Arian backed away. "Now, Tristan, I don't know what depravity you're contemplating . . ."

"You promised," he reminded her, his sensual mouth betraying the hint of a sulk.

Arian frowned. "I did?"

He nodded solemnly.

Arian searched her dazed brain for a clue, finally remembering that moment of weakness when she'd begged him to release her from her torment. "Oh!" she cried. "You can't mean to . . . ?"

He did.

At first Arian thought there was nothing so terribly depraved about the provocative kisses he was scattering along her breasts and belly. But that was before his hands gently urged her thighs apart. Before his tousled, golden head disappeared between her legs. Ignoring her shy moan of dissent, that devilish tongue of his whipped her into a frenzy of delight.

When she once again lay limp, sated, and totally at his mercy, he lifted her in his arms. She wrapped her legs around his hips and laid her head against his shoulder as he carried her not to the bed, but the shower. They kissed endlessly beneath the twin shower heads, the hot water coursing over their entwined bodies generating clouds of steam.

It was there, sheltered by that billowing veil, that Arian found the courage to reciprocate some of that blinding pleasure Tristan had so selflessly given her.

When she turned him away from her, urging him to splay his hands against the frosted-glass door, he cocked a suspicious eyebrow, but did not protest. His protest came when she pressed her naked breasts to his back and reached around him to leisurely rub a fresh bar of soap over every inch of his magnificent body. Her eager hands celebrated the differences between them, discovering that his muscular thighs and calves were sprinkled with the same tawny down as his chest and arms. When the bar of soap slipped from her hand, leaving only her fingers to shyly stroke that part of him still stiffened with need for her, he threw his head back with a guttural groan.

God, how she loved this man, Arian thought fiercely. She would do anything for him. Let him do anything to her.

Driven by a primitive urge to prove her pledge, she set him free from his bondage and dropped to her knees before him.

As Tristan watched Arian's generous lips enfold him, he thought the sheer erotic beauty of it just might drive him insane with pleasure. He tangled his fingers in her hair, but could only bear a brief eternity of such exquisite torment before he was compelled to cup her buttocks in his powerful hands and take her hard and fast against the wall of the shower stall.

When the last sweet, shuddering aftershock had passed, he gathered her against him as if he would never let her go, and hoarsely whispered, "That, my darling, was magic."

29

When Copperfield burst into the bedroom the next day without bothering to knock, Tristan simply groaned, rolled to his stomach, and burrowed his head beneath his pillow. Arian sat bolt upright, blushing to the roots of her hair, and tried to jerk the satin sheet up to her nose. Unfortunately, most of its sinuous length was wrapped around Tristan's lean hips, and she barely succeeded in shielding her breasts.

"Good morning, Arian," Cop said cheerily, as if not the least bit surprised by her presence or her nudity.

"Good morning," she squeaked, still tugging vainly at the sheet.

He pried the pillow off Tristan's head. "Wake up, sleepyhead. This is no time to lollygag in bed all day."

Only one of Tristan's eyes was visible, but its bloodshot depths glared murder at him. "Didn't I fire you?"

"No. I quit."

"Then you're fired." He retrieved the pillow, but Cop snatched it right back, his bronze face glowing with excitement.

"I need you both in the lab right away. I think I've found the key to proving Arian's innocence."

That lured Tristan to a sitting position. He shot Arian a wary glance that only deepened her blush. He had already proved her innocence with devastating success—at least in one area.

Cop jerked his head toward the bathroom. "I'll wait in the living room while you two shower."

They both blushed at that, neither wanting to be the first to meet the other's eyes.

"That won't be necessary," Tristan growled. "We'll be right there."

Peeling back the sheet, he threw his legs over the side of the bed and staggered into the bathroom, as unabashed in his nakedness as Michelangelo's *David*. Arian dragged the sheet *over* her head.

Cop beamed down at her shrouded form. "I really should have warned you. He's an awful grump until he's had his first eight cups of coffee."

The inner sanctum of Tristan's lab was exactly as Arian remembered it. White. Sterile. Deserted. She wryly noted that the hole she'd blasted in the floor with her amateur lightning bolt had been repaired.

She had forsaken the colorful suits Tristan had bought her when they were engaged in favor of black leggings and a black cowl sweater. If she was still on trial, then she wanted to look the part. The image of accused witch was complete, all the way down to the black cat nestled in the crook of her arm. Tristan's stormy glower warned her that he wasn't completely oblivious to her symbolism.

Cop thrust a cup of steaming coffee into Tristan's hand before shepherding them over to a long counter built to double as an impromptu conference table. Arian was only mildly surprised to find Sven admiring his reflection in the shiny countertop.

Tristan scowled at him. "Didn't I fire you?"

Sven snapped to attention, brushing back his silky mane. "Yes, sir."

"Good. Then you're hired."

Arian sat, depositing the sleeping kitten in her lap. Tristan nursed his coffee while Cop paced around the counter, obviously too excited to sit still. It was precisely that excess of nervous energy that made Arian suspect he must have had even less sleep than she and Tristan in the past forty-eight hours.

"When I got back to my loft the other night," he said, "I couldn't concentrate and I couldn't sleep. So I finally came back to the Tower and forced Montgomery to let me monitor his experiments on the amulet."

Tristan took another sip of the coffee. "That's what I get for not making you turn in your ID badge. I would have ordered Sven to toss you out on your ear, but he was too busy playing knight in shining armor to my runaway bride."

They all three glared at him and he subsided, gazing sulkily into his coffee.

Copperfield slapped a thin folder down in front of him. "Here are Montgomery's results."

Tristan opened the folder and examined its contents. It didn't take long. His disgruntled expression revealed his frustration. "There's nothing here. The carbon dating on both the necklace and the broom yielded inconclusive results. My researchers in Massachusetts are being forced to sift through three centuries of obscure documents, most of them too fragile to be handled by human hands. There's absolutely nothing here to prove"—he spared Arian a cautious glance—"anything."

Cop leaned over his shoulder to tap the bottom of the page. "Except for this."

Tristan read, " 'The microprocessor was encased in an unidentified alloy . . . ' " He cast Copperfield a helpless glance. "So?"

"Gordon Montgomery has memorized the chemi-

cal formulas of every alloy known to man. If he can't
identify it, then it hasn't been discovered yet."

Tristan rose and began to pace in a counterclock-
wise circle. Arian grew dizzy each time his path bisected
Copperfield's. She shifted in her chair, eliciting a sleepy
grunt of protest from Lucifer.

"So you're suggesting this alloy could only be from
the future," Tristan said.

"Precisely! And if Arthur Finch could travel to the
future, then he could travel—"

"To the past," Tristan finished for him. They both
wheeled around, meeting face-to-face.

Arian's heart began to whisper a melody of hope,
but she still felt compelled to remind them of the theory's failings. "That doesn't explain how my mother could
have stolen Warlock from Arthur Finch twenty years
ago."

Copperfield held up a finger, riveting them all.
"Not twenty years. Three hundred and twenty-eight
years. Use your imagination, Tristan. It may be a little
rusty, but I know you used to have one."

Tristan sank back into his chair, rubbing his unshaven chin.

Cop said, "Suppose Arthur traveled to sixteen
sixty-nine ten years ago, lost Warlock to some irate
hooker he'd stiffed for the bill—sorry, Arian—then
spent the next twenty years searching for it."

"Would it have taken him that long to locate this
woman? Or her child?" Tristan asked.

Cop nodded. "Possibly. You have to remember that
this was before the days of mass communication. He
couldn't exactly slap her picture on a milk carton. And
at the time of their encounter, she wasn't some re-
nowned courtesan. She was simply a common—"

"Whore," Arian gently provided.

Cop winced. "I sincerely doubt that Arthur wanted
to draw attention to himself by reporting the theft to the
local authorities."

Tristan nodded, conceding the point and encouraging Cop to continue.

"Even if Arthur had found the necklace, that wouldn't mean he would have had to return to the present exactly twenty years after he left. He could have programmed Warlock to deliver him right back to nineteen eighty-five. He'd be twenty years older, but you'd still be that same shy, gullible boy. Or he could travel back to nineteen sixty-three and prevent you from ever being born."

Arian shuddered and Tristan reached across the table to take her hand.

Cop's gaze drifted between the two of them, his voice losing its edge as if to lessen the impact of the coming blow. "If Arthur's been stuck in the seventeenth century for twenty years, his daughter has had ample time to come of age."

Daughter.

The word had such a grim finality to it. Tristan kept hold of her hand while he studied her face as if searching for some elusive hint of his old friend. It was not a pleasant feeling. Although Arian had entertained frequent fantasies about the father she'd never met, she could derive little comfort at the prospect of being the daughter of a man her husband despised.

When Tristan drew back his hand, her heart did a painful little backflip.

He looked at Copperfield, then at Sven. "Would you please excuse us?" The men filed out quietly, leaving them alone.

Arian was the first to break the awkward silence. "Did you find a family resemblance? If you'd like, you can check beneath my hair for horns."

Tristan offered her a ghost of a smile. "If you were hiding a forked tail, I think I would have noticed it last night."

"I'm not so sure about that."

He simply gazed at her, all that had passed between them in that misty bathroom darkening his eyes.

She sifted her fingers through Lucifer's silky fur. Keeping her voice light was becoming more of a struggle. "Copperfield failed to point out the obvious. If I am Arthur's daughter, isn't there a chance that I've been in league with him all along?"

"Have you?"

Arian had wanted Tristan to laugh, to scoff aloud at the ridiculous notion, not fix her with that level stare of his and ask her the one question she should never have had to answer.

She bowed her head, no longer knowing if last night had been about love, revenge, or magic. Even if she still possessed the amulet, there was no spell to make Tristan believe in her, no spell to erase the shadow of suspicion from his eyes. His trust would have to be given freely. She would not beg for it.

Scooping Lucifer into her arms, she rose to her feet.

Tristan's face betrayed his bewildered anguish as he reached across the table and caught her hand, his grip rough with desperation. "I need time, Arian. Can you just give me a little time to get used to the idea?"

Arian smiled down at him through a veil of tears. "Take all the time you need. I've certainly got more than I can use."

She gently withdrew her hand and slipped from the room, feeling Tristan's tortured gaze follow her every move.

Arian huddled on the settee, her fingers buried in Lucifer's soft fur, and watched the shadows of twilight creep across the living room. The salad Sven had sent up nearly two hours ago sat untouched on the coffee table.

She'd never felt more like a prisoner, not even when she'd been jailed in that tiny shed in Gloucester.

She could not bear to go into the bedroom with its rumpled sheets that smelled of Tristan's cologne and the leisurely spell of loving they'd shared at dawn. The bathroom was even worse with its scattering of damp towels and evocative memories.

Cruel doubts spun and darted through her mind, torturing her. What if Tristan didn't come? What if his loathing for Arthur Finch was stronger than his love for her? What if he would never be able to look at her without seeing the echo of Arthur's sneer in her smile? Perhaps he feared spending the rest of his life casting her sidelong glances, wondering when she was going to plunge the knife into his back.

It would not be easy for him, she knew. He had never trusted anyone completely, not even himself. And she was asking him to trust her with a treasure so precious and fragile he'd been hoarding it ever since his mother had left him on the steps of that orphanage—his heart.

Arian reached automatically for the amulet as she had done so often in times of trouble. Her hand closed on empty air. The emerald was gone, but if she had learned anything in the past few weeks, it was that the world was brimming with magic.

Not the superficial sort of magic children dreamed of with wish-granting genies popping out of bottles and lonely beasts turned into princes by a kiss, but a magic born of true love and hope for the morrow and the grudging smile of a man to whom smiles did not come easily.

Bowing her head and squeezing her eyes shut, Arian wished, harder than she'd ever wished when she was a little girl. She no longer wanted to summon some noble prince to her arms, but simply a man with all of his flaws and strengths.

Her man.

The elevator chimed. Arian jerked her head up, almost daring to believe it the tolling of some celestial bell. Her heart soared in anticipation as she settled Lucifer on the pillows and jumped to her feet.

She was at the elevator doors before they could even begin to part, wanting the first thing Tristan saw to be her welcoming smile.

She was still hovering there, that tender smile trembling on her lips, when Sven's limp body rolled over her feet.

Tristan was standing in the courtyard when the feeling of utter calm came stealing over him. He had been standing there for a long time, hands in pockets, gazing at the ice-clotted fountain, yet feeling no cold. It was so quiet he could hear the snow falling, each flake muffled against the ermine cloak spread over the courtyard. The serene silence gave the desolate wonderland the air of a tomb, a paradise fallen.

One minute, he was trapped in a vise of indecision, the next, all his doubts were banished, his fears soothed. His spirits rose, free to soar for the first time in a decade.

He adored his wife. She adored him. They would work out the rest. It didn't matter if Arian was a time-traveling Puritan or Vlad Dracula's daughter. All he knew was that he wanted to spend the rest of his life proving his faith in her.

He threw back his shoulders, brushing the snow from them. He would bundle Arian into the limo tonight, he decided with a smile. He would offer his chauffeur the rest of the week off and drive her to Connecticut himself. He would book a room at some rustic country inn and give her the honeymoon she had always deserved. Perhaps if the snow thawed and their cozy bed didn't prove an insurmountable enticement, they would even go out hunting for land. Surely together they could find a little chunk of heaven to build their dreams upon.

He turned toward the bank of glass elevators, desperately eager to join his bride.

Cop stood there, clutching a cordless phone in his white-knuckled hand. Tristan's own heart seized up at the sight of his friend's bloodless face.

Cop held the phone out to him. "It's Wite Lize. He wants to trade Arian for Warlock."

30

Ninety-six stories above the courtyard on the roof of the Tower lurked a far more brutal world with no gently falling snow or crisp winter breeze. The wind here was a roaring, battering dragon, whipping its tail so hard against the Tower you would almost swear you could feel it shifting beneath your feet.

As soon as Tristan burst through the fire door, he realized the truth. Hell wasn't hot. Hell was standing on the roof of a New York skyscraper in a subzero wind chill with snow being driven into your eyes like slivers of glass. Satan was a dragon who breathed ice, not fire, and for a bone-numbing minute, as Tristan sucked that glacial blast of brimstone into his lungs, he thought he was going to die.

But with his next breath, he learned that hell was the sight of Arian standing there on the edge of that roof with no coat and no shoes, just Wite Lize's frail old body to shield her from the dragon's wrath. He would have almost sworn he could hear her teeth chattering.

His blood boiled with rage. He wanted to howl with

it. Wanted to march across the roof, snatch his wife from Wite Lize's scrawny arms, and slap the old fool sense-less. But the snub-nosed revolver pressed against Ar-ian's jaw froze him more effectively than any dragon's breath.

Wite Lize beckoned him closer, and Tristan knew none of their vocal chords would stand much pounding by this ruthless wind. He complied, inching forward until he was near enough to see the frantic gleam in Arian's eyes, the bob of her milky throat as she fought to swal-low her terror.

If she went so far as to muster a brave smile for him, he thought he just might cry for the first time since Bambi's mother went down under that hunter's bullet.

"Did you bring what I wanted?" Lize bellowed, his theatrical training serving him well, even on this bleak, windswept stage. He was wearing flowing white robes like some sort of second-rate Merlin from a bad sword-and-sorcery movie.

Tristan drew Warlock from his pocket, dangling it by its chain in a tantalizing arc.

"Don't try anything cute," Lize warned, tighten-ing his arm around Arian's waist. "I promise you that I can pull this trigger before you can even think 'abraca-dabra.' "

Tristan might have considered doing just that, but Arian was the only one who knew how to work the damn thing. He could hardly afford to jeopardize her life by turning himself into a goat or conjuring up a pair of tur-tledoves.

"Don't you dare give it to him," Arian shouted, struggling to be heard above the wind. "He'll destroy you if you do. He'll destroy us all. He's an even bigger wretch than his son."

"Why, thank you, my child," Lize crooned. "I find your flattery quite scintillating."

Good girl, Tristan thought. Prod his vanity. Get him talking and buy them some more time. Time for

Sven to secure his ropes and come crawling over the edge of the roof. Sven, who had a sore jaw and a score to settle with Lize for coldcocking him with the butt of the revolver. Maybe even time for the SWAT team from the NYPD Special Forces Unit to battle their way through the snow-clogged streets.

All they had to do until then was keep the old man talking. Tristan deliberately laced his voice with withering scorn. "Don't believe anything the senile old fool has to say, Arian. It was Arthur, not Lize, who masterminded the entire scheme."

Lize sputtered his indignation. "I think not! It was my idea to befriend you in the first place. Not that it was any great challenge. You were so eager, so pathetic, so starved for any crumb of affection."

The truth had lost its power to sting. "And I suppose it was your idea to murder me, too."

"Most certainly. Then Arthur had to go and bungle it. I told him, 'Wait until he's asleep, bash him in the head with a blunt object, then put the pillow over his face and smother him.' But no! He had to go all artistic on me and fetch the carving knife. Blasted boy never did have any respect for authority."

Tristan shook his head in mute disbelief. All these years, he had harbored poisonous guilt for corrupting his friend, never realizing that Arthur had been rotten to the core from the beginning. Arian had twisted around to gaze at Wite Lize's face, her own expression more horrified than his. She was probably wondering just how deep this strain of family madness ran. Tristan feared she was about to find out.

Wite Lize shook the revolver in the air. "I'm the one who deserves the magic! I'm the one who's been booed off every stage between here and Pasadena! Just think how impressed my audiences would be if I could actually saw my assistant in half, then piece her back together again."

Arian shuddered.

Tristan stiffened as he saw Sven's blond head emerge from the darkness. Despite his size, the Norwegian's motions were a study in stealth. He came creeping over the edge of that roof just like one of the heroes in the action movies he'd always longed to star in.

But Lize's voice had changed, become amiable, almost cajoling. Its sickly sweet tones sent a chill down Tristan's spine that had nothing to do with the cold. "But I really can't take credit for everything, you know, since it was my darling granddaughter here who delivered the coup de grâce. She was the one bold enough to beguile you with her feminine wiles." He gave Arian a tender glance. "I'm surprised you didn't notice the family resemblance. I recognized her the moment I laid eyes on her. Like father, like daughter, I've always said, but you saw only what you wanted to see."

"Why, you miserable old wretch! Don't believe him, Tristan!" Arian cried out, beginning to struggle in earnest. "I never conspired against you. He's only bluffing!"

She slammed her fist into Lize's chest, then stomped his toes, utterly heedless of her own safety. Sven paused in a crouch, not daring to intervene for fear of hurting her.

"Arian, don't!" Tristan shouted, terrified the old man would lose patience and simply shoot her.

Ignoring Tristan's warning, Arian broke away from Lize's grip and ran straight for her husband's arms. But ice had slicked the roof's surface and she went skidding, her feet careening out from under her. She landed on her stomach with a nasty thud that knocked the breath from her lungs. For a moment there was a silence so profound she could not even hear the wind.

When she could breathe again, she dragged up her aching head and opened her eyes. Tristan stood less than ten feet away, and from his fierce expression, she could almost convince herself that he longed to run to her—to pick her up and dust her off and kiss the tip of her nose. But what was stopping him? Was it because he believed the terrible things Wite Lize had said about her?

She twisted her head to peer behind her. It must be the gun. The gun pointed at her back. Pointing the gun at Tristan would not have stopped him, and Wite Lize knew it. Arian squinted, wondering if she was only imagining the immense shadow creeping across the roof toward Wite Lize.

The magician stomped his foot like a petulant child. "Give me Warlock! I want Warlock now!"

Tristan grinned and drew back his hand. "Here you go, old man. It's all yours."

Everything seemed to happen in a blur. The amulet went sailing over Arian's head in a glittering arc toward Lize's outstretched hand. Just as his gnarled fingers closed around it, Sven came out of nowhere to smash his fist into the old man's jaw.

But then the gun went off and Sven dropped, clutching his thigh. Blood blossomed between his pale fingers.

The amulet in one hand and the gun in the other, Wite Lize cackled triumphantly, his white robes rippling against the inky sky. "She's my granddaughter, you dolt. Do you really think I'd be heartless enough to shoot my own granddaughter?"

Wite Lize brought the barrel of the gun around and Arian realized he had never planned to shoot her. He was going to shoot Tristan. He was going to finish the job his son had botched all those years ago.

"You wouldn't dare," Tristan said. He did not cower or flinch, but stood tall and proud, his tawny hair whipping in the wind, as Lize aimed the gun straight at his heart.

Arian half crawled, half lunged to her feet, intending to knock Tristan out of harm's way. But her feet could find no purchase on the icy roof and she skidded right into his arms. She heard the dull report of the gun an instant after the bullet ripped through her back.

A wild cry tore from Tristan's throat as Arian crashed into him. He caught her in his arms and they both went down, just as he and Arthur had done so long ago. Her eyes fluttered shut, her lashes dusky crescents against her pallid cheeks. Her curls spilled over his lap like a gleaming shroud as he tried to staunch her bleeding with his bare hands.

An irresistible darkness was spreading through Arian's veins, dimming everything around her and dulling the pain in her back to a nagging throb. Something wet struck her face. Bewildered, she struggled to open her eyes, to ask Tristan when the snow had turned to rain.

When she finally managed to pry apart her heavy lids and blink away the swirling fog, Copperfield was there and Sven and oddly enough, Wite Lize, standing over them all, the smoking pistol hanging limp from his liver-spotted hand. Arian knew instinctively that they had beaten the old man. Warlock would be returned to its rightful master before this night was done. The realization filled her with peace. She sighed, snuggling deeper into the delectable warmth of Tristan's arms and letting her eyes drift shut. Perhaps she would just steal a tiny nap.

"She's my granddaughter," Lize whispered, tears welling in his rheumy blue eyes. "I never meant to harm her."

"Heal her, then," Tristan snarled through bared teeth, gathering Arian's limp form to his breast. When Lize just blinked stupidly at him, he roared, "The amulet! Use the godforsaken amulet!"

Wite Lize opened his other fist as if he'd forgotten his ill-gotten treasure. "Ah, yes, the amulet," he murmured. "Very well. I suppose I can manage some suitable spell. After all, I've spent my entire life preparing for this moment."

As Tristan rocked back and forth, using his own

body to shelter her from the wind and cold, the old man mumbled a few words beneath his breath that sounded suspiciously like pig Latin.

"There now," he said, beaming brightly. "That should do it."

Hardly daring to hope, Tristan peered over Arian's shoulder at her back. Although blood still dripped from his fingers, the dark, pulsing wound was slowly shrinking, closing inward on itself until no trace of it remained. Tristan wrapped his arms around her and held her as if he would never let her go.

He barely felt Cop's worried tap on his shoulder. "Uh, Tristan?"

"Mmm?" he murmured, burying his face in Arian's silky curls.

"She's fading."

"I know the wound is fading. For once in his miserable life, Lize has done something right."

The panic in Copperfield's voice mounted. "No, Tristan. Not the blood. Her. Arian is fading."

Tristan shot him a wild look, then glanced back at his wife. Copperfield was right. Arian had always been pale, but she'd never been transparent. He could already see the faint outline of his own legs beneath her.

Lize took a step backward. Then another. But Sven had already staggered to his feet to block his escape.

Tristan shook off the horror that threatened to paralyze him and tried to gather Arian close. Her flesh felt as insubstantial as the scent of cloves lingering in his nostrils. Was it his imagination or was that fading as well?

"What did you do?" he shouted at Wite Lize. "What in the hell have you done?"

Wite Lize sniffed piously. "You needn't be such an ingrate. I simply sent her back where she belongs. At her father's side."

Tristan would have lunged for his throat then and there, but he was desperately trying to cement his grip on Arian's ebbing flesh. He grabbed her arm with a force that should have wrenched it from its socket only to have his hands close on empty air. Sven let go of his wounded leg long enough to snatch the amulet from Lize's hand and toss it to Tristan, but before Tristan could breathe a wish, Arian was gone, vanished like a sweet, poignant dream, only half remembered at dawn.

Tristan staggered to his feet and sent a blast of raw power hurtling at Wite Lize before collapsing with a hoarse wail in Copperfield's arms.

He never even saw the cops come swarming over the roof, never felt it when they dragged him out of Copperfield's frantic grasp, tore Warlock from his hand, and slapped a pair of handcuffs on his bloodstained wrists. Never heard the officer solemnly intone, "You have the right to remain silent . . ."

All he could hear was the wind roaring in his ears and the gentle reproach in Arian's voice when she had smiled through her tears and whispered, *Take all the time you need. I've certainly got more than I can use.*

31

Arian was falling, hurtling backward through time. Her arms shot out to snatch at the moments speeding past. *Tristan*. Always Tristan. In love. In anger. In passion. Lowering his lips to hers through a veil of steam. Plucking an orange blossom from her hair while her kitten scampered around their feet. Scowling at her across a deserted lab. Stroking her aching brow with his strong, slender fingers, the ice in his eyes thawed by tenderness.

The images vanished, hurtling her into utter darkness.

Overwhelmed by a crushing sense of loss, she curled herself into a tiny ball, clenching her eyes shut against a hot rush of tears. End over end, she flipped, dropping like a stone into the uncaring void. Then with an impact that slammed the breath from her body, she crashed through an invisible barrier into something wet and warm. At first, she thought it was her own blood.

Steely hands clamped on her arms and legs, propelling her upward into night air oppressive with the odors of smoke and sweat. Those same hands pounded her back, forcing her to breathe when she would rather have died. Coughing weakly, she opened her eyes to a blur of orange light and pale blobs viewed through a clinging web of hair.

"The witch lives!" a man cried.

"Satan saves his own," hissed a woman.

Arian closed her eyes as a roar steeped in madness pounded through her brain. Despair buffeted her as she realized she had traveled so far only to arrive right back where she'd started. A firmly muscled thigh flexed beneath her cheek. A gentle hand drew the tangled skein of hair away from her face. Jerking away from the possessive touch, she tossed back her head and sucked in a ragged breath.

The Reverend Linnet gazed down upon her, his smile as beatific as an angel's, his sparkling dark eyes malicious twins of her own. "Hello, my child."

"Hello, Papa," she snarled before driving her fist straight into his smirking lips.

A hand was tenderly stroking her curls. Beguiled by the soothing touch, Arian snuggled deeper into the familiar satin sheets. "Oh, Tristan, I had such a grim dream," she murmured.

"Poor lamb," he crooned. "Tell Papa all about it."

Arian shot straight up in the bed, shaking off a shroud of drowsiness. She slowly turned her head to discover she wasn't having a dream, but living a nightmare. 'Twas not Tristan who sat on the edge of her bed, but the Reverend Linnet.

"Ah, Sleeping Beauty stirs," he said, smothering a yawn behind one flawlessly manicured hand. "How wonderful for a man to wake up each morning with such a pliant creature in his bed! Tristan always did have all the luck."

"And all the charm," she snapped, scooting as far away from him as the sumptuous bed would allow.

Linnet's sly smile warned her she had revealed too much. Her head felt as if it were stuffed with more feathers than the mattress. Massaging her leaden limbs, she slid toward the edge of the bed. The scratchy homespun of her night rail snagged on the sheets. A quartet of gilt cherubs leered down at her from the massive canopy.

"A bit decadent for a Puritan preacher, don't you think?" she asked.

Linnet shrugged. "Charity Burke found it quite delightful. In our little interlude here, I'd say she was moved by the spirit as never before."

Arian shuddered, sickened anew by the notion that she could be the daughter of such a loathsome creature. God only knew how many other innocent young women of Gloucester he had debauched in this secret attic. A narrow skylight was nestled beneath the sloping eaves, revealing a thin belt of slate-gray sky. The stifling silence was broken by the gentle sputter of a costly wax candle that perfumed the air with the scent of lilacs.

As Arian dragged herself to her feet, Linnet followed suit, studying her every move with his glittering dark eyes.

She gripped one of the gaudy bedposts for support. "I demand to see my stepfather. Marcus deserves to know the truth."

"And which version of the truth would that be? That you spent the past two days in a drugged stupor dreaming of mysterious towers and your golden-haired incubus of a lover? Or that you traveled to the future and spent the past month in New York City screwing my former business partner?"

Arian flushed hot, then cold. "How did you . . . ?"

He slung one arm around the opposite bedpost. "Oh, I know all about your little adventures in wonderland. You have an endearing tendency to chatter like a magpie while under the influence of laudanum."

Arian quailed at the thought of her most tender and

intimate secrets being prey to his lascivious scrutiny.
"How dare you drug me!"

"I had no choice but to sedate you after your vicious attack on me." He gingerly fingered his lower lip.
Arian noted with no small amount of satisfaction that it
was puffed up to twice its normal size. "At least a hundred witnesses saw you try to strangle me after I so be-
nevolently rescued you from the pond."

"I wish to God I'd succeeded," she spat.

"Why, daughter, you wound me! Are you truly so
eager to be an orphan?" He shuddered in mock fear.
"Why don't you just cast one of your clever little spells
on me?"

Arian reached for the amulet, prepared to do just
that. But Linnet's snide smile reminded her of what she
would find. The amulet was as out of her reach as Tristan—three hundred and seven years in the future.

She forced herself to meet his mocking gaze with
cool aplomb. "I may not have Warlock any more, Papa,
dear. But neither does your bumbling father. And neither do you."

Linnet's smile slowly faded. Arian suppressed a
genuine shudder at the utter absence of expression that
replaced it.

"I suppose you still think it was your ridiculous
little spell that sent you careening into the twentieth century. Haven't you figured out that I'd already programmed the chip to send *me* there as soon as I'd settled
things with you? Your incessant babbling must have activated the program. If that wretched crone hadn't stolen
the amulet and dropped it in the water, I'd have been rid
of Tristan by now."

"Why then? Why nineteen ninety-six?"

"Why not? Ten years should have been ample time
for Tristan to amass his fortune. All I would have had to
do was arrange a nasty accident, conjure up the necessary paperwork, reveal myself as his silent partner, step
in, and take over."

"Why bother with all that when you could just conjure up a fortune for yourself?"

Linnet's sneer revealed the ugly depths of his envy. "Ah, but it wouldn't have been *his* fortune."

"He was your friend!" Arian cried. "How many times are you going to betray him?"

"As many times as necessary. Friends are expendable. As are rebellious offspring."

Arian relinquished the bedpost, each of Linnet's well-timed blows only making her more determined to stand on her own two feet. "I cannot conceive how any man, however detestable, can speak so casually of murdering his own daughter."

"His bastard, you mean?"

Arian tried not to flinch, but failed. This was hardly the loving reunion she had once fantasized about. "Better to be a bastard by birth, sir, than by disposition."

He sketched a mocking bow. "Touché. If your mother had been possessed of such wit, I might not have bored of her after only one night. Unfortunately, Lily was only tolerable with her legs open and her mouth shut. I trust Tristan discovered the same thing about you."

"Tristan loved me!" The words spilled from her raw throat before she could bite them back.

Linnet's laughter sent chills down her spine. "Everyone in the twentieth century *loves* everyone else. On good days, they love someone of the opposite sex and the same species. On bad days, well . . ." He lifted his shoulders in a flawless Gallic shrug that betrayed the number of years he'd spent searching for her in France.

"Don't apply your impoverished moral standards to an entire century," Arian snapped.

"Then don't apply your childish sentimentality to Tristan. While under the spell of the laudanum, you babbled something about him believing you betrayed him. As I'm sure you've already learned, Tristan is not a forgiving man."

Arian was haunted by the memory of that night of

passion they'd shared in the penthouse. She might never know now if Tristan had been motivated by love or revenge. 'Twas almost as if he'd sought to punish her with pleasure. To rob her of both her will and her soul with a dark and sensual sorcery that rivaled any warlock's enchantment.

She lowered her eyes, but not before they could betray a flicker of doubt.

Linnet pounced on it with unerring precision. "The game's not over yet, my dear. Nor is it too late to change sides. If I was as eager to be rid of you as you seem to think I am, I would have snatched Warlock from your careless little paw the night I saw you fly. Or fled this provincial hell the minute I had it in my hands. Instead, I offered you shelter and gave you every opportunity to swear your allegiance to me."

"You had me thrown in jail! You manipulated my stepfather and the mob, turning them against me until you believed I'd have no choice but to come begging to you."

Linnet's buckled shoes whispered across the hardwood floor as he closed the distance between them. "Ah, but my brave, beautiful Arian wasn't going to beg, was she? Not even when I had her cast into the water. I really believed you'd come up gasping for air and sputtering some pathetic plea." He touched a tapered finger to his swollen lip, shaking his head with reluctant admiration. "But not my daughter."

"Your bastard," she reminded him, refusing to succumb to his ruse of charm.

His eyes hardened. "Why should you give Tristan your loyalty when I'm the one who searched for you for twenty years?"

"You weren't searching for me. You were searching for Warlock, for a way back to the twentieth century."

"Oh, seventeenth-century Paris had its charms in the beginning—a dizzying array of sensual delights, eager women, an unregulated opium trade."

"French pox, wig lice, the plague," Arian countered sweetly.

"If you're implying the dubious charms of this century have begun to pale, then you're more perceptive than I realized." He bit off each word with increasing antagonism, his European drawl giving way to a clipped New York cadence. "I want to soak in a steaming Jacuzzi, sip Grand Marnier, and smoke a big, fat Cuban cigar. I want to brunch at the Four Seasons with dear old dad, then watch the Giants beat the Raiders on a lazy Sunday afternoon. I want to smell the scent of shampoo in a woman's hair instead of woodsmoke." His upper lip curled in a snarl as he shoved his face next to hers. *"I want Warlock."*

Arian forced herself not to recoil from the cloying sweetness of his cologne. "Warlock doesn't belong to you. You didn't invent it. Tristan did."

"But he wasn't man enough to use it. I am. As you'll soon discover." His glower was vanquished by a sanctimonious smile as he turned away.

Linnet's words chilled her anew, but Arian could not stop her heart from thundering with a hope so far-fetched she hadn't even dared to contemplate it.

She rushed forward to grab his sleeve. "What are you saying?"

He disengaged his sleeve from her grasp with insulting gentleness. "You'll find one of Charity's dresses in the armoire. We have a date with the magistrates in one hour." He reached down to stroke her throat, his fingers tightening with each mocking caress. "Don't overestimate my devotion to hearth and family. If you say one word to expose me, I'll hand you over to the man with the nearest noose."

Arian didn't even dare breathe again until he'd slid open a hidden panel in the far wall to reveal a staircase winding down into darkness. She hated to trust her sweetest dream and darkest fear to words, but the hoarse whisper escaped her anyway. "If you truly believe

Tristan despises me, then what makes you think he'll come after me?"

Linnet cast her a pitying look. "Don't flatter yourself, child. Tristan wants revenge as badly as I do. He won't come for you. He'll come for me."

32

Arian awaited her summons in a ladder-backed chair, her dry-eyed gaze fixed on the brooding slice of sky visible through the skylight. She had confined the unruly tumble of her hair in an austere bun. Her hands lay folded against the black homespun of her skirt. Just as the first raindrops splashed on the skylight, the panel slid open and Linnet crooked a finger at her. Arian rose and followed him down the steep, narrow stairs.

She groaned inwardly as Constable Ingersoll's booming voice floated out of the parlor. "How can anyone deny we are righteous men beset by demons? Our charter was torn away from us. Pirates plunder our coasts. Even the French have turned against us. Mark my words—'tis demons and witches seeking to drive us out of the land the Good Lord gave us."

As Linnet and Arian entered the parlor, the two black-garbed men sitting with Ingersoll rose.

Linnet took her elbow. "Miss Whitewood, these two gentlemen are John Hathorne and Jonathan Corwin, two of our Boston magistrates."

Arian inclined her head. Mr. Hathorne cleared his throat, blinking pink-rimmed eyes like a nervous rabbit while the portly Mr. Corwin compressed his thin lips to a disapproving line.

A fourth man stood at the window with hands in pockets, watching the night sky spill the rain that had weighted the day with gloom.

"Father Marcus!" Arian cried.

She twisted out of Linnet's grasp and ran to her stepfather. He looked older than she remembered. His eyelids drooped with fatigue and his shoulders slumped as if encumbered by a ponderous weight. As she stood on tiptoe to press her lips to his grizzled cheek, she realized for the first time how much she had missed this simple man. Now that she'd been forced to relinquish her childhood dream of a loving papa, she realized what a fine father Marcus had always tried to be to her.

But it seemed her appreciation had come too late. Marcus stood stiffly in her embrace. When Arian's arms fell away, he turned back to the window without a word.

"Miss Whitewood," Linnet prodded with obvious relish. "You may return to the fire and take a seat."

Arian obeyed, dropping into the chair Linnet indicated, her lips pursed in sullen rebellion.

Linnet leaned his chair back on two legs, a study in careless elegance. Arian could still see traces of the fop in his white shirt with its brass studs and frilled cuffs.

"Gentlemen," he said, "we all know why we are gathered here tonight. You've already heard the evidence presented against Miss Whitewood. I've told you how my timely intervention saved her from the mob's misguided wrath."

Arian crossed her legs at the ankles to keep from kicking his chair out from under him.

"Hang her," Constable Ingersoll snapped. " 'Thou shalt not suffer a witch to live.' "

Mr. Hathorne's nose twitched as he leaned forward. "There does seem to be a respectable body of evidence against the young lady."

"Hogwash," snapped Mr. Corwin. "Why should the chit be hanged for a bit of childish mischief?"

Arian smiled at the stern old man, caught off guard by his defense.

"Hang her!" bellowed the constable. "She is a woman. She is French. She is a witch. Need we more evidence? Everyone knows the French are descended from demons."

Arian could not argue with Ingersoll on that point. She *was* descended from a demon.

The leering constable launched into an impassioned recitation of the many documented flaws of the French character. Mr. Corwin disputed him on every point while Mr. Hathorne cheerfully agreed with whoever was speaking at the moment.

"Gentlemen!" Linnet's chair crashed down to all four legs. "I fault myself for letting you come to this disagreement." He stood and began to pace around their chairs, his hands locked at the small of his back. "Alas, I fear I have been remiss by not providing you with all the facts of this case."

"Or any of the facts," Arian added.

Linnet passed close enough behind her to give a loose strand of her hair a vicious tweak. She gritted her teeth.

"In the day and night since I rescued Miss Whitewood from the pond, it has been necessary to sedate her heavily." He plucked a piece of lint from his waistcoat. "There are witnesses in the village who will attest to the fact that while I was carrying her back to my home, she threw her arms about my neck and tried to choke me."

Arian stared at her shoes, trying desperately not to smile at the pleasant memory.

"To protect both her and myself from her demon-provoked convulsions, I summoned Dr. Stoughton to administer a strong dose of laudanum. It was while she was under the effects of the drug that Miss Whitewood's tortured ramblings revealed to me a dark and terrible secret."

"He's lying!" Arian shot to her feet.

Linnet clapped his hands on her shoulders and shoved her back down in a pretense of kindness. "Strength, my child. Resist the demons that torment you."

She clamped her lips together, determined to resist the torments of only one demon.

Linnet crossed to the hearth, took up the iron poker, and stirred the flames to crackling life. Shadows leapt across his features as he looked each man full in the face. "I cannot even bring myself to describe the contortions I witnessed in that bedchamber."

"Do try, sir." Ingersoll leaned forward, his florid brow sheened with sweat.

"While possessed by one of those terrible fits, Miss Whitewood grabbed my hand and dragged me into the bed with an inhuman strength." A flattering flush spread across Linnet's regal cheekbones.

Arian gaped, too captivated by his performance to predict what he would say next. It was easy to understand how he had made his living on the French stage all those years.

"While she had me in her grasp, she did whisper to me a grim tale, indeed." He passed his hand over his eyes. "She confessed to me that the night before the swimming, a dark spirit overcame her in the woods. He took her flying on a pulsating broomstick and worked his dark ways with her until she cried out in agony and mortal pleasure."

"An incubus!" Ingersoll hissed.

"That's rubbish, you blathering Beelzebub!" Arian cried, springing out of her chair once again.

"Sit down, girl." Marcus's command froze her where she stood. He had been so quiet she had nearly forgotten he was there. "Let the good Reverend finish. We will have no more of your impudence."

Arian sat, shifting her gaze to the rafters to keep the tears in her eyes from falling. Somehow Marcus's betrayal was the most bitter of all.

Mr. Corwin cleared his throat. "So now we have the opium-induced ramblings of a young girl in the budding flower of womanhood. Do you have any physical evidence to condemn this child, Reverend?"

Arian wanted to hug the crotchety old magistrate. But Linnet's smooth smile sent ice coursing through her veins.

"Oh, yes, Mr. Corwin. I have evidence. After suffering one of these fits, Miss Whitewood slipped into a stupor. It was at that time that I decided 'twould be wise to have Dr. Stoughton examine her body for Devil's Marks."

Arian's cheeks burned with mortification. Everyone in the parlor knew such marks were only found in the most intimate areas of the body.

Linnet offered her a mocking nod to acknowledge the quickened pace of her breathing. "The examination was conducted properly, Miss Whitewood. Goodwife Burke was present in the chamber at the time."

Ingersoll whipped a kerchief from his pocket and mopped his brow. "I cannot imagine why I wasn't summoned to witness this examination."

"Did you find any such marks?" Mr. Corwin demanded.

Linnet shook his head sadly. "We did not. But we discovered something else." He pursed his lips. "I know of no delicate way to phrase this. The girl was not . . . intact. She is no maiden."

Arian's outraged gasp was drowned out by Ingersoll's whoop of triumph. The constable's round face split in a wolfish grin. "She is a witch and a harlot. Arrange a trial and hang her."

Mr. Corwin shook his head. "A trial would be of

no use now. We cannot hang her if there is the slightest possibility that she could be with child."

Linnet arched an eyebrow. "Is there that possibility, Miss Whitewood?"

Arian gazed into her lap, remembering the hot rush of water over her naked flesh, the steam rising from Tristan's golden skin, his hoarse moan of satisfaction as he joined his body with hers. Her hand twitched with the urge to cup her belly, to savor the irresistible notion that her womb might even now be quickening with Tristan's child. Even though she knew she was playing right into Linnet's cunning hands, she could not summon even a shadow of shame.

Lifting her head, she met his eyes with a pride that bordered on arrogance. "Yes."

Mr. Corwin rose, his distress visible. "Miss Whitewood, if some lad in the village has compromised you, now is the time to name him. This is not a disgrace you should bear alone."

Arian shook her head mutely, regretting that she could not meet his earnest gaze.

Constable Ingersoll lumbered to his feet, convinced a decision had been made. "I have a set of shackles on my horse. I shall escort the smutty tart and her litter of demons to the jail."

"No," Mr. Corwin said, the authority in his voice halting Ingersoll in his tracks. "I will not have this delicate child spending the next month, or the next nine months, shackled in a filthy cell."

Marcus opened his mouth, then closed it.

Linnet rescued him, clucking sympathetically. "We can hardly expect Goodman Whitewood to take the girl back into his home. She has already tried to kill him once. If Miss Whitewood agrees, she may stay with me until her fate is decided." He knelt before her and clasped her hands in his, his eyes as brown and winning as a pup's. "Would you care to abide with me, my child, or would you rather accompany the good constable to the jail?"

Ingersoll licked his bulbous lips in anticipation.

"How could I refuse such a kind offer?" Arian replied without blinking an eye. "Of course I would choose to stay with you, Reverend."

Muttering something about saucy wenches and devil's issue, Ingersoll slapped on his hat, threw open the door, and charged into the rain.

"I should speak to the constable before he incites another mob." Mr. Corwin offered Arian a pained smile of farewell. The wind whipped his cloak into a flapping frenzy as he disappeared into the night, Mr. Hathorne fast on his heels.

Marcus shifted awkwardly from foot to foot. "I'd best be getting home as well. There is stock to be fed." He ducked into the rain without a backward glance at Arian, slamming the door behind him.

Marcus huddled beside his horse, gazing back at Linnet's house through a chill curtain of rain. A pair of oil lamps shone through the front window, brightening the night with their cozy glow.

An iron kettle went flying past the window. Above the spill of the rain, Marcus heard an outraged shriek and the terrible clatter of metal against stone. Linnet stumbled into view, reeling as the lid to a butter churn smacked him upside the head. He snarled and started back the way he had come only to be forced to dive behind a chair as a porcelain platter shattered on the wall behind him.

Marcus shook his head. There was nothing bewitched about the way those things were flying through the air. He had witnessed enough of Arian's tantrums to know that it took only her dainty hands to reduce the tidiest room to a shambles. Following another enraged shriek and a masculine bellow of pain, he mounted his horse and kicked it into a trot, drawing the brim of his hat over his thoughtful eyes to shield them from the rain.

The hidden panel slid open. Linnet slipped into the attic, his dark eyes smoldering beneath the pristine folds of a plaster bandage. Arian sat propped against the bed pillows, her hands folded demurely in her lap. With her face framed by the stiff ruffles of the homespun nightgown, she could have been an angelic twin to the gilt cherubs floating above her.

Linnet stared down at her. "You're not worthy to be my daughter."

He spoke in flawless French and Arian replied in kind without even realizing it. *"Merci beaucoup, mon père."*

His sneer sharpened. "If you ever lift a hand to me again, I'll hang you myself."

"And risk everything? After all, why would you have bothered to earn me a stay of execution if you didn't need me? You must not be as confident of your ability to lure Tristan to his doom as you pretend to be."

Linnet's laugh was even uglier than his sneer. "Tristan wouldn't cross the street to help you, my dear, much less three centuries. I'm the one he'll be looking for when he comes. You're only insurance. A man of Tristan's immense ego would sacrifice much to protect his heir—perhaps even his life."

Arian suppressed a shiver of foreboding. "What if your plan fails? What if there is no child? What if Tristan doesn't even bother to come?"

Linnet hesitated for no more than a heartbeat. "Then the magistrates can try you for witchcraft . . . with my blessing." He snapped off a crisp bow. "Good night, daughter. Sweet dreams." The panel slammed shut with bleak finality.

Arian locked her trembling hands together, torn between praying that Tristan would come soon or that he would never come at all.

33

CRIME SCENE. DO NOT CROSS.

Copperfield brushed aside the tattered warning banner. It fluttered in the bruising January wind like a garish yellow kite, mocking his grief.

A herd of wooden sawhorses cordoned off the block surrounding the Tower, making the hustle and bustle of Fifth Avenue seem a world away. A bleak cloud of desertion hung over the entire structure. It had been abandoned by its employees, its residents, its visitors, even by the press, after weeks of vigilance from their mobile units and helicopters had failed to pierce the veil of mystery surrounding the disappearance of Tristan Lennox's beautiful young bride.

Copperfield's footsteps echoed as he crossed the deserted lobby. The Tower reminded him of a tomb—"a whited sepulcher full of dead men's bones." But the only bones buried in this mausoleum were Tristan's.

He bypassed the main elevators for an express, already knowing where he would find what he was looking for.

Before he stepped off the elevator, he turned up the collar of his coat, as if it might protect him from more than just the icy gusts of wind battering the Tower roof. At least it wasn't snowing this time. The sky was as barren as the face of the man who stood at the edge of the roof, searching its cold, gray vault with his shadowed eyes.

Copperfield nearly flinched at his first sight of Tristan in over a month. His friend's face was haggard, his eyes hollow from lack of sleep. Etched in that stark visage was a phantom of the embittered old man he would become. If he lived long enough.

Cop joined him in his vigil. Tristan wore no coat, but seemed impervious to the cold. Copperfield tried not to embarrass himself by shivering.

He nearly jumped out of his skin when Tristan broke the silence first. "How's Cherie?"

Cop bit back a besotted smile. "Just fine. I gave her an engagement ring for Christmas, but she says marriage is a big commitment and she needs some time to think it over."

Tristan's smile was bleak. "Tell her not to wait too long. She might end up with an eternity."

Cop jammed his hands in his pockets. "Brenda's been calling nearly every day to check on you. She sounds pretty frantic."

Gentle mockery laced Tristan's voice. "She probably wants to make sure I've included her in my will."

Well, that certainly gave him the introduction he'd been looking for, Cop thought wryly. "I talked to the judge today. A trial date has been set."

Tristan's expression didn't even waver.

"You are aware that New York reinstated the death penalty in the fall of ninety-five?" Cop asked, desperate to jar him out of his apathy.

That only earned him a halfhearted shrug.

"I don't understand why you won't let Sven and me testify on your behalf."

Tristan snorted his disdain. " 'Excuse me, Your Honor, but I'd like to make a motion that the charges against my client be dismissed since I myself and the other star witness for the defense observed Miss Arian Whitewood being sucked through a vortex in time on the night of her alleged murder.' " He shuddered. "No, thank you. You'd only succeed in getting Sven deported and yourself disbarred. You might as well call Wite Lize to the stand." He shot Cop a rueful glance. "And we both know what condition *he's* in. Given my prior history, I'm afraid the judge won't be quite so inclined to overlook key pieces of circumstantial evidence—such as the fact that my wife has been missing for over two months and my hands were stained with copious amounts of her blood. Oh, yes, and we mustn't forget that half of New York saw us have a violent quarrel in the middle of our wedding reception."

He had effectively disarmed every legal argument Cop had prepared.

Tugging his ponytail in frustration, Cop paced away from him and back again. "You have an answer for everything, don't you? Except for the one question that's been haunting me ever since she disappeared. Why won't you use Warlock to go after her and bring her back? I know you despise the damn thing and fear its power to corrupt, but isn't a woman like Arian worth risking your soul for?"

Copperfield had finally succeeded in provoking a reaction, if not precisely the one he had expected. Tristan grabbed him by the lapels of his coat, his eyes burning with passion in his gaunt face. "I'd sell my soul to the devil himself for a chance to hold her in my arms one more time before I die! How dare you imply that I wouldn't?"

"Then why?" Cop whispered, helpless to understand.

Tristan let go of him to reach into his pocket and pull out a worn sheet of paper. He handed it to Cop. "This was waiting for me on the day you picked me up at the jail after you finally convinced the judge to set bail. The day they returned Warlock to my possession."

It was a fax dated 11/26/96—the day after Arian had vanished. The fax had been sent from the city courthouse in Gloucester, Massachusetts, at 0800 hours and looked like a Xeroxed copy of some obscure historical document.

He cast Tristan a bewildered glance. "I thought your research team was turning up nothing but a lot of dead ends."

"They were," Tristan said softly. "Until Arian went back."

Suddenly, Cop didn't want to read the fax. Didn't want the stark words to imprint themselves on his brain. But trapped beneath the spotlight of Tristan's uncompromising gaze, he had no choice.

Swallowing the knot in his throat, he gently read, " 'On the thirty-first day of October in the Year of Our Lord sixteen eighty-nine, an accused witch by the name of Arian Whitewood was hanged by the neck"—his voice faltered—"until dead." Cop crumpled the paper in his fist. Tears seared his eyes.

"They hanged her, Cop. They hanged my beautiful, funny little witch." Tristan gestured to the empty sky, his voice bleak. "If she was out there somewhere, lost in time, don't you think I'd know? Don't you think I'd feel the whisper of her breath? Smell the scent of her hair on the wind? She's dead," he bit off savagely. "She's been rotting in her grave for over three hundred years. All because I was too damn stubborn to trust her. She had to prove herself worthy of my faith by throwing herself in front of a bullet."

The fax fluttered from Cop's fingers, but Tristan didn't try to stop it. They watched it drift over the edge of the rooftop like a wisp of cloud.

Copperfield held his silence for as long as he could

before blurting out, "Oh, why the hell don't you just jump?"

Tristan recoiled as if he'd been struck. "What?"

Cop swept out his hand toward the edge of the rooftop. "Why don't you just jump and save the taxpayers the expense of executing you?"

Tristan blinked, looking mildly dazed. "I always knew lawyers were a cynical lot, but doesn't advising your client to commit suicide cut down on the chances of your collecting your exorbitant fee?"

"I'd rather forgo my fee than watch you mope around the Tower like some brooding Heathcliff from a high school production of *Wuthering Heights*. If you're too busy feeling sorry for yourself to get off your pathetic ass and go rescue your wife—"

"Didn't you hear a word I said?" Tristan shouted. "Arian's dead!"

Cop thrust out his lower lip. "I can't believe you'd let a little thing like that come between you."

Tristan was staring at him, visibly torn between anguish and hope. He took one step toward him, then another, backing him toward the edge of the roof. "If you're cruel enough to offer me hope without foundation," he said hoarsely, "as God is my witness, I'll throw *you* off the roof."

"You won't have to," Cop promised his friend, his lips curving in a lazy grin. "If I'm wrong about this one, I'll jump."

"Devil's slut!"

The raucous shout assailed Arian the minute she emerged from the front door of Linnet's house. She drew the hood of her cloak forward to veil her face.

"Satan's whore! Going to meet your lover, aren't you? So he can plant another demon whelp in your belly!"

Clutching the bundle beneath her arm, she ducked her head and started across the dirt road, praying she could reach the edge of the woods without being accosted. A ball of mud spattered across the back of her cloak.

She whirled around. Two boys crouched at the other side of the road, scooping up handfuls of mud and patting them into missiles. In the past three weeks, she had seen them and many others like them lurking around Linnet's cottage, hoping to catch a glimpse of her. If the sky hadn't been threatening rain again, there would have been more.

The tallest boy cocked his head, his broadcloth coat marking him as a rich man's son. "G'day, witch. My cousin says you should give up your phantom lovers and give a real man a taste. He would be more than happy to meet you in the woods some afternoon and show you—"

He yelped as the fistful of mud Arian hurled hit him squarely in the nose. Both of the boys burst into tears and fled, sobbing that the evil witch had cast a spell upon them.

Arian sighed and shook her head. She could hardly blame children for parroting the malice fostered by their elders.

She slipped into the forest, thankful to escape the oppressive atmosphere of Linnet's house for a few hours. The underbrush clawed at the hem of her cloak, its fingers stripped to bone by the looming promise of winter.

Arian sank down on a fallen log and laid her supper of a warm beef pie beside her. Linnet had given her free rein to wander, knowing full well that more than three steps in any direction would summon a mob intent on doing her more harm than his mocking smirk could ever do. His confidence that she would not run away galled her. They both knew she had nowhere to run.

Arian reached for her supper. The log was empty. She peered beneath it, but found nothing but beetles burrowing into the black soil. She straightened, frowning. There were no wood sprites or gremlins in Gloucester that she knew of.

A contented slurp from behind a nearby bush proved her wrong. As Arian crept toward the bush, it quivered with trepidation. But before its occupant could flee, she reached beneath the prickly branches and seized a black-stockinged foot. She dragged out a wrinkled gnome of a woman, recognizing her as the Scotswoman who had saved her life by stealing the amulet from Linnet and dropping it into the pond.

Arian plucked a shriveled leaf from the woman's hair, relishing the novel sensation of towering over someone. "You're a dreadful thief, Becca. 'Tis no wonder they were going to hang you."

The old woman swiped at the beef juice running down her chin. "I'm as bonny a thief as ye are a witch, lass."

Arian smiled wryly. " 'Tis God's truth you speak. I'll probably be executed long before you will."

Becca licked her gnarled fingers, her sly gaze snaking downward to Arian's belly. "Not if there be a devil's seed within as the village folk are sayin' "

"Oh, Becca," Arian chided. "I expected better of you."

The woman's weathered face split in a grin. "The only devils plantin' them kind o' seeds are bonny, silver-tongued devils. Who dishonored ye, lass? Was it one o' them strappin' Churchill lads? Or that wild Burroughs boy?" Arian's face clouded and Becca's tone softened. "Don't be thinkin' o' the fellow too harshly. To tumble a comely young maiden, many a fine man has made promises he couldna keep."

"My man made no promises," Arian whispered bitterly. *Unless you count his wedding vows.*

"But he loved ye well, didn't he? No need to blush, child. His only shame lies in not comin' forward to claim ye before the mob does." Becca reached out and patted

Arian's stomach. "I was a midwife in the Old Country. I'm sorry, lass, but there's no babe growin' in yer belly."

Becca's words only confirmed what Arian had suspected, but she still felt a sharp stab of loss for that shy, golden-haired child she might never have. She sank down on the log, propping her chin on her palms. "He may not come for me at all, I fear." Saying the words aloud made her feel worse than she had ever imagined. "We had a misunderstanding. He had reason to doubt my loyalty."

"He thinks ye let another toss up yer skirts?"

"Oh, no! A different kind of loyalty."

Becca shook her head. "There's no other kind o' loyalty 'tween a woman and a man. At least none worth dyin' for. And die ye will, if he don't come." Her voice deepened to a hoarse croak. "That devil-eyed preacher ain't plannin' no trial, lass. Just a lynchin' on the night o' no moon when darkness hides even the foulest deeds."

Arian stared up at the tiny woman as the woods grew darker, as if a shadow had fallen over them. "But the magistrates from Boston . . . Mr. Corwin . . . Mr. Hathorne . . ."

Becca caught Arian's chin in her bony hand, her grip surprisingly firm. "No fine magistrates from Boston, lass. Just the mob and the rope and ye. Summon this lover, demon or no, before 'tis too late."

Arian followed the old woman's gaze skyward. Between the brittle branches, the moon was materializing as little more than a sliver of ivory in the afternoon sky.

34

The bruised veil of the sky rippled and tossed. A chipmunk prowling the damp leaves stood on his hind legs, his nose quivering with curiosity in the eerie silence. With a rending tear, the fabric of the sky split, sending the tiny creature scurrying for safety.

Wrapped in a gush of winter wind and New York smog, Tristan spilled through the gaping hole, his limbs flailing wildly as he crashed through a latticework of bare branches. He slammed into the ground, cursing the fallen leaves for not being as soft as they looked.

Just when he was about to catch his breath, Copperfield appeared, plunging out of the sky with alarming speed. Tristan flexed his body to roll, but before he could, Cop landed on his chest. When Cop finally recovered enough to roll off him, Tristan grunted out an oath.

"Cheer up," Cop said. "If I'd have landed a foot lower, you wouldn't have needed Arian—or any other woman."

Tristan sat up, tossing a handful of leaves at his friend's head. A faint wind whispered through the trees.

The hole in the sky had closed, sucking in the last traces of industrial pollutants and exhaust fumes. In its place hung a chill canopy of darkness, devoid of all but a few stubborn specks of light. The moon was nowhere in sight.

Tristan wondered if Arian had felt this bereft when she first arrived in New York City. He wasn't sure what he missed the most—the noise pollution or the air pollution.

He checked his pocket to make sure Warlock had survived the jolt while Copperfield pawed through the leaves. "Damn. I can't find my tomahawk."

Tristan joined the search. "It's made out of rubber. What good could it possibly do us anyway?"

Cop sniffed. "That's easy for you to say. You didn't have to comb through every theatrical store in New York trying to find costumes for a Pilgrim and an Indian. If we don't have these things back by Monday, the owner's going to charge us double." He grunted with satisfaction as he found the missing prop.

Tristan clambered to his feet. "I think you should demand your money back. You look just like Tonto."

Cop adjusted his leather headband, grinning rakishly. "I am Tonto. And you, *kemosabe,* are Miles Standish."

Tristan tugged at his starched collar, thinking it was no wonder the Puritans were so repressed if they always had to wear this many layers of clothing. The only possible advantage would be in allowing Arian to gently strip away each layer with her graceful fingers until . . .

The wistful image provoked a fear so terrible he could only whisper it. "What if it's November the first, Cop? What if we're too late?"

Copperfield clapped a bracing hand on his shoulder. "I see a light up ahead. It might be a house. Shall we go take a look?"

Thankful for his friend's matter-of-fact demeanor, Tristan nodded. He, too, could just make out the faint glimmer barely visible through the trees. Copperfield ducked beneath the maze of branches and Tristan followed, swiping stray twigs out of his hair. At the edge of the woods, they paused, mesmerized by the sight of a charming little clapboard cottage. A cozy arc of light shone from its front window, holding the dark at bay. Two doll-like figures were framed by the glass expanse.

Exchanging a wary glance, they darted across the damp grass in one accord and sank to a crouch beneath the lumbering branches of an oak.

The scene inside the parlor could have been a primitive painting, so still were its players, so cozy its props. Steam rose in merry puffs from an iron kettle hanging over the hearth. The pewter candlesticks on the mantel gleamed as if they'd just enjoyed a vigorous buffing. A man sitting in a straight-backed cane chair dipped into a wooden bowl and brought a handful of fluffy popcorn to his mouth, his gaze never straying from the black book resting in his lap.

"Such a portrait of domestic bliss," Tristan murmured, his hand curling into a fist against the oak's trunk.

In a rocking chair across from the man he'd once known as Arthur Finch sat Arian, her dark head inclined toward a scrap of embroidery. She worried her bottom lip between her pearly teeth, all of her concentration centered on drawing a delicate needle through the thick linen. A modest white cap perched atop her frizzled curls, covering all but the most rebellious of them.

Tristan's first sight of her—vibrant, alive, and keeping what appeared to be a most agreeable company with his sworn enemy—struck a massive blow to his heart.

As they watched, Arthur lifted his head and spoke. Arian rose, smiling her sweetest smile.

"I'll kill her," Tristan said evenly. "They won't have to hang her. I'll strangle her with my bare hands."

He started up. Copperfield caught his coattails. "Would you hold on just a minute? Watch!"

Tristan dropped back to one knee, stroking his jaw, and watched Arian glide to the hearth. She wrapped a towel around her hand and unhooked the heavy kettle. Steam flushed her face just as his loving had once done, making his gut knot with a longing doomed to go unrequited for all eternity.

Arthur laid the book aside and favored her with a paternal smile. Tristan growled beneath his breath.

The unrelenting sweetness of Arian's smile should have warned him. Arthur held out his mug. Arian upended the kettle and cheerfully dumped a golden river of hot apple cider over his head.

Tristan grinned.

Arthur jumped to his feet, his face purpling with rage. Arian backed away from him, clapping her hands to her cheeks with an expression of dismay that could have softened even the flintiest heart. Her lips flew and Tristan could well imagine her mocking apologies.

Arthur flung his chair away and stalked her with a mute snarl. He cornered her against the hearth and drew back his fist.

Tristan didn't realize he was halfway across the yard until Copperfield's weight slammed him into the dew-dampened grass.

Cop's breath burned hot with desperation against the back of his neck. "He didn't hit her. Do you understand? He wanted to, but he didn't do it."

They both held their breath as a door slammed a short distance away and Arthur's shoes clattered on the stoop. He passed within a few feet of them, muttering a steady stream of curses, the black book still clutched in his hand.

When he'd disappeared down a narrow path, Tristan rose and gave Cop a shove. "Follow him," he whispered. "Don't let him out of your sight and make sure you stay out of his."

Rubber tomahawk in hand, Cop obeyed, darting through the shadowy trees with the fleet grace of his Cherokee ancestors.

Tristan's heart contracted as he turned back to discover Arian standing at the window only a few feet away, her fist pressed to her mouth. Her gaze searched the murky sky as if any scrap of starlight might cheer her. Her silent sigh fogged the glass, then she was gone, leaving the parlor in a sprawl of overturned chairs and spilled popcorn.

Arian's tread was weary as she climbed the stairs to her bedchamber. She'd been banished to Linnet's sparse bedstead after her first night in his care. He preferred to have his secret attic with its perfumed candles and satin sheets readily available if he chose to return from the village with one of his whey-faced chits in tow.

She rested her candle on the table and sank down on the stool in front of the mirror. Her own spitefulness had exhausted her. She plucked off her cap and ran a brush through her hair. The warped glass threw back her reflection in foggy waves. Was it her imagination or was her image growing more blurred around the edges? Even the mirror seemed to know her time was running out. The sliver of moon that had kept her hopes alive throughout the week had finally waned to darkness.

Even making her father's life a private hell was losing its charm. The wolfsbane she'd slipped into his broth last night had failed to provoke even a tiny thrill of excitement. Perhaps she was becoming as wicked and jaded as he.

The brush tangled in a stubborn curl. Arian blinked back tears, terrified of losing her reflection in their mist. She laid the brush aside, too heartsick to lift it for another stroke. Preying on her weakness, Tristan moved through her mind like a shadow.

She closed her eyes, her longing so miserably keen she could almost smell the wintry scent of his cologne drifting through the open window, almost feel his warm fingers brushing her nape. A familiar weight settled between her breasts.

Her eyes flew open. The emerald amulet nestled against the stark bodice of her dress, glittering with brilliance even in this dim light. She lifted her astonished eyes to meet Tristan's gaze in the mirror.

He stood behind her, yet did not touch her. Arian's hands began to tremble. Encroaching madness must surely have conjured such an impossible vision. Tristan with the close-cropped hair of a Nordic prince. Tristan with gaunt hollows beneath his cheeks that spoke of endless days and sleepless nights. Tristan with a sandy beard framing his sensual mouth. Unable to resist the temptation, Arian reached behind her to touch it.

It felt prickly and soft and indisputably real to her disbelieving fingertips.

He caught her hand and brought it to his lips. "Now, love, you're free to use Warlock to blast me into infinity if you'd like. I can't say I don't deserve it."

Arian sprang to her feet, snatching her hand back. "How nice of you to drop in!"

His mocking shrug was endearingly familiar. "I was in the neighborhood."

To occupy her shaking hands, she marched over to the window and slammed it. She hugged herself in the lingering pocket of chill air. All the tender reunion scenes she had envisioned in the past month seemed to have gone up in a puff of smoke at Tristan's abrupt appearance. Instead, she felt feverish and contrary, much as she had after surviving a bout of cholera as a child.

The man had just crossed three centuries. The least she could do was offer him some common courtesy.

Tristan watched in helpless bewilderment as Arian twisted the window curtain into a useless rag, her shoulders even stiffer than her collar. "I'm afraid my father has stepped out. You may wait for him in the parlor if you like. I'll fetch you some cider."

"No, thank you," he replied, a smile spreading across his face as he realized what was troubling her even before she did. "I've seen you pour." He dared to draw nearer, near enough to inhale the intoxicating scent of woodsmoke and cloves from her hair. "I didn't come for Arthur, Arian. I came for you."

She blew her nose on the curtain, her voice suspiciously muffled. "Well, you took your own sweet, bloody time about it, didn't you!"

Groaning, he slipped his arms around her waist and rubbed his bearded cheek against her smooth one. "Oh, Arian, turn me into a frog or fry me with a thunderbolt, but for God's sake, please don't cry. I don't think I can bear it."

She melted into the cradle of his arms. "I hope you don't think I'm going to forgive you just because you hold me this way. You can kiss my ear and rub your face against my throat all you want, but I'm not . . ." Her voice faded to a breathless sigh. She lifted her head, baring her throat to the prickly caress of his beard.

"Arian?"

"Mmmmm?" she murmured as his lips found hers.

"I love you."

Tristan drew her into his embrace, kissing her sweetly parted lips before they could utter a protest. He spread his palms against her slender back, caressing her warmth beneath the scratchy homespun. Her hands crept around his neck. He tasted salt in their kiss and knew that one, or maybe both of them, was crying. They might have kissed like that for the next three hundred years if a rock hadn't crashed through the window in a shower of leaded glass.

Tristan hurled her to the floor, shielding her with his body.

"Come out, devil's whore! Come out and bring your demon lover!"

Bits of glass tinkled from her hair as Arian lifted her head. "Oh, no! Not Goody Hubbins!"

Tristan dove for the candle, extinguishing it between two fingers before peering around the edge of the curtain. Even from where she huddled, Arian could see the sea of torches bobbing on the lawn below.

"Join us, witch, and face the righteous wrath of God!"

Arian saw Tristan's face stiffen with raw hatred at Linnet's sanctimonious shout. She crawled to the window, her knees cushioned by her thick skirts, and tugged at his pants leg. "Let's go, Tristan. Now! We'll use Warlock to flee to the future. Back to New York, where we both belong."

"We can't," he said flatly.

"Why not?"

"Because the bastard has Cop. He was supposed to follow Arthur without being detected."

Arian peeped over the window ledge. "And a fine job he's doing, I'd say."

Copperfield hung next to Linnet, caught in the burly embrace of a tanner. The man's meaty fingers were poised at Cop's throat, as if he'd like nothing better than to snap his neck like a twig.

Arian rose, gazing up into her husband's shadowed face. "So you weren't interested in Arthur, eh? Only in me?"

He shot her a guilty glance from beneath his gilt-dusted lashes. "I had to know when he was coming back to the cottage, didn't I?"

She tightened her lips. "You have an answer for everything, don't you? Well, why don't we give your precious Arthur a taste of the wrath of God?" She stroked the amulet, its familiar contours imbuing her with courage. "I daresay a lightning bolt between the eyes would singe that smirk off his face."

Tristan drew her away from the window, his grasp on her shoulders both firm and gentle. "Can you guar-

antee you won't accidentally singe off Cop's ponytail? Or
turn that hulking thing that's got hold of him into a man-
eating crocodile?"

She nodded hopefully, then shook her head, knowing Tristan was right. They could hardly afford to trust
Cop's life to the erratic performance of the amulet.

Tristan's eyes narrowed as he considered their dilemma. "I want you to go to the window. Tell Arthur
you'll surrender peacefully if he'll come and escort you
down. Alone."

Unable to bear the thought of losing Tristan so
soon after finding him, Arian gripped his coat in her frantic hands. "But if he knows Copperfield is here, he must
suspect that you're here."

"That suits me just fine," Tristan replied, sliding
his hand beneath his coat. It emerged gripping Sven's
sleek Glock 9-millimeter. The modern weapon looked as
out of place as he did in this provincial time.

"What about Warlock? We can't risk him getting
his hands on it again."

Tristan assessed the sparse room, his gaze brightening when he spotted a loose plank in the floorboard.
"Hide it under there. We'll come back for it as soon as
we rescue Copperfield. It shouldn't take very long.
Those self-righteous prigs will probably scatter once we
expose Linnet for the miserable fraud he is."

Arian obeyed, feeling a twinge of loss as she tucked
the amulet beneath the board. But Tristan was there to
press a fierce kiss of encouragement to her trembling
lips.

Drawing in a bracing breath of his cologne, she
stepped up to the window.

"Saucy bitch!"

"Demon's concubine!"

"Satan's whore!"

She flinched as she recognized Constable Ingersoll's bellow. Behind Linnet, Charity Burke fell to the
ground, her nubile body writhing and twisting in a con-

vincing travesty of a fit. The curses swelled to screams, then died abruptly as Linnet cut his hand through the air, demanding silence.

"Miss Whitewood," he called up to the window. "The righteous folk of Gloucester have suffered enough beneath the burden of your malicious attacks. Now we have captured this stranger who confesses to knowing your name. You summoned him from hell, did you not?"

" 'Tis common knowledge demons love to take the form of Indians," Goody Hubbins shrieked.

The tanner gave Copperfield a meanspirited squeeze.

"Enough!" Arian cried. "I shall entrust myself into your hands if the good Reverend will come and escort me down."

Disapproving murmurs rose from the crowd. A crowd of men surged around Linnet. He inclined his head to hear their pleas, then pushed his hat back, baring his high forehead.

His voice rolled like thunder over the enthralled crowd as he closed his eyes and lifted his arms heavenward. "Oh, mighty and merciful God, grant me your power! Bless me with the strength to resist the wiles of this cunning child of Satan."

Behind her, Tristan growled.

Linnet lowered one hand. A sturdy Bible was slapped into it. "I march into battle against wickedness alone and unarmed except for Your most marvelous and holy Word." He opened his eyes and met Arian's gaze, smiling tenderly. "Do protect thy most humble servant from the rampant hag that lies in wait for him."

He darted for the front door. The mob trailed behind, shouting encouragement. As Linnet's footsteps pounded up the stairs, Tristan caught Arian around the waist.

"Behind the door," he commanded.

She obeyed, pressing herself to the wall while Tristan braced his shoulder against the door. Her heart slammed against her rib cage. She pressed her eyes shut, whispering a fervent prayer of her own.

A firm knock sounded on the door. Linnet's voice was just loud enough to carry to the expectant ears of the mob. "Open the door, my child. I have come to escort you to your destiny. Put yourself in the Lord's merciful hands and you will be cleansed." He shifted to a hissed whisper. "Let me in, you miserable brat or I'll have them send up that meddling Indian's ponytail—with his head still attached to it!"

His expression resolute, Tristan stepped back from the door and nodded to her. She reached out and swung it open, using the sturdy oak as a shield. Instead of the quivering female he had expected, Arthur found himself face-to-face with the man he had once tried to murder. A man who had aged only ten years to his twenty, still retaining the full vigor of manhood while his own was already beginning to fade.

He drew in a choked breath and Arian had to bite her skirt to keep from bouncing out from behind the door just to see his face. She contented herself with fixing her eye to the crack between door and frame, although that gave her little more than a restricted view of the enormous Bible clutched in Linnet's white-knuckled hand.

He recovered himself with admirable aplomb. An icy sneer chilled his voice. "Why, hello, Tristan. Did you come all this way just to see little old me?"

Arian could almost see Tristan's lips slant in a mocking smile, almost feel the flawlessly balanced weight of the gun as he leveled it at Linnet's treacherous heart with deadly grace. "I wouldn't walk across a New York alley to spit on you, Arthur. I came for my wife."

Joy and pride surged through Arian's heart.

"Soon to be your widow," Linnet snapped, "if you don't hand over Warlock."

"Now, Arthur, I'm not that same gullible boy you

left in New York. Surely you don't think I'd be stupid
enough to carry it on me."

"I've already searched the Indian. I know he
doesn't have it. That just leaves you and my devoted
daughter. And if you don't tell me where it is, I can promise you she'll be begging to tell me before this night is
done."

"Oh, yeah?" Tristan drawled. "What are you going
to do? Bludgeon her to death with that Bible?"

"Ah, my poor misguided brother," Linnet said gently. "You should never underestimate the mighty power
of the Word of God."

The Bible thumped to the floor to reveal the flared
muzzle of a blunderbuss. There was no time to warn
Tristan. No time to scream. The click of flint striking
steel echoed in her ears at the exact moment she
slammed the door on Linnet's wrist.

His howl of pain was cut short as the blunderbuss
exploded right next to Arian's ear. She sank against the
door, clutching her head in a vain attempt to silence the
bells ringing inside of it. Tristan sat on the floor where
the blast had knocked him, his lips moving in a soundless curse. A smoking crater marred the plaster a few
inches from where he had stood.

His face was ashen. "Sweet Jesus, I thought Puritans only carried muskets."

Realizing her hearing had been restored, Arian
scrambled over to him and threw her arms around his
neck. But there was no time to explain the primitive
magic of gunpowder and flint, no time to rescue the
Glock from the dusty corner where it had landed after
spinning out of Tristan's hand, no time to pry Warlock
out of its hiding place and use it as a weapon.

The door crashed open and men swarmed around
them. Linnet watched, his wounded arm cradled to his
chest and his mouth set in a gratified sneer, as they tore
her out of Tristan's grasp. It took five of them to do so
and she knew Tristan only surrendered her then be-

cause he feared her arms would be wrenched from their sockets.

"Arian!" he shouted as they bound his wrists behind him with a raw length of hemp. "What day is it?"

Trapped in Constable Ingersoll's relentless grip, she flung back her hair, shooting him a tormented glance. "Friday? Saturday?"

"No! What day of the month?"

Her ears were still ringing. She shook her head, trying desperately to clear it of an echo from the past. Tristan's laughing voice saying, *Don't you know that tonight is the night when werewolves howl at the moon and witches take to the windy skies on their brooms?*

" 'Tis October the thirty-first!" she shouted. "All Hallows' Eve!"

Bleak dread seized his features, only to be replaced by a composure so absolute it chilled Arian to the marrow.

He refused to even meet her gaze as they were led past a smirking Linnet and shoved down the stairs into the waiting arms of the mob.

35

The mob surged around them, herding them toward the forest in a pulsating prison of flesh. Faces twisted with hatred shoved themselves at Arian. She recoiled from their hot breath only to slam into the stalwart bulk of Constable Ingersoll's chest. His fingers dug into her bound wrists, shoving her into Copperfield, who was still being dragged along by the tanner.

"Hello, sweetheart," Cop murmured. "I had hoped we'd meet again in less dire circumstances."

"As did I," Arian muttered, craning her neck in a frantic attempt to spot Tristan.

As she was shoved up the mossy bank into the woods, she caught a brief glimpse of his rigid back. Not once did he glance over his shoulder at her.

Dark shapes swelled and receded in the smoky light of the bobbing torches. Some of her tormentors had thought to disguise themselves, like the man who stalked past, his cape rippling around his ankles and his hat brim drawn down to shield his features. Others like Goody Hubbins screeched their accusations openly.

Deeper into the woods the mob danced, driving them along with pinches and taunts. As they spilled into a deserted clearing, the jeers died to a silence broken only by the shuffle of feet and the death rattle of the leaves against their skeleton branches.

A scaffold blacker than the moonless sky loomed in the middle of the clearing. The noose looped around its crossbeam twisted in the wind.

A terrible numbness crept through Arian's limbs. She could already hear the tragic tale Linnet would tell the magistrates from Boston. *I did my utmost to save the poor child from the mob,* he would say, dabbing a tear from his eye with his bandaged hand. Mr. Corwin would shake his head in genuine regret and Mr. Hathorne's nose would quiver as he agreed it was an ugly end to a lamentable story.

No trace would ever be found of the scaffold. Following the executions, the brush piled beneath the rough-hewn planks would be torched. The flames climbing into the night sky would consume the last trace of Arian Whitewood with no one the wiser that the man now climbing the steps to the scaffold had ever had a daughter.

Tristan mounted the steps behind Linnet with no visible trace of faltering, his hair gleaming like spun gold in the torchlight, his hands relaxed beneath their bonds.

Or a partner.

Rage swept through Arian, washing away the paralyzing terror.

"Bring the witch, Constable," Linnet called out.

Arian kept her head held high as Ingersoll jerked her to the foot of the scaffold.

Linnet smiled down at her. "Let her watch her demon-lover die first."

Arian's anguished cry was drowned out by the cheers of the crowd. Tristan watched helplessly from the scaffold as she struggled to wrench herself out of Ingersoll's grasp. He wanted to shout at her to stop before she ruined everything, but he did not dare. So he simply averted his face and studied the grim reality of the noose dangling a scant foot from his head.

After Arian had been subdued, Arthur pointed at Tristan with his uninjured hand. "We hang this stranger first lest he summon a legion of demons to torment us. Tonight we shall know the righteous satisfaction of watching his soul descend to hell to meet its master."

The mob roared its approval. Tristan yawned.

His deliberate nonchalance was rewarded with Arthur's bitten-off words. "Have you anything to say in your defense, *warlock*?"

Arthur was baiting Arian and Tristan knew it. The wretch was just waiting for her to start babbling, to confess Warlock's location in a futile attempt to save her husband's life. Little did he know that Tristan Lennox's bride was made of sterner stuff. At least Tristan fervently prayed she was.

Refusing to let Arthur have the last word, he stepped forward, summoning the same cool charisma that had allowed him to rule a modern empire. Even with his hands bound, there was enough menace in his demeanor to send the crowd scuttling backward.

Acid mockery laced his words. "Good folk of Gloucester, I do have a confession to make." He waited for throats to be cleared, brows to be wiped. "If you hang Arian Whitewood this night, you hang an innocent girl. Innocent in that she had no choice but to succumb to my demands. I bewitched her."

The mob erupted into shocked exclamations. A withered old woman hovering at the edge of the scaffold howled at his blatant confession of witchcraft. Tristan felt Arian's startled gaze burning into him, but he refused to look at her.

Shooting him a murderous glare, Arthur lifted his hands in a plea for silence. "Beware this scoundrel's dark enchantment! He seeks only to free his whore!"

The crowd fell silent, but this time their rapt gazes

were locked on Tristan, not Arthur. He stepped to the edge of the platform and looked straight into Arian's eyes.

The crowd was so still that the husky timbre of his voice could be heard from every corner of the clearing. It was almost as if they knew he was speaking from the heart. "From the first moment I laid eyes on Arian Whitewood, I knew I had to have her. She fought for her virtue wisely and well." A wry smile curved his lips. "So I was forced to cast my web of spells to beguile her. When she would have turned me away, spurning my lustful attentions, I stripped her of her will and worked my dark magic on her until she was helpless to resist. I vow to you, she is innocent. Even now, she cannot remember the worldly acts I forced her to perform."

Arian bowed her head, tears sparkling on her lashes. Tristan knew she remembered only too well the tender attentions he had lavished on her willing body.

"Hang him quick!" Ingersoll bellowed. " 'Tis just as we feared. He is an incubus come to bring forth a new generation of witches. Hang all three of them before they join forces to destroy us all."

Tristan swore as the tanner thundered up the scaffold stairs, dragging Copperfield behind him. This wasn't going exactly as he'd planned.

"No!" A man in a long cloak shoved his way through the crowd to Arian's side.

Tristan had no idea if the stranger's appearance boded ill or well, but from Arthur's bitten-off curse and the flicker of hope in Arian's eyes, he suspected the latter.

The man pushed back the brim of his hat to reveal a stolid, weatherbeaten face. "If this wizard speaks the truth, then my stepdaughter is innocent. She is no witch, only a victim of this warlock's lust. She is no more a servant of Satan than Goody Hubbins or Charity Burke. If she is hanged, then must they not be hanged also?"

A young girl slid to a faint in her mother's arms.

Tristan suspected she just might be the aforementioned Charity Burke.

"Cover your ears. Do not heed this man!" Arthur shouted. "The witch has cast her wicked enchantment over him as well!"

Arian's stepfather rested his hands on her shoulders. "Speak up, girl. Tell them what this man is to you."

Arian lifted her gaze to Tristan, her eyes welling with unshed tears. His jaw clenched of its own volition, as if awaiting a blow he was helpless to dodge.

"I know him not," she said softly. "I've never laid eyes on him before tonight."

Tristan bowed his head. He knew he should be grateful to Arian for taking the out he had offered her. But her denial cut deeper than he had anticipated. Copperfield touched the small of his back with his bound hands.

Arthur bolted down the steps, knocking Marcus aside to capture Arian's shoulders in his hands. He gave her a harsh shake. "Do you know what you're saying?"

A sob tore from her throat. "I cannot remember him, good Reverend, truly I can't! My head aches from trying."

A malevolent smile curved his lips. He drew a dagger from his coat and sliced through her bonds. "Then prove your innocence, my child. Follow me and condemn his soul to hell for all eternity."

Linnet turned and mounted the steps. Arian trailed after him, twisting her skirt in her hands. The tanner reached for him, but Tristan jerked away, moving to stand beneath the noose on his own.

As Arian drew near to him, Tristan would have sworn he could feel the warmth of her body, smell her sweet scent. He closed his eyes briefly to keep himself from burying his face in her disheveled cloud of hair.

The mob held its breath, spellbound by the sight of the dark elfin beauty facing the tall golden warlock.

Arthur jerked slack into the noose and laid it across Arian's trembling palms.

Tristan inclined his head as if waiting to be crowned.

"Now, daughter," Arthur whispered, just loud enough for Tristan to hear him. "Do it and I'll spare your life. We'll take Warlock and return to the future. You'll inherit every penny of his wealth and we'll rule New York together. We'll create a dynasty of witches and warlocks, you and I."

Arian stood on tiptoe and slipped the noose over Tristan's neck. A sigh passed like a wave through the crowd.

Tristan smiled down into Arian's eyes. "Would you grant a dying man a last request, Miss Whitewood? A kiss from your honeyed lips to carry his wretched soul through an eternity without you?"

Before Arthur could slip between them, Tristan bent his head and brushed his lips against hers, reminding her for the last time just how good it could have been. Arian burst into tears and fled down the steps to her stepfather's waiting arms.

The tanner dropped the other noose over Copperfield's head. "Hey!" Cop wailed. "Don't I get a last request?"

The mob swarmed around the bottom of the scaffold, waving their fists and chanting a demand for witches' blood. Arian's stepfather whipped off his cloak and wrapped it around her slumped shoulders. Tristan watched them melt into the woods, his wife's small form tucked beneath her stepfather's arm. When she was gone, he closed his eyes and kept them closed until he could open them without crying.

36

A booming request for prayer rose above the shrill cries for blood. Arthur bowed his head, keeping one eye open and on Tristan. He sped through the Lord's Prayer with such haste that he left out half the words and mispronounced the rest.

Tristan stared straight ahead, the coarse rope chafing his neck. "I'm sorry about this, Cop. I didn't think it would end this way."

"Don't kick yourself. I'm the one who invited you to this party. If there is a next time though, I'd advise you not to make your wife so angry she leaps at the chance to drop a noose over your head."

An unfair pang of anger at Arian's desertion stabbed him. "We shouldn't have to worry about a next time. I predict that Arthur's desire to see us dead should override even his love of being the center of attention."

He was proved right as Arthur shot out a garbled "Amen" and danced across the scaffold, nearly tripping in his haste.

"I'd like to register a formal complaint," Cop said

"I was not offered a last request. It is well within my legal rights to demand a final cigarette or a kiss from one of those comely wenches screaming for my blood or maybe just a piping hot pepperoni pizza."

"Shut up, Injun," Arthur hissed, pretending to offer up a pious prayer for their soon-to-be-departed souls. "You and the golden boy here will wake up in hell before you know it."

"I'll be waiting for you there," Tristan promised. "When you crawl through those gates, mine will be the first face you see."

Arthur arched an eyebrow. "Then I shall endeavor to make the best of the time left to me on this earth. I can't help but notice what a lovely young woman my daughter has turned out to be. Of course, no one in New York knows that Arian is my daughter so I doubt there will be much gossip when we take up residence as husband and wife."

"Why, you perverted son of a—" Stymied by rage at the depth of his ex-friend's depravity, Tristan drove his knee into Arthur's groin.

"Hang them," the good Reverend croaked, sinking to one knee.

The platform shuddered with each of the tanner's long strides. Arthur crawled backward, supporting his weight on his good hand. Tristan pressed his shoulder to Copperfield's, as if he could somehow buoy him up when the trapdoor separating them from death swung out from beneath their feet. He lifted his gaze above the frenzied crowd to the ebony canopy of the sky, remembering a glittering New York skyline and the sweet warmth of Arian's body nestled against his own.

Fire streaked across the horizon like a ray of hope.

Tristan blinked. He might have believed he had imagined it had Copperfield's elbow not dug into his ribs with jarring force. The mob sucked in a collective gasp as the fire plummeted, then shot skyward, blazing itself across the sky in an arc aimed straight for the clearing.

A maniacal cackle of laughter that would have done the Wicked Witch of the West proud raised every hair on Tristan's nape to tingling life.

His heart swelled with pride as the broom swooped out of the sky, giving him his first clear look at the angel-faced witch perched astride it, a flaming torch clutched in her hand.

The mob scattered at her approach. A shriveled old woman dropped to her stomach, shrieking with fright as Arian's rippling cloak passed over her prostrate form, reeking of fire and brimstone. Arthur dragged himself to his feet, his skin clinging to his sharpened bones until his face resembled a death mask.

The broom darted upward, circled the clearing twice, then dove straight for the scaffold.

"The lever!" Arthur screamed. "Pull the god-damned lever!"

The tanner's hand was already gripping the lever, but the huge man stood transfixed by the ball of fire hurtling toward him out of the darkness. Arian was near enough for Tristan to see the mischievous sparkle in her eyes before the giant lost his nerve and leapt off the scaffold, bellowing in terror. Arian swooped past, her hair billowing behind her in a dark cloud of retribution.

Her voice floated back to him. "I'll be back . . . don't go anywhere . . ."

"I wasn't planning to," he muttered, tugging vainly at the cord binding his wrists.

Arthur lurched toward the lever, one hand cupping his groin. Cop stuck out his foot and he tripped, falling with a jolt that shook the scaffold.

Arian swooped past again, hanging upside down by one knee. "Tristan, help! I'm not very good at this! What should I do?" Her screech faded and she was gone again.

"The rope, Arian!" he shouted. "Burn the rope!" His cry was nearly drowned out by the terrified shrieks of the fleeing mob.

Arthur raised himself to hands and knees. Cop tangled his hands in Tristan's bonds and jerked, a steady stream of profanity pouring from his lips. Arthur's arm stretched toward the lever.

"Aaaiiiiiiieeeee!" Arian swept past, right side up, but backward. She took a frantic swipe at the rope securing the nooses with her torch. The odor of burning hemp flooded Tristan's nostrils.

He and Copperfield jumped as one man at the precise moment Arthur caught the lever and jerked it down. Finch fell against the post, slumping with relief as he heard the rhythmic bang of the trapdoor against the bottom of the platform. Swiping his damp palm across his mouth, he peered over his shoulder, eager to savor the destruction of his enemies.

But instead of two bodies twisting in the wind, he saw two men grinning in perfect accord. He whipped a dagger out of his coat, but it went clattering to the boards as Tristan's booted foot caught him soundly in the rump. He went sailing off the scaffold, arms flailing at empty air.

Cop snatched up the fallen dagger and sawed through their bonds. Tristan crouched on the edge of the platform. Arthur was sprawled below, his face buried in a mound of leaves.

"Give me the dagger," Tristan said, reaching behind him.

Cop hesitated for a heartbeat, then slapped the hilt in his open palm. Tristan prepared to spring off the scaffold.

Copperfield tapped him on the shoulder. "If I'm not mistaken, your wife seems to be in need of some assistance."

Tristan jerked around, following the path of Copperfield's pointing finger to the ever-widening loops of fire unfurling on the horizon. He squinted, barely able to make out the tiny figure draped over the broomstick, arms and legs flopping with each flip of the broom. Centrifugal force had to be the only thing keeping her aboard. He glanced back at Arthur. Arian's shrieks floated to him on the wind.

Shaking his head in bemusement, he tossed the dagger to Copperfield, then jumped up and down, waving his arms in the air. "Over here, Arian! Aim the stick this way!"

The broom made a wobbly dart for the sky, then swung around and shot toward the scaffold.

Tristan pulled off the heavy coat and shimmied up a support to the top of the crossbeam.

Cop's mouth fell open. "Surely you don't plan to—"

"If Finch moves," he commanded grimly, "kill him."

The wind tore at Tristan's shirt and stung his eyes as he squatted atop the crossbeam. The broom shot straight toward him, growing in size and speed with each passing second. Arian's mouth worked in helpless dismay, warning him to get out of the way. Her terrified eyes loomed in his vision; the flapping of her cloak nearly deafened him.

Tristan stood, balancing on the balls of his feet, and stretched his arms straight in the air. The broomstick dove for his chest. Arian screamed. As she jerked up on the end of the stick with all her might, the torch tumbled from her hand to land in the brush below the scaffold.

She passed between Tristan's outstretched arms like the breath of a dream. He snatched at the stick just above the bristles and held on, gritting his teeth as every muscle in his arms howled a protest. The broom shuddered, then went soaring upward into the moonless sky. Copperfield's whoop of triumph spurred Tristan up and astride the broom.

Arian's pert derriere was draped over the broomstick in front of him.

"Tristan!" she shrieked.

"Well, I have to hold on to something, don't I?"

She twisted around to glare at him. "Would you

consider pulling me aboard? This view is growing quite tiresome."

"On the contrary." Tristan ran his hand lightly up the creamy expanse of thigh exposed by her billowing skirt.

She squealed in outrage and he pulled her up, wrapping his arms around her waist. The miracle of flying was nothing compared to the wonder of holding her in his arms when he thought he never would again. He gave her a gentle squeeze, assuring himself that she was real, that he hadn't conjured her from his lonely dreams. She turned her head and his lips captured the corner of her mouth in a lingering touch of flame. A slow fire ignited in his belly, born of too many nights without her.

Tristan opened his eyes and for one deliciously lazy moment thought the reddish glow below merely a pale reflection of his blazing hunger for the woman in his arms. A closer look revealed a scaffold licked with flames and a figure in rented buckskins hopping up and down and shaking his fist at the sky.

"Uh-oh," he said. "If we don't pick up Cop soon, I'm afraid he's going to get a little hot under the collar." He folded his hands over Arian's, guiding the broomstick downward.

As they descended, the leaves around the scaffold burst into flame, engulfing the structure in a crackling inferno. Copperfield scrambled up a support to escape the flying sparks. Flames shot into the night sky, forcing Tristan and Arian to squeeze their eyes shut against the merciless heat. At the very last second, Arian jerked up the end of the broomstick, her nails digging convulsively into the wood.

"We missed him," she wailed. "I didn't dare go in blind."

"The way you maneuver this thing, blindness would be a virtue." At that dry comment, they both swiveled around to discover Copperfield hanging on the back of the broomstick, his knuckles white with effort. His feet were slapping the tops of the trees. "Couldn't you have stolen something a bit more roomy? A flying carpet? Or maybe a minivan?"

Tristan grabbed the leg of his buckskins and hauled him aboard.

"I did the best I could on such short notice," Arian retorted. "After your brilliant boss here so nobly offered to die for me, I barely had time to sprint back to the cottage and fetch Warlock. We were doing just fine until we picked up all this extra weight," she added spitefully.

As if to prove her point, the broom dipped in a dangerous arc, circling the clearing. Tristan's eyes watered as he struggled to see through the shimmering heat.

Cop rested a hand on his shoulder. "I'm afraid I failed you. True to character, Arthur slithered away into the woods when the fire started."

Tristan felt Arian stiffen against his chest. His hands were resting on her rib cage and he could feel each thud of her heart as if it were his own.

"I had very little time with my stepfather," she said softly, "but once I convinced him that the good Reverend was my father, he was only too willing to believe that he was also a fraud who had been seducing the innocent girls of the village. Marcus is on his way to Boston this very minute to fetch the magistrates. But if you want to go back for Arthur, we will."

Tristan understood the question underlying her words far better than she did. Her heart fluttered in the cradle of his hands—fragile and more infinitely precious than any dream of revenge. Arthur would never have Warlock again. He would be forced to survive in this primitive society using only his wits. If they didn't hang him for all the harm he'd already done.

Tristan watched as the scaffold folded inward, collapsing in a cascade of flames. A sense of peace enveloped him. "Your father made his own private hell in this century. Let him burn in it." He rested his chin on Arian's shoulder. "By any chance, Mrs. Lennox, do you remember the spell that first carried you into my arms?"

She rested her dark head against his fair one. "Why, of course I do!" Dismay colored her voice. "But Arthur claimed that he had programmed Warlock to deliver him to your doorstep and my ridiculous little spell had nothing to do with—"

"Concentrate!" Tristan barked, folding the fingers of her right hand around the amulet. "How do you expect to win a million dollars and establish yourself as any sort of respectable witch if you're distracted by every skeptic who pokes fun at you? Don't you have any more faith in yourself than that? You'll end up scrubbing toilets in Grand Central Station for a living if you can't show me any better magic than this. Watch it! Our feet are dragging. That's it now. Pull up and squeeze the amulet. And don't think wiggling your adorable little rump and batting those eyelashes is going to get you anywhere with me. You'll be a bony old hag one of these days and forced to rely on your talents to keep me enchanted. Watch out for that bush! And don't—"

"Time halts but keeps on flowing!" Arian shrieked, desperate to drown out the nagging rumble of Tristan's voice. "The winds cease but keep on blowing. Love hates but keeps on growing."

The broom dipped, then made an erratic dart for the tops of the trees. Copperfield threw his arms around Tristan's waist.

"Why, Cop," Tristan shouted. "I never knew you cared."

Arian chanted,

> *A door opens, slamming shut.*
> *A knife seals, then makes the cut.*
> *The witch says absolutely . . . but . . .*

The broom gathered speed. A ribbon of road unfurled beneath them. The night wind roared in their ears.

With hellebore and eye of newt,
Belladonna and ginger root,
Griffin's claw and ash and soot.

"What abominable poetry," Cop muttered into Tristan's shirt. "Root doesn't rhyme with soot."

They shot toward the far horizon. But Arian's squeal of triumph deepened to a cry of dismay when the broom did a sudden nosedive, sending them hurtling straight for the yawning chasm of a deserted lake.

There was no time for panic. No time for regrets. Tristan simply closed his eyes and buried his face in Arian's hair, wanting his last breath to be drawn from her scent. As they crashed through the surface of the lake, the water exploded into flying fragments of darkness and they went soaring upward through a veil torn asunder into a sun so brilliant it blinded them all.

37

Arian dragged in a breath of air so cold and crisp it made her giddy. The rising sun of the winter dawn dazzled her eyes. She blinked and the pink and azure sky poured over her senses, washing away the fog of night from her color-starved mind. She felt Tristan's fingers curl over her shoulders, heard Copperfield's crow of triumph, and laughed aloud as the broom soared in a miracle of weightlessness.

The state of New York unfolded beneath them in all of its awakening glory. They soared over a mountain, shivering in the delicious chill of a snow-capped peak. As the broom dipped into a valley, their feet skimmed the periwinkle-blue of a lake, sending a spray of rainbow-colored water shooting into the air. They glided upward again only to find themselves lost in the marshmallow cotton of a cloud. Tristan's arm crept around her waist. As soft as the caress of the cloud itself, his lips brushed her cheek.

They burst out of the cloud to find the vast city prawled beneath them. As Arian spotted the steel spire of Lennox Tower looming on the horizon like the pinnacle of some enchanted castle, her heart soared. Then plummeted as she remembered she still hadn't the foggiest notion of how to land the broom.

Before she could open her mouth to warn Tristan, the tail of the broom caught a downdraft and dove into a spin that sent them careening straight for the walled courtyard in a tumble of curses and shrieks.

The blanket of snow that broke their fall wasn't nearly as fluffy as it looked. Arian opened her eyes to find herself cradled across Tristan's lap. He was gazing down at her with a tenderness that melted her heart. For a stunned instant, she thought time had tricked them, sending them back to the moment when they had first met.

"Does your head ache?" he murmured.

She shook her head, reaching up to brush the snow from his hair. "My heart."

His warm fingers glided down her throat and into the bodice of her dress in search of that elusive organ. "Does this help?"

She moaned at his exquisite touch. "Oh, yes. I feel much better already."

"Good." He drew her into the curve of his shoulder and brushed his lips against hers. She surrendered the softness of her mouth, inviting him inside to wash away the bitter taste of Gloucester.

A hoarse groan interrupted their sweet communion. Copperfield lay with his head in the fountain and his legs sprawled in the snow. His eyes were still closed. Tristan untangled himself from Arian's arms with pained reluctance and went to tap him on the cheek.

"Oh, Cherie," Cop mumbled, bringing Tristan's hand to his lips. "You smell so good."

"That's my aftershave, you dolt," Tristan replied, jerking his hand back.

Cop's eyes shot open. "Sorry. I thought you were

someone else." He sat up, rubbing his head. "I guess you could say our landing was a crashing success."

Arian's jaw dropped as she noticed the stone statue towering over him. It perched in the center of the fountain as if it had always been there. But it hadn't.

She climbed to her feet, peering up at the snowy mane of white hair and flowing robes. The pursed lips had been frozen for all eternity in a pious smirk that would be just perfect for goldfish to leap through once spring arrived.

"Why, it's the spitting image of Wite Lize!"

Tristan shot Copperfield a sheepish glance. "I hadn't really noticed."

"It was Sven's idea to move him off the roof," Cop confessed. "He was scaring the pigeons."

Arian's tinkling laughter faded as a squadron of uniformed cops burst into the courtyard, flourishing guns.

"Freeze!" shouted their commander.

Tristan rolled his eyes. "Oh, for heaven's sake, this is getting just a little bit redundant."

"Shall I?" Arian whispered. She nodded to the amulet, her eyes sparkling with wicked mischief.

Tristan shook his head. "Why don't we just let my lawyer handle it? That is what I'm paying him for."

Copperfield tried. But he quickly discovered that it was difficult to intimidate a badge-flashing member of the NYPD when dressed like a cigar-store Indian.

"Out of the way, Geronimo," snapped one of the officers as he slapped a pair of handcuffs on Tristan's wrists.

"I'm Tonto, you idiot!"

"Yeah, well, I'm the Lone Ranger and I'm going to haul you down to the station if you don't jump on Silver and hi-oh your ass into the sunset."

Cop gritted his teeth in frustration. "Could you at least tell me what my client is being charged with?"

"Resisting arrest and skipping bail." The officer

dismissed Copperfield, focusing his full attention on Tristan. "You have the right to remain silent . . ."

Arian tapped the officer on the shoulder.

"Just a minute, ma'am," he said without turning around. "Anything you say can and will be held against you . . ."

Arian tapped him harder. "Pardon me, sir?"

He shot her an annoyed look. "Please do not interfere with my duties, ma'am. This man is a dangerous felon accused of murdering his wife." He turned back to Tristan. "You have the right to an attorney."

"But I am his wife!"

The cop did a double take. Arian crossed her arms and smiled sweetly at him.

"Shit, Eddie," muttered one of his companions. "I've seen her picture. It is her."

The officer shoved his cap back on his head. "Well, I'll be damned . . ."

Tristan rattled the handcuffs at him, his smile pleasant enough to blister. "Would you mind?"

The officer's bulldog face turned pugnacious. "No, as a matter of fact, I wouldn't. Cuff them all," he barked. "We'll straighten out this little mystery down at the station."

Ignoring Arian's wail of protest, Copperfield's belligerent threats to sue for false arrest, and Tristan's resigned sigh, his men hastened to obey. As they were being led from the courtyard, the officer paused just long enough to glance up at the fountain and murmur, "Nice statue. My wife has a dwarf just like it in our garden."

It took Copperfield nearly fourteen hours to sort out the various legal dilemmas posed by their respective disappearances. By the time Arian stumbled into the penthouse bedroom and flipped on the lights that night, she was yawning with exhaustion.

Which was why it took her a baffled moment to realize that the scraps of paper scattered across the bed and floor were one-dollar bills. A million one-dollar bills to be exact. Lucifer came capering across the field of green to greet her.

She scooped him up with a cry of delight, astonished by how much he'd grown in two short months. His woolly little belly was rounded beneath her hand.

"He missed you. But not half as bad as I did."

Arian whirled around to discover Tristan leaning against the doorframe, hands in pockets. He had stopped at his office to shave and change out of the quaint shirt and knee breeches he had worn in Gloucester. He now resembled the Tristan Lennox who had first taken her into his arms—a portrait of irresistible elegance in a two-thousand-dollar suit.

A wave of shyness washed over her and she wondered if he would ever truly cease to be a stranger to her. She gently deposited Lucifer on the bed and held out a handful of dollar bills. "I can see you've redecorated since I've been gone."

He shrugged. "Since I didn't have to waste my one phone call calling my lawyer, I called Sven. It turns out he used to be an interior decorator before he became a hairdresser and a—"

"Demolitions expert?" she finished for him. She gazed around the room in utter bewilderment. "I don't understand."

Tristan drew a paper from his breast pocket and handed it to her. Arian unfolded it, recognizing it as a copy of the prenuptial agreement he had destroyed prior to their wedding.

"I'm willing to backdate it if you like. You'll still be entitled to the million dollars, the chateau in France, and the monthly stipend." His gaze dropped to the carpet. Or where the carpet would have been were it not buried beneath a mound of bills. "Even if you should choose to remarry."

Arian sank down on the bed, struggling to absorb his words.

His face was an expressionless mask. "I won't contest the divorce. I can't imagine how you could possibly want to stay married to me after I demonstrated such an abysmal lack of faith in you. I almost got you killed."

"You also saved my life."

Suddenly, Arian understood. Tristan was offering her a freedom he believed she desired. No matter what the cost was to him. And she knew now beyond the shadow of a doubt that it would be far more than a paltry million dollars. Reaching up, Arian drew the amulet over her head.

"Keep it," he ordered, his voice cracking beneath the strain of maintaining his veneer of detachment. He could not quite hide the anguished longing in his eyes. "You've already proved you have a heart too pure to be corrupted."

Ignoring his command, Arian drew off the amulet and marched into the bathroom. She had to give him credit. He didn't come running until he heard the chortling flush of the commode.

Arian faced him, a wistful smile tugging at her lips as she touched her bare throat. "I don't need Warlock anymore. And neither do you. Our love is the only magic we'll ever need."

Tristan's aloof mask slowly cracked in a smile. His legendary reserve crumbled as he whooped with triumph and snatched Arian up in his arms, lifting her over his head.

Arian laughed down at him, knowing that for the rest of her life she would be content to fly only in his loving arms.

Tristan and Arian didn't emerge from the bedroom until very late the next morning.

Still wrapped in her husband's embrace, Arian drew the door shut so as not to disturb a napping Lucifer. "I wish . . ." she murmured.

"Careful now," Tristan chided, kissing the tip of her nose.

She trailed her lips along his freshly shaven jaw. "I wish you would love me forever."

He tipped her chin up, gazing into her eyes with solemn tenderness. "Don't waste your wishes on what you already have, Mrs. Lennox."

She squeezed her eyes shut. "Then I wish I had a million . . ."

"Dollars? Goats?" he offered, cringing in mock alarm.

Her eyes popped open. "Orange blossoms!"

Tristan swept her into his arms, laughing aloud at her frivolous notion. She had been right. They no longer needed Warlock. Not when he was only too eager to spend the rest of his life granting her every wish and making all of her dreams come true. But their tender embrace was interrupted when he sneezed. Twice.

They both glanced at the closed bedroom door before staring at each other, their eyes widening cautiously.

Tristan was the first to shake off the bizarre fancy. "Don't be ridiculous. That would mean you really were—"

"A witch," Arian whispered, unable to suppress a tiny giggle.

Tristan reached for the doorknob first, but her hand closed over his at the same instant. Exchanging a silly grin, they shook their heads at their mutual whimsy, shared another lingering kiss, then started for the elevator hand in hand to seek out some breakfast for their growling stomachs.

If they had opened the bedroom door at that precise minute, they would have seen Lucifer standing on his back legs in the middle of the bed, his tiny paws batting at the shower of orange blossoms drifting down from the ceiling in a fragrant cascade.

Epilogue

From the front page of the *Global Inquirer,* New York
City, January 26, 1997:

BOY BILLIONAIRE WEDS
MYSTERY BRIDE FOR
SECOND TIME!

After tenderly renewing their vows before a small
audience of friends and family, the beaming billionaire
and his squealing bride departed in a waiting helicopter
for destinations unknown. The generous pair shared
their joy by circling the city to scatter one million orange
blossoms and one million one-dollar bills over the cheering throngs of well-wishers.

Although reports of her premature death appear to
be greatly exaggerated, the bride wore black.